IT'S ALW

When Stan fii... impressed. He's digging the scene at the Treble Clef and Royal, this thin little guy two seats down, is so boiled he can't get his cigarette up to his mouth. But they start talking music, and Stan introduces him to Walt and Berte. And before you know it, with Royal's unique arrangements, they have a jazz combo. But Royal is no ordinary jazz pianist—this guy plays from somewhere *out there*. Stan and Walt have a hard enough time just keeping up with him, and Berte— well, she's so in love with Walt, she's just happy to be the singer. And, man, some nights, they really soar! But it can't last. Because Berte is a woman with a mission, and Royal is a man with a past.

IRON MAN

Coke Mason is a tough fighter. He's got a great left hook, and he can take the punishment. His manager George Regan knows all his strengths and weaknesses—hell, they've known each other since they were kids—and uses them to his advantage to get Coke fired up before every fight. Coke is headed for the top. But he's got one weakness that Regan can't use—Coke's love for Rose, his manipulative wife. Rose has Coke twisted around her finger so tight, Coke can't see straight. But that doesn't bother Coke. Whatever Rose wants is okay with him. Until suave hustler Paul Lewis enters the scene, with a proposition of his own.

W. R. BURNETT BIBLIOGRAPHY

Novels
Little Caesar (Dial, 1929)
Iron Man (Dial, 1930)
Saint Johnson (Dial, 1930)
The Silver Eagle (Dial, 1931)
The Goodhues of Sinking Creek
  (Raven's Head, 1931)
The Giant Swing (Harper, 1932)
Dark Hazard (Harper, 1933)
Goodbye to the Past (Harper, 1934)
King Cole (Harper, 1936)
The Dark Command (Knopf, 1938)
High Sierra (Knopf, 1940)
The Quick Brown Fox (Knopf, 1942)
Nobody Lives Forever (Knopf, 1943)
Tomorrow's Another Day
  (Knopf, 1945)
Romelle (Knopf, 1946)
The Asphalt Jungle (Knopf, 1949)
Stretch Dawson (Gold Medal, 1950)
Little Men, Big World (Knopf, 1951)
Vanity Row (Knopf, 1952)
Adobe Walls (Knopf, 1953)
Big Stan (as by John Monahan;
  Gold Medal, 1953)
Captain Lightfoot (Knopf, 1954)
It's Always Four O'Clock (as by
  James Updyke; Random, 1956)
Pale Moon (Knopf, 1956)
Underdog (Knopf, 1957)
Bitter Ground (Knopf, 1958)
Mi Amigo (Knopf, 1959)
Conant (Popular Library, 1961)
Round the Clock at Volari's (Gold
  Medal, 1961)
Sergeants 3 (Pocket, 1962)
The Goldseekers (Doubleday, 1962)
The Widow Barony (UK only;
  Macdonald, 1962)
The Abilene Samson (Pocket, 1963)
The Winning of Mickey Free
  (Bantam, 1965)
The Cool Man (Gold Medal, 1968)
Good-bye Chicago
  (St. Martin's, 1981)

Essays
The Roar of the Crowd
  (Potter, 1964)

Screenplay Contributions
The Finger Points (1931)
Beast of the City (1932)
Scarface: The Shame of a Nation
  (1932)
High Sierra (1941)
The Get-Away (1941)
This Gun for Hire (1942)
Wake Island (1942)
Crash Dive (1943)
Action in the North Atlantic (1943)
Background to Danger (1943)
San Antonio (1945)
Nobody Lives Forever (1946)
Belle Starr's Daughter (1949)
Vendetta (1950)
The Racket (1951)
Dangerous Mission (1954)
I Died a Thousand Times (1955)
Captain Lightfoot (1955)
Illegal (1955)
Short Cut to Hell (1957)
September Storm (1960)
Sergeants Three (1962)
The Great Escape (1963)

Uncredited Screen Contributions
Law and Order (1932)
The Whole Town's Talking (1935)
The Westerner (1940)
The Man I Love (1946)
The Walls of Jericho (1948)
The Asphalt Jungle (1950)
Night People (1954)
The Hangman (1959)
Four for Texas (1963)
Ice Station Zebra (1968)
Stiletto (1969)

IT'S ALWAYS FOUR O'CLOCK

FOUR O'CLOCK

IRON MAN

BY W. R. BURNETT

AUTHOR OF THE ASPHALT JUNGLE AND HIGH SIERRA

STARK HOUSE

Stark House Press • Eureka California

IT'S ALWAYS FOUR O'CLOCK / IRON MAN

Published by Stark House Press
2200 O Street
Eureka, CA 95501
griffinskye3@sbcglobal.net
www.starkhousepress.com

ISBN: 1-933586-24-9
ISBN-13: 978-1-933586-24-3

Text set in Figural. Heads set in Interstate.
Cover design and book layout by Mark Shepard, SHEPGRAPHICS.COM
Proofreading by Rick Ollerman

First Stark House Press Edition: November 2009
0 9 8 7 6 5 4 3 2 1

W. R. BURNETT: A VERSATILE HARD-BOILED MASTER

BY DAVID LAURENCE WILSON

"'It's the only live art in the world today,' said Royal.

"'You know what I mean?

"'...'I've been thinking about it for years. You see, all the other arts are just repetitions of what was done in Europe, or even Rome and Greece. Look at painting. Same old stuff. Take the novel. You read much?'

"'...'Well it's the same old thing over and over. Never anything new or original, all derivative. Well, jazz was invented in America. It's the true expression of American civilization. That's what I mean.'"

From *It's Always Four O'Clock*, 1956

For a literary giant, he was as approachable a man as you'd want to meet, a streetwise wise guy whose haunts were now limited to the few blocks around his home, the mean streets of Marina del Rey, the King's Harbor. W. R. Burnett had never learned to drive, he never flew, and he had never gone to the ceremonies for the Academy Awards, not even when he was nominated. Now his eyesight was lousy. These days he'd go out for a walk with his dog carrying a golf club but no balls. Burnett wasn't a golfer. He wasn't going out to practice his swing. Not unless he had to.

Burnett was born in 1899 in Springfield, Ohio. He attended Ohio State University and worked as a statistician for the State of Ohio, 1921-1927. He wrote plays—then he began writing novels. He wrote for eight years without acceptance. Only then did he become an overnight success, with the publication of *Little Caesar* (1929). A year later he received the O. Henry Award for "Dressing Up," judged the best short story of 1930.

Along with Jim Tully, Carey McWilliams, Robert Joyce Tasker, John Fante and James M. Cain, Burnett wrote for H. L. Mencken's magazine *The American Mercury* during the nineteen thirties. He wrote for *Harper's Magazine* and *Collier's*. He was considered a sophisticated intellectual.

To put it bluntly, Burnett was hot, and he was hot for a long time. He cooled off but then he got hot again. This happened more than once. He probably made more money in the writing game than any other three or four Stark House novelists combined.

The novels in this collection are unencumbered by the expectations of one-sheets and movie clips, Edward G. Robinson or Humphrey Bogart. They are outside the context of Hollywood legend and runaway best-sellers. *Iron Man* (1930) and *It's Always Four O'Clock* (1956) give us a chance to applaud Burnett on the page, as something both more and less than a phenomenon. This is the versatile Burnett, a man engaged with the world around him. The stories are long unpolished gems.

□ □ □

By 1981, when I met Burnett, it had been decades since he had made the big money, spending all he made and more, estimating that at one time he'd spent about a quarter million a year on his landscaping alone.

"I've been lucky," he told me. "I'm a lucky bastard."

It's a laughing fate that gives fortunes to men destined to be poor. Burnett would not be the first successful writer to remark upon how wealthy he could have been without his vices, passions, or children. For Burnett it was gambling. It was also a subject, grist for his mill, in *Dark Hazard* (1933) and *Tomorrow's Another Day* (1945). Gambling and comments on the art of gambling are frequent in his stories.

In 1981 Burnett was downsized but comfortable, particularly pleased at the initial reception for his new novel, *Good-bye Chicago*. Younger writers were showing up to pay homage and Burnett felt vindicated, even after a decade with no new novels published or films produced. Now there were suggestions that *Bitter Ground* (1958) or *The Cool Man* (1968) might be purchased for a film.

Burnett was still a garrulous man at eighty-one years of age. Like so many other survivors, he was able to laugh as well as scowl. "As long as there's an Earth I can sit around and talk," he said. Though he didn't know it, in his eightieth decade, Burnett was taking a last bow after receiving the 1980 Grand Master Award from the Mystery Writers of America.

"I never wrote a mystery in my life," he said.

But he enjoyed the honor, long overdue, however unexpected.

Good-bye, Chicago (1982), Burnett's thirty-fifth and last novel, was his first book published in fourteen years. It gave his fans an excuse to toast all the classics he had written during the past fifty years. For *Mystery* magazine, I wrote: *There are no mysteries in this elegiac novel about the survivors of the Chicago gangster wars. At first one is surprised by the matter of fact, idiomatic tone of this story. It is a surprisingly breezy pace for this veteran writer, a tale told without ellipsis or foreshadowing, without reflection. Burnett is analytical rather than emotive. There is no gore, little sex, and so many interlocking characters that one is tempted to reach for a scorecard."*

Well, OK. Nearly thirty years later we'll simply state that *Good-bye, Chicago*, like *Little Caesar*, was a matching bookend surrounding Prohibition era crime. Burnett had become both the first and the last of the hard-boiled novelists.

The *Los Angeles Times* had written him up and there were articles and reviews in magazines in the U.S. and overseas.

Burnett was enthusiastic about an even more recent effort, *The City People*, a collection of new short stories and vignettes. He was confident that it would be his next book to be published. It sounded reminiscent of Ben Hecht's *1001 Afternoons in Chicago* (1922), the life of a city: "The crime in this book appears the way it would appear in an overall picture of the city," Burnett said, "There's no crime accentuated. There's a robbery—an attempted robbery of a White Front restaurant—an all-night diner... and there's a story called "Stakeout" - in which a cheap crook is caught— there's one story about a real top criminal, called "Home for Christmas Eve"—and that's it! The rest of the stories deal with business... Vietnamese refugees... everything! It's every layer of society, from a bum to a multi-millionaire. It's just what you have in the city."

In the 1980 reference work, *Twentieth Century Crime and Mystery Writers*, George Grella, an Associate Professor of English, at the University of Rochester, summed up Burnett's career: *"The fact that his metaphors derive from a context of violence and treachery, rebellion and disorder, the violation and corruption of the law, should not shock any alert, informed observer; his world demonstrated Burnett's profound and accurate insight into his country and his age."*

That doesn't sound too bad.

Despite this, most of the profiles and essays made a point that Burnett had been "forgotten." If Burnett had been forgotten it was only because we are a nation without memory.

It was suggested that Burnett had become blind, and had given up on the writing. This would have been a surprise to those close to him. He was still working, still reading, still writing books, songs and his thoughts on the day's news, four hours a day spent exercising his craft. Sometimes he'd write about books or music that he had listened to.

His eyesight was deteriorating, but he never complained. He continued to read and write with the aid of magnifying glasses. "I've always typed my books," he said. "I even type now when I can't see what I'm typing. I can write with my eyes shut... and they practically are shut.

"I've tried dictating but it's no good. I wasn't nearly as good. It's not natural to me. But I may have to do it now. It's possible."

Retiring didn't seem to be an option.

□ □ □

If you spoke to Burnett's contemporaries you wouldn't hear a lot of stories about him. Burnett was a Midwestern Everyman who was distinguished more by his success than by any personal style or adventures. It was his reputation and his success that escorted him in Hollywood. Despite stories of an occasional confrontation, usually spread by Burnett himself, he was a pro, a renegade who usually sided with the ownership.

It was hard to imagine him casual, in an undignified photograph. Always in a suit, a writer as a professional, a mercenary with a pen.

There wasn't much physical description of this fella. He had a nearly life-long mustache, he was a little heavy.... Really he looked like he belonged in one of his own novels. If you know where to look you can find him on the internet in promotional shorts for the films adapted from *Iron Man* and *Dark Hazard*. In the latter film Burnett and Edward G. Robinson just happen to meet in a bookstore, as if they had synchronized their shopping hours. Burnett has a greyhound with him but it is not just any greyhound, it's "War Cry," the national champion. The dog looks a little out of place—it's a new, not a used bookstore, and the dog is much more familiar with a racetrack. Burnett himself is quite a bit more shy than the boisterous Edward G., a hat covering the top of his face and head, one hand hidden in his pocket.

The truth is that there is not much of a history on Burnett, no biography, no collection of his letters. In the early years he enjoyed the racetracks. Later there were children and season tickets to the Dodgers.

For five decades Burnett would be measured by the success of his first big hit. He was an example to other writers, both by income and by his ability to continue simultaneous careers as a novelist and screenwriter. No one was more capable at juggling the two parallel careers. LITTLE CAESAR... HIGH SIERRA... SAN ANTONIO... THE ASPHALT JUNGLE... THE GREAT ESCAPE... in their time these were the titles on the marquees and Burnett's films and novels were as well known as Shakespeare.

Burnett was a keen observer of his time and a generous critic of the writers of his generation. In 1981 he was engagingly modest but he was also quite confident about his place in American fiction. *Little Caesar* was the book that ended the age of F. Scott Fitzgerald.

Burnett put in his time at the typewriter but he also wrote fast. There was no other way to get his name on the cover of 35 novels, in the credits of forty or fifty films. "When I tell people how fast I write a novel they don't believe me," he said.

Did this make him a commercial writer? Only by chance. Coincidentally, it would seem. Burnett used the screenplays to finance his career in novels. Nevertheless, he was popular. Even Gloria Swanson had a copy of *Iron Man*.

"With *Little Caesar* I created a style of my own," Burnett said. "It's hard to realize the shock of that book! Readers were surprised to find that my hero was a villain—a murderer. Critics were outraged by my effrontery in having such characters, and in humanizing them. But you see, that's what I do best. I humanize people that other writers don't even write about. Or if they do, they're just names, they're not people.

"You see, what I did was—number one—throw out everything that they'd put in novels before—and use no—practically no description at all. Everything shown through action and dialogue, and in the language... approximately—stylized... the language of the people. Not literary English at all. Just American English, the kind that people really speak.

"I had already experimented. *Little Caesar* was my sixth novel. When the others were turned down I threw them away. They were approaching the style of *Little Caesar*, but I was still fooling around with old literary language. *Little Caesar* was finished in two drafts, so I had it pretty well in mind.

"What my objective was, and I'm still at it, has been to give as close a picture as is possible of my time, and the time previous to me. It dates from the Civil War to the present," Burnett said.

By the time he had finished his ninth book, Burnett's publisher was describing his novels as "Americana" and dividing them into categories: "Night Life: *Little Caesar*, *Iron Man*, *The Silver Eagle* (1931), *Dark Hazard*; Midwest: *The Giant Swing* (1932), *The Goodhues of Sinking Creek* (1934), *Goodbye To The Past* (1934), *King Cole* (1936); Old West: *Saint Johnson* (1930)."

□ □ □

When you shook the hand of W. R. Burnett you were shaking the hand that shook the hands of the writers Dashiel Hammett, William Faulkner and Horace McCoy, the Hollywood directors Raoul Walsh, John Huston and John Sturges, producers and publishers: Jack Warner, Howard Hughes and Adolph Knopf. Three more screenwriters he liked: Tom Reed, Steve Fisher and Fredric Faust, who wrote as "Max Brand." They were his contemporaries. The great writers of the past, his models, were Balzac, Guy de Maupassant and Anatole France.

Burnett saw James M. Cain occasionally at the offices of their agent, H. M. Swanson, but they weren't particularly friendly.

McCoy was a pal, though Burnett considered him to be basically an unhappy man, no surprise to the readers of McCoy's fiction.

Burnett and Hammett met just once, two titans beside a wall of books. "I went in a bookstore and here was this tall, slender, rather scholarly looking gent," Burnett said. "He was the last guy in the world you'd think was Hammett—but it was him. The bookseller introduced us and we went back and sat and talked for the whole afternoon. Very polite."

Hammett, of course, was Hammett, of the Continental Op, Sam Spade, and Nick and Nora Charles: six classic novels and a pile of short stories that are always in print somewhere. But Burnett would write thirty-five novels, lots of movies and plenty of novellas. How'd you like to listen to that shoptalk?

"Hammett didn't write many novels," Burnett said. "Blanche Knopf told me that they'd do their best to get a book out of him but they just couldn't do it."

Burnett dedicated four novels to his first wife, Marjorie Bartow, and ten to his second wife, Whitney Forbes Johnston. Three more novels were dedicated to his sons, James and William. Others were dedicated to Adolph Knopf, Frank Harris and Stephen Crane. Burnett was not a provincial. The novels contained references to Machiavelli, Jean Cocteau and Salvador Dali.

When I spoke with him, that long day in 1981, he suggested that I should interview John Fante, whose writing he admired.

The length and span of Burnett's career was unprecedented: no athletic star could trump him, with thirty years at the top of his game, two bestselling crime novels, *Little Caesar* and *The Asphalt Jungle*, twenty years apart.

Whatever the merits of his stories, so many years later, Burnett must be noted for his historical role and his influence on American crime, western and adventure storytelling. You could put in a strong claim that he had written the first gangster novel and the first big heist caper. You chase those ripples for a couple decades and you come up with Donald Westlake's pseudonym Richard Stark and the sunny-side up amorality of his character "Parker." Burnett was not nearly so dryly mechanical, however. He wrote more about the relationships than the crimes committed.

"I was interested in crime as a social phenomenon, as a left-handed form of normal endeavor," Burnett said. And the criminals? "They're just businessmen who don't abide by the rules."

Burnett was the right kind of guy in the right time and place. He had the right experience and the right attitude. And he had talent. He wrote about down to earth gangsters with a commonsense approach. He was one of the first of a phalanx of Chicago writers, including Ben Hecht, Jonathan Latimer, John Bright, Kubec Glasman and Howard Browne, who came west to write the gangster films.

In the movies, primarily at Warner Brothers, Burnett's characters were unforgettable. If the writer had faded over the decades the characters he created remained constant: Edward G. Robinson as "Rico," the "Little Caesar" of the book's title, his hand covering a gunshot to his arm, the window behind him pockmarked by machine gun bullets. Humphrey Bogart as "Mad Dog" Earle, a graying bank robber, an associate of the notorious John Dillinger, one man against a latter-day posse, cornered in the rocks above Whitney Portal. Steve McQueen, the captive, endlessly throwing a ball, bouncing it against a wall with a determination that this wall too, will one day fall. These were some of the great scenes in American films.

Burnett was among those who defined Hollywood film making. Perhaps it is only fair that Burnett may be best known for his contributions to motion pictures, despite his distaste for the medium.

Burnett was a ubiquitous figure in both worlds, a unique link between American film and literature. His style and story structure were perfect for the newly talking medium. He moved his stories forward by characterization and dialogue; his plotting was worked smoothly into conversations. It is disarmingly packaged but always utilitarian.

In his best years Burnett was an unimaginably wealthy writer who would still tell stories about the little guy. He would celebrate the hoi polloi without quite joining it. The narrator stood back a little, observing, the quintessential "fly on the wall," the ultimate novelist of time and place. Burnett wrote about outsiders, the common man in the city, a crowd, a growing outlaw nation.

He wasn't as flashy as the paperback writers, subordinating everything to character in a naturalistic style. He could still come up with a zinger every once and a while, as in *High Sierra* (1938): *"Louis smiled and sat up. He'd been sitting there in silence, resenting Roy, who, for some reason, made him feel small. Big hick at that! But he was looking better; he'd lost that pale, flaccid look he'd had when he first came out; he was sunburnt and seemed hard and fit. But his dark hair was shaggy, his tie was crooked, his shoes scuffed, and his clothes looked as if somebody had stood across a room and thrown them on him. Louis was wearing his expensive sport-coat and he was hurt that neither Mac nor Roy had noticed it."*

Both Burnett's characters and his prose were characterized by the Midwest. He was always writing, literally, about the atmosphere: the sky, sun, moon and stars. California was full of transplanted Midwesterners yearning for a family farm.

Burnett also wrote wonderfully subtle, Grant Wood like descriptions of Southern California, his adopted home: *"They drove in silence for a long time through the seemingly endless suburbs of the huge city, passing through little remote neighborhoods with crowded streets and cars parked bumper to bumper, through labyrinthine factory districts intersected by railroad tracks where switch-engines panted and hooted and held up traffic, and at last they came out into a flat country with farms and long rows of eucalyptus trees bordering the roads, and far in the distance they could make out tier after tier of vague blue mountains, towering up into the misty sky."* from *Romelle*, 1946

□ □ □

Iron Man was written in Chicago before the publication of *Little Caesar*. It is a love story, deep and bittersweet, though not necessarily the relationship you might expect. It came from an era when prizefighting was mass entertainment, a subject of novels and short films. When Burnett wrote *Iron Man* he was hanging around the gyms and boxing rings of Chicago.

Burnett was no more a prizefighter than he was a strong-arm man or a gangster king. He was very nearly a newspaper reporter, however, the way he dealt with realism, like an Ashcan painter. In *Iron Man* his prose was sparse and "hard-boiled," the same way he described his boxers. He wrote like a novel was a physical effort, as if sweating and sighing were part of putting the words down on paper. His plotting was as straight forward and well-surveyed as a treasury building.

There are a lot of characters in *Iron Man*; it's a very crowded boxing ring. Consequently, we don't get quite as much as we'd like to get of any of these characters during this extended snapshot. Burnett leaves the reader wanting more, which is not necessarily a bad thing.

To give away the plot, it's an old theme... it's "Rise and Fall": a warrior brought low by time and matrimony. It's Samson and Delilah. The novel was filmed three times, a level of success that would be the highlight of a career for most writers. The titles for the movies IRON MAN (1931 and 1951) and SOME BLONDES ARE DANGEROUS (1937) are not contradictory.

Iron Man rattles with xenophobia and racial and national epithets. Most of them are in the form of dialogue. These were, after all, men who planned to fight one another. Maybe the adrenaline and the trumped-up anger might help them.

In the "complete and unabridged" 1949 Avon paperback reprint these terms were modified with no great harm or advantage to Burnett's prose. What had read like hate was now reduced to condescension. In this Stark House edition—both an entertainment and a historical document—the novel has been returned to its original form. Sometimes it is good to remember even the inconvenient aspects of American culture.

You can sense Burnett's disdain for the new "talkies" in *Iron Man*, even before he made his own leap into the scenarios: *"The picture was on when the usher led them down the aisle. Regan wanted to sit in the back, Jeff wanted to sit in the middle, and Coke wanted to sit up front. Coke was the most obstinate of the three, so the usher seated them in the sixth row. Coke immediately fell into a daze; there were but two things, excluding women, that interested him: fighting and the movies. Jeff was capable of following only the simpler sort of movie and as this one was full of plots and counterplots and dukes and revolutionists, he grew confused and began to fidget. Regan went to sleep with his head on Jeff's shoulder.*

Coke... sat tensely waiting for the inevitable last minute appearance of the hero, a democratic grand duke. At last the hero appeared, sent the bad revolutionist to the mat with a wild uppercut that a blind man could have dodged, took the heroine in his arms and dried her glycerine tears. Coke sighed and relaxed.

"That's a cute blonde," he said to Jeff, "but you ought to see my wife."

For Burnett, who seldom wasted a scene, the diversion is a plot point, as well as an exercise in character. All of it is revealed in casual conversation. Even the boxing matches were described by dialogue. Coke, the middleweight prizefighter, is a legitimate contender and the Iron Man of the title. As he leaves the theater he spies a photo of his estranged wife in a lobby card. It's obvious that his Achilles Heel is in his heart.

Burnett described the scene around Coke Mason's camp: *"Bums from all over the world turned up there; ex-safe blowers, now prominent bootleggers, took rooms in a nearby hotel and scandalized the proprietor and his other guests. Gate crashers, bunco men, smalltime and big shot gamblers, a noted gunman from Chicago, and a scattering of burlesque comedians of the old school could be seen sauntering through the village streets."*

□ □ □

When Burnett visited Southern California in 1929, he was a hot young writer and the studios, desperate for dialogue, were vying for his services. Burnett turned them all down, though he had already purchased a big house near Glendale for his mother and father. Eventually Burnett and his wife Marjorie would move in with his parents. They would separate in 1931 but Burnett would remain in Southern California for the rest of his life.

"It wasn't the money," he said. "It was the climate. I was born in the Midwest, where you freeze in the winter and bake in the summer. This was paradise for me." Later he purchased a home in Redondo Beach for the summer, where he'd swim and bodysurf with the lifeguards.

Though Burnett gave in to the studios, to him it was always a temporary thing. Even fifty years later, when he looked back at his contributions in at least sixty films... it was a means to an end.

The first time was when Warner Brothers asked for his help on THE FINGER POINTS (1931), a story about Jake Lingle, the Chicago newspaperman who insinuated himself between the law and the gangsters and ended up a murder victim. Burnett was more than familiar with the episode. He had already met the screenwriter on the film, John Monk Saunders, the author of WINGS (1927), a suicide in 1945 at the age of forty-four. Burnett would describe Saunders as the smartest writer he'd meet in Hollywood. Warner's asked him how much he'd charge to come in and talk. Burnett thought of the highest figure he could imagine— $1,000 a week—and Warner's matched him.

Later, Saunders called him a fool for accepting the $1,000 a week salary. The studio would have gladly paid him $2,000.

The younger writer began educating Burnett about Hollywood. "He spoke about Hemingway—he knew him," Burnett said. "For a thousand a week, we talked about everything.

"What helped was his approach, his general attitude towards the producers. He thought they stunk—and the only way to deal with them was to con them, which he did as successfully as anyone I've ever seen.

"One week passed, then a second. After three weeks we got a call from the front office. They wanted us to come in that afternoon, to tell them what we'd done. I thought the gig was up but Saunders told me not to worry. He told me to sit and nod my head, to agree with him no matter what he said. I was scared, but then, when we got there, he ad-libbed the entire story. They sat there and said, "Wow! You guys are doing fine!" But as far as I was concerned, we hadn't done a goddamn thing."

Did Saunders write the script after the conference?

"Well, no, I did the writing," Burnett said. "I had to do it. It wasn't the same story he had told them but it had some of the same elements. After all, it was my first screenplay, and winging it, it wasn't too good.

"We were living modestly, my wife and I, in kind of a nice house, but nothing exceptional. Johnny said, I'm going to have some people over Friday—would you and your wife like to come out? I said, Sure! What time? He said, Well, let's see, about eight o'clock.

"I had a heap, not much of a car, but we drove out to Beverly Hills, to the address, and we started looking around, and here's this great big house, all lit up. Cars out in front. Valets out parking the cars. I said, That can't be it—but it was. Saunders had made quite a bit of money. I said, They're not going to park this car! So I parked down the street and went in. The first guy I saw was William Powell. And then Charlie Chaplin. We just walked around, you know. Everybody was there."

In the thirties Burnett worked on several films while producing nine more novels, including his first western stories, *Saint Johnson* and the Civil War novel *Dark Command* (1938). *Saint Johnson* was the first novel about the Earp-Clanton shootout in Tombstone, Arizona, an event no less mythic than Chicago's own St. Valentine's Day Massacre. The film version of *Dark Command* would be Burnett's first association with director Raoul Walsh, who would ultimately make five films from Burnett's scripts and stories.

Despite this production and success, Burnett went broke in 1938. "In spite of all the money I made, with practically no taxes, I went broke gambling—horses and dogs," Burnett said. "At one time I owned eighty dogs. On top of that I was betting on horses.

"For a while, when I owned "War Cry," the National Champion race dog, they'd pay me fifteen hundred dollars a week just to bring him to a track, where he'd race against time. I was making more money racing dogs than I was writing. But then they knocked greyhound racing out of California and I had to ship to Boston and Florida. Pretty soon it became too expensive.... I went broke. I owed everybody."

□ □ □

In 1940 Knopf published *High Sierra* and it started all over again. *High Sierra* sold to the movies three times and was filmed as HIGH SIERRA (1941), COLORADO TERRITORY (1949) and I DIED A THOUSAND TIMES. (1955).

In the next decade Burnett turned increasingly to screenplays. He wrote a number of movies during five years under contract at Warner Brothers, including WAKE ISLAND (1942), CRASH DIVE (1943), ACTION IN THE NORTH ATLANTIC (1943) and BACKGROUND TO DANGER (1943). It was also a decade that featured the crime novels *The Quick Brown Fox* (1942), *Nobody Lives Forever* (1943), *Tomorrow's Another Day, Romelle* (1946) and *The Asphalt Jungle*, all for Knopf.

In 1943 Burnett married his second wife, the former Whitney Forbes Johnston, with whom he shared a complementary, bantering relationship. Two children, James and William Riley Burnett II became the couple's social life. Baseball games or attending an occasional play were diversions from work and parenthood. Burnett had always been a sports fan and one of his last publications was *The Roar of the Crowd* (1965), a collection of his baseball essays originally published in *Rogue* magazine.

During the nineteen fifties Burnett seemed to specialize in western set-
tings, writing five period novels containing a variety of points of view. Burnett also began to write for television. In the years to come he would con-
sider his two films with director John Sturges, SERGEANTS 3 (1962) and
THE GREAT ESCAPE (1963), his most satisfying efforts on the screen.

□ □ □

Chicago was a city. Burnett could never quite seem to give Los Angeles
the same respect. At best it seemed a collection of neighborhoods and separate towns, its tanned citizens all pressed together, somehow even less
predictable than his gangster characters.

He defined Southern California by fog, fire and earthquakes. His character Royal in *It's Always Four O'Clock* certainly doesn't react like a "native"
when he feels a trembler begin"

"'*Earthquake!' yelled Royal, and he jumped off the piano bench, tore past me like
a dash-man in the Olympic Games, then out into the hall and out the front door,
leaving it open. We could hear him running down that quiet Beverly Hills street ...*"

Another quote from *High Sierra*, was tragically predictive: "'Yeah,' said
Marie. 'This is the kind of weather when they have brush and forest fires. I nearly got caught in one down around Santa Monica once. It was just this time of year.
It got so dry my lips cracked. A strong offshore wind was blowing and you could
see for miles. All of a sudden the brush caught on fire.'*"

November 6, 1961, was the date of the Bel Air-Brentwood Fire, considered the worst brush and chaparral fire in Southern California history.
Four hundred and eighty-four residences were destroyed, including Burnett's. His books, his correspondence, and all his unpublished manuscripts
were destroyed, including all 29 copies of his latest manuscript, *Young
Casanova*.

Burnett and his wife got out with pets and clothing. The only unpublished manuscript to survive the event was a novel titled *The Pilot's Seat*,
about airline pilots who view a UFO. This manuscript was written in 1951
with a pseudonym, James Vance Colwell.

"About all you can do is forget it," Burnett said. "That's what I did."

He worked on FOUR FOR TEXAS (1963), ICE STATION ZEBRA (1968)
and STILETTO (1969), and he wrote episodes for television series: "Naked
City," "The Asphalt Jungle," "Legend of Jesse James," "Off to See the Wiz-
ard," The Virginian" and "Bonanza." He turned down an Elvis Presley picture and ROBIN AND THE SEVEN HOODS.

Then there was the fadeout.

The flow of books slowed. In the fifties Burnett published eleven novels,
including *Underdog* (1957), which he rated as his best crime novel. The

pace slowed in the nineteen sixties, when eight novels were published but seldom without revisions. The novelization for *Sergeants 3* (1962) was probably written by Tommy Thompson, a prolific pulp and paperback western writer. *Conant* (1961) and *Round The Clock At Volari's* (1961) appear to have been written as much longer books, intended for hardback then cut for a shorter paperback length. *The Abilene Samson* (1963), a long, funny and philosophical folk tale, was likely untouched. It read as an immediate precursor to Thomas Berger's novel *Little Big Man* (1964). *The Winning of Mickey Free* (1965) may have been ghostwritten or revised by the prolific novelist Robert Silverberg. The intriguing but little known Fawcett paperback, *The Cool Man* (1968), was cut by an editor, since it had been written for a hardback. To find that uncut manuscript is at last one fan's Holy Grail.

Then nothing until *Good-bye, Chicago*.

Burnett hadn't stopped writing. He wrote almost every day. What he had done was to stop publishing.

"For me, it's never been a matter of confidence or doubt," he told me. "Writing is an impulse. It's what I've done with my life."

For Burnett, the book seemed cheap if the cover bent. Appearances mattered. Burnett had never written for the pulps and he didn't intend to begin writing paperbacks in his sixth decade.

"That's when I said, 'the hell with it!' I just kept writing and putting them away. All those novels. I wasn't going to stand on a street corner and beg. So I've got a lot of them upstairs. There's all sorts and most of them haven't even been copied."

Along with *The City People* and *The Pilot's Seat* there were two western screenplays, THE BRUTAL LAND and THREE GLORIOUS BASTARDS.

Night At Shark Bay and *Oil* were short novels that Burnett intended to package with *Zulu Sea*, originally printed in *Redbook*.

The manuscript titled *The Limelight* was about a famous Hollywood actor who had gone downhill and deserted his family. He owns and manages a supper club in the Midwest while his son searches for him.

There was *Babylon, Horses and Men, Night Without Morning* and *Children of the Age*.

Burnett died in 1982 leaving behind a pile of unproduced plays and unpublished books.

□ □ □

"'Four A.M. It's when the world slows down. It's when things look worst. It's when most people die.'

"'You'll never make the Hit Parade with that,' I said, laughing.

"'I'm not with it now,' said Royal. 'I've got a different slant.'"

From *It's Always Four O'Clock*

Burnett loved many forms of music: classical, jazz, the singing of Nat King Cole.... There was always an upright piano in his homes. During the 'forties he began writing song lyrics, as a break during the long hours in his studio office. He said that it never took him more than five minutes to write a song, that anybody should be able to do it within ten minutes.

In the 'fifties Burnett purchased an electric keyboard.

In the 'seventies Burnett gave his friend Dennis White a copy of the ICE STATION ZEBRA soundtrack, describing it as "good music but horrible orchestration." White gave him the soundtrack for TAXI DRIVER and Burnett called it mediocre music but brilliant orchestration. Burnett may have been picky but when he found something he liked he was loyal. And he liked jazz, in all its forms.

At his funeral Burnett's friends and family were consoled by his favorite songs, "Springtime in Paris" and "What's It All About, Alfie?"

Burnett had always had an interest and respect for the power of music, and he used it in his storytelling. There was Rose Mason, in *Iron Man*, singing and dancing. There was Doctor Riemenschneider in *The Asphalt Jungle*, trading his freedom for nickels in a jukebox, and *Romelle*, the story of a café singer told from the woman's point of view.

The Giant Swing, Burnett's fifth novel, was the first in which he wrote about this power of music and creation. Though it contains many characters all hustling for attention, Burnett's protagonist in *The Giant Swing* is the pianist Joe Nearing, who plays in the danceband at the park in Middleburg. As he awakens to his own talents Joe becomes passionate about the sounds of the city around him. He wants to incorporate those sounds into his own music.

Twenty-four years later, *It's Always Four O'Clock* was a rare pause among Burnett's popular stories of western dust and urban gunpowder. It was published by Random House with the name of a new author, "James Updyke." This was another of Burnett's alternate societies; a jazz trio, a republic of three. Maybe the beginning of another genre: a hard-boiled story about musicians.

This would be Burnett's only attempt at a first-person story. The most striking character among the trio and their associates is Royal Mauch, pianist and composer. The novel is an insider's look at working-class musicians and their uneasy acquaintance with genius. Jazz musicians could read it just as enthusiastically as a hood might read *Little Caesar*. Writing about music is almost as hard as writing about a color, but Burnett did it well.

The novel swings. In many ways the leading character in *It's Always Four*

O'Clock is a continuation of this iconoclastic composer from *The Giant Swing*, now improvising in Santa Monica. This time Burnett traces the moments when the combo comes together as a group, those "middle" moments that had been left out of *The Giant Swing*.

Both of these novels, twenty-four years apart, were dedicated to Allen Marple, a shadowy figure with almost no internet footprint at all. Was this the doomed, tragic pianist who had inspired these stories?

Not quite. Marple was the editor who brought Burnett to Harper's for five novels in the early 'thirties. None of them were typical crime stories. Later Marple wrote short stories, like "Act Your Age" and "A Very Modern Girl" in the early fifties and *Write It And Sell It* (1964), a book on the craft and business of writing. He was known for his aphorisms: "The best story is no good until it's on paper."

Marple was initially uncomfortable with *The Giant Swing*, in which Burnett's character Nearing leaves Middleburg for New York. Then Burnett cuts to his return, as the successful composer of "The Giant Swing" and other musicals. Marple suggested that Burnett visit New York City and its theatrical district on a research trip so he could fill in that nine year gap in the center of this story. He also tried to talk Burnett into rewriting perhaps his most experimental novel, *Goodbye To The Past*.

Perhaps Burnett's dedication was a way to jab an old contemporary.

□   □   □

There was still more history to come between this writer and his muse. In the 1986 publication *Backstory: Interviews with Screenwriters of Hollywood's Golden Age*, the interviewers Pat Gilligan and Ken Mate credited Burnett with writing 100 songs. The credit was picked up on web sites and a story on Burnett in *Firsts* magazine. The cover of this Stark House volume credited Burnett as a songwriter.

It was always a hobby, however. It was like adding fly fishing or bowling to a resume. It was recreational rather than professional.

On the other hand, Burnett seemed to enjoy the idea of developing a musical version of *Little Caesar*, a theme he may have missed when he turned down ROBIN AND THE SEVEN HOODS.

Ultimately Burnett's professional attachment to music went no further than the pages of his novels. Nowhere are there the lyrics of a song written by Burnett. They may have never been written down. Those that were written may have gone up in smoke. No one will ever produce a rockabilly gangster opera with lyrics by W. R. Burnett.

Still, there remained a connection between Burnett and music, like his affection for a particularly melancholy form of jazz.

In 2005 the Zurich "dancefloor punk" band "Asphalt Jungle" released its second album. According to those in the know: "The new album has everything that experienced urban cowboys and cowgirls need: it rocks, it's danceable, sometimes dreams, with subsidy... sexy and ironic...."

In New York another pair of musicians recorded as "Asphalt Jungle" and composed music for television.

There is also this, a curious inscription from Burnett on my own copy of *It's Always Four O'Clock*:

"Believe it or not, I almost turned out to be a musician.

Sincerely, W. R. Burnett"

This is the life that could have been. A lot of us have dreams like Burnett's and some of us, writers and readers, have the chance to make them "real" within the pages of a book.

DOWNIEVILLE, CA
JULY, 2009

IT'S ALWAYS FOUR O'CLOCK

BY W. R. BURNETT

To Allen Marple

It was a real cold night and this big trainshed of a place they called Memorial Hall was damp and drafty. You'd think three or four thousand people all huddled together would stir up a little warmth—but this big town on the river was like Siberia in the winter and the cold sneaked in every place. People barked like seals all around us, and there was a loud humming and rustling all through the joint that began to bother me and make me jumpy. Anyway, I felt as out of place as a blind man at a burlesque show.

What was I doing here? I knew damned well what I was doing here. But it's just the kind of question you ask yourself when you're nervous and beat.

We were all there, in the same row—a motley crew, as the fellow says. Frank Guardi, in a tux that had probably set him back three hundred dollars, Walter Flick, or, rather, Walter Hanneman, as he was now calling himself, turning his big handsome face about, and looking a little sheepish, I thought, and Berte Evers, shivering in her mink coat and holding onto Walter's arm as if she was afraid he'd suddenly sail up like a balloon in the big auditorium and take off for outer space. Which he might. And right next to me—Mrs. William Ward Jones III, with her blond hair short as a boy's and her jeweled cheaters flashing under the lights. Yeah, we were all there.

Now the buzzing blew up a storm, the lights came down, and the conductor took his place on the—what do you call it?—podium? Sounds like a cure for acne.

The conductor waved his stick. There was a crash, and the big band—a hundred or so strong, and all glad they were working—took off. I say "took off." But I don't mean it. I really mean "laid there." They were playing "Vahgner." My ears wouldn't listen.

I just sat there thinking about Royal while the noise went on....

...As there seemed to be nothing better to do, Royal and I copped Walt's car and drove down to Castle Rock, on the beach. We took out the car seat and sat on it in the sand. It was early summer and a weekday, not many people around, just some mothers wading in the surf with their squealing little kids. A bunch of gulls came over to see if we had anything to eat, we didn't, so they flew away, squealing like the kids in the surf.

Royal just sat there, looking at the water. I began to feel drowsy. But in a moment I sat up with a bang. Here came a chick—and, oh, what a chick!

About maybe twenty, in a red bikini. She had a tan like pale saddle-leather and long, for-real blond hair, not the kind of phonied-up white-blond hair Frank Guardi's blonds always had. And what a chassis—like it was pumped up to just the right size with a bicycle pump.

"Yowee!" I yipped, and Royal gave a jump.

"What's the matter?" he yelled, like it might be an atom bomb—a real jittery guy.

I pointed to the bim. We watched her pass. She looked up at the gulls, off at the waves, every place but at us, all the same she waggled her little caboose very nice for our entertainment.

"All that meat and no potatoes," said Royal.

And I winced at the old tired gag.

"Did you ever notice the waves?" asked Royal. "They've got a beat. A regular beat."

I said: "You watch the ocean, kiddo. I'll be back quicker than I hope."

I jumped up and started down the beach after Miss Inner Tube. Royal didn't seem surprised. Half an hour later I was back, happy as a weeded-up sax player. I had a phone number.

"It's got something to do with the numbers seven and nine," said Royal, looking up.

"You're wrong, kiddo," I said, smelling a gag. "It's a Crestview number and it's got no sevens nor nines."

"The waves," said Royal patiently. "They've got a regular beat."

♮ ♭

I could go on like this about Royal for days and days, but you'd just get confused. You wouldn't know who Royal was and you wouldn't know who was talking. I don't mean I want to start off and go right through. That's boring. But I think we ought to get a few things straight so we'll all know where we are—that is, as near as anybody knows where they are nowadays.

Me, my name is Stan Pawley. I am twenty-four years old and I play the guitar—pretty good, I think—for money, when I can get it, and for fun when I can't. I did my time in Japan—Army I'm speaking of—and I got back without so much as a bad cold. Not that I liked it, you understand. Who does?

I wasn't born with my present name. I was born Stanislaus Pawloski. I didn't mind the Stanislaus so much because that came out "Stan." But I sure as hell got tired of that "Stan *what???*" routine. So now I'm Stan Pawley. But I'm no foreigner. My Old Man was born in South Chicago. I grew up there and around Gary, where the Old Man worked in the steel mill before he and another guy took over a big bakery route, and made a lot of moola. Yeah, the Old Man's pretty well fixed, but there were eight kids in the family and it was rough for a while.

I was always queer for the guitar. When the other guys were playing football I was playing the guitar. I got called a sissy quite a lot but I can fight when I *have* to—who wants to?—so I did all right. By the time I got through high school I was a kind of celebrity around the neighborhood. Why? Because I'd already played some with a pretty fair Chicago band. I was launched on my career, as it says in the movie mags. Some career!

When Uncle Whiskers got through with me I took a quick trip back to Gary, told the Old Man I was going to settle on the West Coast. He was relieved. He'd always figured me for a bum—a musician, for God's sake!—and is he so far wrong? Yeah, he'd figured me for a bum, and if I stayed around Gary he was pretty sure he'd have to keep me. Now in spite of the fact that he was born here, the Old Man's still a Pole—got small ideas about money. He used to get in a lather over two-bits. I used to say to him: "Wake up, Pop, you're in America." Then the gaskets would all blow. "My own son!" he'd yell, he could get pretty dramatic in a cornball way. "He'll be calling me a Polack next!" And if I was real sore and pretty sure he wasn't going to give me any money, anyway, I'd come back with: "If it fits, put it on."

However, fathers and sons always battle. The father's going and the son's coming, and that's bound to make an uneasy situation. I liked the Old Man in spite of all our squabbles. He was a hundred per cent good man. Boring as hell, but good. I still like him—as long as I stay away from home.

I was lonesome in L.A. I got some jobs, playing with little combos—and after I'd sat out my time, I did some work around the movie studios and also in television. I was making a living. I had a little room you could just barely swing your arms in. And I had a few pretty fair telephone numbers. I wasn't exactly what you'd call living it up, but it could have been worse.

I met my best friend, Walt Flick, playing a date. He was, as he said, a "bull fiddle rassler." We clicked some way. It's hard to say how. Those things are funny.

I'll tell you about it. You might almost say that Walt and I didn't have anything in common except music. Walt was a college guy, graduated from a big Midwestern university. And a real handsome schnook. Big, like a football player, with curly dark-red hair, very off-beat, and he had one of those smiles. You could just see the chicks warming up when he turned it on. Now, me—I'm run of the mill every way. I've only got one asset with chicks—confidence, and there's a lot of wishy-washy babes in this world who don't know their own minds, I score big with them. But what I mean is, they don't flock. With Walt, they flocked, or would if he gave them a chance.

But the main thing with Walt was, he wasn't petty. And neither am I. If you want to find out what somebody is like, live with them for a while—brother, that's the test. Well, Walt, who was always a lucky guy, was handed this apartment he had, it belonged to a singer friend of his—Al Darby—who was working in New York, doing big. Two bedrooms yet, a nice living room, and all the rest. North of Sunset, off the Strip, and up high. You could see all the lights of L.A., Hollywood, Bev. Hills, etc., etc.—if you wanted to see them, I never did, particularly.

I really flipped when Walt asked me to move in with him. It don't happen! I said okay quick, and moved in that day, before he could change his mind. I kept wondering why he wasn't shacking up with some doll-face, he could have had his pick. But then I got to know Walt, and all became clear, as it says in the movies. He kept his sex life separate, if you know what I mean. He seldom talked about it, never mentioned a doll's name, didn't hang around with them, and didn't want them cluttering up the apartment. Every once in a while I'd see him with a doll, on the street, or in some bistro. The first time, I joined him. He didn't like it, I could see. I never did it again.

Now here's a funny thing. They all looked alike. Brunettes, dusky ones, a little on the expensive call-girl side. Just sex. Just a lay, as the fellow says. Walt was all business when it came to dolls. It was just a necessity to him, and that was that!

Sometimes I get sloppy over dames. Not Walt!

As I say, he wasn't petty. I'd lived with guys before and it always ended up in a row about who didn't pay for the milk or who lost the laundry or who left the window open or forgot to lock the door—you know what I mean, petty stuff. Walt didn't give a damn if the house fell down. He was easy to live with, good-natured and not in the least boring. That's another thing. After a week or so, most guys bore you till you want to bust the guitar over their conks, and they're feeling the same. Let's put it this way. We didn't bore each other. Walt had a good sense of humor. There was no corn in his make-up—except one thing: maybe it's corn and maybe it's not, he always wore his fraternity pin. (He wore a vest, this joker, maybe just for the pin.) But he never talked about college—no rah, rah—and, another thing, he never talked about the Army. He'd done his time in Germany with the Seventh, and like me, he just wanted to forget all about it.

And he had a beat-up Ford coupe, that I could use now and then when I had a heavy date and had to squire the broad a little before the pass.

We were living it up, big Walt and me.

Another thing. He had no ambition. Now a real ambitious guy will drive

you daffy. He's always biting his nails over something, this or that is happening to him, or *not* happening to him, as the case may be. Walt played
his dates, took his dough, and relaxed, like myself. We were going
nowhere, and liked it that way.

Sometimes you can't help running into one of these old guys who gets
to bleating about what bums the new generation is. They got no ambition,
they don't get out and fight for the buck, they're low slobs, who want to
live on the State. You know what I mean.

Man! I was out of the Army two days when I ran into one of these wind-
bags. I'd've belted him, only he was forty-five years old. A guy gets dragged
into the Army before he's old enough to get started and when he comes
out the income tax starts eating him up, and he sits waiting for the atom
bomb. Ambition, my ass! I just turn my back on such jokers now!

And speaking about the Army.... Who, me? No, not me. But Walt, Royal
and myself were sitting around in the apartment one night with some
musician friends, and there happened to be one of those guys. He'd heard
a couple of guns go off in Korea and he thought they should have tossed
bouquets at him all over the place when he got back. He yacked it up pretty good, and I could see Walt was getting ready to clear the joint and I did-
n't want it cleared because we'd been going very fine on music until Hero
gets off on his spin.

Finally Hero turns to Royal, who hadn't been saying anything, or even
listening. "How about you, chum?" asks Hero, who's been looking kind of
askance at Royal, anyway, he's the kind of guy you look at askance, believe
me! "Where did you do your stretch?"

"I told them I was a fag," said Royal.

Wham! Hero's crew-cut stood up like a porcupine's quills. Big Walt
leaned back in his chair and started to laugh. He told me later that this was
when he really began to like Royal.

Hero was flexing his muscles now. "Well," he said, pretty nasty, "are you?"

"No," said Royal. "I never went that route."

I didn't know Royal very well at the time, and I wasn't sure why he had
made such a remark in the first place. Was it to take this Big Hero down?
Was it to cover something up? And then the way he said: "No, I never
went that route," as if he were saying: "No, I never bowled," or something
trivial like that. He was a real puzzler, this boy.

Well, time has passed since then and I'll tell you what I found out. Royal
had been rejected for the Army: bad eyesight, underweight, general debil-
ity, I guess. And as for his remark about "that route"—well, Royal never
condemned anybody for anything. He just didn't seem to think like other

people when it came to morals and manners, and things like that. He was the most tolerant guy I ever met in my life, and the least hypocritical.

Yep, tolerant is the word—except for one thing: music. Here he was intolerant. He just couldn't stand sloppiness or mediocrity in music. It drove him daffy!

♮ ♭

When I think about the first time I met Royal, it reminds me of a cute kid I used to run around with. Her name was Sandra Bernstein but she called herself Sandy Burns, and she really looked like an Irish girl, with blue eyes, fair complexion and black hair—her girl friend, Stella Meyer, always referred to her as a crazy mixed-up Yid. (A lot of stuff is getting into this story that don't belong in here. Or maybe it does. Who knows what belongs where? Is there a law?) Anyway, Sandy was kind of a conventional girl—that's why she gave me the brush, finally—and anybody or anything that didn't fit in with her scheme of living she called an "oddy." She didn't think I was an oddy—don't misunderstand me—she thought I was a bum. But oddies she shied away from.

You know how you get influenced by the people you go around with. Well, from then on weird people were oddies to me.

And the first time I saw Royal, I said to myself: "There's an oddy."

It happened this way. I'd played a big party in Bel Air and was loaded with caviar canapés and wine the servants had snuck out to us. I got a ride in with a friend of mine: Sig, a trumpet player.

Sig talked all the way in, taking those Sunset Boulevard curves like he was a stock-car racer—with me grabbing anything handy. "Man, that's living it up!" he yacked. "I'll bet that brawl cost five thousand round ones. And did you see them chicks? How about the blond that fell on her keister on the porch doing the mambo. Man, I didn't know where to look! And them canapés—I'll bet I et two dozen. And did you see the butler drinking that wine? He won't come down for two days." Sig went on and on.

As soon as I could get a word in, I said: "Sig, it's not two yet. Let's go catch Lonny at the Treble Clef. I want to get those mambos out of my ears."

Lonny Boyle had a slick trio, played fast post-bop. I liked it, especially as a change.

But Sig said: "Man, not me! I'm for the sack. I want to lay there and dream about that blond and that house and that living! That's for me."

"If you had to pay for it you might have a different slant."

"Get out of my dreams, spoiler. Let me alone."

So Sig dropped me off at the Clef.

There was hardly anybody in the place. It's one of those real dark joints where other people eat off your plate and drink your drinks. It was getting toward closing time and Lonny was tired and just kicking it around, soft-like, with his two boys. I slid into one of the bench seats opposite the trio, put my case on the floor, and ordered a Scotch and water.

Lonny saw me, shrugged and raised his eyebrows. His boys nodded, then they took off with one of those fast, intricate ones, for my benefit. It was like a machine running good, all oiled and nice. It listened fine.

Then I saw Royal. He was sitting one seat down from me, and he was so boiled he had a hard time finding his mouth with his cigarette. An "oddy," I says to myself. His blond hair was cut real short, not a crew, just kind of butchered. He was a little thin guy, and it was hard to judge his age, he seemed about like myself. He wearing an old gray flannel coat and a loose white silk sport shirt, mussed and dirty-looking. He had on black horn-rimmed glasses with very thick lenses, later I got used to that fish-eyed look. Now it was just part of the "oddy" business.

He looked like maybe he might be a musician, if anything. Lonny jumped into "Chinatown, My Chinatown" and I saw Royal wince. I liked the way Lonny played this great oldie. Why the wince?

I caught Royal's eye. "Okay, eh?" I said.

"Going no place and fast," he replied, in a very sober voice.

"You don't like it?"

"It's smooth, smooth," he said.

Kind of superior, I thought, so I said to myself to hell with this bum and turned away. But in a minute I saw him heading for the can.

Well, it was closing time. Lonny and his boys came over and sat with me and we yacked it up. The hat-chick went home with her boy friend, who'd come to pick her up, and pretty soon the manager delicately hinted that it was time to close the doors. "Come on, boys. Screw," he says.

Just as we were going out I remembered the "oddy." I says to the manager: "There's a guy back in the can. Drunk."

"There is not," said the manager, "I was just back there."

This jolted me. "Is there a back way out?"

"Double-bolted and locked with a key," said the manager, beginning to look at me kind of strange.

"Well," I said, "I saw him go back there."

Laughing, Lonny and his boys took off. Why I waited I don't know to this day. I'm sure glad I did. The manager lammed into the back and pretty soon he turned up, leading Royal by the arm.

"I got a notion to call the cops," said the manager. "He was hiding back there in the storeroom."

Royal didn't say anything. He just stood there, not struggling, looking up at the manager, who was a big rough moose.

"Maybe he was going to frisk the joint later," said the manager.

"How about it?" I said to Royal. Now no matter how odd this character looked, he didn't look like any sneak thief. He had class—and if you ask me what that means I'll say this: I can't tell you but I know.

Royal gave sort of a grimace. "I was looking for a place to lie down and sleep."

"He's drunk and bushed," I said to the manager.

I could see the big lout was turning it over in his mind: the police—trouble—wasted time—for what? So he said: "Okay. Get him out of here," like I'd brought him in.

"I never saw him before," I said.

While we were arguing—about what?—Royal walks out the door, turns to his left too sudden, and falls on his hands and knees. I hurried out. The manager slams the door, cursing. He's got to go and check the cash register now with the bartender and he's tired and fed-up. I understand his viewpoint. It's no picnic running one of those plush saloons.

I picked Royal up and asked: "Where do you live?"

And he told me. It was only a block away. I said: "Why look for a place to sleep in that joint if you live so close?"

"That was a routine," he said. "I was going to hide around and use the piano after everybody'd gone home."

This got me. You can understand that, can't you?

He lived in a basement. I didn't know anybody lived in basements outside of Greenwich Village. I wasn't even sure they lived in basements there, I'd never been to New York. Well, it was under an old grocery, a real old building for Hollywood—an ex-grocery, because it was some kind of rooming house now. It was damp—a real creep joint.

His door was unlocked, of course. He stumbled in and turned on the light and I looked around: a bed—unmade, two chairs, a table, a few books and magazines—nothing!

"Thanks," he said, as much as to say: "Good-bye, Good Samaritan. Get lost."

But he puzzled me. "Are you a musician?" I asked.

"Amateur," he said.

Oh, amateur! That did it. "Well, so long," I said. "You better sleep it off." I was turning away when I suddenly remembered what he'd said about Lonny Boyle. "You don't like the trio at the Clef?"

"Tired technicians," he said, throwing it away.

This didn't sound like an amateur comment. But it did sound like some of that longhair stuff you're always hearing about jazz, and reading in some of those silly magazines.

"Lonny's one of the best," I said.

"Well, he's earning a living," said Royal.

"You mean, that's all he's doing?"

"That's what I mean," said Royal.

There was some truth in it, too. Every once in a while I got the feeling that Lonny was tired and bored and just going through the motions.

"You play piano?" I asked.

"Not to speak of," said Royal. "I just kid around with it."

This guy not only puzzled and interested me, he irritated me, too. "Look," I said, "we got a piano over where I live."

Then I told him who I was and gave him the address of our pad.

"My name's Mauch," he said. "Royal Mauch. When I was in military school they called me Royal Pudding."

"When you were where?"

"Reform school," he said.

This was the beginning. You were never sure about anything he said.

Well, here's the topper. Worrying about this joker, I'd forgot my guitar. It was on the floor of the Clef and the Clef was locked tight when I got back. This guy could get you in more trouble.

When I got back to the apartment that night, Walter wasn't alone. He was drinking with Frank Guardi and a girl I'd never seen before. I looked her over pretty carefully, wondering who she belonged to, she wasn't Walter's type and she wasn't Frank's type. Both these guys were in a rut: Walt with his gypsy brunettes, and Frank with his second-team Marilyns.

This girl—well, she looked like a lady. Don't ask me what a "lady" is, I don't know. But that's the way she looked to me. She was about twenty-five, slender, with natural dark-blond hair, cut pretty short, and a sort of narrow, high-nosed face, a little on the delicate side. Let me put it another way. I'd never waste a minute on this chick. Why? Because she's repulsive? Far from it, chum. It's simple. She would never give me a tumble in a hundred years. I know about these things. I've had practice.

But she certainly liked big Walt. I don't mean she was giving with the feminine corn. You know. "Oh, you drate big mans!" Nothing like that. She was just enjoying herself in his company. So I figured she was Walt's— after all, a guy can change.

But she wasn't. She was with Frank, which was another puzzle.

All I found out for the moment was that her name was Berte Evers.

Well, I guess I'd better tell you about Frank. His father was a millionaire. Don't jump. They're common in Beverly Hills and West Los Angeles. The old man had made all his money in the agency business—he was now president of American Artists Associated, A.A.A.—and he was a sick man and practically retired. He would like to have had my stomach. I would like to have had his money. But we couldn't make the switch. Frank was about thirty, a very smoothly handsome Italian boy: olive complexion, curly black hair, big black eyes, and white Hollywood teeth—you know, so beautiful they look false.

He used perfume. Now, I'm prejudiced. I shy away from guys who use perfume. It bothers me. But don't get me wrong. I don't think a guy should stink. I'm not against baths. But there's a happy medium. (What's a happy medium? Do you ever stop and think how many things we say and write without even knowing what they mean? Parrot stuff! I'll try to keep it down.)

Well, Frank was a nice boy—maybe too nice. It always seemed to me he was acting the part of a gentleman—at least, his idea of a gentleman. He was one of Walt's best friends—or Frank thought so, anyway. He had made all the advances, puzzling Walt quite a bit at first. You see, fags have given Walt a whole lot of trouble. He's wary. But the last thing in the world Frank is, is a fag.

He's something maybe worse—a frustrated singer. Yes, believe it or not. With all that money and that big home in Beverly, his ambition was to be a singer. So he chased around after musicians. He'd had some bad experiences. There are a lot of freeloaders and goldbricks in my "profession," take my word for it—I know, because I'm one of them—and they'd go out to Frank's big house and eat smoked turkey and drink his booze and make fun of him.

Walt didn't object to the freeload, himself, but it wasn't a passion with him, as the fellow says, by any means. Walt could always do all right on his own, so Frank got to liking big Walter so much he was always calling him, taking him to lunch, bowling with him, etc., etc.

Also Walt could fake the piano pretty good, and he'd play accompaniment for Frank to sing, and sometimes I'd go along—for the smoked turkey and booze—and bring the instrument with me.

Frank had a pretty good Italian tenor voice. But he was inclined to flat— which drove me wild—and he insisted on singing "I Got My Love to Keep Me Warm" when he should have been singing "O Sole Mio."

He thought Tony Martin was a bum. Frank could be pretty trying at times. I'd just keep thinking about all that money he had, and wondering what made him such a sad schnook!

Now there are loud bores, drunken bores, belligerent bores and wise-guy bores. Frank was a quiet, smiling bore. I listened to the boring conversation that ensued and tried to keep from yawning. One trouble was, Frank had no sense of humor at all. Of course, occasionally he'd give with a gag he'd heard on television or from a friend, but it was an effort, and pretty soon he was right back on his own level, dead serious, giving weighty thought to everything. He read the papers a lot. He'd even get upset over the editorials. Oh, well. I guess I've said enough about Frank.

Pretty soon we got around to music and I found out that the doll, Berte Evers, had played a few club dates around town in some of the flea-bags where the meals they give the "artists" are more important than the money they pay. She was a singer. She did not look like a singer. Maybe she really wasn't, I thought, playing joints like that at her age. You think I'm joking? Twenty-five is not young for a female entertainer, believe me. And thirty, while we're on the subject, is not young for a sideman. The kids come up fast and in droves! It's what they call a rising tide all the time. It's also a rat race, this business. You hang on by the skin of your teeth and hope for the best.

So she was a singer. She looked more like a doll who would be sitting ringside at Ciro's. I don't mean some Big Wheel's kept mink. I mean a doll with money of her own.

Well, I won't keep you in suspense, though I found this all out later. Her name was actually Hildegarde Dehn. Her old man was a real big Beverly Hills attorney, and Leo Guardi's best friend. Leo was Frank's father. So it was one of those things. The old boys got their heads together and says to one another let's arrange it so that the "young people" see a lot of each other and maybe.... But it didn't work. Berte and Frank were very polite in their attitude and went around quite a bit together, socially, I'm speaking of. In a way, she was a sort of convenience for Frank, because Frank was in the Social Register and he sure as hell couldn't drag any of his regular babes to the high-nosed parties it was hard for him to avoid—any one of them, after a few snifters, would begin to give out with that "up to my ass in daisies" type of conversation.

Yeah, she was one of those society singers. Like Frank, she didn't give a damn for what she had and wanted what she really wouldn't want if she had it. I guess we're all that way, more or less—except for real bums like Walt and me.

But as I said, I didn't know all this at the time. I couldn't figure her.

Well, the minutes dragged on, and finally Frank and Berte persuaded Walt to go hit a few late drinking spots with them. I hit the sack. Royal had completely slipped my mind.

♮ ♭

Walt woke me up slamming the front door. It was daylight—nearly eight o'clock, as a matter of fact. I went out into the hallway and began to work him over for waking me up, kidding, of course. Walt was feeling no pain.

Walt drinks like a gentleman, no bother, no fuss, he just gets this silly look on his big face—that's all.

"I'm hungry," he says. "Let's stir something up."

We made coffee and sandwiches and sat down. The damned California sunlight was killing me, so I pulled the blinds down.

"What's with this Evers chick?" I asked.

"That's trouble, trouble," said Walt, grinning, then he told me all about her. "She likes me."

"I don't know why."

"I don't either," said Walt, "because I'd run a hundred miles from that one."

"Let's not get to bragging so early in the morning."

"You don't get me. That's not a casual, man, believe me. That's for life. And a real fine chick. She'll end up marrying Frank maybe at that."

"And they can sing duets."

Big Walt choked, he laughed so hard. There is nothing like a drunken audience to build up your ego. Finally I remembered my own little adventure and told Walt about Royal.

"Sounds like a psycho," said Walt.

"Are you so normal?" I asked, irritated.

"Man, I'm abnormal as hell," said Walt. "I'm the pathological wolf type— the Don Juan, the Casanova. According to all the books, we're undercover fairies."

"I always wondered about you, asking me to live here and all."

"I ain't got around to you yet," said Walt. "I'm a busy man. According to the books, the honest-to-john he-man is a real dull bastard who marries one woman and lives with her for fifty years."

"Well, it saves him a lot of trouble," I said.

And Walt laughed again as if I'd come up with something real funny. He didn't seem to take any interest at all in my story about Royal.

I forgot all about Royal myself.

Well, one night Walt begged me to come with him out to Frank's. "He keeps asking me," said Walt. "I feel like a heel. He means well. I'll bet I've turned him down a dozen times the last few weeks."

"Any smoked turkey?" I asked.

"I guess so. There'll be something, you can bet."

"You mean, it's a party?" I asked, recoiling.

"Party? Hell, no," said Walt. "Frank wants to sing a little and sit around and yack. Nobody'll be there."

"All right, let's go," I said. I was at loose ends. A job had blown up, and my best telephone number, my newest, had gone home to Azusa, the big wicked city being too much at last for little home-town girl! (Man, what a town Azusa must be if this chick was typical—Sodom and Gomorrah!)

"Take the guitar," said Walt. And when I balked, he laughed and said: "Frank's bought a new double-bass so he can have it around when I'm out there. Keep me happy, I guess."

"Oh, these dirty aristocrats," I said. "Throwing money away. I can hear the tumbrils distantly rolling."

Walt gave me such a surprised look that I got sore. "I read a book once, you superior bastard," I yelled.

"What's a tumbril?" asked Walt, breaking me up.

Well, he persuaded me with the bull-fiddle business. Maybe we'd get a chance to kid around a little together. Maybe Frank might even get laryngitis. I got out the old battered case—my baby. Where would I be without it? Oh, where?

Then I got a shock. Royal was in the lobby looking for me. I pointed him out to Walt, who took one quick look and said: "Let's creep out, creep."

But Royal saw me and came over. "Going out on a job, Pawley?" he asked. He even remembered my name, and when I got to know him better I wondered how that had happened.

"Well, not exactly," I said. Then I introduced him to Walter and they shook hands limply, and nodded.

"I won't keep you," said Royal. "You mentioned the piano and I just thought...."

Walter started to edge away, but I had one of those brilliant flashes of stupidity that have been the guiding principle of my life. I turned to Walter. "Let's take him with us," I said. "He plays piano. He's a lot better than Lonny Boyle."

"I didn't say that," Royal put in, showing a quick flash of anger that kind of surprised me.

"Okay. So he's as good as Lonny Boyle. We'll...."

Royal looked me over as much as to say: "I was sure wrong about you, chum", then he started out. I felt embarrassed and ashamed—yes, I'm not kidding. There was something about Royal.... It wasn't that he was pathetic, exactly. He was more like a five-year-old kid who'd had his feelings hurt.

I took hold of his arm. "I was just ribbing," I said. "We'll be glad to have you. Eh, Walt?"

Even Walt was a little uneasy now. "Sure, sure," he said, wanting to kill me at that moment, I'm pretty certain.

To tell the truth, after the way I'd acted, I was a little surprised when Royal decided to come with us. Of course, I didn't know at the time how lonesome this poor guy was, and what a bad state of mind he was in.

Royal never failed to be a big surprise. Frank's enormous, elegant, old-fashioned house always made me feel like going back to the apartment—it wasn't for me and I didn't belong in it. I'd been raised in a little old dirty frame house full of yelling kids. The Japanese butler in the white coat bothered me. I felt like I should have come to the tradesmen's entrance. I was always afraid I'd break something, or make a shameful fopah. I couldn't get easy.

But Royal—he walked in, not even noticing anything. He smiled at the butler, who gave him a little bow. He was introduced to Frank, took it in stride with an air, and then was introduced by Frank to Berte Evers. And he said: "How do you do?" as easy as Beau Brummel in the movies.

A wallop—this boy. Within fifteen minutes even Walt was proud of the stranger we'd brought with us and kept looking at him.

We hadn't expected Berte to be there, and Walt gave me a side look, as much as to say: "What did I tell you, chum?"

As a matter of fact, I think Walt was right. Berte had arranged the whole business, making Frank think, of course, that it was all his own idea. Oh, these chicks!

Things went along fine. All the same, I wasn't easy. Remembering Royal's reaction to Lonny Boyle, I shuddered to think how he'd react to Walt's sketchy piano and Frank's singing.

However, he just sat there with a tall drink in his hand while Frank punished "I Got My Love to Keep Me Warm" and topped it off with "Smoke Gets in Your Eyes."

"I think I'm getting a little better," said Frank. "Don't you, Walt?"

"Yeah," said Walt. "I liked it better tonight."

Royal still said nothing. Finally Berte turned to him. "What do you play, Mr. Mauch?"

Mister—for cryssake!

Royal shook his head. "Nothing," he said.

"Aren't you a musician?" asked the doll, a little surprised.

"There's a difference of opinion about that," said Royal. "I just kid around on the piano a little. Amateur. College piano player, you might say."

"What college?" asked Walt quickly.

"Slippery Rock Teachers," said Royal.

Walt got a little red when I laughed. Berte dames are quick about these things—saw that her hero was embarrassed, so she jumped right in. "Walter, will you play for me?"

"Sure. What'll it be?"

"'Moonlight in Vermont,'" said Berte.

Frank sat down and sulked quietly and handsomely. He wanted to be the
Big Singer. Good God, wasn't this his own house? If he couldn't be the Big
One here—where, then?

Berte and Walter had trouble. They zigged at the wrong time. They
laughed. Berte couldn't get the ship off the ground.

"That's the wrong key for you," said Royal, and everybody looked at him.

"I always sing it in that key," said Berte. "I sang it around every place in
that key." Every place! Three or four of L.A.'s seediest traps!

Fed up, Walt asked: "You want to take over?"

"If it's all right with Miss Evers," said Royal. "Maybe I could help her a
little."

Walt got red again and Berte threw him a quick, veiled, loving look.
What did she care about keys, etc., etc.? She cared about Walter. That was
the whole reason for the evening.

Walt got up, and Royal sat down and ran through a few bars of "Moonlight in Vermont." My head jerked at the same time Walt's did. Was he kidding? This sounded like "Moonlight in Vermont" upside down or something. But it took a musician to do it, an oddy.

"There's your key," said Royal.

Berte, looking a little confused—as well she might—tried it. "Yes," she
said, surprised. "You're right."

They took off, and my hair began to stand up. Walter's mouth dropped
open, and finally he looked at me and jerked his thumb at Royal's back, as
much as to say: "Get him, man!"

But Berte stopped in the middle, lost, and said: "I'm sorry, Mr. Mauch. I
just can't follow you. It's too complicated. I lost the melody."

"Let him play," said Walter. "You can sing later." It was a real brush-off
and the doll was hurt, I could see.

"No," said Royal quickly. "I'm sorry. I'll simplify it. Or maybe you've got
your own arrangement with you."

"No, I haven't," said Berte, confused and almost ready to cry. Her big red-
headed hero had certainly let her down—and with a real loud public bang.

"Let's try it again," said Royal.

They tried it again. Royal kept it very simple, except the bass would take
off toward the ozone now and then, and a counter melody would knock
the hell out of this pretty good tune and make it sound oafish.

Berte gave up.

"I'm sorry," said Royal. "I thought I could help you. I'm out of practice."

"You better help her, Walt," said Frank, absolutely oblivious of what had
happened. He had no more ear than the average opera singer.

Royal got up and went back to his drink. But Walt and I were sweating
to hear some more piano from this strange little guy.

♮ ♭

You know, there is a funny thing. It occurs to me that Frank and Royal had a couple of traits in common. I mean, Frank was serious-minded, so was Royal. Frank gave out with tired gags, so did Royal—"All that meat and no potatoes." "Slippery Rock Teachers." But if you would notice this and get to thinking it made them similar, man, how wrong you would be. Frank was serious-minded about everything, Royal just about music. Frank gave with the gags to show he was one of the boys and could hold up his end in a yacking contest, Royal used old bad gags to baffle you, to cover up, to get you off on the wrong track. Royal had a lot to hide. Frank, nothing.

There couldn't be two guys more different. Actually, Frank was a very conventional guy. And as for Royal—well, if there is another one like him anywhere on this globe, I'd like to meet him. If you know of any, you can reach me c/o Musicians' Union, Hollywood.

This Royal—he broke everything up into pieces. The word "fracture" was invented for him. I don't know anything about Art—with a capital B, standing for Bushwa, to be polite about it—but if Royal had ever decided to paint, he would have painted those cockeyed-looking things where the woman has two eyes on one side of her face and looks like she was cut out of marshmallow with a cleaver. The things he could do to a tune.... It sounded as though he was changing keys every other bar—but he wasn't. If your ear was good enough—but whose was?—you could tell he was still in the same key. He used to play "Chinatown, My Chinatown" for me and I'd try to follow him and get lost after eight bars—this was at first, I'm speaking of. And I'm no mug, believe me. Bop never fazed me. The chord combinations always sounded all right to me and I couldn't understand why so many people held their ears. But I held my own ears over Royal at first.

Well, music is a hard thing to write about. Almost impossible, in fact, it's just something you listen to—so I won't bend your ears with too much talk about it. But take my word for it, music was never before fractured to the same extent as it was by Royal, not in my hearing, anyway.

Maybe I can put it another way. He was always twisting words around, particularly street names and the names of cities. Royal wanted them *his* way. La Jolla turned out La Majolica, and I'll let you wrestle with San Luis Obesity, La Sinandgaga Boulevard, and La Debris Avenue.

One time Walter said: "If Royal looked on the outside like he is on the inside, he could play the Hunchback of Notre Dame."

And if you get what he means, it's a pretty shrewd remark.

♭ ♮

Okay. Back to Scene, as they say in Hollywood.

Yes, Walt and I were sweating to hear some more piano from this strange little guy.

But it took some time.

Frank sang again, then Berte, with Walt faking on the piano and goofing more than I'd ever heard him goof before. He was nervous on account of Royal.

Once in the middle of a song—a loud yelling one: "Gambler's Guitar"—Frank turned and gave Walter one of those beautiful Ipana smiles, and said: "Baby, you made a bubu."

This baby almost fowed up.

So it went, with Royal sitting there getting mildly plastered, saying nothing, just looking at the floor. He was so lonesome at this time that he would have sat around on the night watch with a bunch of morticians at Utter McKinley—but I didn't know this, of course. I was just surprised that he was so quiet and polite about the whole business.

Just as Frank's and Berte's pipes began to tire and I was thinking, "Man, here we go," the butler came in and told Frank that the "buffet" was ready. Needless to say, I forgot all about Royal and took a tight rein on my passions—as it says in books—so I wouldn't trample Berte on the way to the dining room.

"Does my father want anything?" Frank asked the butler.

"Just some milk, sir," said the little Jap, bowing.

When I got a gander at that "groaning board" I really felt sorry for poor old Mr. Guardi. Me, feeling sorry for a millionaire? But I did. He was way up on the second floor in the back of this huge house, with round-the-clock nursing, and fourteen specialists tapping his bankroll and telling him what *not* to do. Yeah, I felt sorry for him. Milk, for God's sake! Man, was I glad that I was twenty-four years old, with a strong stomach and few scruples.

Baked ham, smoked turkey, smoked shrimps (Did you ever eat smoked shrimps? Man, you haven't lived!), the best rye bread I ever tasted, a whole big silver bowl full of little globs of butter in ice, a salad I can't put a name to—something like potato salad, but off-beat someway, and all the other fixings, you know: ripe olives, celery, pickles, relish, etc., etc.

In fifteen minutes my stomach was out to here, but I went back for more. And you should have seen Royal eat. And I thought to myself he doesn't look like a guy who would eat like that. And I was right, he wasn't. It just happened that he hadn't been eating regular for a week or two. This little guy was famished. And big Walt—well, you've heard talk about trenchermen! This guy invented it.

And naturally, Frank and Berte hardly ate anything. But being polite, well-raised people, they pretended to horse around with one thing and another until the Three Bears had finally stowed away enough to hibernate on.

Well, while we were in the dining room loading up, the butler had carried the bull fiddle into the music room at Frank's orders and there it was, waiting.

I could see Walt wanted to unfasten his belt and unloose the top button of his pants as he did around the apartment after he had scoffed everything in the joint, as was his ungentlemanly habit once a day, but as there was a lady present, he decided to suffer. I had my own trouble, struggling with burps. But Royal was a new man. There was color now in his pale face, and his eyes didn't look quite so fishy behind those thick lenses.

Walt grabbed the bass and began to kid around. I got my case from the hallway and took out the instrument. Finally Royal wandered over to the piano.

Yowee! Murder! We couldn't follow him. It sounded like ladies' night at a Turkish bath when a Peeping Tom looks in the window.

We stopped.

Frank smiled one of his smiles and started to put his foot in his mouth. "Maybe it would be better...." He was obviously going to say something like "Wouldn't it be better if just Walt and Stan played," but Walt saved him.

"I don't excavate this tiger," said Walt. "Make it simple, will you, chum?"

Berte and Frank stared in unbelief.

We tried it again. Royal made it simple, according to his lights, and we stumbled through "You Took Advantage of Me"—a hell of a swell tune. But not the way we played it.

Frank and Berte didn't know what was going on.

We horsed around for an hour, getting real snatches here and there, and then all of a sudden—wham! Royal had come up with an oldie that must date back to about 1916 or '17—"There's Egypt in Your Dreamy Eyes"—and we jelled, man, I mean, we really left the platform and headed for Mars!

Walt took a break like I've never heard before—and you should have heard the bridge Royal came up with. I began to weep. And finally, when we were through, Walt jumped in the air and kicked up his right leg.

"Man, man!" he shouted.

Frank looked at us dumfounded, smiling sort of uneasily. Berte was staring at Walter—the hell with music, what do dames really care about music when they're after the Big Moment. Yeah, she was staring at him, wondering if he was crazy or what. A big romantic hero like that acting like a weeded-up colored boy in some Central Avenue dive!

Royal got up and quit—and he was right. After that, it would all be downhill. He was grinning like a little boy with a new top. He patted us both on the back. "You boys," he said, "you're pretty good."

"Good, hell!" I said. "We're terrific."

"We might make that into something in a week or so," said Royal.

Get him! But he meant it. This oddy was a perfectionist.

Well, we headed for home, the three of us. I was a little embarrassed for Walter, who seemed sort of punchy after that last number. You see, Berte was angling for him to take her home and he didn't even get it, the big goof! If he'd been dodging it, that would be something else again.

Royal gave us two more surprises before we saw the last of him that night. As we were driving down the Strip and I was making uncomplimentary remarks about a singer who was billed in big letters at Ciro's, Royal said: "You know, fellows, that Miss Evers has the makings."

"Of what?" asked Walter.

"A singer," said Royal. "She has a very good ear and a natural feeling for phrasing. Trouble is, she's been taught all wrong. How she could sing at all, with either one of us playing, stops me."

What he meant by the last remark was, that he himself couldn't play for singers, his style was too individual, and Walt just couldn't play, period.

"I never noticed anything out of the way," said Walt, surprised.

"Well," said Royal, not arguing—he never argued—but just quietly stating what he thought, "first thing is, she always sings in the wrong key. A key too low for her voice. She thinks that's the way to sing, because it's fashionable. And the arrangements she's got must be murder, if I'm any judge. Besides, some teacher has taught her how to break the notes up— you know, that sophisticated hillbilly stuff that there ought to be a law against, and then that Billy Daniels speaking stuff, and the moan. Murder! I could make a singer out of her in a few years."

"A few what?" asked Walt.

"Years," said Royal. "Oh, I'm not suggesting it. I'm merely stating a fact. I don't teach singers and she wouldn't listen to me if I did. I've been through all that."

"How about Frank?" asked Walt, the nasty man.

There was a pause, then Royal broke us up. "I can't understand," said Royal, "why he isn't a success right now."

Walt and I howled. People leaned out of cars to look at us. This was the most brutal criticism of popular singing that either one of us had ever heard.

A few minutes later we got our second surprise. As Royal was getting out of the car at his corner, he asked: "Say, have you fellows got any loose money?"

Walt recoiled. I could feel him do it. Hollywood was full of bums who five'd and ten'd you to death. There was always an epidemic of it in our business.

"Why? What's the matter, Royal?" I asked.

"Well," said Royal, "I forgot to see about any money. And the man's got my door locked. I can't get in. I was going to mention it at the hotel but you fellows were going out and...."

Wow! Walt never said a word, but I knew what he was thinking. Either we dug up some money for Royal or we took Royal to the apartment with us—and we were stuck with him. Now it's one thing to be crazy about the way a guy plays piano, but it's another thing altogether to play papa and mama for him. A guy like Royal could easily drive you daffy in a few days if you had to live with him.

"How much do you need, Royal?" I asked.

"Well," he said, after some thought, "I think twenty-five would see me through fine. Then I'll see about some money."

We dug it up. It killed both of us. That was a lot of money for us, but I think we were both feeling the same way about the business. At this point we were a little afraid of Royal. Who was he? Where had he been? How did it happen a guy who could play piano like that hadn't been heard of? We had a feeling like maybe he was a Voodoo Man. Does that sound silly? All right, let's put it another way. This guy was from Mars, maybe. He didn't belong here. I'm not exaggerating when I say that this boy made Lonny Boyle, considered the best around, seem conventional. Nothing added up. Nothing figured. So we gave him the twenty-five.

He just said: "Thanks, fellows," waved, and disappeared.

"Well," said Walt, as we drove on, "there's an original mooch if I ever saw one."

"This guy, Walt," I said, "is not a mooch."

"Well, at least he's not the usual gimme-five type. He says gimme twenty-five. Suppose he'd said a hundred."

"You could always hock this car."

Now big careless Walt began to get back in character. First he chuckled, then suddenly he burst out into a roar. We both roared, remembering now what Royal had said about Frank.

"Well," said Walt, finally, "many a time I've got less good out of more money."

But there was a topper. Three days later a check appeared in the mail. It was the dirtiest, smeariest-looking check I ever saw in my life, but it was good, and it was for fifty dollars.

There was a note with it written in pencil on a torn-off piece of yellow copy paper.

Dear fellows:
        Thanks for the fifty. It was swell of you.
                    Royal Mauch

"Fifty?" cried Walt, staring.

"That's pretty close for Royal. A mooch, eh?"

"Let's look him up, give him back twenty-five."

"Okay. But if it was anybody else...."

We couldn't find him. He'd gone away some place. But he'd kept his room. The dirty old guy who ran the joint said proudly that "the gentleman was paid up to the nickel," and he went on to explain that he'd had a little trouble with his tenant but that that was a thing of the past, there'd be no more trouble "because this young man is a perfect gentleman."

♮ ♭

Well, with one thing and another we lost Royal. Then we found him again. He came over to the hotel one afternoon. I was listening to the rebroadcast of an Eastern ball game. He surprised me. He knew quite a bit about baseball. We sat around with our feet up, listening. He didn't look so good, and I asked him if he'd been sick.

"No," he said, and left it at that.

Naturally you don't argue with a guy if he says he's not sick. He looked it, though. When I gave him back the twenty-five, he seemed bewildered. He said he was certain he'd tapped us for fifty.

"Fifty's what I needed," he said rather vaguely. Finally we got that straight.

Walt showed up just as the ball game was over and he seemed really glad to see Royal. We sat around yacking.

"You owe me twelve-fifty," I told him, which was very unwelcome news to him at the moment, as things had been slack, so he brushed me off.

Then he began to talk to Royal. "Couple days ago," he said, "I ran into Frank and Berte. It was out in Beverly. We went into the Luau for a drink and one thing led to another, so I told Berte what you said. She lit up like a police switchboard on Hallowe'en."

"Well, it's true," said Royal.

"We got to go out there again one of these nights," said Walt. "I'm glad you turned up. Where've you been? We went over to your place."

"Oh, I had to go away for a while," said Royal.

And I thought: "I'd like to see Royal on the witness stand. Like trying to get blood out of a turnip."

Well, we yacked some more, then Royal got up and said he'd have to go.

"Why," I said, "you got a date?"

"Date? No."

"How about the piano? It looks kind of lonesome over there."

Now this is the kind of thing no musician ever says to another. Music is hard work. Most musicians want to forget all about it whenever they can and go out on the town with their wives or somebody's wives, or go to a ball game, or bowl, or go to a movie, or even just work around the house, cut the grass, and maybe take junior and the missus out for a ride in that nice Southern California traffic where it's bumper to bumper for twenty miles in any given direction.

But I had a strong yen to hear that cockeyed piano-playing of Royal's again.

"No, thanks, Stan," he said. "I'm not with it lately. I've hit a post."

He really looked low. This is the first guy I ever worried about before in my life. I couldn't understand it. So I says, "Let's all go get some sandwiches, and then maybe we can bowl or something."

"Count me out," said Walt.

I knew what that meant—a dusky brunette. So Royal and I went together, just the two of us. It was not a success. Royal just sat there staring while we ate, and when we'd finished and were outside and the lights were just coming on along the boulevard, he said: "Well, so long, Stan. Thanks for the eats. I'll see you."

He walked off. I just stood there, watching him. He had a very young walk, like a high-school kid.

A few days passed. One evening Walt said: "Stan, will you see if you can dig up that piano player? I can't dodge Frank much longer."

"You mean Berte."

Walt thought for a while before he spoke. "Yeah, Berte, too. I don't know, Stan. This is a fine, nice girl. I like this girl. But she's trouble, brother, and no neck in the noose for me. On principle."

"That girl's got everything, chum," I said. "Are you crazy? Even money."

"I know, I know," said Walt. "It worries me. Some nights I can't sleep."

I laughed so hard at this I almost sprained my jaw. Walt! He was the original buzz saw. I could hear him snoring at night with all doors closed.

He got sore as hell at me, and then he came to himself, as he usually did, and started laughing.

"Love in bloom," I said.

And he got sore again. "It's a word, a word," he yelled. "I don't even know what it means. I'm no movie writer. They put out all that corny love crap. They made it up. Look, let me explain. A girl sees a guy she wants, so she goes after him hot and heavy, if she wants him bad enough, the sky's the limit. It's a battle. If the guy gives in and lets her tie the rope on him for good, everybody says he's a nice fellow, but to hell with that he's hooked, ain't he? But if he blows after he's had the use of the girl for a while and the heat's over, they say he's a heel. You can't win. No matter what you do, you lose. To hell with it."

"Walter, Walter," I said. "You can tell your mother. Is it really that bad?"

He went for me. We belted each other pretty good for a while, laughing, then we went out and belted the Scotch at the nearest bistro. And along about eleven Walter walked off with a big smiling brunette he'd never seen before.

At three the next morning he came in singing. Then he rushed into my bedroom and pulled me out of bed by the heels. Just as I was hitting the floor with my caboose, he said: "Stan, will you find that damned piano player for me?"

But it wasn't easy. And to tell the truth I didn't strain myself over it. I had other problems, jobs and telephone numbers, etc., etc. And then one after- noon Royal walks in. Walt and I are sitting around like a couple of char- acters from Tobacco Road. It's a hot summer day. We've got on pajama pants and we've got our big ugly bare feet up on the table.

As usual, Royal is a shock. He's got on a Brooks suit, tie, everything.

"Who died?" I asked.

He gave such a start at this that I was surprised.

"Died?" he asked, kind of funny.

"Well, look at you."

"Oh," he said. "I bought some clothes. I've been running low and I just didn't get around to it."

"What does he use for money?" I wondered. It was useless to ask, and how could you, anyway?

He sat down and we kicked it around, and finally Walt brought up going out to Frank's.

"All right," said Royal.

So Walt got on the phone.

"Smoked turkey, here I come," I said, my mouth watering. While we were getting dressed, later, we heard the piano.

A short, very odd piece took off, exploded and then stopped.

Royal played it again. It was like nothing I'd ever heard, and yet it was jazz, of a kind, just as Dixie, swing, and bop are all jazz, in various phases. But it was a hell of a lot stranger and very fast.

Walt ran into my room with his suspenders hanging. "Did you hear that?"

"Yes. And there it goes again."

We went back into the living room. Royal looked up at us kind of sheepish and began to play chopsticks, but even that started to sound weird and he took off with it for a moment, then stopped.

"What were you playing?" asked Walt.

"Oh, just something I kid around with."

"You mean, you were improvising?"

"No," said Royal. "It's something I... well, it's a little jazz piece I wrote. 'Beating the Birds to the Cherries.'"

"Let's hear it."

Royal played it. Then got up. It made you feel very strange, like anything new or mysterious does. You know, when you say to yourself, "Now what in the hell ever made him think of that?"

We just stared. Then Walt broke me up. "Has it got lyrics? It would make a fine encore for Frank."

Royal was pleased by Walt's remark. Walt was catching on.

"Man," said Walt, "that one really runs. Did you write it down?"

Royal nodded.

♮♭

On the way out to Frank's I got to thinking about the night Frank and Berte dropped by our place and insisted on taking us out to dinner. Us? They wanted Walter, that was all, but being polite people, they asked me to go along. Well, let's put it this way: I was hungry and Frank was buying, so I went.

While I was getting dressed, Walt came back and said: "Leave off the sweater and put on a tie. We're going to Romanoff's."

Romanoff's! I used to know an out-of-work drummer who parked cars there. I felt defiant about the whole thing. Okay, Romanoff's! It's a free country, I'm a citizen. What is Romanoff's? Just a place where you scoff.

But when I got there, I didn't feel so defiant. For Frank and Berte it was routine, just as Pete's Broiler would have been for me. And as for Walter, well, he's a college man and he's got his fraternity pin—and to hell with all peasants. Me, I'm one of the peasants!

I had a feeling the headwaiter was looking me over and thinking: "What's that bum doing in here?"

And while we were having a cocktail, Mike Romanoff himself came over and shook hands with Frank and smiled at all of us, and I thought he was eying me, rather surprised, as if to say: "Why didn't these nice people leave the chauffeur in the car!"

I gulped down a martini too fast and began to feel hot all over, so I gulped down another one. After the third, I was feeling no pain and began to look around at the chicks. Wow!

Then we got to talking about Royal, and that's what we talked about through dinner.

Frank didn't dig him at all, and he asked Walter what we saw in him.

Walt says: "He's the best damned piano player I ever heard. He's way out there, he's on a new kick."

"You mean, like Sauter-Finegan?" asked Frank—oh, he was a hip kid.

Walt thought this over for a while, then he said: "No. I think it's natural to him, he can't do it any other way. Sometimes the Sauter-Finegan outfit sounds like it's trying too hard to get off on a new kick."

"Well," said Frank, "I've got a wonderful ear, myself, and I've been singing ever since I was six years old, but most of this stuff we're talking about baffles me. Could it be an affectation?"

Get him! Walter avoided my eyes and damned if he didn't flush a little.

"It could, it could," said Walt, quickly brushing it off, then he tied into the sole, which was cooked with bananas and almonds. I had it, too. Does that sound gruesome? It melted in the mouth!

"I like him," said Berte, jumping in—the little woman—taking up the slack. "There's something sort of... well, sad about him. He's a very gentle person, I think."

Full of martinis and Mars-type food, I got into the discussion. "It's like this," I said, and I could see Walter was getting ready to kick me under the table, like as if we were married and he was a woman ashamed of her blabbermouth husband, "say a guy's got astigmatism real bad. Without his glasses, the world's a completely cockeyed place. Well, Royal's got astigmatism every way, not just eyes—if you know what I mean."

Frank did not know what I meant. "You mean he's whacky?"

"What's whacky?" I asked. "Who's crazy? Who's the judge? Maybe the wrong people have got the right people locked up."

Frank smiled indulgently at this, but I meant it. Take a look at the world and then think it over. It's possible.

"Look," I said. "Take the Army." The Army? Me? But it was only to make a point. "They draft all these young guys, make soldiers out of them. But a hell of a lot of them don't fit. So do they say, 'Hell, this guy will never make a soldier in a hundred years, he's not cut out for it'? No. He's right away a psycho."

I was getting a little too serious for Walter, on account of the martinis, I guess, so he said: "Well, they didn't find you out. What are you yelling about?"

And we all laughed.

But I wasn't through. "Look," I said, "they set up a pattern, not only in the Army—every place. And if you don't fit it you're a psycho."

"Stop apologizing," said Walter. "It's all right. We like you."

"I think he's a very nice boy," said Berte, meaning Royal. "He was trying very hard to help me. And he has excellent manners."

So she noticed things like that. It made me kind of uneasy again.

"I don't know," said Frank, baffled. "It always seems to me that maybe it's just affectation."

So we ate our Baked Alaska in silence, and the point of all this is, once you met Royal you kept talking and wondering about him, even a guy like Frank Guardi, who was so conventional in his thinking that he didn't even realize that he himself was trying to break out of the pattern.

You see, Frank was a born agent and impresario, like his old man, and the old man expected Frank to take his place eventually, but Frank wanted to sing.

Funny world, eh?

Well, at Frank's we had another "Royal night," as Walt and I were beginning to call it.

Frank sang as usual and insisted that he was getting better, to which Walt agreed. Then Berte sang and I noticed Royal squirming around in his seat, finally he got up and went to the piano. Apparently he'd been giving Berte some thought. Here's what he did. He played the melody with one finger, indicating the way the tune should be phrased, and Berte caught on little by little. Then Royal began to explain to her that the mannerisms she'd picked up, second and third hand, were very, very bad, and that she was to sing in her natural voice and cut out the grunts, groans, sighs, moans, slides for home base, and the arm-waving.

"Most of these singers," said Royal, "you tie their arms they couldn't sing. It's stupid."

But occasionally Royal would forget himself and begin to chord and then Berte would get lost.

But it was wonderful. Both Walt and myself felt we'd been taught a lesson. This guy *knew!*

And then the buffet, which I won't go into, and then finally Royal, Walt and myself began to horse around. After about half an hour we did pretty good with "Three Little Words" and a slow "I Can't Give You Anything But Love, Baby." Then Royal began to dig up the oldies, the real oldies, I mean: "Siren Song," "Japanese Sandman," "Allah's Holiday," "Babes in the Woods," "Poor Butterfly," and finally one I'd never heard of—a waltz, "Underneath the Stars." A waltz? Royal broke it all to pieces and reassembled it. We just listened, with Walt hitting an obvious bass-note now and then.

But Royal had saved the best till the last, and pretty soon we were tying into "There's Egypt in Your Dreamy Eyes"—and Hi-O, Silverberg, away!

It was better than the other time even. Walt's face was red as a tail-light, and I began to get ready to cry... when, wham! the lamps started to shake, the pictures jumped on the wall and my chair rocked sideways—a straight chair, I'm speaking of—and I said to myself, "Man, we couldn't be that good!" And then I noticed the big chandelier swinging kind of wild in the hallway.

Frank and Berte were standing now. And then all of a sudden something began to bang and rattle some place in the house.

"Earthquake!" yelled Royal, and he jumped off the piano bench, tore past me like a dash-man in the Olympic Games, then out into the hall and out the front door, leaving it open. We could hear him running down that quiet Beverly Hills street—north of Sunset, naturally, would Frank live any place else?

"What the hell?" cried Walter, swaying with the big bass as if they were both drunk.

But I took out after Royal. I can run pretty fast but I didn't get to him till he was almost to Sunset. I had to grab him and hold him. He was all to pieces, pale as chalk, shaking all over, and crying, with his face all screwed up like a little kid.

I said: "Where the hell do you think you're going?"

He wasn't thinking and he didn't know where he was going. He kept trying to get away from me and run some place—any place. I considered taking him over to the Polo Lounge at the Bev. Hills Hotel for a drink. It was close by. But I changed my mind about that quick. Once they got a look at Royal, they'd bounce us both out.

Well, the earth quieted down and stopped rocking. It had seemed like a rough one to me—but the papers didn't give it much of a play the next day, so maybe it wasn't as rough as I'd thought.

I finally got Royal back to Frank's house and put him in Walt's car, then I kept honking the horn for Walt, I wasn't going to leave that joker alone for one second in his condition.

Well, we took him back to the apartment, with Walt driving and looking at him kind of uneasy from time to time.

And to get a little ahead of myself, Royal would never play "There's Egypt in Your Dreamy Eyes" again.

I put him in my bed. He was in real bad shape, and pretty soon he asked in a funny-sounding voice: "Have you fellows got any stuff?"

"Stuff?" cried Walt, drawing back.

"Yes, you know," said Royal.

Walt backed farther off. "You mean, weed? Hell, no, we don't touch it."

"You on it, Royal?" I asked. You could have knocked me over with a piccolo.

"I was," said Royal, "but I beat it. I was even on the Big Kick for a while."

"You mean 'H'?" I gasped.

"Yes," said Royal.

"You're crazy," I said, without thinking.

"No," said Royal, calming down. "That's not it. I just had some... well, some big disappointments. I...." He let it go at that.

"Have you really got it beat?" I asked.

"Yes," said Royal.

"Then let it stay beat. We'll get you straightened out. You stay here, Walt. I got to use the phone."

Walt was shying like a big nervous horse, but he stayed. And I went in and called a doctor I knew who was a good guy and liked jazz, and looked after Mose Baylor for free when Mose tried to take the hard way out with a .22 rifle and just succeeded in blinding himself in one eye. Mose was okay now, and some of his friends had finally managed to give the doctor at least a few bucks—after two or three years. This doctor never dunned a musician.

♮♭

His name was Wallace and he was about forty, a nice, quiet-looking guy. I briefed him about Royal, and then he went in and stayed with the guy for about an hour.

When he came out, he joined Walt and me in a drink of booze.

"Well?" said Walt, pretty nervous himself. You see, this big Walt—this moose—didn't know what it was to be sick and sickness scared hell out of him.

"Oh, he'll be all right," said the Doc. "But keep him off the stuff if you can. He's not strong, and he's very nervous. Born nervous, I mean. It's in his system. Why? Don't ask me. He ought to sleep ten or twelve hours. I slugged him slightly. It'd be a good idea if he stayed in bed for a day or two, but he probably won't. If he wants to, let him."

"What do you think of him, Doc?" I asked.

"Think of him?" said the Doc, surprised. "I don't think anything of him in particular. Why?"

"Well, he's a pretty special guy in some ways. The best piano player I ever run across in my life."

The Doc laughed. "Stan," he says, "those things don't show on the outside."

It was a wise remark.

Back a ways, I said: "Funny world, eh?" as if I'd made a smart remark. But it is a funny world. How about this? Later, it turns out that Frank, Walter, and Royal all belong to the same fraternity, different chapters, or something, though. Walt still had his pin—on his vest, I mean. Frank probably had his put away in a box in a dresser drawer. But if Royal ever had one—which I doubt—he had lost it long ago, you could bet on that.

I just throw this in as a mighty strange coincidence.

Well, we were stuck with Royal, as we were afraid we'd be the night we dug up the twenty-five for him, and it was damned inconvenient. It interfered with everything. Walt and I were used to doing things our way, going and coming as we pleased, you know what I mean. Every time I wanted to change my clothes, there was Royal, lying in the bed. Every time I wanted to run out for a sandwich I'd start worrying about how Royal was going to get a meal.

However, we did the best we could, and in three days—which seemed like three years—it was all over. What I mean is, Royal got up, said he was okay, and moved into the living room, which made things a lot easier all around. At night he slept on the couch. This didn't bother anything because he never complained about us coming in late and banging the doors, or about the noise or the lights going off and on, or anything.

In the morning when I got up—actually it was afternoon, about twelve-thirty or one—he'd have the living room all straightened up and he'd get my breakfast. He was used to living alone, so he whipped up a pretty good meal—even hot cakes.

He seemed to go out of his way to try to please us, and it was sort of embarrassing, like a poor relative struggling to hang on with you, when he knew you didn't want him around any longer. We wondered why he didn't take off now to his own place, which wasn't far away. Why spend his nights on a couch in the living room?

The thing was, he *wasn't* okay and he knew it, and he didn't want to be alone. He was still pretty jumpy. And even we noticed it at times. But being a couple of iron-nerved slobs, we didn't draw the right conclusion.

I only found out later what all this meant to Royal.

We had dinner at home one night, the three of us—and Walt and I were not looking forward to the evening because neither of us had any place to go or anything to do. We were restless as cats, and I mean real cats.

Royal was looking much better. There was color in his face and he'd dressed up in his Brooks suit and a necktie.

After Walter had finished his second piece of pie, he got up and began to walk around pulling at his curly hair. Finally he looked at me and asked: "You want some smoked turkey?"

"How can you talk about food after what you just ate?" I came back, turning the idea over in my mind. The longer I thought about it, the less I liked it. I just did not want to hear Frank sing "I Got My Love to Keep Me Warm" again.

"Listen, fellows," said Royal, "would you like to hear some music?"

"What kind?" asked Walt, turning.

"All kinds. Any kind," said Royal. "Records."

"I don't know," said Walt dubiously.

"Anything's better than listening to Frank sing," I put in. "What's the pitch, Royal?"

"I get hungry for my records," said Royal. "I haven't played any of them in months."

"Special records?" I asked.

"Well, it's my collection," said Royal. "I've got three or four thousand."

"Three or four thou...!" Walt began, then he laughed. He never failed, this boy Royal. "Where do you keep 'em, at Bekin's Storage?"

"No. Out at Palos Verdes."

Now Palos Verdes was to hell and gone from where we lived, twenty miles, maybe even further. I began to laugh. "Walt," I said, "this is for us. Clear to Palos Verdes to listen to records."

"Come on," said Walt. "What are we waiting for?"

♮♭

Palos Verdes is a very nice residential section down by the ocean, but it's dark as hell, hilly, desolate at night, and it's like living in the woods. I looked around at the far-apart houses with trees, hills, and darkness in between and wondered who in the hell would want to live in a place like this. Me, I like boulevard lights and drug stores on every other corner.

We still didn't know why we were going to Palos Verdes, but, of course, that was the kind of thing that bothered neither Walt nor me ordinarily. But finally Walt asked, "Who lives down here?"

"Must be rhinestone hill-billies," I said.

"No," said Walt, "I mean, where the hell are we going? Whose house?"

"Some people I know," said Royal. "They keep my records for me."

"Yeah. But how about us barging in?" asked Walt. I could see he was a little nervous. This Royal frazzled him, like.

"Oh, that's okay. There's nobody here."

"How do we get in?"

"I've got a key."

Well, we wound up and up and up till I began to get dizzy. All of a sudden we made a turn in the road and right in front of us was the whole coastline with the lights stretching away to hell and gone along the shore, maybe away up to Santa Monica. Man, we were really up there—and no street lights!

Now I began to get nervous. "Are you sure you can find this place, Royal?"

"Find it?" he said, like I was an imbecile. "Sure."

And he found it, and there it was. What a place! A big, one-story modern house stretching along the top of a hill, dark as the inside of a coal mine, with the shoreline lights kind of glistening way off behind it, in the distance.

"This is a *house!*" said Walt, as we parked in the drive and got out. "I can't even see the end of it."

"Oh, it's not so big," said Royal. "It just looks big."

There was no answer to this, so we said nothing and followed Royal through a kind of archway and along a wonderful porch like you'd expect to find at a swank hotel, with plants in pots, and chairs and... well, you know: class.

Then came the Royal touch. He'd forgot the key.

"Oh, fine," said Walt, laughing.

"We'll get in some way," said Royal. "Don't worry."

But we *did* worry, while Royal ran around to all the windows, trying to get in. Then he disappeared around the corner of the house in among the bushes.

"Say," said Walt, "this is silly. I don't like this. He bothers me."

"Well, we've come this far," I said, "why back up now?"

"The jailhouse is cold," said Walt.

Time passed. Insects chirped all around us and pretty soon an owl began hooting in a tree right near us: "Whoop! Whooo!"

"Who dat?" cried Walt.

And I laughed like hell. I was kind of hysterical. I'm strictly a city boy and don't go for insects and dark nights in the woods and owls.

All of a sudden the porch light came on and we jumped. The front door opened and Royal looked out. "Come on in, fellows," he said, calm as you please. "Sorry to keep you waiting so long."

♭♮

According to the trades, Hollywood is full of Personalities with a capital P. You know what I mean? Do you ever read the *Hollywood Reporter*—the gossip column? "Jan Gootz just winged in from N.Y. for a huddle with the brass at Repulsive." Who is Jan Gootz? Why, you dope, he is a Personality! How come? Well, he hired a press agent, man. Don't you know *nothing?*

I always get a picture of Jan Gootz "huddling," and it always reminds me of the old football gag, about the quarterback who couldn't recognize any of his teammates unless they had their backs to him and were bending over. You think that gag doesn't fit Hollywood?

Yeah. "Will Lotys Wishfort return to Sock Cummerbund?" So it says in the column. Who is Lotys, and who, oh, who, is Sock? Personalities, chum. With press agents.

Well, Royal was a real *Personality*—and he didn't *need* a press agent.

You don't mind if I sort of get off the subject now and then, do you? Like talking about a Hollywood gossip column? They tell me this is what's called a digression. It's kind of like what a musician might call "kidding around," instead of sticking to the melody. Lawrence Welk sticks to the melody. Guy Lombardo sticks to the melody. Boring, isn't it? Except that maybe you might come back at me with that old one, fifty million Frenchmen can't be wrong. But don't give me that! A *hundred* million Frenchmen, or any other kind of people, can be wrong. And if that's anti-democratic, put me in the hoosegow.

All right.

So Royal let us in. Man, this house was a monster.

Walt took one look and said: "Dis mus' be de plaze!"

"Come on back here, fellows," said Royal, leading us through a kind of hallway—I don't know what else to call it—with glass partitions, or something, and copper gadgets on the walls with ferns and stuff in them, and pale indirect lighting. Man!

"When does the floor show start?" asked Walt, and Royal looked around at him and grinned.

"I don't like it much myself," he explained.

"You don't like it?" cried Walt. "Kiddo, you better go see a head-shrinker. Man, I'd like to own this pad. What a place to bring chicks to! Dance! Party!" All of a sudden Walt stopped and stared, then he cried: "Shangrila! Get that scenery."

Words, words, words! And I'm stuck for some to use. Words are like painted marbles, they get all the stuff rubbed off of them. Take "great." What does it mean? It means "great," you donkeyhead, you yell back at me. All right. So now we got "great" movie actors, and "great" automobiles, and "great" refrigerators and even "great" lipsticks. So what are you going to call George Washington? Do you dig me now?

One time I got to talking about words with Royal. It's always a mistake to talk about anything with Royal if you've got any doubts. This was no exception. "Take 'red,'" Royal said. "There's no such thing as 'red.'" "What do you mean?" I yells. (He was "great" at getting people to yell.) "There's a color. We named it 'red,' that's all. Like you number something. Take you, for instance. You are a young animal, aged twenty-four. Your number is Stan Pawley. But you are really not Stan Pawley, at all. It's only for convenience." "Sure, sure," I said and then I walked away and thought this over for several days.

Well, I'd better stop thinking about words or I'll never get this thing written at all.

I was just trying to find some words to describe the view from this big, long playroom, or whatever it was. A huge view-window ran the whole length of the outer wall. In fact, the whole wall was glass. And framed in this glass was a... oh, the hell with it. I'm just trying to say you could see all the way up the coast, considerably past Malibu, Royal said. Maybe thirty miles or more. And the lights were shining along the shore and making zigzags in the water, and we were away up high above all of it—and it looked like a night background in a stage play, only better. I'll let it lay. I won't say any more except to remark it made you gasp, and if that makes me sound faggy I can't help it.

But Royal didn't even glance out the window. He was running around like an agent at an actors' convention, opening doors, grabbing up bottles and glasses, getting out ice cubes, slamming things down on tables.

Walt just stood looking out the window with his mouth open. Finally he turned and looked at me.

"Man, we just don't live," he said, sort of puzzled.

"We live."

"We exist," said Walt. "Not that I'm queer for luxury and big houses. Frank can have his. But, *this* pad!" He began to sing "Dream" and Royal stopped in his scrambling around, turned and listened.

"You see?" said Royal. "Nobody needs a voice to sing. Walter knows how to sing."

"Thanks," said Walt, a little surprised I could see.

"How about *me* singing?" I asked, jealous. "I know a wonderful number. 'Everybody's Got Somebody, But I've Only Got You.' Naturally it was written by a musician's wife."

Royal smiled indulgently.

"That's good patter," said Walt. "I'll remember that."

"Any time, any time," I told him, having come off first, at least in my own estimation.

"Look," said Royal. "I'm a lousy host. There's the liquor, water and soda, and the glasses and ice. Help yourselves."

"Lousy host, he says," laughed Walt, pouring himself a hooker that would have jolted a mule. When there was free liquor going, Walt was a real musician. And what about me? I did likewise. And, oh, that Scotch was smooth. Over the rocks is the way we drank it when it was somebody else's liquor. Few rocks, much booze.

The record player was in the wall, naturally, and just as naturally it was a Hi-Fi deal. Royal was sitting on the floor, flushed and happy, like a kid at home surrounded by his toys after he'd been away for the weekend.

We listened. We drank. We didn't give a damn what he played. But it was the usual stuff. Bix. Louis. Mugsy. Benny. Red. Tommy. Duke. You know what I mean. I won't say I was bored, because it is very hard for me to be bored and drunk at the same time. Let's put it this way: I was listless. And so was Walt. This was all stuff in the past tense, like looking at the valentines your mother had saved from when she was a girl.

But Royal sat there with his head lowered, really listening.

It went on for hours, with Royal still sitting on the floor and us still spraddled out in chairs, and the Scotch running out in a couple of bottles—we each had one—like sand in an hourglass. And then it stopped.

Royal didn't say a word. He'd hardly had a drink. Finally he got up and stretched. "You know what that is, fellows?" he demanded.

We didn't know what he meant, so we didn't say anything.

"It's the only live art in the world today," said Royal.

"In your hat," I felt like saying. God, how I hate that highbrow cackle. And Walt gave me a worried, puzzled look. He didn't dig that kind of talk any more than I did, and it made him uncomfortable.

"You know what I mean?" asked Royal.

"You been reading the *Saturday Review?*" I said.

"No," said Royal mildly. "I've been thinking about it for years. You see, all the other arts are just repetitions of what was done in Europe, or even Rome and Greece. Look at painting. Same old stuff. Take the novel. You read much?"

"I like girly books with naked chicks on the covers," said Walt.

"I read," I said, and Walt snickered.

"Well, it's the same old thing over and over. Never anything new or original, all derivative. Well, jazz was invented in America. It's the true expression of American civilization. That's what I mean."

I was sure surprised at Royal—you always expected something unpredictable, something original from him, but to me this was just the old drivel, and Royal was repeating it like he'd thought it up. Who cares? Music—jazz music—is either for kicks or loot, or both. Why make a federal case out of it?

Royal looked from me to Walt and back again, then he clammed up. He seemed kind of hurt, I thought.

Walt's quart was empty and Walt was pie-eyed, with that silly expression on his big face. I was only about three drinks behind him and my feet were beginning to get numb.

I could see Royal was trying to make up his mind whether to play any more records or not, and just as he was opening a new cabinet, a car came buzzing up the drive, crunching the gravel, and I saw a flash from the headlights on all the glass in the hallway for a moment.

Royal straightened up and listened. We heard voices, car doors slamming. "Oh, Christ! Piggy!" Royal said in disgust. "I thought she was going to stay in Santa Barbara for two more days."

"Who's Piggy?" asked Walt, sobering and beginning to get worried.

"My damned sister," said Royal.

Royal's sister! "This I'll have to see," I says to myself.

Then there was a key in the lock, the big front door swung open—I could see it away down that long glass, metal, and fern hallway—and a fairly tall, slim woman walked in with a mink coat draped on her shoulders. A middle-aged chauffeur in a blue cap and a plain blue suit was carrying two bags, and beyond them was a middle-aged maid with her hat on sideways and her hair sticking up in wisps.

"Royal!" shouted Piggy, down all the length of the hallway. Her voice sounded surprised and pleased.

Walt looked at me and I looked at Walt. There was money written all over this combination. Maybe Royal was broke, but it was a damned good cinch his sister wasn't.

The chauffeur and the maid—husband and wife, I found out later—turned off some place in the world-of-the-future hallway, and Piggy came on alone.

It was obvious right away that Piggy, like her brother, was a character. She was about thirty, slender, flat-chested, narrow-hipped, elegant, expensive and homely, but with *something*—don't ask me what! Her blond hair was cut as short as mine—I don't go for the crew, myself, I'm more the duck-tail type—and, being very near-sighted, like Royal, she had on slanted jeweled cheaters that gave her a kind of Mongolian look. A dyke, I says to myself right away—you know how you make those snap judgments.

But as soon as she saw the Male Animal—Walt—I began to realize I was wrong. She really looked him over. Now I don't mean she was on the make for him, don't get me wrong. But she was sure conscious he was there.

I just sat there like the bum I am, but Walt, a college man drunk or sober, had got up right away and stood waiting respectfully to be introduced.

"So you're the boys," said Piggy, as I stumbled bleary-eyed to my feet. "Kip's been telling me about you. So nice for you to come."

Walter even bowed, though that was overdoing it, because he was taking one awful chance of falling through one of those glass-topped tables.

"I'm Kip," said Royal. "This is Piggy. Her name's Mrs. Bill Jones."

"God, I hate that name," she said mildly. "Call me Piggy."

"I'm sorry," said Walter, giving with another little bow, "but I could never call you Piggy. How about Slim?"

I don't know. Sometimes I wonder how this boy does it. If I'd've said that, the broad would probably have been insulted, at least it would have sounded awful silly. With him, it sounded like Sir Waiter Raleigh, or maybe Rubirosa.

"All right," said Piggy, giving Walt a pleasant smile—she had good-look- ing teeth, I'll say that for her. "Swell. And what do I call you?"

I jumped in now. "Lover Boy," I said. "Or maybe Peter Pan."

"You're Stan, aren't you?" she said, giving me one of those oh-so-you're- here-too looks I often get when I'm in company with my wonderful big pal, that man's man and woman's delight, Walter Flick.

"I'm Stan. He's Walt," I said, pointing us out.

She looked us both over, then she looked down at the forlorn bottles that once had been so full of smooth and lovely Scotch, then she laughed.

"If you've had enough to drink," she said, "how about something to eat?"

"Roger," I said, and Walter gave with a fiendish grin that would have made Harpo Marx envious.

This grin made Piggy laugh. "Okay," she said. "Ellen's worn out and Pat's got rheumatism because it was so damp at Santa Barbara, and they've gone to bed, so I'll have to get the food myself."

"Could I be of any assistance?" asked Walter. Trust him!

"Oh, definitely," said Piggy. "Follow me."

Walt followed her. They disappeared. From time to time we could hear faint laughter coming in through the ventilators or some place.

"He sure is a card," I said sadly.

"Walt?" said Royal. "Nice fellow. He better look out for Piggy. She's the domineering type."

"He's the eel type," I said. "Anyway, she's married, isn't she?"

"Divorced," said Royal. "But Bill keeps trying to get her back. God knows why."

Royal's attitude toward his sister struck me as very humorous and I began to laugh.

"It's not funny," said Royal. "She ought to wear riding boots and carry a whip—and then you'd know what she was like."

While we waited, Royal began to talk about his sister. He was such a close-mouthed guy that this sort of surprised me. But he was feeling it, man, he was feeling it, and it came out. He wasn't just being coy, or put- ting on an act, or talking for effect, he meant it. I could see that there was a real antagonism between him and Piggy. "This Bill Jones," he was telling me, "is a wonderful fellow—or used to be till he married Piggy. She just married him to get away from home. She and my father hate each other like cats and dogs, and she couldn't take it any longer. You see, it makes a bad situation when two people in one house want to dominate."

"Must be in the money, this Jones boy," I put in, curious.

"Yes," said Royal. "His family's very rich. Gas company money. And of course Piggy had none of her own. Dad wouldn't give her a penny. But she's got plenty now."

I could still hear the laughing coming in through the ventilators or some place. Walt could really make the dames laugh. With an all-female audience he'd be a riot on any stage in the country.

♮♭

We ate in what I guess you would call a kind of breakfast nook in a normal house. But what a nook! It was a long, narrow room, sort of semicircular, with a leather seat running all around the curved part. The flat side, the wall, was just one great big window. The moon was looking in now, and we heard that owl again, whoo-whooing some place.

"Who dat?" cried Walt, with his face full of omelet.

And Piggy laughed, put her arm across his shoulders and patted him. This was one smart chick, I could see. She had Walt's number already. She did not take him seriously at all. She treated him like he was a big St. Bernard.

Royal was mighty subdued, pushed his food around on the plate, and kept compressing his lips like a preacher in the South Sea Islands, disapproving of all this paganism. But Royal was really only disapproving of his sister—just a kind of family disapproval. I'm from a big family and I ought to know. As far as his sister was concerned, he'd had it, apparently. Everything she did or said seemed to irritate him—and let's let it go at that.

Finally Royal piped up: "Well, fellows, I guess we'd better be getting back."

"And leave this mess?" cried Walt. "Oh, no. I'm going to help the little woman clean up."

"He's a doll," said Piggy, patting him.

Walt gave with one of those fiendish Harpo Marx grins, and wiggled his big ears. They really wiggled. It was one of his many parlor tricks.

Piggy pointed at him and roared with laughter.

Royal took off his glasses and began to wipe the lenses with a handkerchief. His hands were shaking. Boy, did he look lost and bewildered without those glasses.

"Come on, glamorous," said Piggy to Walt, getting up. "I accept your offer."

And while she and Walt got things straightened up, Royal and I just sat there. I never saw a guy look more forlorn.

Well, Royal didn't go back with us. He stayed with his sister—at her request. Request? She practically dared him to leave. "I come clear out here to Southern California," she told us, "to look after him. I buy this house so he will have some place to stay. And what happens?"

What happened was, apparently, that Royal had run off and got himself a dirty basement pad in Hollywood. Anyway, we were shut of him now and we were glad. Three was a crowd in that joint of ours.

Piggy shook hands with us and told us to be sure and come again, but Royal just stood there silent with his lips compressed.

In the confusion, we forgot to ask Royal how to get back to town. Walt just drove along through the darkness, talking. The food had sobered us somewhat, but not too much.

"That's a real screwed-up family situation," said Walt. "Royal's mother was a kind of invalid—in and out of bed ever since he was born. Royal was a mama's boy, I guess, didn't like his father. Piggy didn't like the father either, or the mother, as far as I can make out. Piggy marries some rich guy and blows the family."

"Royal's family rich, too?" I asked.

"I don't know," said Walt. "She didn't say. Well, the mother died and Royal went all to pieces and ran away from home—came out here. By this time, Piggy's divorced, so she comes out here to look after Royal. She thinks he's kind of whacky and she's worried as hell about him. She also," Walt added, after a long pause, "thinks he's a genius."

"Thinks he's a *what?*" I yelled.

"A genius," said Walt. "A musical genius. Oh, she's an odd chick. She's only got one idea. She's going to look after this joker whether he likes it or not. She says he'll be a famous man by the time he's thirty. It's her duty to look after him, she says." A long pause. "That's what the lady said."

"Now here's some top-secret stuff," Walt continued, while I was digesting what he'd already said. "She found out where the boy's pad is, but he doesn't know that. How? Private dicks."

"Oh, no!"

"Yes. This chick is a real determined chick. Don't ever sell her short. And we're supposed to keep this under our hats. We're in the conspiracy now, chum. I'm loaded with telephone numbers. Hers. A lawyer's downtown. And another lawyer's back in the Midwest, where these odd characters came from. Just in case."

"Just in case what?"

"Just in case Junior runs amuck, I guess. And look! She thinks we're great. She thinks we snapped Royal out of it. He's been in a bad way since his mother died. She loves us, kiddo. So... we co-operate."

"Okay, okay. I'll co-operate—providing it don't interfere with my normal life too much."

"Your *what* life?"

"Touché—as the fellow said when he got hit by the truck."

"She says Royal talks about us all the time. She says Royal hadn't talked about anything, hardly, since his old lady died. Stan, this guy's been around. He's studied music at the Conservatory in Cincinnati—and also in Paris. He's a real serious musician. She says he's been working on a big piece—I don't know what—for over two-three years. He got drunk one night and tried to burn it. She took it away from him. She's got it in a safety-deposit box now."

"Boy, sounds like you made this up," I said, and then I began to wonder, did he? "Are you leveling with me, Walter? Or building up to a big gag?"

"I'm leveling," he said.

Well, finally the yacking stopped and we woke up and found out that we were lost, winding around in some damned dark road at the end of no place.

"All we need is a flat now," I grumbled.

"Don't whammy me," yelled Walt, sore. "I got no spare."

Pretty soon we saw a town up ahead. It might have been Singapore, for all we knew. Sure didn't look familiar. And it wasn't when we got there. The streets were deserted, the lights dim. Must have been about three in the morning. Finally we saw a guy crossing a street on foot, and Walt pulled up beside him.

"Excuse me," called Walt. "But where are we?"

This old guy gave us a dirty look. "You're on So-and-so Street," he said. "Where the hell do you think you are?"

"No," said Walt. "I mean, what town?"

Now the old guy stared, smelling a rib. "You drunk?" he demanded.

"Yeah," said Walt. "But what's that got to do with it?"

"You're in San Pedro, California," says this wise guy, "in the United States of America on the North American Continent."

"Thanks," said Walt. "That's close enough." The old guy went on, shaking his head. "San Pedro, eh?" cried Walt. "Let's go look at the boats."

In case you don't know, the San Pedro-Wilmington area is one of the greatest ports in the world, and to hell and gone from Los Angeles.

"We'll look at no boats," I said. "It's the middle of the night and this is one really tough town. You can get your head knocked off here."

"Coward," said Walt.

Well, I won't bore you with the rest. Somehow we managed to get back to our cozy little pad in Hollywood by way of Long Beach and half a dozen other towns I'd never heard of before.

Broad daylight, it was.

Time passed. Not very much. Maybe three weeks. We didn't hear any-thing from Royal. I was very busy, with a real good run of jobs and a new chick—from Georgia—hi, y'all! And Walt was filling in the end of an engagement for a bass player who had cracked up his jalopy on the Holly-wood Freeway and was now lying in a hospital with both knees up and an ugly nurse—he'd crapped out for sure!

I went over to see Walt once or twice. Now I am not a tender-hearted character, but I couldn't take this. Walt was playing bass with a corny piano player in a slick Sunset Boulevard bar. People sat in a circle around this piano player and he gave with the quips and played "requests"— everything from "Papa Loves Mambo" to "Oh, How I Miss You Tonight." One evening when I was in there some drunken middle-aged creep asked for "The Prisoner's Song." And I wondered where he'd been doing a Rip Van Winkle.

"Oh, well," said Walt, "it's money—and it's only for two more weeks."

The piano player did not like Walt. He was a slick-haired Texas wolf and he was used to the broads being on the make for him. Now they started to go on the make for Walt. The piano player tried everything, he even broke down and got a crew-cut. It didn't help. He and Walt ended up not speak-ing. Walt also ended up almost getting shot because this Texas boy was real rough and sometimes packed the difference. The trouble was the Texas boy's *wife* came in one night and threw a pass or two at Walt. Sometimes I'm glad I have to make all the advances. In a way, it saves you a lot of trou-ble.

Oh, yeah. I forgot. Frank and Berte used to turn up at this bar and sit in the intimate circle, watching Walt work. Now of course the Texas wolf knew who Frank was, in fact, Frank's father's outfit—A.A.A.—handled this bum, and the Texan laid himself out to be nice to Frank. But Frank ignored him in his quiet, polite way. And the Texan could see that Frank thought big Walt was the nuts and palavered and smoked with him dur-ing intermission. Believe me, before this engagement was up, there was at least one bewildered and resentful Texan in So. Cal.

Okay. So much for our world-shaking activities.

Well, came one of those nights. I played a private party in Beverly Hills, at a huge mansion north of Sunset. I got so plastered I fell on the floor. Luckily the party was thrown by movie people, so I wasn't tossed out into the street. In fact, I was the life of the party—they told me later, after lit-tle Abe, the drummer, had given me the ice-cube treatment. Boy, the way the servants sneak you those drinks. They'd just hand me something and I'd drink it. Old-fashioned, daiquiri, martini—whatever was going. Man!

I got home at three A.M. and I was still up in that balloon. Well, it seems I'd stood Hi, Y'all up, she was waiting for me in the lobby. This doll had a very fiery temper. She tried to hit me with a big glass ashtray. It wasn't love. Don't get me wrong. She was a real pretty chick and it irked her that a nothing like me would stand her up. The night clerk, a very brave fellow—who argues with a heated-up Southern belle but a very brave fellow?—finally got her into a taxi and out of my life forever. Man!

Funny part was, I'd simply forgotten all about the date when I got the Bev. Hills job at the last minute. I never stand up a good-looking chick. It's not cricket. It's not even ping-pong.

All right.

Now I find out from the night clerk that Walt has been trying to get me on the phone since midnight. He didn't know about the quick pickup job. But I'm bewildered. I live with Walt, don't I? Why don't he just wait till he gets home? I'm still oiled, too, which added to the confusion. The night clerk explains patiently. I'm to call a certain number no matter what time I come in.

I gander the number. Somehow it looks familiar. I call it. It's Frank Guardi's house. At three-thirty A.M.? Frank gets on the phone, then Walt. I'm to take a taxi and get out there right away.

"It's nearly two bucks from here," I yell.

"You charge it to Frank," said Walt.

"But I'm loaded and I want to hit the sack."

"Get out here, you bum, right away," yells Walt, down the wire.

So I did. I woke up just as we were passing the Beverly Hills Hotel.

"You had a nice snooze, pal," said the driver, snickering.

♮ ♭

Did you ever walk into a wide-awake, enthusiastic, sober gathering of friends when you were drunk, tired, disgusted, sleepy and ready to knock your head against the wall?

Then you know what I mean.

Berte, Frank, and Walt all talked at once, very loud and fast. About what? I couldn't make out. Walt got very, very exasperated with me.

"You need a drink," he said.

"Oh, no!" I cried, falling down in a chair and burying my face in my hands.

There was another guy there. His name was Stuart Goldenson. He looked like what most Gentiles think of as a Jew. A short, squat guy with dark kinky hair, sallow complexion, big dark eyes, big nose, etc., etc. Now why this is what most people think a Jew looks like I don't know. Our profession is full of Jews—and I look more "Jewish" than most of them. They've got blue eyes, blond hair, red hair, fair complexions—some of them are as big as Walt and just as rugged. It's a funny thing. But this Goldenson guy was a real kick. With that kisser of his he wore a crew-cut, conservative but very elegant and expensive foreign clothes, and spoke with an exaggerated Duke of Windsor accent. "Wrong sound track," Walt said. Actually, the guy was from Australia or New Zealand and he was one nice guy. Sharp as hell—why not?—but okay.

Well, it turned out Goldenson was opening a swank little bistro in Beverly Hills for upper-class drunks, and he had come to Frank for advice, Frank being a bridge-table friend at some club or other. Stu wanted something fresh and new in the way of music. "They don't listen to it, of course," he explained. "But I want something sophisticated, something chic, in keeping with the decor and the atmosphere."

Get him!

Hearing about all this through Frank, Berte had come up with a brilliant idea, and had sold Frank on it. She'd also sold Stu. Stu had social ambitions, and hobnobbing with Frank and Berte came under the heading of getting up there, as they say in the trade. Here was the world-shattering idea. A trio. Royal, Walt, and me—with Berte as singer.

"I've even got the name," cried Walt. "Flick, Mauch, Pawley and Chirp."

Stu winced. "Oh, no, old boy," he said. "That won't do at all. Too crude."

"I was ribbing," said Walt, giving Stu a look.

Now Berte chimed in. She was pretty excited, believe me, and her eyes— well, what do you say?—shining like stars? Isn't that a little corny? Anyway, they were mighty bright. And you know why. She was looking forward to working night after night with big Walter. She'd made up her mind long ago to capture the unicorn—and what a chance this was!

"I've got it," she cried. "The piano player's first name is Royal. Why not 'The Royal Trio'?"

"King George won't like that," I said.

"King George is dead," said Walt.

"But it's perfect," said Stu. "I'll buy that, Miss Dehn." He wasn't going to call her "Evers," not him! Evers meant nothing at all, Dehn meant a hell of a lot, not only in Bev. Hills, all over Southern California.

"Yeah," I said. "But wait a minute. Let's not be Chuckling Charlies. What about Royal? I don't think he'll go for this."

"Why not?" asked Berte. "He needs work, doesn't he? I always felt that...."

"You felt wrong, Berte," I said. "He does not need work—besides, he hasn't even got a card. He's an amateur."

"We can arrange that," said Frank, meaning A.A.A. could arrange it. And he was right. A.A.A. could arrange almost anything anybody could imagine or dream up in any branch of show business.

"Well..." I said, dubious. Personally I wasn't so keen on this thing myself, but then at the moment I was drunk, disgusted, tired, flipped-off.

The next day it looked swell. A fine bistro in Bev. Hills—say, from about nine to two—with the rest of the day free. Fair pay. Good guys to work with. Hell, why not? I greeted Walt with my changed attitude when he got up about two in the afternoon and stumbled around in his pajama bottoms, his red hair standing up all over his head in curls and his eyes like two poached eggs. But he wasn't having any. He called me some rather interesting names, then he took a shower, drank some coffee, ate thirty or forty good-sized hot cakes—and was himself again.

"This Stu—he's okay," said Walt. "He's heavy with loot, Frank says. But he's stage-struck, and anyway the joint will be a tax write-off if it loses— and it sure as hell will."

"With us in it, it can't miss showing him a very fine loss."

"You're so right," said Walt. "The only thing is—Royal. What do we do? I make you vice-president of the Royal department."

"We could get another piano player. How about your Texas friend?"

Walt merely looked at me.

"Okay. Give me the phone number. I'll call him."

But this was not something you could explain on the phone, so Walt and I ended up driving down to Palos Verdes again. Royal had sounded mighty limp over the wire, like he didn't care much about anything.

And he didn't. He was sitting out in a huge kind of super-patio at the back of the place, wearing dark glasses, a Hawaiian shirt that must have been designed for a heavyweight wrestler, pink shorts, and regular black shoes. His legs were thin, white, and covered with long curly blond hair. Jerry Lewis couldn't have looked funnier.

He explained about the shoes. "I can't find my sneakers," he said. "And I can't go around without shoes. Even with heavy socks on, the pavement burns hell out of my feet."

Piggy was out horseback riding, it appeared. "She's got to be bossing something or somebody all the time," said Royal, "even if it's only a poor damn horse." He seemed to feel pretty sorry for the horse.

We gave him the pitch, first me, then Walt. Royal didn't say a word. He didn't even nod or shake his head. I wasn't even sure he was listening. But I did notice that his color had improved—he was pale as hell when we got there—and that he seemed a little more relaxed.

Finally he said something. "It would take an awful lot of rehearsing, fellows."

He was in. Just like that. I was surprised. Then I had an idea. It would give Royal an excuse to get away from Palos Verdes, and that was it.

Funny world, eh?—as I've said before. You go in a joint and see a trio playing. You just listen, and like it or not, as the case may be. But you never think what might be behind it. A dame on the make and trying to get a very slippery character into a corner, a boy who wants to get away from a managing sister, a guy who is an agent at heart and doesn't even know it, agenting in spite of himself, and a promoter trying to get into show business because he's stagestruck and also killing two birds with one stone—tax writeoff. Me? I got no motives. I might call myself a rebel. I might call myself a vanishing American, the last of the Free Souls. But dat ole pappy of mine maybe was closer to the truth—just a bum! Hi, y'all!

Pretty soon we heard a car coming up the drive. Piggy! "Don't say anything to her," said Royal quickly. "I'll thrash it out later."

Piggy was wearing a loose shirt, tight pants, and riding boots. She was sure a skimpy broad. All that vigor—that moxie—in such a little space. In her riding clothes, she looked like an advertisement for a swank winter resort, a place where they've got to know about your grandfather.

"Hi, boys," she said, gesturing with her riding crop.

"Hiya Slim," said Walt.

"This is an unexpected pleasure," she said, sitting opposite us on a bench.

"The pleasure is all ours, Countess," said Walt.

Royal began to squirm.

"Good God, look at you!" cried Piggy, getting a real gander at her brother now. "What are you made up for?"

Royal swore and grumbled under his breath, then he got up abruptly and went in the house. We could hear him taking a shower in a little room just off the super-patio. This joint had everything but a pool, and you could practically spit in the ocean from the top of the cliff.

Piggy wanted us to stay to dinner, and we had no objections, but we could see that Royal wanted us to blow, so he could rassle with his sister about the trio deal. So we blew.

Piggy walked between us to the jalopy with her arms through ours. "Good God," she said. "What a car!"

"It gets us there," said Walt. "I'm thinking about buying a Jaguar. Just thinking, you understand."

Piggy laughed. "How would you get into a Jaguar? There's too much of you."

"Too much?" asked Walt.

"Well," said Piggy, "too much for the Jaguar."

Piggy was a wit among other things. This remark really handed us a laugh.

♮♭

Royal tried to reach us for hours. But we were out horsing around, doing nothing: bowling, watching TV in a bar, yacking with a couple of musicians we'd bumped into—so run our lives away, as the fellow says.

We got home around midnight, and the night clerk told us about all the calls from Palos Verdes.

I finally got Royal on the phone. He yelled so loud I had to hold the receiver away from my ear. "She's all for it," he screamed. "Can you beat it, Stan? She's all for it. I can live in town, do what I like. Boy, oh, boy."

He sounded like a con who had been sprung after eight years in the big house.

So... that's how the Royal Trio was established.

Now here I am stuck for a word again. "Nightmare" is not exactly the right one, but I guess it's close enough.

It was like this. We rehearsed at Frank's house. It was late in August and a hell of a hot summer for Southern California—we had a couple of days above a hundred degrees. Frank's father had gone to Canada to get out of the heat, and rest—Banff he went to, I think—so we had the run of the place. Nobody there except the Japanese servants, and I often wondered what they thought. You could never tell, of course.

A guy gets so that he forgets that So. Cal. is a desert.

Well, during this time I'm speaking of, we remembered. We always had the big French windows wide open. There wasn't a cloud in the sky and the stars looked like you could reach out and pick one. It was dry as powder and the air was full of electricity. The rugs in Frank's house were three or four inches deep, you'd walk across them, generating electricity, then you'd touch metal by accident and get a hell of a shock. I damned near dropped the guitar a couple of times. And outside I could hear the vegetation rustling like pieces of sandpaper being rubbed together. It was really something! We were all charged up and nervous.

The first night, Walt and I just tore into it when Royal gave us the nod. We were grinning and confident—you know, man, a ball! Royal soon fixed that. He stopped and gave us a quiet little lecture. We tried again. He stopped us. This went on and on and on.

Now don't get me wrong. He wasn't nasty, he didn't lose his temper, he was very, very quiet and reasonable, but patience can irritate hell out of a guy and so can calmness—especially when he wants to flip and throw his guitar through the window—and so can persistence, taking the same phrase over and over and over and then hear Royal say: "I'm sorry, fellows, but that just isn't it."

Walt sweated like a bull and kept wiping his head with a handkerchief. This went on night after night after night.

With Berte it was even worse. After all, if I do say so myself, Walt and I are pretty good musicians, right up with the top sidemen on the West Coast, but Berte—well, Berte had talent, but she was an amateur. Royal was so polite with her it was embarrassing, but patient, persistent.... Good God! It was enough to drive a nun to drink!

Every night—usually toward morning, it was—Berte went home pale and nervous and holding onto Walt like she'd just collapse if he wasn't there.

That was the routine now. Walt took Berte home. And Royal would drop me off. Piggy had bought Royal a new Ford.

On the way home I'd just sit there holding my case and staring at nothing. Royal would gab on about new numbers, new attacks, etc., etc. It didn't figure. Me, I'm pretty rugged. Royal, well, Royal was a pale, skinny little slat. But he'd be roaring on at three in the morning after hours of rehearsal as if he'd just bounced out of bed.

The business even got to Frank, and one night I heard him grind his teeth. And for him that was something. The same as if Walt had set fire to the house or kicked out the big front window. Frank was a very polite, restrained guy.

But poor Stu! He thought we were all daffy, especially Royal. He was used to businessmen. Finally he took to staying away altogether. Once in a while he'd call up and ask timidly how things were going.

They weren't going at all, if you want to know.

And then there was the business of Walt and Berte to really complicate things and louse it up good. Berte was a hundred per cent female with a hundred per cent female ways and thinking. So naturally she got the idea I was against her. Here's the way she figured. Walt and I lived together and did as we pleased. She resented this, of course, because she wanted Walt to do *her* way, not his, which is normal procedure with chicks. So, being a chick, she figured that I wanted Walt to do *my* way. She was interfering, see, in her opinion, so she was dead certain I resented her and wanted her to hell out. You get it? The truth was, I'd always thought it was kind of silly of Walt to run away from Berte. She was a good kid, good-looking and rich. What the hell does a guy want?

But Berte had her mind made up. I was against her. And this just added to the tension, the nervousness, and the hysteria.

And on top of everything else, Walt wasn't himself any more. Little by little, this persistent chick was throwing him off balance.

Well, one night I got a bellyful and said I was through for the evening.

"Why?" asks Royal, giving me a puzzled look.

So I lied. "My fingers are sore," I said. "And if I don't give them a rest I'm going to have real trouble with them."

It was a Saturday night. "Okay," says Royal. "Sorry, Stan. Rest them till Monday night."

It was like getting out of prison. Royal wanted me to come over to his place—he had a new pad, a room in a little hotel near us—but I begged off. I'd had it. I didn't want to hear any more talk about music. So he dropped me off at a little bistro and took my guitar with him to keep for me.

The joint was jumping—juke box playing and a few drunks dancing around the tables. I got a spot up at the front end of the bar and ordered a double Scotch—on my own dough, too, I needed a bracer so bad. Man, I felt loosened up after that first drink. No more rehearsing till Monday night, and Monday night was a long ways off.

I was nipping at the second double Scotch when three people walked in, oiled and arguing. Two chicks and a guy. The guy and one chick were really boiled, staggering and holding onto each other. The second chick was just a little flushed up. I liked her right away. She was medium-sized and slight, with a cute, narrow little waist, which she was proud of and showed off by wearing a wide leather belt. She had black hair, cut very short, and a turned-up nose, her eyes were black and slanted a bit. Kind of Japanese effect. (Okay, so I'm partial to the Japanese look. I served my time in Japan, remember? And it's not true what they say about Oriental girls!)

Anyway, Jackie was a real cutie-pie, no doubt about it.

And she was in trouble and knew it. She kept trying to get away from this other couple but they kept grabbing her and arguing very loud. Finally she looked over at me and as soon as she did, I says, "Hi," as if I was very glad to see her.

She did a slight take, then right away she waved and said, "Hi"—oh, this Jackie was a sharp kid—and came over.

"Drunk trouble?" I says.

"Yeah," she says. "I got to get rid of 'em."

"Okay," I says. "How about a drink?"

"Rum and coke," she calls to the bartender.

I saw the couple coming over.

"My name's Stan Pawley," I whispered to her. "I'm a guitar player."

"Jackie Downs," she whispers to me, as the couple got nearer. "Check-girl at the Mirage. Off tonight."

She introduced me to the couple. They looked me over like I was a leper. I ignored them. "How's it going at the Mirage these days, Jackie?" I asks.

"Oh, same as usual," she says. "How's the old music business?"

I began to tell her about how we were going into the Intime pretty soon. The couple got sorer and sorer. Finally the guy grabs Jackie by the arm. "Come on," he says, real tough, "Don's waiting for us. Let's go."

"That bum," says Jackie. "Go away, will you? I'm talking to Stan here."

The man made a remark I can't repeat, only maybe like this : "...Stan!"

I got set to clip him, but he'd talked in a very loud and vulgar voice and the barkeep had heard him. "Cut out that goddamned lousy kind of talk or get out of here," says the barkeep to this big drunk.

Well, finally the couple left. And that is how I met Jackie.

"I got trapped," she explained. "This girl friend of mine brings that big bum over to my place. I had to work 'em out, so I managed to get 'em over here, where I've usually got friends." She lifted her glass. "Here's to you, Stan, kiddo."

A real pert chick.

We got along fine. In fact, Jackie and I had a ball till Monday night.

But then the nightmare started all over again. We'd been doing very well on "Babes in the Woods"—and I kept saying to myself, "Well, we got one, at least, in the book," but all of a sudden Royal was trying it a new way again and pretty soon "Babes in the Woods" went out the window with all the other numbers.

I don't know what to say. It was like getting locked into a funhouse. Nothing made sense and you couldn't get out.

We went over the same phrases and over them and over them—and we got worse all the time, at least, that was my opinion.

What Royal's opinion was, I couldn't make out. But I did know that Walt was getting about ready to blow the whole thing and I think he would have if it hadn't been for Berte, who half the time seemed on the verge of a nervous breakdown.

♮ ♭

One night, after another week of this torture, Frank, wanting to relieve the tension, I guess, put us all into one of his big Cadillacs and drove us over to Stu's new place. The sign was up already, but not lighted: STU-ART'S CLUB INTIME. The place sure looked mighty fine on the outside, and even better on the inside.

Stu and another guy, a decorator or something, were in their shirt sleeves, shoving things around. Stu was sure having himself a ball. Here was a guy with a million bucks or so playing with dolls. What else? Boy, did that place smell—paint, varnish, new upholstery. God knows what! But real good, if you know what I mean. I began to feel kind of nervous about the whole thing. I wanted it to go. Surprised? I was a little surprised myself. Because with me a job is a job. But this was a kind of family thing, in a way. Not exactly professional. That made it different. The only ones involved who needed the cabbage and were working strictly for it were Walt and me. Funny setup, eh?

Stu explained that you pronounced the name "An-Teem."

"Maybe so," said Walt. "But to the musicians it's going to be In-Time."

This seemed to worry Stu. "Do you think so, old boy?" he says, wrinkling up his face.

"I know so," said Walt. "But so what? People will either come or they won't. A successful place never had a bad name yet."

But I could see Stu was kind of disappointed. He'd apparently been giving the name a lot of thought. However, the sign was up and paid for, and Stu isn't the type who just uselessly throws money away.

It was a real nice place. Small, compact. With a low wall dividing the bar from the tables and booths. A guy could sit on a stool in the bar and gander the musicians, and listen in peace, without barmaids stumbling over his feet, hustling drinks. The "decor," as Stu put it, was up-to-the-minute, ultra-modern as hell and good-looking. The lighting was dim and kind of pinkish—a good kind of light, flattering to chicks—but not too dim. You wouldn't have to bring a flashlight in order to see if you were getting screwed when the bill came round. All the seating was low—the tables, the booths, the chairs. It had a nice lounging kind of look to it. You come in, relax, listen to the music, and get fractured in comfort.

One of the barmaids turned up for rehearsal, or something. There were going to be three of them. She was a voluptuous, dusky brunette, in a white silk blouse, tight black velvet toreador trousers, and ballet slippers. Man! She had what it took to sell drinks and keep the male customers happy. Only one thing. If she'd turn around too sudden she'd knock all the glasses off the bar, or black a guy's eye.

Her name was Rita.

I looked at Walt. Walt looked at Rita. Berte looked at Walt. Frank looked at Berte. Dynamite! A slight wind began to rise in the place. So I looked at Royal. Royal was looking at the floor. He was leaning on the bar. I could see that he was tapping out something with his fingers. Good old Royal!

Rita gave with a pretty smile. Then she smoothed her black hair. Then she gave with a pretty wiggle.

I looked at Walt again. He had that expression!

At a rather curt suggestion from Stu, Rita disappeared into the back.

Walt looked at me and his eyes said: "I see the plot now."

Everybody saw the plot. And I must say it was a great relief to all, except Royal, who didn't have the faintest idea that a crisis had passed.

I couldn't believe it, myself. But little by little we began to get the hang of quite a few numbers here and there—just a glimmering. The only trouble was that as soon as we got this glimmering, Royal would change his mind, and we'd try it another way.

In regard to Royal, I began to get what I guess you might call a roaring inferiority complex. I always thought I was pretty good, but as far as Royal was concerned, I couldn't seem to do anything right.

He'd play the phrasing over with one finger. He'd sing it. He'd whistle it. And finally I'd get the phrasing and then I'd goof on the harmony.

This can get pretty trying.

Well, one night—the hottest night I've ever seen in Southern California, it must have been nearly a hundred degrees at midnight—all of a sudden I'd had it. Without a word, I just packed up my guitar, put on my hat and left. They all ran after me. Berte grabbed my arm. I'll never forget the look on her face. She was scared blue.

"Talk to him, Walter. For heaven's sake, talk to him!" she kept saying.

But Walter'd had it, too.

I walked fast down that dark street toward Sunset Boulevard. I knew I could pick up a cab at the Beverly Hills Hotel.

But pretty soon Royal caught up with me and walked along beside me. And I remembered the night I'd chased him down this same street after the earthquake.

We didn't say a word. When we got to the cabstand he just got in the cab with me, forgetting all about his own car, which was parked in front of Frank's house.

We were passing the Mocambo before he said anything. Then he jolted me, because I'd expected him to beg me to reconsider, which at that moment I wouldn't have done for a permanent job and a lifetime pension. "Look, Stan," he said. "Stop in with me. I want to play a record for you."

If it had been anybody but Royal, I would have belted him right there in the cab. I never said a word. But by the time we got to Royal's I'd cooled off a little, so I did what he wanted.

He had a little record player in his room now. I sat down and lit a cigarette and waited. Royal put a record on, and adjusted the gadget. It was a long-playing record and I groaned to myself. I was in no mood to listen to some goddamned, long-winded....

"Look, Stan," he says, "the singing is in German, so don't pay any attention to it. Just listen to the music."

The singing was in German, yet! Trust Royal. Well, it started. It was the goddamnedest music I ever heard in my life. The singing was like nothing

I'd ever heard before, a cross between talking and moaning. And the background...! Well, what can I say? This music bothered me. It made me nervous. It scared me, kind of. I don't know what to say.

"Had enough?" asked Royal, after about ten minutes.

"Hell, yes," I said, sweating. So he stopped it. "What was that?" I yelled.

"It's a German opera, called *Wozzeck,*" said Royal. "It's over forty years old."

"That's over forty years old?" I couldn't believe it. You know. You listen to Stan Kenton—pretty advanced stuff. Hell, Stan Kenton was like finger exercises compared to this stuff. "How could it be forty years old, Royal?"

"Well, it is," said Royal. "I just wanted you to hear something unconventional—and then maybe you wouldn't get so damned sore at me because I'm trying for something a little different."

I just sat there, staring at him.

"Look, Stan. Most popular music is childish—ricky, ticky little tunes that a small boy could make up on the piano. All right. We take these tunes. We try to do something with them."

I still said nothing. What are you going to say?

"Now, Stan," said Royal, "how about trying it again? Believe me, we're improving."

So I said okay. What else?

If I live fifty more years—and I might, if they don't drop that egg—I'll never forget the last night. It was hot, man, it was hot, and a strong, dry wind was blowing outside. Even Frank was in his shirt sleeves—and that is saying something.

Royal had a loose white silk shirt on and it was sticking to his back. He was just as quiet, patient, and persistent as he'd been all along—and just as fiendish, if you know what I mean, as if I'd never blown up and he'd never talked me into giving with another try.

Frank kept rushing in Tom Collinses. We poured them down and they poured themselves right out again—through our pores. The music room began to smell like juniper berries.

Finally Berte got off the ground, and real good, with "Moonlight in Vermont"—and Royal got up and kissed her on the cheek. Berte burst into tears and got hysterical. Walt and Frank carried her over to a couch and put ice on her head.

And it wasn't just one of those corny feminine acts. Berte had been so worried she hadn't slept for three nights, she told me so later. She didn't tell me why. But I knew. She was afraid the whole thing would blow up, on account of Royal's quiet fiendishness, and she'd lose her big chance to put the horse-collar on Lover Boy.

We weren't through yet. Shortly after three A.M., Royal put his head down on the piano and began to cry. Then he got up and made a speech. We were all great. He loved us all. He was full of gin, of course, but he was also full of sincerity, this boy. I doubt if he ever had a crooked thought in his life. He meant what he said, drunk or sober. Of course, he'd eel around a little at times to hide his own hurts and things, but that's something else again.

Well, leave it to Walt. He picked Royal up, put him on his shoulders—like you see in those pictures of aquaplaning—and ran around the room with him, yelling and kicking up his big feet.

What an evening!

Berte was so exhausted she stayed at Frank's house all night. Oh, perfectly proper, believe me. Out in front, Walt, Royal, and I stopped to talk a moment.

"Well, we're ready, fellows," said Royal.

"Yeah, it's kill or cure now," said Walt.

"No. We're in," said Royal, then he grinned, waved, and walked away to his car.

"Did you ever see such an odd bastard as that?" asked Walt, as we drove off. I agreed heartily, as the fellow says.

♮♭

After quite a play in the saloon columns, we opened. A Friday night. The joint was packed by eleven o'clock. And Rita and her two helpers were buzzing around like card-girls in a bingo joint. The people even listened to us. Several times a loudmouth, who insisted on talking, was shushed by the patrons.

This was a good sign.

About one o'clock the musicians began to wander in. Now here's a funny thing. The lay people liked us, accepted us, but the musicians were bewildered. Lonny Boyle sat down front and stared blankly. Lonny was doing a local show on TV now and was getting a little upstage. I saw him shaking his head.

During a break he cornered me in the alley outside the place.

"What's with this?" he asked. "Who you kidding?"

"It's a job," I said, not liking his attitude.

"That broad can't sing," he said. "I've seen her around. And where did you get that jerky piano player? He's for the birds—or else that piano's out of tune."

"Or else you've got a tin ear," I said, fed-up. It's pretty silly for a starving sideman like me to talk to a guy like Lonny Boyle—a big name, a potential employer—like that. But let me repeat—I am a Free Soul. My name may be Pawloski, but I'm more old-time American than any guy called Smith you know. I will just not take any crap from anybody!

Lonny turned pale. He was used to pawing and bouquets from hungry musicians. "Why, you p...!" said Lonny. He called me a name I don't like. I like it so little I won't even repeat it.

"Lonny," I said, "you've got a nice Irish kisser. Keep it that way."

Lonny decided to keep it that way. He went back inside.

Pretty soon Walt came out. Before he could speak, a window opened in the alley and Rita stuck her head out.

"Mr. Flick..." she said in her low cooing voice and I could see Walt's ears trembling slightly. "I got a drink for you, honey. Some man's buying for the band. You want Scotch?"

"Not bar Scotch, gorgeous."

"Don't you worry, honey," said Rita. "I'll look after you."

She gave with that slow smile, she patted her hair, but we couldn't see the wiggle—the window was too high.

"Nix, chump," I said, still feeling belligerent. "That's Stu's bounce."

"I know, I know," said Walt hurriedly. "But I got to be nice to the girl, don't I?"

"Why?" I snapped.

Walt looked me over carefully. "What's with you?"

I told him about Lonny. He made no comment. Just shrugged.

Now the alley door opened and Gorgeous Creature appeared with the drink. Before she could smile, pat, or wiggle, Berte brushed past her and joined us. Walt took the drink and nodded rather coyly at Rita, then he clinked glasses with Berte.

"What's the matter with *me?*" I yelled. "Don't I get a drink?"

Rita's eyes popped and she looked hurt. (Actually, this big Rita was a very nice kid. Her only trouble was that boys had been flocking after her since she was thirteen and she was not exactly what you might call of strong moral character.)

"Why, sure, Mr. Pawley," she said. "Excuse me. What will you have?"

Berte was foot-tapping by now. Berte also is a very nice kid. But war among women.... Brother, let me out! Are they cruel—even nice kids like Berte!

"This drink is awful," said Berte. "Take it back!"

Rita's "niceness" disappeared pretty quick. She snatched the drink. She forgot about mine. Oh, we were having a ball.

In the middle of this, Royal wanders out, calm and happy as a little lamb. "Well, fellows," he said, "maybe we didn't fracture them but we're doing very, very fine."

I patted him on the head. What a comfort he was—this unworldly little fellow!

During the last set, the place was loaded with curious musicians. We sailed. I mean, we really sailed.

It was a picnic, watching the musicians. Some of them hated us—we were working, weren't we, and in a plush joint. Some of them didn't dig us at all, and looked bewildered or suspicious, like we were pulling a gag. Some of them dug us only too well—they looked pale. Lonny was one of them, in spite of his cackle. He stayed till we signed off. Our signature was "Beating the Birds to the Cherries"—Royal's piece.

Lonny buttonholed Walt. I had my back turned, but I listened. I got rabbit's ears, believe me, when I want to use them.

"You guys kidding?" he said.

"People seemed to like it," said Walt.

"It was an opening. Goldenson managed to get good publicity. If you're not careful, you're going to chase 'em away with that stuff."

"Ah—maybe," said Walt, indifferently.

Lonny couldn't let it go. He was burning. "Where in hell did you get that crummy piano player?"

"I think he's good," said Walt. "However, it's all a matter of opinion."

"Where did he come from? Who is he?"

"Name's Royal Mauch. He's from the Midwest."

"He better go back."

I turned. "Come on, Walt. Let's go."

Lonny gave me a look and blew.

"He won't sleep tonight," I said.

"What's this 'let's go' business?" said Walt. "I got to run the chick home."

"Which one?" I asked.

Walt looked me over, then patted me on the shoulder. "Just stop eating meat for a day or two. You'll be all right. Can't Royal take you home?"

"Yeah," I said.

I was flipped-off for two days. I'm not sure just what it was. A combination of everything, I guess.

Well, we were a success. We got nice notices, and we got good crowds. And I mean listening crowds, not loud-talking drunks. The young Bev. Hills kids liked us, movie people would turn up now and then, and even the musicians would show late at night: drink-nursers all—when they themselves were buying.

Now don't get the idea we were a Big Success. Lawrence Welk is a Big Success. We had about as much chance of being a Big Success, playing the stuff we did, as an Arab combo on Fairfax (local joke). But we were a Little Success, appreciated by the Happy Few.

Stu was pleased as hell with his venture. "You boys should have heard the comments," he'd say in that British Royal Family accent. "They like you." The fact that he might make money out of the business after all didn't seem to worry him.

♮♭

As I told you away back at the beginning, Walt did not confide in anybody about his love life. He tried to keep it apart from everything else. So he didn't say anything to me about Rita. But I had my suspicions. It was a natural, that's all. She drooled over Walt so openly that even Royal noticed it finally. And on top of everything else, she was Walt's type, and besides, believe me, friends, Walt is not a guy who denies himself anything, no matter for what reason.

But I wasn't there, as the fellow says, and I couldn't prove anything.

Well, we were "dark" on Mondays, which was nice, as it gave us all a full day to ourselves. In order to be fairly close to Royal, Piggy had taken a nice apartment in Beverly Hills, and she turned up there two or three days a week. With things going the way they were, it was a cinch Royal wasn't going to get down to Palos Verdes very often, and she still wanted to keep an eye on him.

So this Monday she invites us all to the apartment for a "feed," as she said: Frank, Stu—the whole bunch.

The trouble was Walt didn't show. We sat around drinking and waiting. Berte's face got stonier and stonier. Finally she said to Piggy: "I think we'd better eat. Something must have happened to Walter."

The understatement of the week! Something had happened to Walter, all right, and it didn't take any Dick Tracy to figure out what. It was Monday. The place was dark. Stu was with us. Q.E.D.

So we ate. And believe me, the business didn't bother my appetite any. Piggy had cooked everything herself. Not that it took much cooking: a huge pot of the best vegetable soup I ever tasted, garlic toast by the cord, cheese, all the Chianti you could drink, green salad with oil and garlic dressing. I really laid it away till my belt was choking me.

Berte and Piggy hit it off fine—same kind of people. Frank and Stu hit it off fine. Again, same kind of people. Royal will hit it off with practically anybody, if he's in the mood. I was the solitary, you might say. Though I'm not complaining. The food and I hit it off fine.

We stayed around till after midnight. Royal was pretty relaxed with his sister now. Even patted her on the bottom a couple of times. She was pretty happy, I could see. This Royal was a child, as long as he had his own way he was good as pie.

Well, finally we broke up. Royal drove me home.

"Your sister's okay," I said.

"She has her points," said Royal, and then he began to talk about a new number he wanted to add to the book. I shut him off. I was full of food and sleepy. "Tomorrow, Royal," I said. "Tomorrow."

Lover Boy blew in at six o'clock the next morning and woke me up, slamming doors, singing, and taking a shower. I went in the bathroom and just stood staring at him. He was making with the towel. In the nude he looked like Mr. America. For once I wanted to get into a fight with him—a real one. I wanted to work him over, belt the hell out of him.

Why? you ask me. Shall I be frank? Okay. Envy, that's why. You hear a lot of talk about equality. Brother, it's all talk. Were we equal—Walt and me? In what way? This guy had been born strong, handsome, and with the sex appeal of a bull. How about me? I was okay with dames when there was nobody else handy. You say I'm making myself out a slob. All right. Maybe that's what I am. Yeah, equality. We're all equal but Walter is more equal than others.

He noticed the stare finally. "I went down to San Pedro to see the boats," he said, "and fell in." Then he gave me one of those grins that knock the chicks for a loop.

"Don't grin at me, you tomcatting bastard," I said. "What's the idea waking me up?"

He just laughed. He didn't take me serious. Why should he? I'd often talked like that to him before.

"Everybody was sitting around waiting for you to show," I went on. "What kind of way to act is that?"

"Well, I'll tell you," said Walt. "I thought I'd get away in time, but somehow I just didn't."

"Where's your manners? Don Ameche invented something you could have used."

Now he began to look at me. "Say," he said, "what the hell's wrong with you lately? I thought you were Polish. You're always going around with a chip on your shoulder like some freckle-face mick."

"Don't give me that Polish stuff," I said. "What kind of a name is Flick?"

"German," said Walt. "Pennsylvania Dutch."

"You better call Berte," I said. Did I care if he called Berte? I did not. I was just irritated with everything.

"I will not call Berte, and to hell with Berte," yelled Walt. "And mind your own goddamned business."

He had on his pajama pants now. I belted him and knocked him back into the shower. He belted me and I went backward through the door and lit on my shoulder blades in the hallway.

"Okay, now," said Walt. "Quit playing. I'm sleepy."

I'd had it. Jesus, what a punch. He'd only tapped me before.

Pretty soon I heard him snoring. All of a sudden I started to laugh. "Am I crazy or something?" I asked myself. It began to seem funny.

Walt woke me up at two the next afternoon. He was singing. The breakfast table was loaded with food.

"Well," I said, "what have we got here?" And sat down and laid my ears back.

Cereal, hot cakes, sausage, coffee.

"With my own little pinkies," said Walt.

"You'll make some bum a good husband," I said.

We ate in silence for a long time. Finally, when the plates were as empty as an agent's promise, Walt said: "Look. Was there a lot of talk last night?"

"No. Berte just said she thought maybe something had happened to you."

Walt stared, then jumped up and tried to get her on the phone. She was out. Or at least that was her story. He came back and sat down. He looked glum.

"Listen, Stan," he said. "How does this make me a heel? Does she own me? Who says so? I ought to know. And I say she don't. I own me. Nobody else."

"I'm not arguing."

"Goddamn it," said Walt, "I don't want people making rules for me. I do what I damn please. If I was married to her it would be different."

"It would not be different at all," I said.

Walt nodded. "That's why I'm not going to get married. For what?"

Tuesday night things were more than slightly cockeyed at first. Rita went around with red eyes and a bruised lip. Had Stu belted her? It hardly seemed possible, he just wasn't the type. But you can never tell. Berte goofed with "Moonlight in Vermont," and Royal wrinkled up his face like a monkey and kicked the piano. I was my usual sterling self, and Walt seemed okay, playing his very, very fine bass. I sure liked to hear him when he got in one of those walking moods. When his fingers walked, the bass was better than a drum for driving the band. We hit it big on "Chinatown." Walt really went, and Royal let him take break after break. In the middle of one of them, several guys in the joint cheered. Oh, there were *aficionados* about!

The joint was packed by midnight—and it was only Tuesday. Nice going. Things began to roll, finally, so Royal let Walt sing a number. It was a jump tune, and did that big boy go, smooth, fast, and eccentric. Walt stooped over, spread his feet, slapped his hands, shook his head. And every move original, if you know what I mean. He was feeling it, man! No voice at all, just kind of a husky baritone, with no resonance.

He fractured 'em. You should have seen them chicks. They screamed.

Stu was looking on with his mouth open. Frank had just come in. He also had his mouth open.

Walt had to do an encore. He fractured 'em again.

But what I remember most about that night is a picture of Walt and Berte going down the street together after closing time. She had hold of his arm like she was afraid he'd run away, and was taking two steps to his one.

All is forgiven? Don't you believe it. Just on the surface. A feminine dodge. Getting Walt hooked was a lot more important to Berte right now than blasting him about Rita. But once she got him hooked, then the case would be entirely different. He'd not only hear about Rita, he'd hear about a hell of a lot of things.

Thinking this over, I'd laugh to myself, realizing that in a way I was lucky. Me, I'm no bargain. No chick like Berte is ever going to strain herself over getting me in harness. And let's be fair. It's a lot easier for a guy like me to be a Free Soul, than a guy like Walter.

Now things went along very smooth and fine for a while. When Walt wasn't playing, he was with Berte, or sleeping. I hardly spoke six words a day to him. So Royal and I were sort of thrown together.

He was hardly like the same guy. His color was good, he was always smiling, and he was full of talk. One Monday afternoon we drove down to Palos Verdes in his Ford and had dinner with Piggy. He and Piggy were laughing and kidding each other now. All was at peace.

We saw the view. We heard the owl—I guess he went with the lease. And about nine o'clock Piggy hit the hay—she was going out on a dawn horseback ride or something with some people she'd met at Palos Verdes.

Royal wanted to talk about music, so he put the bottle in front of me and we rared back. That Scotch! I hardly listened. I just sat with my feet up, looking through the view-window up the coast toward Malibu. Walt was so right—Shangrila!

Royal was off on that "jazz is the only live art in the world today" kick again. But I felt indulgent. I didn't argue or say anything at all. I just nodded, and belted the Scotch.

Royal talked, talked, his thin face flushed and his eyes kind of flashing behind those thick lenses. Finally he got up and began to scramble around, looking for some article he wanted to read to me. My feet were asleep, not only from the Scotch but from sitting in one position for so long, so I got up, too, and sort of followed him around.

He opened a desk—built into the wall, of course—and a lot of papers fell out and scattered all over the floor. Oh, what a disorderly guy! I helped him pick up the papers. We were both stooping and grabbing, and he just went on talking. I came up with a thin stack of music paper, bound together with adhesive tape. I glanced at it by accident. The bars were all scribbled over in pencil—hentracks, or Chinese writing, that's the way it looked—but there was a title printed in India ink at the top: *The River. For Orchestra and Tugboat Whistle.* I looked over at the bottle of Scotch, then I read the title again. That's what it said.

He snatched it out of my hand.

"What's that?" I asked.

"Oh, nothing, nothing," he said hurriedly, and threw it back in the desk. But I couldn't let it lay. "What's with the tugboat whistle, Royal?"

He flushed and looked sort of uncomfortable. "Just an effect I want," he explained. "I... I been fooling around with that thing for a long time. I finished it once... then... well, I lost the manuscript. So I've been putting it down again lately, whenever I get a little time."

Now I remembered what Walt had told me about the stuff Piggy had in a safety-deposit box. Was this the new version?

"Is it a jazz piece? What is it?"

"No," said Royal. "For full orchestra. First version ran about twenty minutes."

"Twenty minutes!" I yelled. "That ought to empty the house."

Royal laughed. "Oh, it will never get played," he said. "It's something I just fool around with."

Finally Royal found the article he was looking for and I had to sit and listen to what I believe is called a dissertation by some longhaired creep, who couldn't play an instrument, couldn't sing, couldn't do anything, but could tell you all about it. For the birds! However, as I say, I was feeling mellow.

And then pretty soon Royal began to belt the Scotch and he also began to feel mellow.

First he told me about the river. When he was a boy his family had a house on the river. The lawn went right down to it. They had a boat—little motorboat, I guess. It was tied to the dock at the end of the lawn. Royal used to sit in the tied-up boat, so he could feel the rock of the water, and watch the tugboats going past, pushing the big freight barges up the river.

It was great at night, he said. Royal really felt that river. It was tied into his childhood, I guess, like the steel mills with me. But I hated the goddamned steel mills, and he loved the river.

"'Old Man River,'" I said, finally.

"Yes," said Royal. "The best American song ever written."

That was taking in a lot of territory. But why argue?

Then he took a few more drinks and really began to embarrass me, telling me what we'd done for him, Walt and me, and how much the trio meant to him, and that he'd never before known what it was like to be happy. Never since he'd been grown up, he insisted. And of course since his mother had died... I couldn't take it.

You ought to know by now that I'm not a sentimental guy. But this really bothered me and made me very uncomfortable. Walt and I had done nothing. And the trio was just an accident.

I tried to play it all down. But Royal wouldn't go for it. He had his mind made up. We were saints. We could do no wrong.

"Stan," he said, "I used to hate to get up in the morning. Sometimes I didn't. I'd just lie in bed, because I couldn't face another day. Now I don't care if I sleep or not—I'm just waiting for nine o'clock to come around."

Well, what are you going to do?

All the way back to town Royal talked about new ideas that he had for the trio, new numbers, etc., etc.

It was a good thing he was driving. I kept falling asleep.

Well, one Thursday night Piggy showed up at the Intime with a nice-looking couple—Mr. and Mrs. Aldridge—from Palos Verdes, and I saw that they were taken care of and given a good spot. I don't think the Aldridges ever made the saloon circuit and they seemed a little bewildered by the music, the cheering, and the yacking. But this Aldridge guy was human, all right. How do I know? I saw him taking several ganders at Rita's very elegant caboose.

During a break, I brought Stu over and Piggy introduced him to the Aldridges. Stu sat with them, after that. They were Stu's kind of people, and they seemed to take to him. I could see them laughing at nearly everything he said. Stu had quite an original line, all kinds of quaint quips and expressions from Down Under.

Royal ducked his sister and came out in the alley with me on the second break.

"What's she doing here?" he said, like she'd committed a fopah.

"It's a public place. And you're her brother."

"She makes me nervous," said Royal. He was like a high-school kid having a good time in a poolroom—and then his teacher shows up!

But after all he was a polite guy, so on the way back he stops at the table and meets the Aldridges.

Walt sang a song for Piggy, wiggled his ears at her, and brought down the house.

On the third break, Piggy gave me the high sign and we went over and sat at the bar.

"Royal's having a wonderful time, isn't he?" says Piggy.

"Yeah," I says. "And we're doing better than scale, Walt and me."

Piggy didn't dig this and just looked at me before she spoke again. "You boys have certainly been a godsend to him. He's like a different person."

"Look," I said, "Royal makes too much of it. Walt and I haven't done anything. It just happened."

"Let him think what he pleases," said Piggy. "No way to stop him, anyway—believe me. I know." She sipped her drink and sat there thinking for a moment. "I'd like to go to Mexico. What do you think?"

"Why not?" I asked, surprised.

"The Aldridges want me to go with them. However, I don't know. I kind of hate to go that far away from Royal."

"He's okay. What could happen?"

"Well," said Piggy, "I'll talk it over. But I'm surely glad to see him so happy. And he plays very well, don't you think?" She seemed dubious about it. I was flabbergasted.

"Plays well!" I gasped. "Listen... there's only one Royal."

"Really?" said Piggy. "You see, I can't even carry a tune. I know he has great ability with serious music. Professor Mencken told me so, he's at the Conservatory. But popular music... it sort of surprises me."

"Royal is just one big surprise."

Piggy laughed. "And so is Walter. He looks like a movie actor and he acts like a clown. He killed me with that song. God knows what the Aldridges think. They're so conservative."

The guy's not conservative about broads, I thought, but I didn't say anything.

Anyway, Piggy was sure pleased about the way things were going with Royal.

♮♭

The entertainment business is a funny thing. If you've never been in it, it's almost impossible to explain. I mean, the way things happen. It's like gambling, sort of. In the way of streaks, I'm speaking of. If you've ever shot craps you'll begin to dig me. In gambling there is a simple explanation: luck. All of a sudden a cold guy will get hot, and do the impossible with the dice. Like a miracle. What you call it in show business, I don't know.

Take a for-instance. Before I met Walt I was playing with an ordinary little combo. We were going nowhere. But one dull night, with about six people in the place, a big blond doll walks in with an older guy. Expensive people. How they got in this joint I don't know. Their car must have run out of gas.

The barmaid puts them in a booth up front, right opposite us. The doll likes music. She keeps encouraging us. And all of a sudden this dull outfit takes off for outer space. None of us could believe it. What happened? Where did it come from?

I'll say this. It never came back.

It's an odd thing. When you're playing with a combo on a regular job, every night is different, in a way. Some are funny. Some are dull. Some are so scrambled up, you think you'll never get untangled. And then all of a sudden there will come a night—and that's what I'm getting to.

It was just another Saturday night, or seemed so. Crowded, and very noisy when we weren't playing. We had been in the joint over a month now and had built up a regular trade, mostly hip people. Of course, strangers wandered in from time to time, just out of curiosity or just to get a drink on the way home. But on the whole we were surrounded by fans. The young guys came in in droves and fought for seats up front. Royal was their hero. When we were going, they never took their eyes off him. Except when big Walt sang, they didn't think he was much of a singer, but he fractured them just the same. With Berte, they were polite. After all, let's face it, she was the weak spot of the outfit, but nobody was complaining, including Royal.

Well, there had been a big football game in town and the whole area was jammed with outsiders. Also, as we found out later, there were three conventions, one batch staying at the Beverly Wilshire Hotel, not too far away.

Little by little the place began to get packed with strangers, outsiders, a lot of middle-aged men and women good and drunk, and letting it slide, as they were away from home—and to hell with it—whoopee!

What an uproar!

The young hipsters kept trying to shush the outlanders, but how are you going to shush a self-important middle-aged drunk with his wallet stuffed with money?

Frank, smooth in a tux, showed up with one of his white-haired queens and stared about him in dismay, as if he'd walked into a whorehouse by mistake.

Rita was getting her caboose pinched all over the place by the middle-aged cutups. But so what? That was no novelty to her. It was out there and she wasn't ashamed of it, not that babe.

Now anything could happen with Royal, a dead-serious guy about music. I kept looking at him, worried. He might even get up and leave if this silly uproar didn't stop. But, as usual, Royal came up with a jolt.

He leaned over and said to me: "Ask Frank to sing."

I almost dropped my gee-tar. Then I got it. "Great," I said.

Frank was only too willing. I wish you could have seen those teeth.

"I Got My Love to Keep Me Warm!"

Royal gave him the key, then just sat listening. Walt and I furnished the accompaniment.

The hipsters groaned and sat looking at the floor. No, man, no! But the middle-aged outlanders, men and women, flipped.

We could hardly get Frank off the stand.

One big gray-haired guy in the back kept yelling: "Let the wop sing! Let the wop sing!"

This fractured Frank, who laughed so hard his little white-haired queen had to pat him on the back and get him a brandy. And I sat wondering what that big gray-haired oaf would think if he knew that the wop was a millionaire and in the Social Register.

Children, what a night!

Stu was almost in a state of collapse. He didn't dig this stampede at all. "My *word!*" he said.

Well, we started the next set with a real fast "Babes in the Woods" and the hipsters began to twitch and grin in the front of the house.

A nice-looking middle-aged drunk wandered like a lost lamb through the crowd and stopped beside Walt, who gave him a look and began to shy away.

"Do you boys know the 'Missouri Waltz'?" he asked.

"How about 'Poona, Poona from Altoona'?" said Walt.

"No. The 'Missouri Waltz,'" this guy insisted. Though he was drunk, he looked like what you hoped one of your uncles would look like but never did.

"How about 'Moon over West Los Angeles'?" Walt suggested.

"No," said the man, "I don't know that piece. Couldn't you please play the 'Missouri Waltz'?"

Walt was fracturing the hipsters. But he'd had enough.

"It ain't in the book, mister. Sorry."

We finished the number we'd been playing. But the man wouldn't go away. "It reminds me of my wife," he explained. "She died."

Royal turned around and looked at the man. "'Missouri Waltz'?" he asked. "We'll fake it."

And we did, with Royal playing very simple piano. The man stood there weeping, and when we were through he handed Walt a twenty-dollar bill, and Walt took it.

This Royal—you never knew!

One of the hipsters wandered over to the stand, giggling, and said: "Would you boys mind playing 'Young at Heart'? It reminds me of my dog, Julius. He has fits."

He was not a success. Royal, his hero, glared at him, and he went away, hurt and bewildered.

Then the evening really began. Man, was it rowdy! Stu said something to Frank about calling the police, but Frank talked him out of it. Frank was having a ball. He sang two more numbers, and when he left the stand, some top-heavy old dame—you know, pillow chest, skinny legs—grabbed him and hugged and kissed him. Frank was laughing so hard he didn't even resist. His white-haired queen finally rescued him.

And then some character began to yell: "'Tiger Rag'!" every minute or so. Stu was for having him politely thrown out into the expensive air of Beverly Hills, but Frank soothed him.

Finally Royal turned around to us and said: "Okay, fellows. 'Tiger Rag.' And let's cornball it."

Well, words fail! This time it was the *end*.

We took it fast, hot and corny. Spike Jones would have been proud of us. And you could just feel the electricity coming back at you from the audience. Man, we rambled!

And pretty soon big Walt leaned his fiddle against the wall and jumped out on the front of the stage. He was a savage that night, big Walt. He gave it the treatment, he belted it, he yelled—and those awkward antics of his looked more peculiar and original than usual.

"...Yow—hold that Ti—Grr! Yow—hold that Ti—Grr ! Yow—hold that Ti—Grr...!"

On the final round, Royal played standing, and, shaking his head like Durante, kicked up his right leg on the off-beat.

Well, the ceiling didn't fall. But it damned near did. The outlanders cheered as if we'd just made a touchdown. Even the hipsters looked warm, though mighty disapproving. Finally one of them figured out a way to like us on that number. "Best parody I ever saw," he said. You see, he was an intellectual boy and he couldn't possibly just simply like something. He had to have an explanation for it the man in the street wouldn't understand.

After that it was all downhill, of course. The outlanders had worn themselves out, and they even listened respectfully while Berte quietly sang what to me was always her best number, "I Could Write a Book." From *Pal Joey*. I sure love that number. And Royal and Walt did beautiful intricate tricks with it, between Berte's choruses.

The hipsters were with that one! A couple of them were really twitching, hands and feet both.

Before we knew it, it was two o'clock—and the place still packed. Nobody wanted to go home. Finally Stu and his harem—Rita and her girls—managed to get the customers out.

At three o'clock we were all standing out in front of the place, holding a post-mortem on the wildest night we'd ever had. Frank and his silver-haired queen, pretty as a doll cut out of marshmallow, Berte hanging onto Walt's arm and looking up at him, Stu in a tight overcoat and a little foreign hat—a happy boulevardier indeed! Me and Royal.

Everybody was talking about Royal's act with "Tiger Rag."

Royal seemed embarrassed but happy. "I haven't done that for years," he said. "Some other boys and I used to kid around with that one in college."

"And how about Walter!" cried Frank, laughing. "Tarzan!"

"Wasn't he wonderful!" said Berte, giving with the googoo eyes at her drate big mans.

"Yeah, and how about you, for that matter!" said Walt to Frank. "You killed 'em. There might have been a disaster if it hadn't been for Miss O'Hare." Miss O'Hare was the Snow Queen. She giggled politely. If she'd said a word all evening I hadn't heard it.

Well, that left *me*. But I was happy, too. I had a date with little Jackie, who worked till two and was now waiting for me in her cozy pad.

Anyway, it was the high point.

Pretty soon Berte walked off with Walt, Frank walked off with Miss O'Hare, and Stu went discreetly round the corner, where his El Dorado was parked, to wait for Rita.

"I'll drop you off," said Royal.

We got in the Ford, me and my battered old case, and Royal. I explained where he was to drop me off. He glanced at me, but made no comment.

I felt kind of sorry for him. All alone. "Royal," I said, "it's none of my business, but don't you run around with the opposite sex?"

"Sure," he said. "Once in a while."

I tried to picture it and couldn't. "Look," I said, "Jackie knows a lot of chicks. Want a date now? It might not be fancy on such short notice but it'll be young and probably willing."

"No, thank you, Stan," said Royal. "But I surely do appreciate your thought."

I've been repeating that line ever since.

Yes—that was the high point. After that wild Saturday night something began to go wrong, but I just couldn't figure out what it was. One thing for sure. It had nothing to do with Royal, because he was happy as an actor in front of a mirror, working like a donkey on a treadmill, and coming up with so many new ideas and suggestions that we had to put the reins on him. God, we didn't want to rehearse every day!

No, it wasn't Royal. And it wasn't me. So it had to be Walt. One of the Three Musketeers was holding out, or that's the way I began to feel about it. And then Frank was around almost every night, sitting there, drinking quietly, and two or three times he had a couple of sharp-looking, well-dressed men with him. They just sat and drank quietly, too.

One night at a break a musician I knew, Al, had a smoke with me in the alley.

"What's with the A.A.A. brass?" he said.

Now I don't like to be taken for a guy who doesn't know what is going on, so I throw it away. "I don't know. What?"

"You can level with me, Stan," said Al. "I won't say anything. But I know those guys with Frank Guardi don't just sit around in joints listening to music for the love of it."

But I wouldn't talk, naturally.

"They must have big plans for the outfit, son. Maybe you guys are going to go some place."

"Now where could we go better than this?"

"How do I know? New York. Television. Records. You're going *some* place, that's for sure."

And Walt wasn't leveling with me. I knew that big boy well. He just wasn't. And he wasn't as friendly either. Oh, sure, he laughed and talked with me and all that and we were still living together. But it was just something you feel.

This is the only way I know how to put it. You're going with a dame. She's all over you. What did you have for lunch? Where were you Tuesday night? Why didn't you call me at eight o'clock? Know what I mean? All of sudden, she never asks you any questions about yourself. And then, one night, she's got a headache. A few days later she's promised a married girl friend she'll spend the weekend with her. Or maybe her mother's in town for a few days. You know. The slow, painless, gradual brush.

This is what I thought I was getting from Walt. The slow, painless, gradual brush.

Why?

Walt was away all afternoon that day—with Berte, I guess. Royal and I had dinner together at a little chophouse on La Sinandgaga Boulevard (remember?), then we played a game or two of pool, and then we drove out Sunset at a slow pace, talking. We were early.

When we turned down Doheny we hit the fog. It was coming up the street in long white strands. Down the hill the street lights of Santa Monica Boulevard looked like pinholes of light in a gray blanket. Royal switched on his fog lights and I began to sing "A Foggy Day in London-town." Royal immediately chimed in with the weirdest whistle-obbligato you ever heard.

Yep, we have a lot of fog out here. Sometimes in June you can hardly get around at night, and quite a few times during the fall and winter the air-ports are closed down and all of the shipping along the coast stays in the harbors. One night I was talking with a guy who had served time in the Aleutians during World War II, and I said: "That fog sure must have been bad." And he said: "Oh, about like Los Angeles." And when I argued with him he told me about a map he'd seen charting the fog belts, and the Los Angeles area was marked just as heavy on the map as the Aleutians. Yeah, that's what the man said.

As for *smog!*— Well, let's not get into that. I might want to play a date for the Chamber of Commerce sometime.

We'd loafed all the way out to the joint, and we were slowed down con-siderably by the fog besides, but we were still early. The street in front of the Intime was packed with fog like cotton-wool in a Christmas box and the cars were just barely creeping. "The customers ain't going to find us tonight," I said, as we walked in.

It was a few minutes after eight. Half a dozen regulars were drinking at the bar. There was nobody on the booth-and-table side.

I lit a cigarette and sat down in a booth which was jammed up against the stand and was usually filled with squealing Bev. Hills chicks. We did-n't turn the lights on in the shell. Royal groped his way to the piano and played a cockeyed and muted version of "A Foggy Day." Brother, you could see London. Waterloo Bridge. Big Ben. The Strand. The Houses of Parlia-ment. All standing there in the fog. What do I know about London? I can read, can't I? I've seen Sherlock Holmes in the movies, haven't I? It sound-ed great, and I just sat there sort of... well... dreaming, shall we say? And then all of sudden, I woke up. Royal was now playing something that gave me goose-pimples.

It's not just an expression, "goose-pimples." When I hear something way out there in music, I get them. I know a musician who claims that when he hears real fine and odd stuff, his beard starts to grow. Oh, we're a funny lot!

Well, this thing Royal was playing was in a sort of blues tempo—slow and sad. It frazzled me, like, finally, and I was glad when he stopped and got up without finishing.

He came over to me and I lit his cigarette for him. "I'm not with that any more," he said.

"The piece? What was it?"

"Oh," said Royal, in that offhand way of his, "it's something I wrote." He sat down in the booth and thought it over for a moment. "It's called 'It's Always Four O'clock Blues.'"

"Good title."

"Yeah. You know. Four A.M. It's when the world slows down. It's when things look worst. It's when most people die."

"You'll never make the Hit Parade with that," I said, laughing.

"I'm not with it now," said Royal. "I've got a different slant."

The fog lifted. People came jamming in, and we were off to the races. But Walt was not giving at all, just playing a very ordinary bass, and Berte looked pale.

Came the first break, and Walt and Berte disappeared into the alley right away. Curious, I followed them. But they'd gone away back in the dark part, almost to the next street. Even so, I could hear an argument going on. Somebody sent me out a drink and then a couple of out-of-work sidemen appeared and we yacked about music and the world in general. Royal stayed in the shell.

Pretty soon Berte rushes past us like she's got to catch a plane and goes inside. Finally, Walter comes up, looking a little off-color, both sore and sheepish. He said: "Hi, boys," and went inside, too, without even meeting my eye. Trouble, trouble! I'll say one thing for Walt. He'd known it from the first. He'd predicted it. In fact, I think he'd done his best, which wasn't too good when it came to chicks, to avoid it. Well, it was here now.

"What's with the moose?" said one of the boys.

"Frail-trouble, I guess," I said.

"Hell, that's not news with him, is it?" said the other boy.

"This kind is," I said.

"Oh? Serious?"

"Walt hopes not."

We all laughed. I know I shouldn't have said anything. I'm not usually one to pop off. But Walt and me were getting to be strangers. I didn't have the same feeling toward him at all any more.

The boys left. I finished my cig and wandered in. I saw Rita leaning on her elbows with her back to the bar, away down at the far end where she picks up the drinks. I went over to her.

"Hi, yum-yum," I says.

She just looked at me with those big, prominent, dark, not-too-intelligent eyes. She had sort of a smug expression.

"What are you so happy about?" I asked.

"I think she got told for once," said Rita.

"Oh?"

"Yeah. She's in the sandbox, crying."

"Maybe she has a toothache."

"Maybe."

"Oh, how all you girls love each other. It's war to the knife, from morning till night."

Rita resented this remark very much. "Oh, no, it's not," she said. "I got lots of nice girl friends—buddies. It's just something you men are always saying."

"Yeah," I said, with my best grin, "it's just something we're always saying." I was making a joke of it. Why should I get a dolly like Rita sore at me? You never know. A guy could get lucky.

But Rita did not accept the concession. I'd burned her. "It's like I always say," said Rita in that low, cooing voice which even sounded that way when she was sore, "you can't make a guy do what he don't want to do. And if you can, he's no good."

Rita was not long on logic, but I got the idea. "You're so right, baby," I said, easing up closer to her. She fractured me!

"You can't rope a man like he was a steer," said Rita, "and expect him to stay roped. He's got to *want* to stay roped."

"Got your rope handy, honey?"

She gave me a look, and then began to laugh. She was a big, good-natured kid at that. "Always pitching," she said. "What's the matter with Bobbie? She's between men." Bobbie was the blond barmaid. To me she had an unsympathetic nature. She was always fighting about money—the tips—with the bartender and the two other girls. Stu was a gentleman. He did not cut in on the tips the help got.

"Between men?" I said. "Three in a bed, you mean?"

Rita threw her head back and gave with a loud fat laugh. Just at that moment Berte whizzed past us. Rita stopped laughing and her eyes narrowed. I cursed Berte under my breath. I'd been doing all right. Now I wasn't even there.

I walked away without another word to Rita.

It was not a good night. As I played, I kept glancing at Berte out of the corner of my eye. She was a very sad girl. I began to feel kind of sorry for her. Here was a kid away out of her class. She should have stayed with mama and papa in the ancestral mansion in Bev. Hills. She was not equipped for this jungle warfare. As for Walt, well, he was a big ape, wasn't he?

♮♭

Several nights later when I got home from the job, Walt was already there. This had never happened before, and I was mighty surprised. He was in his shirt sleeves with his tie to one side and his vest unbuttoned. I could see the fraternity pin shining on the vest-tab. He was standing in the middle of the living room, staring at nothing and twisting his hair. When Walt was disturbed, which was damned seldom, I assure you, he always twisted his hair till finally a strand of it stood straight up. He was neither a crew boy nor a duck-tail boy. He got his hair cut once a week and it was of normal length and style. Funny thing about Walt. He wasn't vain. He was no mirror-fighter, in spite of his looks. I don't think he ever gave his appearance a thought and he seemed as unconscious of his clothes as a dog is of its collar. He was always clean and neat, but that was as far as it went.

He was, I guess you might say, a sort of instinctive kind of guy. Normally he acted without thinking. He was healthy and well balanced. He didn't *have* to think. You might almost say he had no alternatives. He was a simple guy, wanting one thing at a time—and something he could get. Life was easy for him.

Well, now he was thinking, and making a mighty rough go of it.

"Hi, junior," he said.

I just looked at him, put the case down, and went out to the refrigerator and got myself a bottle of beer. When I came back he was sprawled out in a chair with one leg up over the arm.

"Want some beer?" I asked.

"No, thanks," said Walt. "I've been drinking too much lately. I wish those guys would stop buying us drinks."

"Oh, come now, Walter. You could take Coke."

He didn't say anything and sat for a long time looking at the floor. "I've been thinking," he said, finally. "You know, this joint's getting mighty inconvenient."

I glanced around at the nest. I could remember when it had seemed like paradise to me. Still did, for that matter. How could I possibly do as well elsewhere on the dough I made? "What do you mean, Walt?" I asked. Did he want me out, was that it?

"Well, you see," said Walt, "things are kind of different for me now."

"If you want me out of here, say so," I put in. Hell, why beat about the bush? If this was it, it was it!

"No, no," cried Walt. "I tell you I'm just thinking, that's all."

"You mean, on account of Berte?"

Walt grimaced and wagged his head from side to side. "I mean, I ought to have a place of my own—that's what I mean."

"Well, that's what I said."

"No, no. I don't want this place," cried Walt. "I should have a new place."

"Okay. Get one," I said. I was beginning to get sore.

"I tell you I'm just thinking," said Walt. "Don't jump down my throat. Can't I think?"

"I wish to hell you'd tell me what's going on," I said. "What is all this, for

Christ's sake? If you want me out of here, I'll get out. If you want a new place, *you* get out. What's tough about it?"

Walt jumped up. "I don't know. I'm not ready. Can't a guy just think?"

He went into his room, banging the door.

The next morning, all through breakfast, I had a feeling Walt wanted to tell me something. I gave him all kinds of leads and a couple of times I thought he was going for them. But he didn't. He went away mumbling something about he'd better hurry, he had to take Berte some place.

Well, the handwriting was up. I didn't know what it spelled out. But it was there, all right.

Monday came round again. I spent the day with Jackie. We were getting to be buddies, Jackie and me. And it wasn't easy, with her. She was only nineteen, but she'd seen a lot in her short life, believe me, and what she thought of men in general couldn't be printed. She was a tough little cookie, always the quip, always the brushoff if you got serious about anything. All the same, I liked her, and we had fun together.

She could generally get hold of a car—from one of her many girl friends—so we drove down to the beach, had lunch at Malibu La Costa, and then drove around the hills overlooking the Pacific. It was a swell day, mild and clear. Gulls were all over the place. I felt low. Jackie kept looking at me kind of funny.

We had dinner at a little French place on Sunset where you could scoff a pretty good table d'hôte for buttons, then we went to a movie. I usually got a big bang out of taking Jackie to a movie. Man, those comments! But this night I wasn't with it. Jackie made a few cracks and then quit. We just sat there.

Finally we went back to her place. Now Jackie is a very sensual little doll when she's in the mood. Usually when we'd get to her place, she'd disappear and come back dressed in a Chinese banker's coat and Chinese slippers. What else? Nothing else, man! But this night she just flung herself down in a chair, kicked off her shoes, and sat with her legs stretched out, looking kind of sullen.

When I didn't say anything, she said: "Why don't you scram?"

"You want me to scram?"

"Well, that's what you want to do, isn't it?"

"Look, Jackie," I says, "I'm just not with it."

"That's what I been thinking all day," she says. "Gwan, scram." I knew her pretty well by this time. Her feelings were hurt, and this is the way she showed it. Where another girl would weep or pout, Jackie would get tough.

"Look, baby," I said, "this has got nothing to do with you." And then I started to tell her about the way things were going with the trio and with Walt.

Jackie had been out to the Intime two or three times, but she'd never made any comments about the place or the trio. Finally she said: "Well, a job's a job, isn't it?"

"Yeah," I said, "but this is kind of special."

Jackie wiggled her toes and stared at them for a while, then she said: "You sure like that big red-haired bum, don't you?"

I was surprised. "Walt? Sure. He's my best friend."

Jackie laughed quietly to herself, real nasty. You know. Yuck-yuck-yuck.

"What's the idea?" I says, beginning to get sore.

"Who am I to tell you your business?" says Jackie. "But that big pretty-boy would sell out his mother."

"That's what you say about everybody."

"Yeah. And I'm always right."

And she damned near always was!

"You don't even know the guy," I argued.

"I don't have to. I can see, can't I?" says Jackie. "He's the kind the gals fall all over. They spoil him. He gets big ideas. Am I right?"

We'd never discussed Walt before, mind you. "More or less," I agreed.

"Well," said Jackie, "if he's got any reason to sell you out, you're sold."

"Okay, okay," I said, sore.

"And now scram!" cried Jackie. "I'm sleepy."

So I scrammed. I went over across the street to a little bar, had a couple of drinks, and thought things over, then I called Jackie.

"What do *you* want?" she said in her gracious way.

I told her where I was. "Come over," I said. "Let's have a drink and relax."

She just slammed up the receiver. But fifteen minutes later, there she was. She didn't say anything. She just sat down beside me.

So we had a few drinks... and then we had a ball after all.

Yeah, the handwriting was up, all right—and what Jackie had said about Walt made my uneasiness worse. She was a real sharpie when it came to guys.

A few days passed—and then... well, I'll tell you about it, just as it happened.

It was about three in the morning, I guess. I got home first, as usual, and was just thinking about taking a shower when there was a real light tap at the door. Who could it be? Royal? I'd just left him. Maybe a message from the management. What else? Nobody ever called on us—we discouraged it—and Walt always carried a key.

I went over and opened the door. Berte! I took a step backward and said: "He hasn't got home yet. I usually beat him."

All the same I was mighty surprised. She'd never been in the place to my knowledge since that night she had come with Frank.

"Oh, he won't be here for hours," she said. "He's with Frank and Stu."

"Oh?" I says blankly. I'm frazzled!

"Aren't you going to ask me in?" says Berte, smiling in that nice, ladylike way. She was looking real fine tonight in a plain dress that probably only cost about two hundred and fifty dollars, and a blue fox stole. Her dark-blond hair was thick and real rich-looking and cut fairly short, and she was wearing diamond earrings in her pierced ears. Oh, a fine, slim, hip, expensive doll!

"The pleasure is all mine," I says, aping Walt.

She came in, sat down, and got out a cigarette. I lit it for her. She was playing it very calm, but she was nervous, I could see, and I began to wonder.

"How about a snifter?" I says, the gracious host.

"Scotch and water, thank you," she says, relaxing and crossing her legs. You know there's something about when you say that a girl is crossing her legs... like, well, you're trying to make a point of it, as if it has a meaning of some kind. You can say that a guy crossed his legs, and who cares? So while I'm on the subject, let me say this: it is one thing for Rita to cross her legs and an entirely different thing altogether when Berte does it. When Rita crosses her legs she really throws one over the other and if you're sitting opposite her in the right spot, yowie! With Berte it's just a graceful movement and as ladylike as everything else about her. Now why, oh, why, did this refined chick have to go for an Animal like Walt?

I bring the drinks and we sit and look at each other.

"Stan," she says finally, fussing with her stole, her cigarette, her purse and her drink. How they can fuss, chicks! Nervous, all of them, nervous, restless, ready to take off, disgruntled, dissatisfied, looking for slights—why? Purely physiological, a friend of mine always says, he's been married four times at the age of forty—and plays tenor sax in his spare time—so maybe he knows. "Stan," Berte said, "I imagine you are Walter's best friend."

"I don't know," I said. "What about himself?"

There was a long pause. "Stan," she said again, "let's cut the funny talk. I'm fed to here with funny talk since we had the trio. I would like to hear a little serious talk."

"You better talk to Frank then," I said. I wasn't liking this, whatever it was. You know the word "patronizing"? I had a feeling this was it.

"Stan," she starts out again, "I know you don't like me, but I like you."

"I like you fine," I says. "You are a very enticing doll, Berte."

"Thank you," said Berte. "But what I mean is... you and Walter, well, you were sort of Damon and Pythias, till I stepped in."

"Let's make it Amos and Andy. I like that better," I says. Get this doll! What a crust! And she was so wrong!

She flushes and I can see that she can just barely keep from stamping her little, narrow, elegant foot at me. "Well, anyway," she says, when she'd recovered, "I'd like to have a talk with you. You might not think so, but where you are concerned, Walter is a big coward."

"Oh?" I says. "Does he know you're here?"

"Oh, no," she says. "And don't tell him, please."

These chicks! "Okay. I won't tell him." Was I getting curious!

"He's also a coward about Royal," she said. "I never saw anything like it. A big man like him!"

There was a pause. I leaned forward and said: "Come on, Berte. Level. What is it?"

"Well," she said, "here's how I want you to do this. You've heard a rumor. You bring it up tonight when Walter gets home. That way, we'll get it out in the open and it will be better for everybody concerned. Right?"

I thought this over for a while. "Look, Berte," I said, "this begins to sound like one of those round-the-mulberry-bush feminine deals. And I don't like 'em."

"All right," she said, "just wait till I tell you. I know you won't let me down then. Well, the big men at A.A.A. think Walter is sensational. He's never had a chance before to show what he could do. They think he's got great talent, as a kind of off-beat singer and as a Personality."

"Well...? So...?" I broke in. "Trouble with Walt is, he's got no ambition. If they think he's going to beat his brains out to be a success like a guy has to do, they're daffy."

"Oh, I can help him there," said Berte, the brave little woman.

"Are you sure?"

"Yes, I'm sure."

"Okay. Go ahead."

"Well, one of A.A.A.'s top comedians is laying an egg on a big hour show out of New York—television. The men at A.A.A. think they can save the show with Walter helping out. It's a crisis, you might say."

"Like the trouble in Formosa, you mean?" I was mad. I didn't dig this talk at all. From Berte?

"Couldn't we please cut the jokes?" asked Berte, with a slight edge to that polite, cultivated voice.

"Sure, sure," I said. "I was just keeping in step. Walt on TV? That's a yack, a yuck, and a big boff!"

"Well, he's signed," said Berte, real calm, like a fencer giving with a quick thrust. Touché—and there goes your head, à la Thurber!

I jumped up, spilling my drink. "Signed! What happens to the trio?"

"That's what I wanted to talk to you about," said Berte, settling her stole and reaching for another cigarette. I didn't light this one.

"You mean it's washed up?"

Berte nodded, struggling with a match, screwing up her eyes, lighting about a quarter of her cigarette—you know how dames do. "As of this Saturday."

"This coming Saturday?"

"Yes," said Berte. "Frank arranged it with Stu. Lonny Boyle's coming in."

I absorbed this slowly. Then I threw my glass at the wall, smashing it. Berte jumped in her chair, then stood up. I went over and opened the door. "Good night, Miss Dehn," I said. "It's been so nice."

She walked almost to the door, then she turned. "Why are you angry with me? Did you want to wait till Saturday night to find out? Walter wouldn't tell you. And besides, it wasn't my idea. It was Frank's. Of course, I'm for it." There was a pause. "Stan, if you come right down to it, the trio itself was all my own idea."

I thought this over for a while, then I said: "Look, this means nothing to me. A job's a job. But it's going to be mighty sad news to Royal."

"Yes, I know," said Berte, though she didn't—I mean, she didn't *really* know. "You've got to break it to him."

Man, did I shrink. "Me? Why me?"

"Who else?" asked Berte.

Yeah, who else!

Berte hesitated, then said: "Look, Stan, believe me, I've got Walter's best interests at heart."

"I couldn't care less," I said. "He's a big boy. He's over twenty-one. I do all my worrying about Stanislaus Pawloski."

"About whom?"

"Not whom! Me."

"Oh," said Berte, giving me an odd look. "That's your name, is it. I see. I didn't know."

"And let me tell you something, if you think you're going to ride Walt from here on in, you'd better get some spurs, a whip, and a curb bit."

Berte didn't get sore at all. She just stood looking at me kind of sad, like. "I know," she said. "Don't worry. I know." A pause. "Stan, please don't tell Walter I was here."

"Frankly, Berte," I said, "I don't know what I'm going to do. I'm so flipped-off, I can hardly talk. I make no promises."

"Well..." said Berte, then she went out.

I slammed the door after her. I had to hold onto myself. I wanted to kick out all the windows. How do you like that Walter?

♮ ♭

Walt didn't get home till five o'clock. He was slightly oiled. He took one look at my packed bags in the middle of the living room, he took one look at my kisser, then he fell down into a chair and just sat there.

"I heard a rumor," I said.

"Yeah?"

"It seems we have a Jackie Gleason in the outfit, and Jackie has got to go on to bigger things and we are out on our asses as of Saturday night."

"Yeah?"

"This being the case," I went on, "I do not want to have anything more to do with said Jackie Gleason and have booked a domicile elsewhere."

"Tonight?" asks Walt, not looking up.

"Right now," I said, and I picked up my bags and started out.

"Listen, Stan," said Walt, getting up, looking kind of sick, "I tried like hell not to let this happen. But they all kept ratting at me. Frank, Berte, all the big guys at A.A.A. I'm a little guy, Stan. I don't know how to say no to those big A.A.A. guys."

"You don't know how to say no, period."

"Jesus, what could I do?"

"You could have told me. This has been going on for weeks. You could have leveled with me and Royal. This is going to break that guy up."

"God, can't you get another bass player?"

"I'm going to suggest it."

I started past him. "Look, Stan..." he began.

"Keep away from me, Walter," I says, "or I'm going to belt you with one of these bags. Lonny Boyle! After the way he talked. Oh, is that mick happy. Man, this is the worst yet."

"God, I'm sorry, Stan," said Walt.

"Look," I said, "we've got to play together through Saturday night. Don't speak to me. Just don't speak to me or there's going to be trouble."

Walt backed off, and I walked out. It wasn't easy. We'd had big times in that place.

♪ ♭

I got a room in a little Hollywood hotel—and what a room!

It's Always Four O'clock Blues.

God, I hated to think about Royal. I didn't know what to do. If I told him now, I doubted if he'd finish out the week. And I didn't want that to happen, on account of Lonny Boyle, who might be called in early to fill in.

I sat there in that poky room staring at nothing till nearly eight o'clock, then I went out and had some breakfast in a drug store. Then I went back and had a bright idea. I called Palos Verdes. I had a hell of a time getting an answer, then Ellen, the maid, came on. Pat, the chauffeur, had driven Piggy to Ensenada, in Mexico: Ensenada Hotel. So she'd gone after all!

What could I do? I had to call her. So I went down in the lobby and arranged with the clerk for my Mexican call. I was in a flea-bag where you didn't bang the phones with long-distance calls on the cuff, believe me. Hollywood was full of bums and deadbeats and these little hotels had had some gruesome experiences.

Some guy on the other end gave with the mañana accent. Madame Jones was staying at the hotel... yes. Her luggage was there... yes. But she had gone on to the south for a few days with a party of friends. Yes... she would be back. I left my number and instructions at what hour to call. Then I paid the bill.

With this Royal it was always trouble, trouble.

I saw Jackie a couple of times that week. I made up my mind I'd have to tell her the truth about the trio, but I just couldn't do it, after what she'd said about Walt. Finally I lied to her about it. I said we were fed up and were asking out, that all of us needed a rest. She gave me a look from under those long black eyelashes.

"You need a rest, all right," she said, finally. "You're not with it. You used to be the liveliest guy in town—a barrel of laughs. But lately you've got to be a real glum character. I am a glum character myself. Two of us is too many."

This worried me. I was getting to feel pretty strong about this tough little Jackie. Yes, I'll admit it. So... I told her the whole business. I braced myself, getting ready for the dirty laugh and the I-told-you-so. But I was wrong.

Jackie came over and patted me on the head. "I'm sorry, Stan," she said. And that's all she said.

God, I sure loved that little chick for that.

♮♭

What a week! Even now, just remembering it, I get that same sweaty, apprehensive feeling—something hanging over you, day and night, like the sword ready to fall. To make it worse, Royal was playing his best and kept yacking to any of us who would listen about three new arrangements he was working on—tops!

With Walt it was even worse. He sure surprised me. I guess you don't really know people after all, you just get a bullheaded idea that you do and stick to it. Instead of just saying the hell with it and forgetting it, as I expected Walt to do, he was all to pieces. If our eyes met by accident, he quickly looked away. He was one uneasy guy. And if I ever saw a person suffering from what they call remorse, it was him. I guess that Walt, size and all, was really a kind of weak guy that could be pulled here and there by other people, in spite of what he wanted to do himself.

Berte—the little woman—was bright and gay, too bright and gay, and her singing suffered. Royal would wrinkle up his face and kick the piano, but he never said anything to Berte, one way or another. She was one of his team, one of the saints, I guess—and could actually do no wrong in his eyes. He was always very gentlemanly and polite to her.

Frank was in and out, sometimes alone, sometimes with the Snow Queen, or another like her, sometimes with one of the boys from A.A.A.

What a conspiracy! Everybody in the place, from the colored porter to Rita, knew that we were finishing Saturday night and they had all been warned not to say anything about it. Royal was not to be told.

The most nervous guy of all, I think, was Stu. He was a real nice gent and he didn't like this ring-around-the-rosie underhand business at all.

As for myself, well, I had a knot in my stomach and no appetite. Need I say more? I kept trying to get Piggy on the phone, with no results. Saturday night began to seem like the end of the world to me. Finally I sent a telegram care of the Ensenada Hotel.

Saturday night came, and with it the usual Saturday night crowd. We rambled pretty good in spite of everything. At ten o'clock Lonny Boyle waltzes in, smiling at the peasants, waving greetings, very well pleased with himself. At the break I took him aside. He kept looking at me askance. He was leery of me since that night I'd told him off.

"Lonny," I said, very polite, "don't crack about coming in Tuesday."

He gave me a funny look. "Why not?"

"It's a long story. Nothing to do with you. Stu's keeping the place dark Sunday as well as Monday and...."

"I know," said Lonny, looking me over. "Say, what's going on here? We should have had some publicity already."

"They break it Monday."

"Yeah," said Lonny, puzzled, "but, hell, a lot of people know I'm coming in."

"I know, I know. But just don't say anything tonight, that's all. As a favor," I added, hating myself for saying it... but, well, there you are.

Lonny liked people to ask favors of him. Lonny was quite a Big Wheel, at least in his own estimation, and it pleased him to grant requests from the lesser orders. "Okay," he said, his face relaxing for the first time, "as a favor to you. Say, Stan, what you got against me?"

"Nothing, nothing," I said hurriedly.

"Man, you were really chomping opening night. I thought you had me in your black book."

"Jittery, I guess," I said.

Lonny seemed mighty relieved and pleased. "Yeah," he said, looking me over carefully. Did he think I was crawling? "Well, be seeing you."

He smiled and went back to join a group of hipsters, who began to "Mr. Boyle" him and ask about his new record album that had just come out.

Well, the night went on and on. I kept saying to myself, what am I going to do? I'd been counting on Piggy all along to help me out of this nightmare. What the hell, if she was so keen on looking after her little brother, why wasn't she around? Two or three times I thought about calling up the lawyer down in Los Angeles—one of the numbers Piggy had given me and Walt—but... well, what was I going to say to him?

I sat playing the old gee-tar and looking about me. Now human nature is a funny thing. For months I'd been taking this pleasant little trap for granted—just a place where you work, boring, irritating, a place you want to get away from and have some fun. But now that I was leaving it, it sure looked good to me, nicest place I'd ever played in. All shining and new and pale-blue mirrored, and nice people, good drinks, no beefs—and there was big luscious Rita moving her big body gracefully about among the customers, leaning over them—just enough to cause male eyes to pop—smiling, polite, efficient. I was going to miss this place.

And I was going to miss Walt, too—goddamn it! I glanced over at him. He was looking at me. He jerked his head around with a quick movement and grinned at somebody in the house. I saw a girl wave to him, one of the hipsters' girls. Walt did a little shuffle and walked the bass. The girl squealed.

Then... all of a sudden Rita was whispering in my ear. She'd snuck up on me, I guess. This was the closest I'd ever got to Rita and I liked it. Her lips almost touched my ear. Her hair tickled me. She smelled good.

"Phone, honey," she whispered. "Mrs. Jones. Important."

Who is Mrs...! Then I got it. I just put the instrument down and walked away from the stand right in the middle of the number. Walked? I ran, back along the crowded bar and into the public booth. Trust Piggy. She'd found me in spite of the fact that like a fool I'd only left her my home number.

"What's the matter, Stan?" she cried, and her voice sounded mighty anxious.

I told her, as briefly as I could. She didn't quite dig it at first, much to my surprise. So we were closing! Then she began to catch on.

"Well," she said, "I didn't know quite what it was, so I came in town. I'm at my apartment."

Was I relieved! "Swell," I said. "Royal and I will be over there around two-thirty, maybe earlier."

I went back, walking like a foot-soldier who'd just got the pack off his back. Berte was singing. She followed me with her eyes as I came up through the crowded place and took my seat. Royal swiveled round to look at me but said nothing. Walt pretended to be clowning with the hipsters down front. It was mighty sad clowning!

Finally it was over. I ducked Walt, I ducked Berte, I ducked everybody but Royal.

"That was Piggy on the phone," I says to him. "She's over at her apartment. She wants us to come over."

"That so?" said Royal. "I thought she was still in Mexico."

"She just got back. Ah... weather's been kind of bad, I guess."

We drove over to Piggy's with me clutching the old battered case. Royal never stopped talking—all these new ideas he had! He'd decided to call a rehearsal for the middle of next week, not only to try some new numbers but to brush up on several of the old ones. "We never have got the best out of 'Babes in the Woods,'" he said. "It's a great tune and we sound ordinary on it. What do you think about 'Rose Room'? Think we ought to add it? It's a dandy."

I mumbled something. God, time was going slow!

There was Piggy, smiling—lounging pajamas, short haircut, jeweled cheaters and all. Was I glad to see her!

"Hi," said Royal.

"Hi," said Piggy.

We sat down. Piggy made some daiquiris and they tasted good. Royal sipped his absent-mindedly, then began to tell Piggy all about the trio, how well we were doing, and what his plans were for the future.

Piggy looked mighty uneasy. I couldn't take any more of it. Now let's talk about bravery for a minute. If bravery is just thick-skulled indifference to danger or trouble, then I'm not brave, I'm a coward. But if bravery is overcoming your natural instinct to dog it, then I'm a very brave guy indeed. I wanted to get out of that place and let Piggy take the rap. My feet would hardly stay there. But finally I said: "Look, Royal. There's something I got to tell you."

Now Royal was a careless, absent-minded guy, but he was also a nervous, sensitive guy. Something about my tone of voice bothered him. He turned around real quick and looked at me. "Yes, Stan?"

So I told him, falling all over myself like a drunken and guilty husband trying to explain to the angry little woman how it happened to be three o'clock in the morning and how he happened to be so loaded with booze he couldn't have hit the ceiling with his hat.

Royal could just not take it in. He sat there with his mouth open. He turned pale. Little beads of sweat began to appear on his forehead and his upper lip. His hands began to shake. He was really taking it hard, harder, even, than I'd expected.

There was a long silence. Piggy kept glancing at him very uneasily.

Naturally I've seen a lot of guys get the rug pulled out from under them. In my profession, it happens all the time. But little by little, a guy gets hardened to it, and gives with the, "Oh, what the hell!" But Royal was just not the type who gets hardened. His nerves were close to the surface, things hit him a tremendous wallop—like the earthquake, that time. Well, here was another earthquake.

"Look, Royal," I said hastily, "I'm going to scout around tomorrow or the next day and see if I can't dig us up a real good bass player."

He didn't say anything. Piggy mixed him another daiquiri, but he wouldn't drink it. Finally he got up and sort of stretched.

"I think I'll go to bed, Stan, if you don't mind," he said.

"No, no," I said quickly. "Go to bed. Sleep on it. Call you tomorrow."

"I was thinking," said Piggy, "you might like to go back to Mexico with me, Kip. I've met some nice people down there and...."

Royal ignored her. He just went into the bedroom and shut the door.

Piggy and I stood there looking at each other. Finally she said: "I'll see if I can get him down to Palos Verdes tomorrow. He can sit in the sun, swim...."

"Yeah," I said.

"Don't feel too bad, Stan," she said. "Matter of fact, there isn't much anybody can do for Royal. He's just the way he is. When he was six, I was nearly thirteen. Mama was almost always in bed. I looked after him. He was always impossible. He gets to liking people, then something happens. It's bound to. Royal's like a child. He doesn't understand how the world is at all."

"It's a rough place even for me," I said.

"And for me," said Piggy. "But we're tough."

We shook hands. I really liked this chick. She was a hundred per cent.

Well, for the first time in my life I borrowed some sleeping pills, and tossed around on the bed till noon, not awake, not asleep. The hell with that! I haven't taken any since. If you're going to have to lay awake, lay awake—at least you know what you're doing.

Piggy called me about twelve-thirty. She and Royal were at Palos Verdes.

"How is he?" I asked.

"You can't tell. He won't say anything. I'm trying to get him to go to Mexico with me."

"Well, good luck," I says.

Man, I felt low.

♮ ♭

The next few weeks was a real rough period for me. Emotionally and financially, as the fellow says. I couldn't get with it. I'm a guy who never saves any money—intentionally, I mean. Sometimes when I'm working steady, it just accumulates. Well, it had accumulated. So I sat back. I passed up jobs. I spent dough on Jackie, in bars and restaurants, and tried to be a Chuckling Charlie for her benefit—though I don't think I was kidding that sharpie much. I was surly with guys. Some of my pals began to duck me in bars. Several nights I got very, very drunk indeed—which is not my usual habit—and Jackie had to help me home. Jackie was out of work, too. But she was just waiting for a new place to open where she had a pretty good deal coming up—a piece of the checkroom. I'm telling you, this was a smart chick, for nineteen.

Finally one night Jackie got so sore at me for the way I was acting that she called me a slob and slapped my face. Being well loaded, I swung back at her—but I missed. Luck was with me. Jackie boiled and told me to get the hell out and stay out.

The next night I called her from a bar and asked her to meet me. She slammed up the receiver like she'd done before. But she met me. I started belting the Scotch right away, but she ordered Coke.

Finally she said: "Look, Stan. I was beginning to think you were okay. But I guess you're just another louse."

This really jolted me. I pushed the half-empty glass away.

"What do you want me to do?" I asks, like a kid talking to mama.

"Straighten up and get a job—and stop being such a slob," says Jackie.

So I tried. I cut my drinking away down. Jobs were scarce—but I got a few pickups. My pals stopped edging away, and seemed glad to see me again.

Funny, eh? What a few well-chosen words from a sharp little nineteen-year-old chick will do?

♪ ♮

Well, one morning I got up feeling pretty good. I'd worked a party the night before and refused the drinks—most of them, that is. No hangover, and I had a few bucks in the bank. I took a shower, singing and whistling, dressed up in a new sport coat Jackie had selected for me, and strutted out for breakfast. It was almost winter now and pretty nippy. I could see snow on the mountains away to hell and gone off to the east some place. A lot of guys I knew went up to the snow on the weekends when they weren't working. But not me! I'd been brought up around Chicago. I'd had a bellyful of snow.

Well, after scoffing a mighty tasty breakfast and a pot of real good coffee, I strutted back to the pad, whistling and smoking a cigar, just like a happy square in from Ioway to get a gander at the sinful and glamorous metropolis of Hollywood. By the way, do you know there is no such place as Hollywood? Honest. There is Los Angeles, there is the Strip, there is Beverly Hills, Westwood, West Los Angeles—but there is no such place as Hollywood. It's just something you talk about. All right. Sue me. As to the cigar—a guy I never saw before gave it to me in the restaurant. His wife had just had a baby that morning. You think that kind of stuff happens only in the funny papers? Well, it happened to me.

But as soon as I got into the lobby I stopped whistling. Frank and Walt were sitting there. Frank was reading a newspaper with his hat tilted back, looking like a big-shot bookie or a real plush hoodlum—a movie hoodlum, I'm speaking of. Walt was just sitting there—nothing else, not even smoking.

I hadn't seen Walt for a long time. It was kind of a shock. How else can I put it? I'd written that joker off the books for good—and there he was, staring into space, waiting for me.

Frank got up and came over right away. "Hello, Stan," he said, shaking hands "sincerely," a real A.A.A. handshake, and giving with the Ipana smile. "You're not really sore at Walt, are you?"

Was I? I wasn't so sure now that I saw him sitting there, the big oaf! "I don't know what I am," I mumbled. "The hell with him. What does he want?"

Frank seemed a little uneasy and nervous. He looked me over, sort of, studying me like he wasn't quite certain whether I was vegetable, mineral, or animal. That made two of us. I wasn't quite certain either. "Well," he said, smiling again, "he's flying East Tuesday. I'm going with him. It's like this, Stan. Berte's going, too. They... well, she and Walt are going to tie the old knot at Las Vegas. Surprised? Yes, they're going to be married."

I looked over at Walt. He was hanging his head like a big dog that had been caught in the kitchen stealing the dinner roast. I don't know how it could be, but all of a sudden I felt sorry for this joker. Also, the whole thing struck me as funny. I began to laugh. I couldn't stop.

This really put Frankie-boy off balance. He was such a conventional guy. I could almost read his mind. He was outraged. Was this a way to greet the marriage announcement of your best pal and severest critic? "What's so funny, Stan?" he asked, staring.

"You going on the honeymoon, Frank?" I asked, still laughing.

Man, I caught him with that one. He's not the stammering type, but he began to stammer now. "Well, I... I... no. You see, Stan, I'm representing Walt now for A.A.A. This is a really big thing, this new contract, and...."

Frankie the Agent!

I looked over at Walt and grinned at him. I couldn't help myself. I just was not sore at the big guy any longer. He jumped up right away, looking mighty relieved, and came over and began to pump my arm like a greeter in a resort hotel when the weather's been bad. Was he glad to see me!

"God, Stan," he said, "you had me worried."

"Hi, Lover Boy," I said. "Well, it looks like the rover has crossed over. When is the blessed event? Oh, excuse me. That's something else, ain't it? And let's hope it's nine months."

Frank was really shocked. But Walter seemed to think I was funny as hell. It was like the old days when he used to come home boiled and laugh at everything I said, funny or not.

"You see," said Frank, trying to stop this line of conversation, "Walter considers you his best friend, whether you like it or not...."

"Oh, I *like* it, I *like* it," I jumped in, giving with the Jerry Lewis bit, and Walt laughed like hell again.

But I didn't stop Frank. He went right on. "...and he wants you to be best man."

I looked at Walt. "Is that on the level, kiddo?"

"Sure it's on the level," said Walt.

"Las Vegas?" I says. "Hell, how am I going to get to Las Vegas?"

"On the cuff," said Walt. "How do you think?"

"All expenses paid?" I asked, clowning, and Frank gave me a very disapproving look.

"Sure," said Walt, "and all you can eat."

"All right, Walt," I says.

Frank now looked relieved. Walt grinned all over his big face and grabbed my hand again and shook it. "God, Stan," he mumbled, "you sure as hell had me worried."

We flew to Las Vegas. I felt pretty good. This was quite a nice junket on the cuff. Good old el cuffo! But I didn't like flying—I'd had a bellyful during my time in the Army—and I didn't like the looks of those big ugly snow-covered mountains we were flying over. What a place to crash-land in! We hit some bad air and I got kind of panicky. Frank and Walt laughed like hell at me and made me drink brandy from a flask. In spite of promising Jackie I wouldn't go on a bender during the junket, I overdid the brandy. My stomach was empty, too—which added to the fun and riot.

But you should have seen Berte. She was so nervous she didn't know what she was saying and didn't listen when you talked to her. You could almost see the wheels clicking in her mind. Would she make it? What could happen now? The unicorn was in the trap at last—but was there a possible chance that he could get away? In spite of the brandy-glow I was developing, I felt kind of sorry for her.

Oh, yes—the brandy. Pretty soon I was lit up like a Christmas tree. So I went on the make for the stewardess—encouraged by Walt, who was getting a big bang out of me. She was a real cute rusty-haired doll with teeth like Frank Guardi. I didn't get any place, of course—are those girls used to the pass!—but I had a lot of fun trying, and managed to forget about those jagged mountains below us.

Finally we landed. Man, I mean, we landed. I turned pale-green and began to shake all over. Give me a helicopter any time.

♮♭

Las Vegas, a desert with slot machines!

What a place! Frantic gambling with the atom bomb just over the mountains. I'm not kidding. I talked to a fellow who was in Las Vegas when they set one of them off. He couldn't even tell you about it without getting scared. His chin trembled. "Jesus, what a flash," he said. "Like nothing you've ever seen in this world, chum. I haven't been the same since."

And the dolls! They talk about Hollywood. It's nothing. You should see the shapely chicks parading through the streets in sunsuits, bathing suits, cowboy pants or any other kind of clothes that are tight enough or skimpy enough to cause male eyeballs to roll. I almost lost mine—my eyeballs, I'm speaking of.

"This eyestrain is killing me," I says to Walt, whose head was turning around like an owl's—fine way to act on his marriage day, I must say!

"Let's buy us some dark glasses," said Walt, so we all went in and bought dark glasses. Berte, too—going along with the gag.

"Good God," I said to Frank, as one of these undressed Las Vegas dolls brushed past me, smelling sweet and looking even better than she smelled, "where do they all come from?"

"It's the big money," said Frank, and after that remark he took us down the street to a big gambling joint and showed us a million dollars being displayed in a show window. You think I'm kidding? Okay. Next chance you get, go to Las Vegas and see the million dollars in the window. The only thing is, it may be gone before you can get there. I kept trying to figure out a way to steal it. And if *I'm* figuring—a reasonably honest guy— you can imagine how many other guys in Las Vegas are figuring the same thing. Anyway, there it was. One million simoleons!

While Frank and Walt made the arrangements, I bucked one of the fifty-cent slot machines. Believe it or not, I broke even. All that fun for free! I also added considerably to the brandy I'd already taken on. I crossed my fingers when I thought of Jackie. Hell, this was a real occasion—once in a lifetime!

Now there was a funny thing about Berte. She did not want one of those "chapel" deals, like most chicks. She wanted to get it over with as fast as possible so it would be a fait accompli (oh, I know some Greek words!), and to hell with the frills.

So she and Walt got married in the basement of the courthouse. I guess it was the courthouse, and I guess it was the basement. I was feeling no pain by this time and things were getting pretty fuzzy for me and I wasn't exactly sure where I was at any given moment.

The judge, or magistrate, or whoever he was, who married them was a nice-looking little guy with a gray mustache and a bald head. Both Berte and Walter were pale. In fact, Walt looked like a guy who was walking that last mile. "I'm not guilty, warden," he might have been saying.

When it was all over, the judge kissed the bride, Frank kissed the bride, I kissed the bride—but by the time she got around to me she was crying so hard the front of my shirt got soggy. Big Walt just stood there, looking a little appalled, as if he wasn't exactly sure what this was all about. And he wasn't!

I got so fractured that night they all had to put me to bed. (Good thing I'd left Jackie in L.A., she'd surely have been flipped-off at me.) These people were really tired of me by this time—and I was tired of them, very tired. It's a good thing the lights went out when they did, because Frank was beginning to irritate me more and more with his quiet ways and his smooth smile, and Berte... well, she hadn't wanted me along in the first place, you could bet on that. She'd given in to Walter so she could get him to Las Vegas with as little trouble as possible, but now, the thing was over—she had the unicorn—so why should she put up with me any longer? I'm not dense, drunk or sober. And her pained smile began to give me a pain in the ass. Yeah, it's a good thing I passed out when I did. I might have really disgraced myself.

But the next morning it was different. I was slightly hungover and I felt mighty sad and all to pieces, as if this was the end of everything. A gale was blowing at the airport and we all had our faces full of alkali dust. When the plane was called, Walt clung to my hand like a drowning sailor hangs onto a spar. He was really getting the rush—every way. Berte had rushed him into marriage. A.A.A. had rushed him into a long-term contract. From time to time, he got flashes of all this, I think. "Sold down the river, massa, I'll never see the Old Plantation again!" He was a worried, badgered guy.

I cuffed him sadly, and he cuffed me. "I'll drop you a line, kiddo," he said, looking like a guy going to his own funeral.

But you should have seen Berte. She looked like an angel now, all sweet and calm. She'd made it!

Frank gave with the teeth and patted me patronizingly on the shoulder. Then they were up and away. I stood, practically getting my pants blown off, looking up at the sky. Good-bye, big Walter, good-bye!

It's a funny thing when you think of it. But not a single one of us had so much as mentioned Royal's name.

Well, here we were back where we started, me and my battered old case, in a crummy room in a crummy Hollywood hotel. I was on the front. Across the street was a big red and blue neon sign that went off and on, off and on, all night long. It was turned off for good about six, and I used to wonder what poor benighted bastard had to get up to turn it off—a former bugler in the Army, no doubt.

I played dates. I took Jackie around—we were getting along together swell now. And about once a week, when I didn't forget it, I'd call Royal up at Palos Verdes. He sounded very limp. I lied to him and told him I was still looking for a good bass player, he lied right back in an all-gone voice and said: "Fine, Stan." Then, little by little he just sort of slipped my mind. You know how it is. A guy's got his own life to live.

But you couldn't forget about Walter. He was the talk of the profession. He was Walter Hanneman now—Hanneman being his middle name. I guess the TV vice-presidents didn't go for the "Flick." And he was doing very well indeed. He was new. He was fresh. He was big, young, and handsome in a sort of crude way. And his antics were original. At first, when people saw the billing, they would ask "Now who the hell is Walter Hanneman?" After a couple of weeks, they were saying: "Gotta catch that Hanneman guy tonight. Have you caught him yet?"

On the hour show Walt was on for about twelve minutes. He gabbed with a broad and got one laugh after another. He did a hilarious bit with the bass fiddle. He sang a jump tune and the boys had had sense enough not to tamper with his style. He belted it, he rocked, he was awkward as an ape, but he felt it and it came across. The star, a big hamola, tried to cut in on all of Walt's time, naturally, but when he was on with Walt he might as well have stood in his dressing room. It was even kind of embarrassing. This star was no chicken. He wore a piece, his teeth were false, and he seemed to me to be put together with adhesive tape. He was so damned boyish. All the same, he looked like Walter's grandfather.

Sad? Yeah. But this is show business, man. They come and they go. And some of them even stay too long, if you know what I mean.

Walt was really with it, and I used to wonder about all the lovelies on the show—dancers—there was quite a flock of them. And then this dolly that he did the routines with was not to be sneezed at either. Was the Little Woman in the wings? If I knew her, she was. And she'd better be!

Jackie's mother lived at Hermosa Beach. She had divorced Jackie's father—a real bum, Jackie said—some years back and had remarried. Jackie couldn't stand her stepfather and she never went near the house when he was around. But—a funny thing—she seemed kind of sentimental about her mother, who she referred to as Old Mom, in spite of the fact that "Old Mom" was just barely forty. I used to hear them talking on the phone once in a while. Jackie was mighty nice with her mother, though I don't think she saw her more than once every two or three months.

Well, Jackie and I were sitting around her apartment one afternoon. It was a real dismal day. No sun, damp, and with a mist over everything. The houses right across the street looked blurred.

"Boy, what a day," says Jackie.

"Yeah," I says.

"You know," says Jackie, "on days like this I get to thinking about Old Mom. She's had a rough life, one bum after another."

"Why don't you call her?"

Jackie didn't say anything for a long time. She had her shoes off and she sat there wiggling her toes and looking at them. She had mighty pretty little feet. "Stan," she says, finally, "I never bother you with stuff like this, do I?"

"Like what?"

"Like Old Mom and family and stuff."

"No," I says, looking at her in surprise.

"You know something?" she says after another pause. "I'd like to see Old Mom today. If I can get a car, will you drive me down?"

I groaned to myself. Clear to Hermosa Beach? "Sure I will, baby," I says, trying to be a gent.

Jackie came over and kissed me on the top of my head. "Swell. You can go and sit in a bar while I talk to Old Mom. I'm not going to inflict that on you. There's a bar right down the street."

So... we ended up in Hermosa Beach, of all places. The bar was right on what they call the Front, and that old Pacific really looked stormy that day. The waves were rolling in ten or fifteen feet high and some of them were so powerful when they hit the beach that this little rickety old bar would shake like there was an earthquake. It was a real dismal, gray day, with a big white fog-bank showing far out at sea. Gulls were flying every place, screaming like parrots. I wished I was home, as I sat there sipping at a highball.

To make it worse, some joker punches the juke box and out comes "Papa Loves Mambo." What a day for it! And then all of a sudden I remembered Royal. Hell, Palos Verdes was only a hop, skip, and a jump away from Hermosa Beach. So I called him up.

He sounded limp, but glad to hear from me. When I told him I was in Hermosa Beach, he asked me to drive up and see him, but when I'd explained the setup, he said, real quick: "Okay, Stan, I'll come down and see you."

I sat there worrying. I wasn't even sure that Royal could find the place, he was such a damned absent-minded, careless kind of guy. But he found it, all right. I looked up, and there he was, peering in the doorway. He had on a Hawaiian shirt —not the wraparound he'd been wearing the day Walt and I braced him about starting the trio—white flannel pants, tennis shoes, and dark glasses.

He shook hands with me, grinning. He looked good, I thought, feeling very relieved, tanned and sort of cheerful. I ordered him a drink and he sat down.

"Swell about Walter, isn't it?" he said.

And I threw him a look. You see, I'd got out of the habit of being with him. And my first idea was, "Is this a crack?" But of course it wasn't. He meant it.

"Yeah. Walt's really living it up."

"He's pretty good, don't you think? I catch his show every week."

"Well, you discovered him," I said, laughing.

Royal looked blank. "Me?"

"Sure," I said, "if it hadn't been for you he'd still be beating that damned old bass all around town. You let him sing."

"You mean he didn't sing before?" asked Royal, puzzled.

"Only when drunk. Only in private before a few select friends—mostly girls."

"I'll be damned," said Royal. "I heard him sing 'Dream' up at the place one night. Not his type of tune, but he's a natural singer." There was a long silence. And then that same damned joker played "Papa Loves Mambo" again. Royal glanced over at the juke box, wincing a little, then he asked: "How are you getting along, Stan?"

"Oh, as usual. A job here and there."

"You should do better than that," said Royal. "You are a very fine guitar player."

"That's what I keep telling them, but nobody listens. How about yourself?"

"Oh—nothing," said Royal. "I'm not with it."

It was the way he said it, I guess. I began to feel uneasy about him again. And I started to realize that the tan, the dark glasses, the sort of cheerful manner was a front. This guy was low, very low.

But what could I do about it?

"How's Piggy?" I asked, just to say something.

"Oh—same as usual. She keeps trying to get me to go some place. First, it's Mexico. Then it's a Caribbean cruise."

"I can go," I said. "I'd sure like to get out of this Hollywood trap for a while. I did get to Las Vegas." So I told Royal all about my trip and Walt's marriage and everything.

"I don't think they'll be happy," said Royal.

I gave him a look. He meant it, as usual. I wanted to laugh, but changed my mind. "Why not?" I asked, curious.

"I think she'll put too much pressure on him. I don't think Walt likes pressure."

"You're so right," I said.

"You put too much pressure on people," said Royal, "and they'll turn around and do just the opposite of what you want them to do—just out of perversity. Do you know what I mean?"

"I do, I do," I says. Then: "Let's have another drink."

So we had another drink. Royal bothered me. I wanted to say something to show I was still interested in the trio, so I said: "I've been looking around for a bass player, Royal. But I can't find one that suits me."

Royal sat shaking his head. "Don't waste your time, Stan. It's no use. It was just one of those things. You and Walt and I... well, it was a perfect fit. There was a spark. I don't know what to say. It wouldn't work again."

"It might."

Royal started shaking his head again. "No, Stan. It's the spirit of a thing that counts. You lose that, it's all gone."

What are you going to say? I sipped my drink, and looked out at the damned gulls swooping around every place over the beach and along the Front. Man, they made a melancholy noise, squealing. And suddenly I remembered Miss Inner Tube that day on the beach with Royal. "All that meat and no potatoes." I hadn't known him very well then. A real puzzler!

Well, we were talked out. We just sat there. And finally little Jackie came hurrying through the doorway, gave a quick gander, smiled and hurried over. Royal got up at once and stood waiting to be introduced.

"Oh," said Jackie, perter than necessary, "you're the piano player."

Royal bowed slightly and admitted that he was. I ordered a drink for Jackie, who sat down and began to give with that feminine routine—

pushing things around on the table, looking in her purse, patting her hair, settling her belt.

Jackie was always sort of nervous with strangers. That was the reason for the extra pertness, and the scrambling around. Male strangers, I'm speaking of, she was relaxed with girls. Another thing. She always got on her face a sort of unnatural expression—a cross between defiance and hardness. I noticed it every time I introduced her to some guy I knew, and it irked hell out of me, because I wanted these guys to see her at her best. Believe me, when she's relaxed, she's a real cute chick, but with that hard, defiant expression, well... it was something else again.

Here's what I'm getting at. In two minutes with Royal she was completely relaxed. In fact, she was more relaxed with him than she was with me. She seemed like a kid of fifteen, she giggled at some of the things he said like they were high-school buddies holding hands in a soda-fountain. Man, I kept staring at her. I was seeing a new Jackie, and a Jackie I really liked, believe me.

You can't beat chicks. It's like they had antennae, or something. She'd called the turn on Walt, without knowing him, and she had Royal's number in two minutes—a real sincere guy, friendly, no digs, no animosity, no struggle. I think you get the idea.

I even felt kind of jealous, in a way. Can you imagine that?

Well, we walked to Royal's car with him and shook hands. "Why don't you drop in and see us sometime, Royal?" said Jackie.

"Maybe I will," said Royal, smiling at her.

On the way back, Jackie didn't say anything for a long time. Finally she turned to me and said: "Gimme a cigarette." I lit one for her and handed it to her. "Nice guy," she said, between puffs.

"Yeah," I said.

"There is one guy," she said, "with no bum in his nature."

"How about me?"

Jackie threw her head back and laughed. "You!"

This burned me. "So I'm a bum."

"No," said Jackie, "but you've got all the makings."

♮♭

Shortly after Christmas—and a real cold night it was—Piggy finally ran me down on the phone.

"Have you heard from Royal?" she asked, sounding very agitated.

"No," I said. "Should I have?"

"I haven't seen him for a week, Stan," said Piggy. "And I can't find him any place."

"I don't know where to look," I said. "Maybe he's gone back East."

"You don't need to look. I've still got the Payton Agency. They're looking. I wired back East, too, and our lawyer there has hired an agency."

Man, Piggy didn't care how much money she spent, apparently!

"If he calls me, or comes over, what do I do?" I asked.

"See what you can find out, that's all. Where he's staying, you know, that sort of thing. I've got to be awfully careful with him. He has the silly idea I want to make a slave out of him. I just want to look after him, Stan."

"Yeah," I said, "and he sure needs it."

I worried about Royal all the next week and then little by little he just sort of slipped my mind again.

One Saturday night when I picked Jackie up at about nine she was all gussied-up in a new dress, she'd been to the beauty parlor—for hours, of course. Chicks and beauty parlors! It's a subject in itself—and, man, she really looked pert and cute. So I took her to the Club Intime after dinner at a good place. As soon as I walked in I began to laugh and chuckle to myself. Saturday night—and it wasn't even half full! And somehow the place had changed, didn't have the glamour it used to. Stu wasn't there— he was in Acapulco having a ball—and Rita had left for greener pastures. She'd had a real bad row with Stu about something or other, so I was told, and she'd blown.

Jackie and I got a seat right down in front of the shell. Lonny Boyle's trio didn't sound right. It wasn't the old Lonny. He was trying something new and it wasn't jelling. Suddenly, with a start, I got it. He was trying to ape us—the Royal Trio—and he just didn't have the horses. Oh, what a laugh! On some numbers, Lonny, that formerly very slick piano player, sounded like a real poor parody of Royal.

He gave me a very friendly nod, and when the break came he sat down with us and offered to buy a drink. Naturally I accepted. "Cold out," he said, looking around him at the sparse, quiet crowd. "People won't come out in Southern Cal. when it's cold."

"You're right, Lonny," I said, playing it straight. Oh, how I wanted to laugh!

"We did great till the cold weather hit," Lonny explained.

"So I hear," I lied.

Lonny didn't dig Jackie. He kept glancing at her. She had that expression I told you about. Lonny was a good-looking, curly-haired Irishman with baby-blue eyes, and he liked to have the chicks fawn. Jackie, to put it mildly, did not fawn. Lonny told Jackie about his new album. "I think you'll like it," he said, giving with the Big Man smile. Jackie was not amused. Nevertheless, it was all very pally.

We stayed for another set. I wasn't going to stay forever—not at those prices. Lonny shook hands with me as we left.

"May call you one of these days," he said.

"Fine," I said, and gave him my phone number. What the hell, it's a business. A job is a job. Work is work. I'd just as leave work for Lonny—if that's what he was getting at—as for anybody else, except Royal.

But I really laughed and had fun on the way home. Jackie made several very tart comments about Lonny that fractured me, and when I explained the whole business to her—Royal getting worked out, Lonny Boyle working his way in and then laying a big egg, trying to imitate Royal—she was as pleased as I was.

"And besides," she said, "I think he's got a touch of fag."

"No," I said, not going for this. "Things get around in the music business. You're wrong."

"A touch, I said," Jackie insisted. "He's too pretty, and did you notice his nails? Polish—like mine. I don't mean he works at it."

"You like 'em rough, eh, baby?" I says, hugging her.

"No," said Jackie. "I like you."

What are you going to do?

There was a hamburger joint across from the trap where I lived, and I used to drop in there late at night to get a snack when I'd come back from a job. Did I say hamburger? The L.A. area is the home of the burger—cheeseburger, nutburger, any kind of burger you can think of. I usually took mine straight. The place was a hangout for early morning drunks and they used to turn my stomach sometimes scoffing those crazy-looking cheeseburgers. No, I'm not delicate. But when a guy's been working hard all evening and... oh, never mind.

Well, this night—a real mean drizzly foggy night—I'd scoffed three hamburgers and I was just starting for the pad when several musicians I knew walked into the place—staggered in, I mean. So I sat down with them while they ate. We talked about this and that and then got onto the subject of big Walter. It caused an argument. One guy said he was great, another guy said he was nothing. The yacking went on and on, with me just listening. Why I didn't get up and go, I don't know. During a lull, a character walked in and asked the badgered guy in the chef's hat behind the counter for a "camelburger." The guy in the chef's hat was a nervous, flighty kind of boy—I'd noticed it many times—and this straight-faced character bothered him.

"What did you say?" he yelled.

"Camelburger," said the character, "and you can't hardly get them no more."

"Beat it," said the chef.

"How about a bearburger? I'm hungry, man."

"Read the menu," said the chef, tapping his foot. He had a long knife handy. He's the type of guy I would never argue with.

"I'd settle for cheese," said the hipster, "but I just had a cheese soufflé at Romanoff's. And as for nuts, I got pecan brittle right here in my pocket."

"Scram!" yelled the chef. Night after night he had to argue with drunks and wags.

"Any spaghetti in the house?" asked the hipster. "I can play it like a harp. I just hold it in my teeth, you know, and...."

"Order, or scram."

God was looking after that hipster. He thought for a moment, then he walked over to us and picked me out. "You got any jack, Jack? I just happened to think—I'm tapped."

"Go home, boy. Go home," I said. "You're safer there."

"This guy with the tall white hat, he's a savage," said the hipster. "Did you see that knife? Man, you could really pare your nails with that."

Finally he wandered out. I heard a car start up and glanced out the window. This character was driving a Thunderbird. How do you figure it? Hollywood at night. All the oddies collect out here.

I remember all this so well because it held me up, and if I hadn't been held up so long—but why worry about that now? When a thing's done, it's done, no use yacking about how it might have been.

♮ ♭

It was nearly four when I crossed the street to my pad. The night clerk was asleep behind a magazine, but he woke with a start when he heard my footsteps. It was his business to wake when he heard footsteps crossing the lobby late at night because some of the boys used to try to sneak out with their luggage now and then.

"Oh, Stan..." he called.

"Yeah," I said, wondering. I was paid up to the minute. I never took any broads to my room. I never caused any beefs. "Somebody's been trying to get you on the phone."

"Who?"

"I don't know. He called first about an hour ago and he's called twice since. Sounds awful drunk. Couldn't get his name."

Well, this could be any of a hundred guys I knew.

"Thanks, Lou," I says.

"You want to talk to him if he calls again?"

"Oh, I guess so," I said. Why not? If it was one of my many drunken musician friends, he'd just keep calling, no matter what.

I went upstairs. I was just taking off my tie when the phone rang. "Here he is," said Lou, "and he's not making any sense at all."

At first I thought it was a rib. I couldn't make out a word the guy was saying except "Stan" and "gotta say goodbye" or something like that. This character sounded like he was in a tunnel and had his mouth full of mush besides. All at once I realized it was Royal.

I began to get nervous. "Royal! Kid!" I yelled. "What is it?"

He mumbled and mumbled for a long time. I couldn't make out a thing. He was drunk, all right, no doubt about that, but he was more than drunk. I just didn't get it. Finally, all of a sudden, he hung up. I stood there with the receiver in my hand, staring. Then I began to sweat. Something was wrong, mighty wrong. I called downstairs. "Lou," I yelled, "any idea where that call came from?" "No," said Lou, sounding kind of startled. "What's the matter, Stan?" I hung up, and sat trying to see if I could make any sense out of the sounds Royal had made, that's about all they were, sounds.

Suddenly I had a bright idea. In all that rigmarole he'd said a word several times that sounded like "cliff," pretty close to that, and I thought about "clef," remembering the night I'd met Royal in that joint called the Treble Clef. Lonny'd been playing there. And Royal had tried to hide till everybody went home so he could use the piano. A real wild crazy idea, you say? Sure was.

I dug out the number and called it. The phone rang on and on, I let it ring. A long time passed, with me sweating and telling myself I was daffy. Finally somebody answered it, said what sounded like "Wa? Wa?" and then nothing. But there was a noise like somebody'd knocked the phone over. I rang the number again. It was busy.

I was panicky now, not knowing exactly what to do. Call Piggy? Call the police? Why? Maybe I was just imagining this whole thing. I grabbed up my overcoat, then called downstairs and asked Lou to see if he could get me a taxi right away. He did.

It was foggy as hell. I jumped into the taxi and says to the driver: "You know a nightclub called the Treble Clef?"

The taxi driver turned around and stared at me. He was a tough-looking monkey about thirty-five. "Sure. But it closes at two, chum."

"I know," I said. "But a guy just called me. I think he's drunk and locked up in there."

"Well," said the driver, staring at me again, "I'll take you there. But, me, I'm not going to get mixed up...."

"Okay, okay," I said. "I'm not going to rob the joint, if that's what's worrying you. And step on it."

"In this fog? You just sit back and relax, chum."

Fog's a funny thing. It makes a town look unfamiliar. Half a dozen times

I thought the driver was going the wrong way and that we were lost. But finally we made it. The fog wasn't nearly so thick here, and I could see the old Treble Clef standing there black and deserted.

I jumped out of the cab. "You wait," I said. "I may need you."

"Look here, chum," said the driver, "I don't like this business. What are you going to do, break in? You pay me. I'm going to scram. I don't like this...."

"You wait," I said, yelling at him.

He scratched his chin, then he took off his yellow cap and scratched his head. These poor taxi drivers—the things they run into at night in Hollywood!

I began to bang on the front door, making one hell of a racket. Then, getting no answer, I ran around to the side and tried to look into a window, but they were too high up and the wall was sheer, no chance to climb. Then I ran around to the back, stumbled over a few empty garbage cans that fell and rolled and clattered about on the cement, and beat on the door, kicked it, yelled. I was like a lunatic. And what if I was wrong?

When I got around to the front again, a squad car was just pulling up.

"Oh-oh," said the taxi driver sadly.

Two big cops came over to us and flashed a light in my face. I tried to explain. They kept butting in. Finally one of them said: "Al, this guy's loaded one way or another. Frisk him."

They frisked me—for weed, I guess. I identified myself and showed them my union card. Then they frisked me again, man. A musician, eh? What a reputation *we've* got!

Finally things quieted down a little and the cops listened.

"Okay," said one. "We'll find the owner."

Well, we didn't find the owner because nobody knew where to look.

"We got to break in," I said.

"Break in!" cried a cop. "Are you crazy?"

I begged, I pleaded. "One of you guys just boost me up. Let me look. There's a night light on in there. A real dim blue light."

The cops talked it over at great length, then at last we went round to the side—taxi driver and all and with the meter running, too—and one of the cops boosted me up and I grabbed the ledge and finally got a gander into the joint. I gave a start and almost fell. There was Royal. He was lying on the floor, just in front of the little raised band platform.

"He's in there. He's in there," I yelled. "We got to get him out."

But the cops were very deliberate. We had to boost one of them up. He must have weighed two hundred and twenty pounds. Man, we were all panting and grunting. "Yeah," he said, "he's in there."

We let him down and he and the other cop had another conference.

"Look, guys," I said, shaking, "this boy's sick. He's not a well man. We ought to get him to a hospital, or something."

God, I just can't go into all the rest of it. Finally one of the big coppers wrapped a couple of handkerchiefs around his fist and broke the window, then he unlocked it, raised the sash, and climbed in. The remaining cop boosted me in, then the taxi driver boosted the cop in.

We turned the lights on. Royal was lying flat on the floor, breathing like a guy who'd just climbed a mountain.

"This guy's in a bad way," said one of the cops. "I'll call an ambulance and we'll get him to emergency right away." He called, all efficiency now.

Good God, I thought, what has happened to Royal!

I had a sudden flash. "Guys," I said to the cops, "do you know the Payton Agency?"

"Sure," said one of them. "Good outfit."

"Well, they're looking for this guy," I explained.

The cop hesitated, then called the agency. It took him only about two minutes to get one of the Payton biggies on the wire. At four-thirty in the morning. That's service. I'd told the cop Royal's name.

He completed the call, then turned and looked at me. "Do you know who that guy is?" he says, pointing to Royal, who was being worked over gently by the other cop.

"Sure I know who he is," I said. "I told you, didn't I? He's a friend of mine."

"Oh," said the cop.

But he sounded funny. "What do you mean, do I know who he is?" I yelled, nervous.

"Ever hear of the Mid-American Steel Company?" asked the cop.

"Sure," I said. "I read the papers. I used to play the market." Big man! But I *did* used to play the market, peanuts, of course. It was something a silly band leader friend of mine got me into.

"I *thought* you didn't know," said the cop. He pointed to Royal. "This guy's old man runs it. President of the Company."

Trust Royal. Always a jolt.

I could write a book about this one damned thing. We couldn't get the doors open. They had to take the front door off the hinges. The cops couldn't find the owner any place. What a mess!

And there was poor Royal, lying on the stretcher, pale as your shirt, and breathing so hard you could hear him fifty feet away.

Payton got in touch with Piggy. Piggy got Royal a suite in a hospital at Santa Monica, and they moved him there from the emergency hospital after he'd been given first aid, or something.

Oh, yeah. I paid the taxi driver. It tapped me out.

Man! I sat there in my crummy room watching that old sun come up. It was a cold morning, still a lot of fog in the streets, but drifting away now. I really felt low.

Well, nobody could figure the thing out, not even me, and I certainly knew more about Royal than anybody else trying to figure it out, including Piggy—in some ways, that is. It's always been my feeling that Royal was taking the hard way out, but got scared and called me. Why in the Treble Clef? You've got me there, except that he was drunk. I don't know. It's a puzzle.

Anyway, he was loaded with stuff. Not only alcohol, but barbiturates— a ton of 'em, so I hear.

Well, it got in the papers, of course. But mighty strong influences were at work, the Payton Agency, lawyers, Mid-American Steel money... and the suicide angle was never touched on. Royal had been in poor health for over two years. He had taken some medicine which didn't mix with alcohol. Ill, he'd gone to the men's room at the Treble Clef and had been locked in by mistake at closing time. That was the story.

I even got my picture in the paper. I even got interviewed by gentlemen of the press, who thought I was the biggest liar they'd ever talked to but couldn't pin me down to anything.

I cut out all the clippings and sent them to Walt. I could just see him reading them and shaking his big head and saying, "That Royal!"

Do you like hospitals? I hate them. They're so clean and shiny white, so antiseptic, and so inhuman. They give me the creeps. When I go to visit a friend in one of them, I can hardly wait to get out. Two kinds of people in the world, I read some place, the sick and the well, and believe me they don't mix.

All the same, I thought I ought to go out to the Santa Monica Hospital and see how Royal was doing. Believe it or not, Jackie, in her quiet way, was kind of upset about the whole business—she'd taken a real liking to Royal—so she borrowed a car from one of her girl buddies and we drove out. Jackie wouldn't go in. She said she hardly knew the guy and it would be presuming, and don't get the idea it was the Mid-American Steel business that she read about in the paper that was worrying her, if Royal had been a car-hop she'd have acted just the same. I always ended up with the heebies after a visit to a hospital, so I was very glad that I'd find Jackie waiting in the car when I came out.

Well, I didn't get to see Royal. He was too sick, with doctors, nurses, oxygen tents, etc., etc. But I saw Piggy. Man, you should have seen the accommodations. Piggy had practically taken over the hospital. She really surprised me, she was so calm. Maybe she was relieved to have Royal in a state where he couldn't run away and she didn't have to worry about that angle at least—for a while.

We sat in a big, good-looking, private sitting room, full of flowers. White wings, male and female, kept going in and coming out of Royal's room. Plush quarters, man. Most of the bums I went to visit were in wards, where there were always creeps who talked or snored all night, and always irritation and beefs. Money's a nice thing, I guess. Too bad I'll never have any of it.

"How's he coming, Piggy?" I asked.

"Oh, pretty well," she said, fussing with those jeweled cheaters. "He never was strong, you know. When he was little he had scarlet fever, and a few months later, inflammatory rheumatism. His heart's not too good, the doctors say."

"He'll be all right, though, won't he?" I asked, getting worried. A guy twenty-four or -five years old don't just up and die. That's for guys in their forties, old guys.

"Well, we think so," said Piggy. "We hope so."

I sat there twisting my hat. What do you say? There was a long silence. A cute nurse, all starched and kind of looking like a nun, crossed the room and went out, giving Piggy a little smile. Then a big, heavy-set man with a red face and a very high forehead (it went clear to the back of his neck, almost), opened the hall door abruptly and walked in like he owned the place. He damned near did. He was Royal's Old Man: S. L. Mauch, President of Mid-American Steel. I couldn't take my eyes off of him: a big, healthy, robust guy, almost sixty, I guess, but full of life. Royal's Old Man? How could it be? And then I remembered his invalid mother. Royal just took after the wrong side of the family, that was all. Apparently Piggy got her looks from the mother and her toughness from the Old Man. Too bad Royal couldn't have.... But the hell with that! Vain regrets.

"This is the boy," said Piggy, meaning me. "This is Mr. Pawley."

The Old Man was very awkward with me. To him a musician was a rara avis. Let's be frank. To him a musician was a bum. He was very nice and polite. I could see that he was trying to make up his mind whether to give me some money or not. He decided in the negative. I guess he was afraid he might hurt my feelings. Don't laugh. He might have, at that.

I could see he didn't think much of Piggy. And I could see Piggy didn't think much of him. There's nothing odd about a situation like this, as a lot of people seem to think. I've got an older sister who wouldn't speak to my Old Man for a hundred dollars. The Old Man did everything under the sun to keep her from marrying some pool-hustling bum. He told her just what would happen to her. It did. So now she won't speak to the Old Man. Families are funny things.

Well, we said this and that, I twisted my hat the other way around for a few minutes longer, then I blew. I was feeling pretty good about Royal. What could happen to him with all those nurses and doctors and all that Mid-American Steel moola?

When I got to the car I could see that Jackie was anxious to hear all about it, so I told her, as we drove back toward Beverly Hills along Wilshire Boulevard, which was really swarming with traffic. I told her about all the nurses and doctors and the money being spent. I made it strong.

"Then he's going to be all right," said Jackie, settling back.

"Sure he's going to be all right," I said. Man, I felt good!

Well, we both felt so good we had a ball that night. I took the rubber band off my roll. We ate at a real nice place, then we went out to the Intime and I sat in for a set with Lonny, taking the gee-tar player's place. While I was playing, I saw Lonny watching me and listening with those sharp ears of his. We did "Babes in the Woods"—Royal had revived it— and I took several "Royal" breaks, and I saw Lonny smiling to himself.

"That's *it*," he cried, hitting me on the back.

Lonny was a happy chappy the rest of the evening. He was grabbing the clue, man!

We didn't start home till after two-thirty because of a post-mortem on the front pavement with Lonny and one of the errand boys from A.A.A.— a kid who looked after small things, like bands and singers.

"He was just kidding around, eh?" said Lonny, finally, referring to Royal—oh, Lonny was mighty impressed! "Mid-American Steel! And here we have to work for it, eh, Stan, old boy?" He patted me on the back. Man, we were pals now! "How is he, by the way?" asked Lonny, as a kind of quick afterthought.

"Oh, he's just fine," cried Jackie, who had absorbed considerable giggle-water. "He's just dandy."

"Good, good," said Lonny.

Jackie and I, laughing and gagging, hit one late drinking spot, then we hustled home to her cozy pad. Man, we flang one. I mean, we really did.

Along about four A.M., Jackie and I were sitting looking out the front window. We had all the lights out. God, it was quiet. Just a taxicab hooting now and then on Sunset.

Jackie's apartment was on a side street, just off Sunset. It was on a slope, pretty high up. We could see the lights of Bev. Hills, Westwood, etc., etc. Jackie was pointing out the places to me.

"You see that string of bluish lights?" she said. "Well, that's Santa Monica. That's where Royal is."

"Good old Royal," I said.

At a quarter after four, the phone began to ring.

"Now who the hell is that?" snapped Jackie.

"Wrong number, probably. Let it ring."

But it's a hard thing to do, let a phone ring. Most people are just too curious. Jackie was. She answered it.

"For you," she said. "Lou, at the hotel."

I didn't get it. What could Lou want with me?

"Hi, Lou," I said. "Is the joint on fire?"

"Sorry to bother you there, Stan," said Lou. "But a Mrs. Jones was trying to get you. I didn't want to give her *that* number, you know. But she was so insistent about reaching you...."

Now who in hell was Mrs. Jones...? Then I got it. Piggy! I just couldn't think of her as Mrs. Jones.

"Yeah, yeah," I yelled, and Jackie's face kind of fell and she came over beside me.

"...so I said I'd give you the message," Lou went on. "She told me to tell you her brother just died."

"Died?" I yelled. "Royal?" I couldn't take it in.

"I don't know his name," said Lou. "She said you'd know all about it."

Man, I had it now. "Thanks, Lou. Thanks a million." I couldn't hang the phone up. Jackie took it away from me and hung it up.

You know what they say—the earth rocked? Well, it did. I had the idea for a moment there was an earthquake and grabbed the table, then I fell down in a chair. Jackie took one look at me, and ran for the whiskey. I took a belt like Walt used to do when the booze was free. Man, I needed it.

"How could it be?" said Jackie, all to pieces. "How could it happen?"

Then we just sat in silence, looking out the window. There was the string of bluish lights, all right—Santa Monica—and Royal was sure there now. He sure as hell was. Man, it was quiet. I had a funny feeling as if all of a sudden I'd been moved to a different city and was looking out the window at a place I'd never seen before. I was really frazzled.

I'll never forget how quiet it was that night—just a cab hooting now and then.

Late in February, I flew back to the big Midwestern city where Royal was born. Piggy had wired me the money, and had explained that the symphony orchestra was going to play Royal's piece, "The River," at the Memorial Hall. She also told me that Walt, Berte and Frank were going to be there. They were flying in from New York. Well, el cuffo again. I guess I can't resist it. Anyway, that's what Jackie said.

I was scared all the way—winter flying is too tough for this baby—and I made up my mind I'd come back on the train.

♮♭

Yeah, we were all there, in the same row—a motley crew, as the fellow says. Me on the end, then Piggy, then Walt, then Berte, then Frank. Cold! Man, it was cold! Your blood gets thinned out, living in Southern California, believe me. And then when you hit that Midwestern winter climate—wow!

By the time the orchestra got to Royal's number I was shivering in my clothes and jumping with nerves and boredom. Why do those so-called serious musicians write such long pieces? Man, they beat a theme to death. They try it every way but upside down. My ears were numb. I could hardly listen.

And you should have seen Walt. He'd tried every position a man could try in one chair. But Frank was sitting there with his arms folded, listening. Maybe he liked it, at that. Who knows?

Royal's number was the last on the bill. Piggy was nervous and kept kicking me without meaning to. "Sokolsky, the conductor, thinks it's wonderful, phenomenal," she said. "Really. I mean it."

I looked at her in surprise. "Why not? You don't have to sell me on Royal."

Well, what am I going to say? I got the shock of my life. This music didn't sound like anything I'd ever heard before, least of all from Royal. It was solemn, simple, slow, and powerful. Man, was it powerful! And it had a color to it—a real color, I mean—at least to me: a beautiful dark-blue.

God, with those hundred guys going all out at times, I could hardly stand it. I wanted to get up and run out of the place. This music scared me, like that German stuff Royal played for me the night I tried to bust up the trio. I'm not kidding. It scared me. And I sat there wondering how that puny little guy could have written it.

I began to shake inside. The music just went on and on, rolling back across that huge auditorium, like a series of shining waves—and all at once I remembered Royal on the beach, counting the beat as the big combers came in. And then, right in the middle of everything, though not connected with anything, came the tugboat whistle. I don't know how they did it. I wasn't seeing so good at the moment. Bassoon, I guess—but

I wouldn't guarantee it. And it was just right. Out of key. I mean, in no key at all. It had nothing to do with the chord. It was a tugboat whistle, that's all. And you could see the dark-blue river with the lights shining on it and the water going under the bridges on and on forever. Old Man River.

Well, at the end there is a brief pause. The tugboat whistle sounds again, and that's it!

There was dead silence in the place. I glanced over at Walt. He was crying, with his handkerchief up to his face, and everybody was looking at him.

I couldn't take it. I blew.

As I was hurrying back through the auditorium, the applause started. It wasn't polite applause: it was loud and spontaneous. There were cheers and bravos. The people liked it. And I kept saying to myself: "Good for them! Good for them!"

♪♭

Well, I pulled myself up in the lobby. Piggy was giving a little supper party at a private room in a downtown hotel. I just couldn't run out on it.

Pretty soon the rest of the party showed up. Walt, looking mighty sheepish, Frank, kind of proud, or something—I couldn't make out what, and both Piggy and Berte, being chicks, fussy and nervous.

"Man, he had me," said Walt, taking hold of my arm. "I mean, he had me."

I just nodded. I was afraid I might start crying, myself.

Well, it was a pretty sad dinner party. Everybody was exhausted. Piggy kept explaining over and over why Royal's Old Man wasn't there. Business. He'd had to fly to Venezuela, or some damned place. I never got it right. But it sounded like Venezuela.

I kept glancing at Walt. He didn't look quite the same, and it puzzled me. He had on about four hundred dollars' worth of clothes, and a big diamond ring—I mean, a rock, man—on the little finger of his right hand. But that wasn't it, he'd always looked good in his clothes and had always worn a ring, though not that kind! Finally I got it. Walt was putting on weight, and it was giving him a kind of self-satisfied look. He'd better watch that waistline! And tonight he sure was. He just kicked the food around with a fork.

Finally, with the dessert, Frank said, like an usher at Utter McKinley: "It's a shame he had to go, Mrs. Jones. A real shame."

Piggy nodded, but made no comment. Finally she said: "Mr. Sokolsky and I have been looking through all of his old manuscripts. 'The River' was the only thing he ever finished. But Mr. Sokolsky thinks that he can piece together a suite out of one bunch of manuscripts. He's so high on Royal. I tried to get Royal to talk to Mr. Sokolsky a hundred times, but he'd never do it. You see, Mid-American Steel is one of the sponsors of the orchestra and... well, you boys know Royal." We all nodded, even Berte.

Yeah. We all knew Royal, us bums!

Well, here I am back in Hollywood, and doing very fine, thank you. Jackie has got her checkroom concession going, and she's really coining the moola—in our small way, that is. And I'm working every night but Monday.

And guess who I'm working for. Lonny Boyle. Guess where I'm working: At the Club Intime. And we are doing big. Lonny is learning fast. He's even picked up a new bass player, a big oaf with a croaking voice who sings pretty good scat, a little like Walter.

I've pieced out a half-dozen of Royal's arrangements for the outfit and we really go on them. We've revived "There's Egypt in Your Dreamy Eyes." Last month there was an article about us in *Downbeat*.

Oh, we are really the boys!

And now I'll say good-bye.

THE END

IRON MAN

BY W. R. BURNETT

To My Mother and Father

SHEPHERD:... the mair I think on't, the profounder is my conviction that the strength o' human nature lies either in the highest or the lowest estate of life. Characters in books should either be kings, and princes, and nobles, and on a level with them, like heroes, or peasants, shepherds, farmers, and the like.... The intermediate class—that is, leddies and gentlemen in general—are not worth the muses while, for their life is made up chiefly o' mainners, mainners, mainners, you cannot see the human creters for their clothes, and should ane o' them commit suicide in despair, in lookin' on the dead body, you are mair taken up wi' its dress than its decease. *March 1829, NOCTES AMBROSIANAE*

Part I

I

Coke sat up, pushed back his hat, took his feet off the bed, and, getting up, stood yawning and rubbing his fists in his eyes. Across the room Regan was playing solitaire on a writing-desk, and Coke's sparring-partner, Jeff Davis, was sitting in a big chair by the window turning the pages of a magazine. Coke walked over to Regan and stood looking over his shoulder.

"Boy, you sure was cutting it," said Jeff. "A buzzsaw ain't got nothing on you."

"Sure," said Coke, "I always sleep like that." He bent over and stared at Regan's lay-out. "Play your ace of diamonds," he said.

Regan pushed him away.

"Don't bother me. I got a bet on this game."

Coke, still yawning and stretching, went back to his chair and lolled, flexing his fingers out of boredom. "Say," he said, finally, "you guys are a hell of a lot of company."

Regan turned to Jeff.

"Ain't that a laugh!" he said. "That guy's been sleeping for the last half hour, and he says we're a lot of company."

"Yeah," said Jeff.

"Well, I'm awake now, ain't I!" exclaimed Coke. "It's a wonder you guys couldn't think up something so I wouldn't get stale sitting around like this."

"Want me to dance for you?" asked Regan.

Jeff burst out laughing.

"Let me do it," he said.

"Think I'll smoke a cigar," said Coke.

"Better lay off them cigars," said Jeff, "you'll cut your wind."

"Let him go," said Regan. "That black boy'll cut his wind for him."

"The hell he will," said Coke, but he made no move to take a cigar.

Regan got up, lit a cigarette, and handed it to Coke. "Now," he said, "don't say I'm always trying to cramp your style. Pull on this and get throat trouble." Coke took the cigarette and sat smoking, perfectly relaxed, his eyes closed.

"That's just what I needed," he said.

Regan went back to his game of solitaire, and Jeff cocked up his feet and began to read an article in the magazine. As a rule he merely looked at the pictures. Coke opened his eyes.

"Hey, George," he called to Regan, "look at Jeff. That boy's gonna ruin his eyesight."

Regan turned and stared at Jeff.

"I didn't know they printed them kind of stories in magazines," he said.

"It's about the champ," said Jeff. "A lot of bunk. All about his knockout record. Who the hell'd he ever knock out except Tuffy Munn? And he was doped."

"Well, he flattened your nose," said Regan.

"Yeah, I slipped and ran into a left."

"Oh, God," said Regan, and went back to his game. Coke sat puffing on his cigarette, then he got up and tossed it into an ashtray.

"I'd like to get a go at him," said Coke.

"Well," said Jeff, "all you got to do is knock Prince Pearl kicking."

"Yeah," said Regan, "that's all he's got to do."

"You think I won't, don't you?" said Coke, leaning over Regan's chair.

Regan put down his cards, opened the drawer of the writing-desk, and took out a pile of newspaper clippings. Coke knocked them out of his hand.

"Good Lord, George," he said, "ain't you been in the game long enough to know that them newspaper guys don't know straight up? The hell with them clippings."

"Well," said Regan, "all the smart money's on the black boy. That's something."

"All the smart money was on Willard once, too, wasn't it?" said Coke, flushing. "You guys give me a pain in the neck."

He went into the bathroom, banging the door.

"Boss," said Jeff, "why don't you lay off of him? You know he's on edge."

Regan turned and stared at Jeff.

"You let me handle him, Jeff," he said. "I know that bird better than anybody in the world. Listen, he's got a chance to win. A small chance, I'm saying, but a chance just the same. It ain't no walkaway like all these guys think. But I don't want him to pass up the only chance he's got by getting overconfident."

"Ain't much chance of that, with you at him all the time."

"All right," said Regan, "but you don't know that guy. Why, when he put on his first pair of gloves he thought he'd be champion in a week."

"Well," said Jeff, "that's the old spirit."

"Yeah," said Regan, "that's the old spirit that leads to busted noses and pretty ears."

"I'll say he's got a kick in that left of his and his right don't tap you," said Jeff.

"Sure," said Regan, "but he's got to land 'em. That black boy's hard to hit.

He'd make a monkey out of the champ if he'd give him a match."

Jeff laughed.

"Don't you never worry about Mike Shay fighting the nigger. He'd left jab him to death."

"Well," said Regan, spreading out his hands, "what do you think he'll do to Coke then?"

"I think he'll decision him," said Jeff, "but Coke won't even know he's been hit."

"Hell," said Regan, "you dumb pugs are all alike. If a guy can take it, why, that's all you care about. You can't win a fight by taking 'em on the chin. If you could, you'd be champion."

"There you go," said Jeff.

Coke came back into the room, scowling.

"Well," he said, "have you fight experts got me knocked out yet?"

Regan went back to his game.

"I'm backing you," said Jeff. "I'm gonna bet a little money on you."

Coke patted him on the shoulder.

"Bet a lot, Jeff," he said.

"Yeah," said Regan, "and I'm setting my checks in on the nigger. He'll have his left in your face so much you'll think it belongs there."

Coke stood staring at Jeff and slowly nodding his head.

"Jeff," he said, "I been that guy's meal ticket for God knows how long. Ever since I left the factory. And that's the way he hands it to me. You bet on that nigger, you cheap shanty mick, and I'll give you the lacing of your life."

"He ain't gonna bet on the nigger," said Jeff. "He's just talking."

"Ain't I!" said Regan.

"Go ahead," said Coke. "That'll be all the more reason for me to paste him. Go ahead."

Regan went on with his game for a moment, then he turned to Coke.

"It's about your bedtime, ain't it?"

Coke glanced at the clock.

"Yeah, but I don't feel much like sleeping."

"Want to play some auction pinochle?" asked Jeff.

"No," said Coke, "I'm off of cards."

"You're about off of everything, ain't you?" demanded Regan.

"Yeah," said Coke, "including you."

Jeff got up and stretched, tucked his magazine under his arm, and started for the door.

"Well," he said, "I think I'll go over to the Majestic and grab me a girl. Want to go along, George?"

"No," said Regan, "I dance like Coke boxes."

"Aw, lay off of me," said Coke, flaring up.

"So long," said Jeff, going out.

Coke and Regan sat in silence for a long time, Regan playing solitaire, Coke sulking. Finally Regan put away his cards and turned his chair around.

"How you feeling, Coke?"

"I'm O.K."

"You gonna fight that guy like I told you?"

"I'm gonna fight him to suit myself."

"I guess you don't want to be champion."

"Listen," said Coke, "if you was such a hell of an expert you'd be out there yourself getting the jack instead of me."

Regan got up.

"All right, swellhead," he said. He went over to the closet and got his overcoat and hat. Coke, sulking, watched him out of the corner of his eye. Regan put on his overcoat and started for the door.

"Listen, George," said Coke, "stick around a while, can't you? I don't feel like sleeping."

"No," said Regan, "I got to be going."

"Come on, George," said Coke, "stick around. Lord, don't you know I get to feeling low when I'm training?"

"Now start your bellyache," said Regan. "To hear you talk you'd think you really did some training. Suppose you had trouble making weight like some guys. Two days on the road and your weight's O.K. Lucky and don't know it."

"All right," said Coke. "I don't train hard, but it makes me feel low just the same. Sit down, George, and let's have a talk like we used to."

Regan sat down without taking off his overcoat. Coke sat staring at the floor.

"Well," said Regan, "you don't seem to be doing much talking."

"George," said Coke, "ever hear anything more about my wife?"

Regan laughed curtly and got up.

"So that's the song!"

"Yeah. You know I get pretty lonesome for that kid."

"You're a hell of a man," said Regan.

"You don't know that kid."

"I know her better than you do," said Regan. "Listen, Coke, if I was you I wouldn't be wasting no time thinking about a dame that ran out on me because I couldn't buy her an automobile."

"Hell," said Coke, "she was used to things, see? You couldn't expect her to settle down and do housework."

"Yeah," said Regan, laughing, "she was used to bum hotels, and day-coaches, and three-a-day on a tanktown circuit. Where is she? Anybody ever hear of her? To hear her tell it you'd think Ziegfeld was begging her to take over the Follies."

"You never did like her, George," said Coke.

"No, I never did," said Regan. "And the biggest break you ever got was when she went away and left you."

"That's what you say," said Coke. "But you don't know how I feel about that kid."

Regan put on his hat.

"I'm leaving you, Coke," he said. "I'm sick of this song. Listen, take my advice, lay off that cowtown soubrette, she'll make a bum of you."

Coke ran his hands over his face and sighed. "I'd just like to see her and talk to her."

"Don't worry," said Regan, "as soon as she needs money, you'll hear from her."

Regan started out the door, but the telephone rang and he turned back. Coke made a move to answer it, but Regan waved him away and took down the receiver.

"Hello," said Regan, "yeah, this is him speaking. Well, I don't see no reason why not. Sure, come on up." He hung up the receiver and stood looking at the floor.

"Who was it?" asked Coke.

"A couple of big shots, Mandl and Riley. They want to see us."

"What do you suppose them bums want?"

"Well," said Regan, "you can bet there's something up, because they don't tag after nobody."

"Maybe they want to look me over before they get their jack up."

"Oh, God," said Regan with his head in his hands.

Someone knocked at the door and Regan went over to open it. There was a bell-boy with the two gamblers, and he stood in the doorway, staring at Coke. Riley and Mandl came in, but the bell-boy didn't close the door. He stood staring at Coke.

"Say, Mr. Mason," he said, "my grandmother's gonna be awful sick the night you fight."

"All right, buddy," said Coke.

The bell-boy closed the door. Regan nodded in Coke's direction and said to Mandl:

"He eats it up."

"Well," said Mandl, "ain't that all right?"

Mandl was short, stocky and dark. His nose was slightly flattened and his lips stuck out like a negro's. His partner, Riley, was small, stooped and pale, with sandy hair and a thin, freckled face. They both wore diamonds and loud clothes. They sat down and Regan poured out a couple of drinks for them. Mandl cocked his head sideways and squinted his eyes at Coke.

"What kind of shape you in, Mason?" he asked.

"He looks in the pink," said Riley.

"He's rounding off good," said Regan.

"Yeah, I'm gonna plaster that nigger," said Coke.

Mandl passed around a monogrammed cigar case.

"Yeah?" he said. "The money's all the other way."

"Ain't nothing new about that," said Coke, scowling.

"No, course there ain't," said Riley, glancing warningly at Mandl, who was never very diplomatic.

"We figure we got a chance," said Regan.

"Well," said Mandl, "you can get all the money you want at three to one. New York's long on Prince Pearl since he stopped Joe Savella, and Chicago's crazy about him."

"Joe Savella ain't much," said Coke.

"Fair boy," said Riley.

"He had his own referee the night he got a draw with me," said Coke, "and at that I cocked him through the ropes in the second."

"He did, that's a fact," said Regan.

"Well," said Riley, "we was aiming to lay a little on your boy, Regan."

"What did I tell you," Coke exclaimed.

Regan massaged his chin and stared at Mandl and Riley. Nobody said anything.

"Well," Regan demanded finally, "what about it?"

Mandl flourished his cigar.

"Listen, Regan," he said, "what do you say we all make a clean-up?"

Regan laughed.

"Well, we ain't passing up no ready money. But what's the game?"

Mandl opened his mouth to say something but Riley beat him to it.

"Regan," he said, "winning don't do Prince Pearl no good. You know that. He can't get a match with no Grade A guys because he's a nigger. Your boy's the only bird that ain't afraid of him."

"I ain't afraid of nobody," said Coke.

"Course you ain't," said Riley, soothingly. "Well, Prince Pearl's been after a match with the champ for over a year now and he can't get it. Mike's afraid of him and anyway nobody wants a shine for champ, see? Well, Pearl's no spring chicken any more. He admits to thirty-five, get the idea? He ain't dead set on winning from Mason, here. He thinks Mason's a good boy that ought to have a whirl at the champ... so...."

"I got you," said Regan. "He's willing to turn a back flip for a consideration."

"Sure," said Riley, "he'll take it easy for five grand and your boy'll get a shot at the champion."

Coke's eyes got big and he began to stare at Riley. Regan glanced uneasily at Coke.

"So there you have it," said Mandl. "It's a pipe. We'll clean up big, all of us, and Mason'll get a shot at the champ."

Regan massaged his chin and stared at the ceiling.

"Nothing doing," shouted Coke. "That nigger don't have to lay down. Where do you dollar boys get that crap? Why, you guys talk like I was a set-up. Listen, this fight's gonna be on the square. If that nigger looks like laying down, I'll take it up with the Commission, by God. I'll spill the whole story. I'm winning this fight on the square. I'm gonna knock that nigger for a home run."

Riley was paler than usual and his little eyes darted from Regan to Coke. Mandl hit the table with his fist.

"For God's sake, Mason, don't be a sap," he said. "It's a chance for a clean-up."

"Well," said Coke, "if you guys want to clean up, why, take all the three to one you can get. I'm putting you wise, see? I'm gonna tie that nigger in knots."

Riley laughed.

"Listen, kid," said Mandl, "you ain't even a ten to one shot. Prince Pearl'll never get through hitting you."

Regan was still rubbing his chin. Riley turned to him.

"Regan," he said, "you always seemed like a pretty smart boy. What do you say?"

"Coke's doing the talking," he said.

Coke grinned at Regan.

"Well," said Mandl, getting up, "you guys are a hell of a lot dumber than I thought you was."

Riley got up also.

"Yeah," he said, "we thought we was doing you a favor."

"Well," said Coke, "what I said goes. If that shine don't fight his best, I'll spill something."

Mandl was furious. His sallow face was flushed and he breathed heavily.

"Yeah," he said, "he don't have to fight his best to lick you, Mason."

"Get the hell out of here you dirty kike," said Coke, taking a step toward Mandl.

Regan took Coke by the arm and jerked his thumb toward the door.

"You guys better beat it," he said. "But tell the black boy what Coke said. If this fight ain't on the square, you'll hear from us."

Mandl went out without a word, but Riley stopped in the doorway.

"Listen, guys," he said, "no use for us to get all het up over a little thing like this. Just a misunderstanding, that's all. So long."

He shut the door quietly. Regan began to laugh.

"What you laughing at?" Coke demanded.

"Boy, if you didn't tell 'em."

Coke grinned, very much pleased.

"I got to hand it you, George," he said, "for backing me up that way."

"We're pals, ain't we?" said Regan.

"You're damn right we are," said Coke, shaking hands with Regan.

Regan put on his hat.

"Well," he said, "I hope you lick that nigger because them wise boys'll have all their dough on him now."

"I'll lick him," said Coke. "Wait till he feels one of them left hooks I been practicing."

Regan stood staring at the floor.

"We sure passed up something though, Coke," he said. "You'd've got a shot at the champ, sure."

"Lord," said Coke, "I don't want nobody laying down for me. If I can't beat 'em fair and square I don't want to beat 'em. I'm in this game because I like it."

"Well," said Regan, "you're about the only one that is."

Regan went out. Coke stood in the middle of the room, staring at the floor, then he undressed slowly, took a shower and got into his pajamas. Someone knocked at the door and Coke went over and opened it. It was McNeil, his trainer.

"Well, Coke," he said, "they tell me a couple of big shots was up to see you."

"Yeah," said Coke, "I showed 'em the gate."

"That's what the boss says. Well, I'll be up after you about six, Coke. We want to get a good stiff workout in tomorrow, then we can ease off."

"O.K.," said Coke.

McNeil left, and Coke shadow-boxed for a few seconds, practicing his left hook. Then he climbed into bed.

"I guess I told 'em," he said, aloud. "They don't have to fix no fights for me."

He turned from side to side. He couldn't seem to get settled. Finally he gave it up and turning over on his back, put his hands under his head and lay looking at the reflection of the street-lights on the ceiling. He thought about his wife. Why didn't she write to him? She used to. Maybe she was sick. Maybe she was dead. At the thought of her lying dead, sweat stood out on his forehead and he sat up.

"I guess I better get up and smoke," he said.

He got out of bed, lit a cigarette, and sat staring down into Sheridan Road. Across the street was the Olympic Athletic Club where he was training. All the windows were dark, but there was a group of men standing down at the front door, talking. He watched them, wishing he could go down and talk "fight" with them. When his cigarette got so short that it burned his lips, he put it in an ashtray and got back into bed.

"I can't be laying awake this way," he said.

II

At the street door of the Olympic Athletic Club there was a sign which read:

COKE MASON TRAINING HERE
ADMISSION 25c

Most of the North Chicago amateurs and semi-pros spent the day there. Gate-crashers and bums from as far west as San Francisco drifted in, and there was the usual crowd of loungers and out-of-work ordinary citizens. But the big shots were watching Prince Pearl, who was training on the South Side.

Three days before the fight the gambler, Riley, paid his two bits at the box-office and sauntered upstairs. It was late in the afternoon and Coke was just climbing through the ropes to spar with Jeff Davis. Riley found a chair, tilted his hat over his eyes, and sat chewing a toothpick. The bell rang. Coke came out of his corner slowly, crouched, his chin on his chest, carrying his left low. Jeff came out fast and drove Coke all around the ring, peppering him with light lefts. Coke made no attempt to return the blows, but parried and blocked. Jeff, who looked in good condition, increased the pace, and continued to pepper Coke, who gave ground, ducked, parried and blocked. Riley shook his head and pushed back his hat.

Regan saw him and came over to talk to him.

"Well," said Regan, "what you doing way out here?"

Riley smiled.

"Just looking your boy over. He ain't much."

Regan took a chair and sat down beside Riley.

"He's getting better. He's just taking it easy."

"Why don't he hit that dub a couple?"

"Wait," said Regan.

Jeff pounded Coke around the ring, but landing very few clean blows.

Suddenly Coke straightened him up with a left hook and banged him against the ropes with a jarring right. Then he went into his shell again. Jeff grinned at the crowd.

"Uh hunh!" said Riley.

He squinted and chewed on his toothpick.

"And listen," said Regan, "you're all wrong if you think that Jeff Davis is any dub. He fought ten rounds with Mike Shay before he was champion, and Joe Savella barely decisioned him. Jeff's getting old or you wouldn't see him in there."

"Yeah," said Riley, "he's a fair boy."

Jeff got Coke into a corner and gave him a lacing, but Coke came out with a rush, landed his left hook again and staggered Jeff with a right. The bell rang. Jeff climbed through the ropes followed by Coke. McNeil threw a bathrobe around Coke and took him back to the dressing-room. Speed De Angelo and a North Side boy got into the ring to give the customers a show.

Riley pushed his hat back and threw his toothpick away.

"Regan," he said, "you know I ain't throwing no money away. I been up and down at this game for twenty years, and I bet with my head. But I got a hunch on that bum of yours. I'm already in on Pearl, but I'm gonna hedge. Coke's got a chance."

"You said a mouthful," said Regan.

"Here's the idea," said Riley. "I been watching the nigger. He's fast as greased lightning and he'll hit that boy of yours so much it'll be a sin, but he won't hurt him, see? And he might run into one of them left hooks."

"He won't have to run into no left hooks," said Regan, "they'll be waiting for him."

Riley got to his feet.

"What do you say you and the kid let me buy you a meal tonight, Regan?"

"You can buy mine," said Regan, "but Coke's gonna stay upstairs where Mac can watch him."

"I'll have his sent up," said Riley.

"O.K.," said Regan, "much obliged."

"That's all right," said Riley. "I'll be over at the hotel."

Riley went out. A newspaper man came over to Regan.

"Say, Mr. Regan," he said, "wasn't that Urban Riley?"

"Yeah," said Regan.

The newspaper man took out a cigar and handed it to Regan.

"What's the good word, Mr. Regan?"

"Coke wins by a knockout."

"Aw, hell," said the newspaper man, "don't kid me."

"Well," said Regan, "that's my story."

Regan stood watching Speed De Angelo and the North Side boy for a moment, then he went back to Coke's dressing-room smiling to himself. McNeil was giving Coke a rubdown.

"Well, Coke," said Regan, "you gonna fight the way I told you?"

"Yeah," said Coke, "I think you got the right dope."

"Well," said Regan, "it ain't my dope exactly. I figured it out watching you fight."

Coke grinned and swallowed the bait. "Yeah?"

McNeil pulled him to his feet and said:

"All right. Get your clothes on. Dress fast."

Coke began to dress.

"So you got the idea watching me fight, eh, George?" asked Coke, eager for more.

"Yeah," said Regan, "but I didn't want to tell you. I was afraid you'd get the swellhead."

"Lord," said Coke, "I ain't that kind of a guy."

"Say," said McNeil, "get them clothes on and cut the chatter."

McNeil's helper came in with a couple of newspapers.

"Boss," he said to Regan, "it's a sell-out."

"What?" demanded Coke, turning.

Regan took the papers.

"The Arena's sold out, Coke."

"Whoopee!" said Coke.

"You never give me them seats you promised me," said McNeil's helper.

"By gosh, that's right," said Coke. "Fix this guy up, will you, George?"

Regan glanced at McNeil's helper.

"All right. I'll fix this guy up. But no more, Coke. You're as hard on tickets as an amateur at his first fight."

"Well, I forgot about this guy," said Coke.

Coke pulled his sweater over his head, put on his cap, and then began to shadow-box, purposely bumping into McNeil, his helper, and Regan.

"Say, for God's sake," said McNeil, "take that hyena out and tie him someplace."

"Whoopee!" said Coke.

"All right, Coke," said Regan, "save some of that for your nigger friend."

"I got plenty," said Coke, bumping into McNeil.

"Yeah," said McNeil, "I heard that story before, and then in the third round you got to use everything but the needle on 'em."

Regan winked at McNeil.

"Listen to this, Mac. 'In spite of the fact that Prince Pearl is an overwhelming favorite in the betting and is almost sure to win, Mr. Mike Herbert, the promoter, announces that The Arena has been sold out. This is a tribute to Prince Pearl, a great fighter who has never got a square deal. The fans are behind him in spite of his color and....'"

"Aw, can that!" cried Coke, standing still and scowling at Regan.

McNeil smiled behind Coke's back and his helper stood staring with open mouth at Regan.

"Listen to this, Coke," said Regan. "'...our opinion is that Mr. Iron Man Mason is all build-up. He has a good knockout record and he has never been defeated, but he has only fought two or three men of any consequence....'"

"Where do they get that crap!" said Coke, scowling. "I fought better guys than that nigger ever fought. He couldn't K.O. a good flyweight. What did he do to Joe Savella? Decisioned him. What did I do to him? I beat the devil out of him. They had him all set to win, and he had his own referee and one judge, but it looked so bad they had to give me a draw."

"Alibi," said McNeil.

"You wait," said Coke. "I'm gonna hit that shine so hard they'll hear it out on the street."

"Well, I hope you can hit him," said Regan.

Coke stamped about the dressing-room swearing.

"He'll hit him, he'll hit him," said McNeil's helper.

"Go on," said McNeil, "you're through for the day."

McNeil's helper went out, looking puzzled.

Coke tore the papers out of Regan's hand and threw them on the floor.

"My!" said McNeil, "ain't he temperamental!"

"Well," said Coke, "it's enough to make a guy quit the game, when he sees his own friends pulling against him. Why, listen, Mac, that guy there's gonna bet on the nigger."

"Don't blame him," said McNeil.

"Wait a minute," said Regan. "I kind of changed my mind on that proposition. I was talking to Riley just now...."

"Riley!" shouted Coke.

"Yeah," said Regan, "he was up watching you work and he thinks you got a small chance to win. His money's smart money, so I'm gonna put some of mine with it."

"Small chance, hell!" said Coke.

"Yeah, that's what he said. Small chance. But that's better than no chance, ain't it? Riley thinks you got a good left hook and if you'll fight cautious, like you was telling me, that maybe you'll land that hook hard, and then maybe you got Prince Pearl."

"Sure," said Coke, "I'm gonna fight my own way, like I said. Cautious for five rounds, and then in the sixth I'll open up."

"Now you're talking smart," said Regan, glancing at McNeil, who was trying to keep from laughing.

"Yes sir," said McNeil, "you just fight your own way like you said, and you got an even chance."

Coke was pacified. He grinned at them and said:

"Why don't you guys lay off of me and give me a break. Ain't I a meal ticket?"

"We're for you, Coke," said McNeil.

"O.K.," said Coke. "I think I'll go watch Speed for a round."

He went out. McNeil stood shaking his head.

"Ain't he awful!" he said.

"Yeah," said Regan, "you got to handle him like he was six years old."

III

"When we was weighing in," said Coke, "he says to me, 'How de do, Mr. Mason. How you feeling?' And I says, 'I feel good enough to knock hell out of you tonight.' And he says, 'I don't doubt it, Mr. Mason.' And then he shows them ivories of his. Oh, he's a nice boy, all right, a nice sweet boy."

McNeil, exasperated, said to Regan:

"For God's sake, George, put a muzzle on this guy."

"Let him talk," whispered Regan, looking down at Coke, who was stretched out on the table getting a final rub.

Beyond the dressing-room the crowd was roaring.

"What's on?" asked Coke.

"Your boyfriend Speed's giving some palooka a lacing," said Regan. "You're next."

"How'd Jeff come out?"

"Draw."

"Draw! Who the devil was he fighting?" demanded Coke, sitting up.

McNeil pushed him back.

"A young kid named O'Keefe. Clumsy and hardboiled."

Jeff came in with a black eye and a grin on his face.

"They tell me you got a draw," said Coke.

"Yeah," said Jeff, "that kid's style bothered me. He's a comer, Coke. He looks clumsy but he's fast."

"Well, you look clumsy and are," said Regan "you ought to have walloped hell out of that kid."

"I'm not killing myself in a go like that."

"You ought to always fight your best," said Coke. "That's how I got where I am."

"That's a fact," said McNeil, loosening up Coke's leg muscles.

Nobody said anything. Regan and Jeff stood looking down at Coke. McNeil worked over him fast. Coke closed his eyes. There was a prolonged roar from the crowd. The dressing-room walls vibrated slightly.

"What the hell!" said Coke.

Jeff ran out of the dressing-room. One of the promoter's men passed him coming in.

"All right, Regan," he said, "get your boy ready."

"What's all the commotion?" asked Coke.

"Your boy Speed knocked a guy out in a ripsnorting go."

"Good for Speed," said Coke.

Jeff came running back.

"Speed won by a K.O.," he said.

"That's stale news," said Regan. "All right, Coke. Let's get going."

"Let the nigger go first," said Coke. "I ain't waiting on no nigger."

He jumped to his feet, shadow-boxed for a moment, then McNeil pulled a big, white sweater over his head and wrapped his bathrobe around him. The promoter's man went out.

"That's all arranged," said Regan. "He's on his way."

"I'm waiting till he's in the ring," said Coke.

McNeil opened his mouth to say something, but Regan motioned for him to be still.

"All right, Coke," said Regan. "Now get this. Mac'll do the talking between rounds. You listen to Mac. Don't forget, Coke. Fight cautious. Back away from him when he lands. Make him think you're afraid of him. If the crowd boos, let 'em boo."

"The hell with the crowd," said Coke.

"That's the spirit," said Regan. "Fight part of the sixth the same way if things go all right. Then open up."

"You watch me," said Coke.

There was a roar from the ring.

"There he is," said Regan. "Are you all set?"

"I'm set," said Coke.

Coke swaggered out of the dressing-room, followed by Jeff and McNeil with the paraphernalia. Regan waited until they got started and then he went to his ringside seat by another route.

Prince Pearl was sitting in his corner smiling and mitting the crowd when Coke climbed through the ropes. Coke got a big hand, which surprised him. He mitted the crowd and grinned.

"You got some friends in the mob," said McNeil.

"Yeah," said Coke.

"Well, that don't hurt none," said Jeff.

Coke sat staring at Prince Pearl, who sat erect and smiling, talking to his handlers. He looked nearly as dapper in his gray robe as he did in street-clothes. His silky hair was carefully brushed and pomaded. He was every inch a gentleman, as the press put it.

Coke was not a gentleman and everybody knew it. His face was red and coarse, his stiff, dark hair stood on end no matter how much he worked at it, and his brow was low and wide. He was too big in the shoulders, too small in the hips, and he had no neck to speak of. His eyebrows, each thick enough to make a mustache similar to the one worn by Prince Pearl, over-hung his eyes, and when he was fighting he peered up through them. To Prince Pearl he was white trash.

The referee climbed through the ropes, followed by Soapy, the announc-er, who began to bawl the usual introductions. Prince Pearl stood up and smiled, Coke followed him. The referee broke open a new box of gloves, the taped hands were examined, the gloves tied on. The referee gave them the usual instructions, stressing the neutral corner ruling, a dozen flash-light pictures were taken, then the referee shoved the fighters toward their respective corners.

"I don't see how I'm gonna keep from killing him in the first round," said Coke, scowling.

"Don't go back on us, Coke," said McNeil. "We all got our dough on you. Get in there and stall, like you said. You can do all your killing in the sixth round."

"I'm on," said Coke.

The bell rang. Prince Pearl ambled out, smiling, and touched gloves with Coke, then he immediately led with his left, caught Coke flatfooted, and banged him on the nose. Coke retreated. There was a laugh from the crowd. Prince stepped back on the defensive, but seeing that Coke had no intention of leading, he was forced to lead. He led cautiously. Coke retreat-ed, making no effort to counter. The crowd sank back. They had expected to see something, but here it was, just another fight.

"Bring on the Iron Man," somebody yelled.

Prince Pearl, puzzled, fought more carefully than usual, hardly using his right at all. Coke stalled around the ring, flatfooted, giving a very poor exhibition of boxing, and taking left jabs on the forehead. He clinched and stalled and took a series of light lefts, then he clinched again, leading but once during the whole round. When the bell rang he walked back to his corner, grinning. The crowd booed.

Prince Pearl sat erect on his stool, staring at Coke.

He suspected something.

"You're right about that nigger," said Coke.

"Don't talk," said McNeil, "just nod or shake your head. You mean he's hard to hit?"

Coke nodded.

"Got a good defense, you mean?"

Coke nodded.

"You ain't tried to hit him much, have you?"

Coke shook his head.

The second, third, and fourth rounds were duplicates of the first. Some of the men at ringside stood up and shouted: "No contest! No contest!" The referee told Coke to mix it, it looked bad. But still Prince Pearl held off, leading and retreating, leading and retreating. He stayed out of clinches as much as possible, and in the clinches he spent most of his time keeping Coke from landing. Once or twice he stung Coke and made him counter, then either by slipping or swaying, he made Coke miss.

But a crowd hasn't any eye for boxing. A crowd wants action and bloodshed. At the end of the fourth round the patience of the crowd was exhausted. Men stood on the seats and bellowed.

A cynical radio-announcer informed his listeners that:

"Coke Mason is just another newspaper tough guy. I could lick him myself."

While Jeff worked on Coke, McNeil talked to him:

"How you feel, Coke?"

"Fresh as when I went in. But so's Pearl."

"Keep it up, Coke. You're doing fine."

"Good God! I can't keep it up much longer."

"Don't talk," said McNeil. "Only one more round, Coke, then you can cut loose. Maybe the nigger'll start shooting 'em this round."

Prince, following instructions from his corner, danced out and immediately began to lead, following up a left with a right. For the first time in the fight he was really using his right. He landed repeatedly, staggering Coke with blows to the head. The crowd bellowed. The radio-announcer got so excited that he said left when he meant right and vice versa, which didn't matter much as he couldn't tell a hook from an uppercut. Coke pedaled backwards, ducked, sidestepped, but kept catching them on the head and body. Prince worked him into a corner and peppered him. Coke clinched and shook his head. The crowd thought he was groggy. The roar from the crowd was steady, men were standing on the seats calling for a knockout. And as far as the radio-announcer was concerned the fight was over. Prince drove a hard left to Coke's mouth and drew blood. Coke backed away and, trying to sidestep another left, slipped and fell. The referee began to count. Then the bell rang.

McNeil and Jeff worked furiously over Coke, stalling.

"I got him," said Coke. "Watch him fold up when I hit him with that left."

Riley, who was sitting behind Regan, leaned forward and inquired:

"Is Coke stalling, or has the nigger got him licked?"

"Wait," said Regan.

When the bell rang for the sixth round Prince leapt into the ring, his eyes blazing. Coke met him and hit him a belt to the body that sent him spinning. The crowd got up and yelled. Prince lost his head entirely and stood in the middle of the ring and slugged with Coke. He threw his punches so fast that Coke didn't even try to parry or block them, he took them. The radio-man didn't know what it was all about and told his listeners that hell had busted loose. Prince started a straight right to the head, but Coke was watching for the blow and countered quickly with a left hook for the body. The blow landed squarely in the short ribs. Prince flinched and backed away. But Coke leapt after him, wide open, throwing punches from all angles. And they weren't wild swings. They landed. Prince folded up with a surprised look on his face. Cushions, hats, and newspapers sailed through the air, and Jeff grabbed McNeil and began to dance. At the count of nine Prince got to his feet and tried to back-pedal, covering up, but Coke leapt after him, flailing him. A hard left hook to the body, followed by a right to the head, sent Prince to the canvas again and he didn't get up. When the referee said "ten" the ring was full. Coke helped carry Prince to his corner, then he mitted the crowd, grinning. The referee held up Coke's hand.

The radio-man seized Coke by the arm and pulled him to the microphone.

"Say something, Mr. Mason," he said.

Coke grinned.

"What?"

"Oh, anything."

Coke stared at the microphone, then said:

"Hello, everybody. It was a tough go and I sure met a tough boy, a good game fighter. I was lucky to win. So long."

IV

"Good God," said Coke, "are you gonna work over me all night! You'd think I was the guy that took the count."

McNeil turned and looked at Regan, who was standing back of him.

"Coke," said Regan, "what's the big rush? You ain't going no place."

"That's all right," said Coke, "but you'd think I was a stiffy stretched out like this."

"Let him look you over, Coke," Speed De Angelo put in. "I had a busted rib once and didn't know it and I had a hell of a time."

"Yeah," said Jeff, "there ain't no rush."

Regan pushed Speed and Jeff toward the door.

"You guys beat it," he said.

But Coke sat up.

"You guys stick around," he said. "You're going with me wherever I go. Good Lord, we got to celebrate some, don't we?"

"The best thing you can do," said Regan, "is to go out to the hotel and go to bed."

"You would say that," said Coke.

McNeil pulled Coke to a sitting position.

"He's all right, George," said McNeil. "There ain't a scratch on him except that little cut on his lip."

"Whoopee!" said Coke.

Someone knocked at the door and Regan opened it.

"Coke," called Regan, "there's a bunch of guys here that want to see you."

"All right," said Coke, pulling on his pants, "let 'em in."

Twenty men crowded through the door, filling the dressing-room from wall to wall: reporters, amateurs, pugs, hangers-on, and plain citizens. One of the reporters came over to Coke.

"Got any plans for the future, Coke?"

"Yeah," said Coke, "I'm going after Mike Shay and make him give me a match."

One of the men pointed at Coke and said:

"Boys, here's your next middleweight champion."

"Yea!" yelled the crowd.

"How come you fought so slow the first four rounds, Mason?" asked another reporter.

"Well," said Coke, "I couldn't seem to get going."

"I thought he had you in the fifth."

"Yeah," said Coke, fumbling with his necktie, "he was sure throwing 'em fast in that round. Prince is a tough boy. Toughest I ever fought."

Regan held up his hands for silence.

"Listen," he said, "I don't want to disturb you guys, but I got to get Coke home, so he don't get pneumonia or something. We're staying out at the Allard Hotel, as you guys probably know, so come out whenever you feel like it and talk things over."

Coke shook all the hands shoved at him and grinned. Speed, Jeff, and McNeil worked the crowd out without appearing to do so. Regan stood with his hat tilted over his eyes watching Coke, who was putting on his overcoat and dancing.

"Whoopee!" said Coke. "Ain't we getting there?"

"Looks like it," said Regan.

"Looks like it, hell," said Coke. "To look at your face you'd think I lost."

"Well," said Regan, "don't get all puffed up. You got a break. If the black boy had kept his head he'd've decisioned you sure."

"Yeah," said Coke, taking Regan by the arm and waltzing him around, "but he didn't. Did you see my hook land in the sixth? Oh, baby!"

Regan pulled away from him.

"Listen, Coke," he said, "put your hat on and let's get out of here."

"All right," said Coke, "but I'm taking the boys out to the hotel with me and we're gonna have a feed or something."

"Sure," said Regan, "that's the idea. You leave it to me."

"Whoopee!" said Coke.

Holding up the skirts of his overcoat, he skipped about the dressing-room. Of a sudden he stopped and stood staring at the floor.

"Well," said Regan, "what took you?"

Coke didn't answer for a long time, then he said:

"You know, George, I was just thinking: I wonder where Rose is? Maybe she's sick or something."

"Well," said Regan, exasperated, "if she needs any jack you'll hear from her."

"Aw, there you go," said Coke. "You never got a good word to say for her. You don't know her, that's what I'm telling you. You don't know her. She's a good kid, George, only she's got big ideas. She wasn't gonna be no palooka's wife and I don't blame her."

"I wonder how it feels to be that dumb?" Regan asked the walls.

"George," said Coke, "sometimes I think you ain't human, the way you talk. Ain't you never been crazy about a woman?"

"I'm paying alimony, ain't I? You sap!"

Coke sat on the edge of the rubbing-table and looked up at Regan.

"George, the night she left me it was raining. I can remember just as well. It was the night that Akron bum decisioned me and they held up my money because they said I wasn't trying."

"I know," said Regan, impatiently.

"I was trying, George, only I didn't have nothing in my legs. You know. I was worried about that kid. I knew she was sick of where we was living and all that stuff. Well, when I got home she had her suitcase in the hall. No sneaking about her. Some guy had got her a job with a show."

"Yeah," said Regan, "one of her part-time boyfriends."

Coke flushed.

"George," he said, "if you wasn't my pal I'd lace you when you talk like that."

"Yeah?" said Regan. "Well, maybe I ain't no good in the ring, but I'm a pretty good rough-and-tumble fighter. You lace me and I'll lace you back."

"Aw, hell," said Coke, getting up and walking toward the door.

Regan followed him and put his hand on his shoulder.

"Listen, Coke," he said, "forget that dame and you'll be O.K. She ain't no good. A dame that runs out on a guy when he's in tough luck ain't no good. If a dame's any good at all, that's when she sticks, see?"

Coke didn't say anything. He just stood there looking at the floor.

"Didn't I stick with you, Coke?" Regan went on. "Everybody said you was a bum and ought to go back to the factory. But I stuck to you and tried to make a fighter out of you. You had it in you, all right, kid. But suppose I'd've said 'I can't be managing no palookas' and let you go to hell. Where'd you be now? Didn't I lend you money so you wouldn't have to go back at that ten hour a day grind? Yeah. I stuck with you, Coke. Now you stick with me. Go crying around after dames and you'll be just another bum."

Coke nodded his head slowly a couple of times, then he went out into the darkened corridor to hide the tears in his eyes. Regan followed him, closing the dressing-room door quietly.

Speed, Jeff and McNeil were waiting for them in Coke's car. Regan got into the driver's seat and Coke sat beside him.

"Well," said Speed, "where we going?"

Regan turned to Coke.

"Where we going, kid?"

Coke sat looking at his hands.

"I guess we better go out to the hotel, George. I'm kind of tired."

V

When Regan came in, Coke dressed in pink pajamas and a dark red bathrobe, was sitting at the window looking down into Sheridan Road.

"Coke," said Regan, "I got all the papers I could buy. They're playing you up big. Looks like Mike Shay'll have to fight you."

"Yeah?" said Coke. "Well, I guess maybe I can make it interesting for old Mike."

"I'll take even money on you," said Regan.

"That's the talk, George."

Regan handed Coke a paper and they sat reading the round by round account of the fight. Coke laughed.

"I never seen nothing like them fight experts. Listen, George: '...the new middleweight contender is a sluggish fighter and has to be stung into action.' Ain't that rich?"

"Yeah," said Regan, "listen to this: '...Mason lived up to his name and showed himself to be an iron man. After going down before a barrage of punches....'"

"I slipped," said Coke.

"'...in the fifth he came back fresher than ever and completely outfought and outgeneraled one of the smartest fighters in the ring.'"

They sat laughing over the papers.

"Hey!" shouted Coke, getting to his feet, "listen: 'Champion Mike Shay discusses next match with reporters. Says he may sign to fight Joe Savella, or the foreign middleweight, Larsen....'"

Regan took the paper away from Coke and stared at it.

"That's only a rumor, Coke," said Regan. "I already wired his manager."

"Yeah," said Coke, "that's good. Trying to dodge me, the dirty mick."

"Don't get all worked up," said Regan. "The newspapers're gonna play our game. Listen to what it says: 'It's hard to figure out why Joe Savella should be given a shot at the championship as he has dropped two decisions to Prince Pearl, and Larsen's record is even less impressive. To our way of thinking Coke Mason is the logical contender.'"

"Whoopee!" shouted Coke.

"But that don't mean we'll get the match," said Regan. "Old Mike's a slick boy. If we do get the match, it'll cost us like hell and Mike'll take all the gravy."

"The devil with that," said Coke. "I'll fight him winner take all. I'll fight him for nothing."

"Aw, talk sense," said Regan.

Coke got up, took off his bathrobe and began to shadow-box.

"Look at that hook, George," he said, "that's the baby that'll put old Mike to sleep."

Regan watched Coke for a couple of minutes, then he said:

"Now run in and take a shower, you damn fool! And then get your clothes on. You ought to have a nurse."

Coke went into the bathroom.

Part II

Jeff lay stretched out on the lounge watching Speed and Regan, who were dancing with a couple of girls from a North Side theatre. Coke was sitting in a corner, smoking a cigar, and a little redhead, another one of the showgirls, was reading his palm.

Regan's partner broke away from him and began to dance by herself. Regan stood by clapping his hands in time.

"Step right up! Step right up!" said Regan. "The big show! The big show!"

Jeff sat up and said:

"Kick 'em up, kid. I want to give my eyes a treat."

"Say," called Coke, "cut out the rough stuff."

They all turned and looked at him.

"Yeah," said the redhead, "we can't hear ourselves think."

"Oh, God," said Regan.

Regan's girl stopped dancing and stood with her hands on her hips, looking at Coke.

"Am I bothering you, Mr. Coke Mason?" she inquired.

"No," said Coke, "you ain't bothering me. But this kid here's trying to read my palm and you got her all flustered."

"I can read your palm from here," said Regan. "You're a big bum."

"Oh, he is not," said the redhead. "He's got a wonderful hand. I was telling him he ought to take up intellectual pursuits."

"What's that?" asked Jeff.

"Don't mind him," said Coke.

"Well," said Regan, "I still want to know."

"He ought to read," said the redhead, "and cultivate his mind. He ought to be a newspaper man or something smart like that."

"Yeah," said Regan, "he ought to write poetry and crochet. That's about his speed."

"There you go," said Coke. "Why don't you lay off of me for a while?"

"Oh, he's only kidding," said the redhead.

"What does she mean, intellectual pursuits?" Jeff asked Speed.

Speed grimaced.

"Why bother me with that," he said.

"Say," said Jeff, "want to read my palm, sister?"

"I'm busy," said the redhead.

"Let me read it," said Regan.

"Oh, let's dance," called Regan's partner.

But the music stopped and a radio-announcer began to expatiate on the merits of a certain remedy for colds in the head. Regan twisted the dial vainly, there wasn't any jazz music on.

"I like victrolas better," said Regan's partner, "then you can get what you want."

"Say," called Jeff, "when you get through with Coke will you read my palm?"

The redhead pretended she didn't hear him. He shrugged and got to his feet.

"Well," he said, "I think I'll go out and get myself a sandwich or something. Who's hungry?"

"I am," said Regan's partner. "I could eat a horse."

"Well," said Regan. "Let's all go out and see if we can't find one."

"All right," said Speed. "Are you set, sister?"

"How about you two over in the corner?" called Regan.

"I'm not hungry," said the redhead.

"Neither am I," said Coke flushing.

"Well, that's that," said Regan. "We're on our way."

They went out. Speed called from the doorway:

"Watch your step, Coke. I lost a watch at a fortune tellers once."

"He's awful," said the redhead.

"All they do is kid people," said Coke. "That's the way they have a good time."

"I get tired of people kidding, don't you?" said the redhead, still holding Coke's hand.

"Yeah," said Coke.

The redhead sat looking into Coke's eyes. He flushed and stared at the floor.

"You know," she said, "when they was telling me about you, I thought you'd be some kind of a roughneck."

"Yeah," said Coke, "most people thinks us pugs is no better than gunmen."

"Well," said the redhead, "that's because they just see you in the ring, beating some guy up. That's the way with us. They see us on the stage showing our legs, see, and they think we ain't respectable."

"I know," said Coke. "I used to know a girl that was on the stage. Fact is, I knew her pretty well and she was as nice as you make 'em."

"Sure," said the redhead. "What I say is: there's disrespectable people every place. On the stage and in the church. It's all the same."

"Sure," said Coke, "that's what I always said."

"Showing your legs don't make you disrespectable as long as you behave yourself. Same as prizefighting."

"Sure," said Coke.

The redhead held Coke's hand and stared into his eyes.

"You know," she said, "it does a girl good to meet a guy like you that don't think all showgirls is you know what. All most guys think about is getting fresh with you!"

"Yeah," said Coke, "that's what this girl I was telling you about always said."

"And she was right," said the redhead. "That's a fact. Always pawing you over, you know, and all that sort of thing. It makes you sick."

"Sure," said Coke, pulling his hand away and looking very uncomfortable.

"Of course," said the redhead, "when a girl meets a fellow that treats her right and isn't always pawing around, why, that's different."

"Sure," said Coke.

She smiled at him and he grinned.

"You look just like a little kid when you grin," she said. "I feel like mothering you."

She got up, sat on the arm of his chair, and ran her fingers through his hair. He sat there for a moment, blushing and biting his lips, then he put his arm around her gently. She slid down into his lap.

"Oh, Coke," she said, "what are you doing?"

Coke tried to smile.

"Nothing," he said. "You ain't sore are you?"

"No," she said. "I know I can trust you."

"Sure," said Coke.

She sat there, looking into his eyes, running her fingers through his hair, talking to him at random. Finally he kissed her. She drew back.

"Bad boy," she said. "After mama trusted you. Mama's gonna get right up."

But she made no move and in a moment Coke kissed her again. This time she said nothing, but as Coke hesitated and drew away slightly, she got to her feet and began to turn the dial of the radio.

"I think we better dance after that," she said.

Coke got to his feet, took her in his arms very carefully and began to shuffle about to the radio music.

Pretty soon he said:

"You ain't sore at me, are you?"

"I ought to be," she said.

"But are you?" Coke insisted. "I'll behave."

The redhead didn't say anything and they danced on.

"Are you?" demanded Coke.

"Not exactly," said the redhead.

In a little while the bunch came back and found them dancing.

"Well," said Regan, "how's the palmist and her victim?"

"Yeah," said Speed, "have you decided to take up them pursuits yet?"

"Aw, lay off," said Coke.

When the girls had gone to make their show, Regan took Coke over to the window away from Speed and Jeff and said:

"Well, did I keep the bunch away long enough?"

"What?"

"Oh, don't act dumb. Did you have plenty of time with the redhead?"

Coke stared at Regan, then he said:

"You got that kid wrong, George. Why, I kissed her a couple of times and she began to get sore."

"Oh, God!" said Regan, holding his head.

"That's the way with you, George," said Coke, "you think everybody's disrespectable. Just because a girl gets up on a stage and shows her legs, why, you think she's in for anything."

Regan looked at Coke for a long time, then he put on his hat and went out.

"What's the matter with the boss?" asked Speed.

"Oh," said Coke, "he's just sore because I told him a few things."

II

Speed pulled a sweater over his head and sat at the ring side, watching Coke and a North Side lightheavy. Coke, who never pulled his punches, was trying to keep from killing the young North Sider. Regan and Riley were sitting near Speed, talking. Since the Prince Pearl go, Riley had been spending a good deal of time with Regan. He thought Coke was the coming champion, and said so. Regan wasn't so sure.

"He's certainly got a mean left," said Riley.

"Look at that," said Speed, turning to them.

Coke had jolted the lightheavy with a left hook and the lightheavy was backing away, holding up his gloves.

"I got enough," he said.

McNeil put a sweater over Coke's head, and Coke climbed out of the ring.

"Hello, Mason," called Riley.

Coke came over to them.

"Well," said Regan, "still picking on cripples."

"My hand slipped," said Coke. "I didn't mean to land so solid."

"How's the legs?" Riley inquired.

"A-one," said Coke.

"Go take a shower," said Regan, "and we'll run over and get a lunch."

"On me," said Riley.

"I'll take you up on that," said Coke. "I could eat sawdust."

Regan turned to Riley.

"It's a good thing that bird's a natural," he said. "If he had trouble making weight it'd be just too bad."

"I like to eat," said Coke.

"Who don't?" said Riley. "I used to be a big eater myself, but my stomach went back on me."

One of the employees of the club came over to Regan.

"Somebody wants Coke on the phone," he said.

"Man or woman?"

"It's a man."

"Somebody want me?" asked Coke.

"Yeah," said Regan.

"Go talk for me, George. It may be that redhead."

"Got the gals chasing him now, hunh?" said Riley.

"Yeah," said Regan, "he's a regular killer."

"Go ahead, George," said Coke.

"It's a man, dummy."

Coke went to talk on the phone.

"Listen," said Riley, "I didn't know you managers liked to have your boys thick with women."

"Well," said Regan, "it's a long story."

"Something special?"

"Yeah," said Regan. "His wife ran away and left him, and he can't get over it. She was just a plain digger, but you can't make him believe that. I thought maybe if I could get him interested in a couple of kids I could watch, he'd be a lot better off."

"Yeah," said Riley, "but it's risky."

Coke came running back, scowling.

"George," he said, "it was the redhead. She had some guy ask for me so I'd come to the phone. George, you got to help me out with that baby. She's sore at me."

"Well," said Regan, "I'll do what I can. Why don't you tell me things?"

"She's gonna sue me or something," said Coke. "Good God, George, you know I can't have nothing like that getting out in the papers. Suppose my wife'd see it?"

Regan glanced at Riley, who got up, lit a cigar, and walked away whistling.

"What's she gonna sue you for, Coke?" asked Regan, trying to be patient.

"Breach of promise or something. Hell, I never promised her nothing. All I did was be nice to her till she kept after me and after me. You know I thought she was one, nice respectable girl, but, say...!"

"Never mind," said Regan. "I can imagine the rest. Listen, Coke, does she know that you're married?"

"No. I never told her."

"Did you ever write her any letters?"

"No," said Coke, "I never had to. She was always calling me up and giving me passes to the show and taking me to meet all her girl friends, and..."

"Never mind," said Regan. "The next time she calls up tell her to go to hell."

"But, good Lord, George," said Coke. "I can't do nothing like that. You can't just tell a girl to go to hell after you been running around with her like I have. She was crying when she was talking to me. She feels pretty bad, George, because I been dodging her."

"All right," said Regan, wearily, "you leave her to me."

Coke put his arms around Regan.

"Boy," he said, "I don't know what I'd do if I didn't have you. She's coming up to the hotel as soon as her act's over. You be there, George, won't you? I'll take a whirl out to The Arena with Speed. There's a couple of boys on the card we want to see work."

"All right," said Regan, "but after this, tell me things, see? Tell me things. It'll save us both a lot of grief."

"There ain't gonna be no next time for me," said Coke. "I'm off of women. Why, to hear her talk you'd think she was the nicest kid that ever lived, but, say...!"

"Never mind," said Regan. "You go take a shower and get a good rubdown."

Coke hugged Regan.

"George," he said, "I got to hand it to you. You're one smart boy."

When he went to the dressing-room, Regan motioned for Riley to come over.

"Riley," he said, "you're my lawyer."

"How come?"

"One of Coke's women has been cutting up and now I've got to settle her. You're my lawyer, see?"

"All right," said Riley, "murder barred."

III

Speed, Coke, Regan and Riley had dinner together at the hotel, then Speed and Coke went back to the club to wait for Jeff. They were going out to The Arena and Jeff had Coke's car. Regan and Riley bought two quarts of gin from a bell-boy and went upstairs to drink it.

At eight o'clock the clerk called up and said that there was a woman downstairs to see Mr. Mason, and Regan told the clerk to send her up.

When Regan let the redhead in he said:

"Hello there, Miss De Vere. Just the lady we wanted to see. Meet my lawyer, Mr. Riley."

Riley got up and bowed.

"Pleased to meet you," he said.

The redhead glanced about the room, then smiled at Regan.

"Where's Coke?" she inquired.

"Coke's awful sorry he can't be here," said Regan, "but he's in a conference."

"Oh, he is!" said the redhead. "Well, that's mighty funny. He told me he'd be here when I got here."

"Well," said Regan, "if you'll have a chair, I'll explain."

The redhead sat down, looking suspiciously at Riley and Regan.

"What you got a lawyer here for?" she demanded.

"That's just the point, Miss De Vere," said Regan. "We chased Coke because we didn't want him to get all riled up. He's gonna fight again pretty soon and we got to be careful."

"Well," said the redhead, "you men are all mighty considerate of each other. But I ain't got nothing to talk over with you two. My business is private."

"We understand," said Riley, pouring himself a drink. "How about a drink?"

"No," said the redhead.

Regan settled himself in his chair and shook his finger at the redhead.

"Listen, Miss De Vere, what kind of a mess have you got yourself into with Coke?"

"Mess! I'm in no mess."

She looked from Regan to Riley and back again.

"Say," she inquired, "what's this all about?"

"Well," said Regan, "my lawyer just got a communication from Sandusky, Ohio—that's Coke's home, you know—stating that Coke was way behind on his alimony and wouldn't pay up."

"Alimony!" cried the redhead.

"Yeah," said Regan, "and if Coke don't pay up, they're gonna send him to prison. But the point is, Coke's broke. That boy gets rid of money faster than nobody else. He no sooner got his split for the Prince Pearl go than he lost half of it on the stock market."

"Yeah," said the redhead, "now I'll tell one."

Regan turned to Riley.

"Have you got them figures with you, Mr. Riley?"

"No," said Riley, "I left 'em down at my office."

"Well," said Regan, "it don't matter anyway, because that don't concern Miss De Vere. But, listen, Miss De Vere, I'll bet you'll be interested in the rest of it. Don't you, Mr. Riley?"

"Yeah," said Riley. "She'd be funny if she wasn't."

"All right," said the redhead, "let's have it."

"Well," said Regan, "Coke's wife has had a guy over here watching him and she's got a full report on everything he does. See? She's got your name and what you do and how much you make."

"What!"

"I'm not kidding you," said Regan. "My lawyer had a long talk with her representative, didn't you, Mr. Riley?"

"I sure did. And he's hardboiled."

"Well," said Regan, "here's the point. Coke's gonna be served with a writ some time this week. But Coke hasn't got a dime. You know what I mean. He's got some money, but not enough. Well, the missus thinks he's been spending his dough on you, so she's gonna get a writ of attachment against your bank account."

The redhead jumped to her feet.

"What! Say, this is a mighty nice mess this dumb pug got me into. Say, he never spent over ten dollars on me at one time in his life. We used to eat at sandwich shops and places like that. Say, what kind of a frame-up is this?"

"Now wait," said Regan, "don't get all excited. Here's the idea. You just leave it all to us, see? And we'll straighten it out. I got a little money and my lawyer here thinks that guy from Ohio is crooked and maybe we can get to him. You just lay low, see, and say nothing. If Coke calls you up or anything, tell him you don't want nothing to do with him, see? You know how dumb he is. He thinks money grows on trees and he'd just as lief be served with a writ as not."

"No fooling," said the redhead, looking from one to the other. "Are you gonna help me out?"

"Sure thing," said Regan. "We ain't gonna stand around and see you get gypped when we know you're O.K."

"Say," said the redhead, "I always did think you were a good guy underneath all that kidding you put on."

"Sure," said Regan. "I kid a lot, but I don't mean it. I'm for you, sister. Only do as I say. Stay away from that dumb pug of mine."

"You watch me," said the redhead, smiling. "If he ever gets near me again it'll be because I didn't see him first."

"That's the talk," said Riley. "Now how about a little drink."

"No," she said. "I think I better be getting out of this hotel. That guy might be hanging around or something."

Regan turned to Riley.

"Smart girl, Mr. Riley."

"You bet your life, Mr. Regan."

"Well," said the redhead, "I'm on my way. Goodbye, Mr. Regan. If you fix me up you got a friend for life. Why don't you drop over to my place and see me some night?"

"Maybe I will," said Regan.

When she had gone Regan turned to Riley and they both burst out laughing.

"Regan," said Riley, "I never heard such a line in my life. It's a good thing that kid's dumb."

"Oh, Lord," said Regan, "it was a lot easier than I thought it'd be. Didn't she grab the bait, though?"

"Yeah," said Riley. "But it's a shame to give a cute kid like that the oil."

"There you go," said Regan.

"I think maybe I'll drop over and talk business with her some night," said Riley.

IV

When Coke came in, Regan was lying on the lounge asleep, and Riley was in the bathroom taking a bath and singing loudly. One of the chairs was overturned, Riley's clothes were piled in the middle of the floor, and pieces of torn-up newspapers were scattered all over the room. Coke took Regan by the shoulders and shook him.

"George! George!"

Regan opened his eyes, stared blankly for a moment, then sat up.

"What's the matter?" he demanded.

Coke shook him hard.

"What do you mean getting drunk!" he shouted. "Don't you know that stuff's poison to you. I thought you told me you wasn't gonna get drunk no more."

"Celebrating," said Regan with a sickly grin. "Where's my lawyer?"

"Aw, shut up," said Coke, pushing him back on the lounge.

He hated to see Regan in that condition. It made him feel queer. When Regan was drunk, Coke felt helpless.

Riley came out of the bathroom with a towel around him, dancing.

"How do you like my figure?" he demanded.

"Say," said Coke, "get your clothes on before you get pneumonia. Say, what was you guys trying to do, anyway, tearing up all them newspapers?"

"Celebrating," said Riley. "We won a great legal battle."

"We had to have confetti," said Regan.

Coke pulled Regan to a sitting position, stripped off his clothes, and, taking him under the arms, carried him into the bathroom and put him under the shower. Regan bellowed when the cold water hit him.

"Take it like a man, you bum," said Coke. "God, I can't go away and leave you a minute, you got to go and get drunk."

"Let me out of here," cried Regan, struggling.

But Coke held him under the shower. Riley came in, half-dressed, to watch.

"Say," said Riley, "don't drown him, champ. He's a good friend of yours. A legal friend. A celebrating, legal friend. Chief confetti maker of legal celebrations."

"Aw, shut up," said Coke, pushing Riley away.

Riley went back and finished dressing. When Regan had begun to come around, Coke took him out and made him put his clothes back on. Regan sat down without a word and lit a cigar.

"Well, Coke," he said, "we fixed the redhead for for you."

"Looks like it," said Coke.

"We did that," said Riley. "We fixed her good and plenty. We are legal gentlemen. Celebrating, confetti-making, legal gentlemen. Where did you say she lived?"

"Riley likes her," said Regan, laughing.

"She has such beautiful eyes," he said.

Riley and Regan burst out laughing. Coke sat glaring at them.

"A couple of fine, whiskey micks," he said.

"Gin," said Riley.

And they burst out laughing again.

"Well," said Coke, "all I got to say is, you sure made yourself at home in my room. By God, it looks like the A.E.F. marched through here."

"Don't get sore, champ," said Riley.

"Don't call him 'champ,'" said Regan. "His head's big enough now."

This sounded more like a sober Regan, and Coke grinned.

"All right, George," he said.

V

"Well," said Regan to Speed, "I guess we might as well break the bad news to Coke now as any time."

"Yeah," said Speed. "That sure is a tough break, George."

"I don't know," said Regan. "It'll make a match with the champ more certain. Mike'll lick Joe to a standstill. You know that."

"Sure," said Speed. "Mike knows it too. That's why he picked him."

"I know," said Regan.

Then he turned to Jeff and said:

"Jeff, go and see if Mac's through with Coke. If he is, tell Coke I want to see him."

Jeff went out into the dressing-rooms back of the fight hall. A couple of North Side amateurs were in the ring swinging wild at each other.

"Look at them bums," said Speed.

"Well," said Regan, "they got to learn. Coke was worse than that when he started. He thought all you had to do to win a fight was to rush in swinging both fists."

One of the amateurs connected and the other got a bloody nose.

"You mind if I go a round or two with Dugan?" asked Speed.

"No," said Regan, "only box, don't fight. If that mick gets sore and starts to swing, tie him up."

"Watch me," said Speed.

Dugan and Speed climbed through the ropes and went at it. Jeff came back with Coke, who was grinning. When he saw the expression on Regan's face, the grin disappeared.

"What's the matter, George?" he asked.

Regan handed him a newspaper and pointed.

Coke read:

"Joe Savella signed for a championship go with Mike Shay."

Coke looked stupefied.

"Well," said Regan, "that's that."

"Yeah," said Coke, "the yellow mick. I told you he was afraid of me."

"You'll get a shot at him, Coke. Just keep your shirt on."

Coke sat down and looked at the floor.

"The newspaper boys are already razzing Mike," said Regan. "If he don't plaster Joe in jig time there'll be an awful noise."

"Well," said Coke, "I don't care who wins. I can lick both of 'em in one night."

"Sure you can," said Jeff. "I can lick 'em myself."

"Sure you can," said Coke.

"Say," said Regan, "cut out the back-slapping, you birds, and let's talk business."

Jeff smiled and struck at Regan, then he got up and stood watching Speed and Dugan, who were bouncing about the ring just above them.

"Listen, Coke," said Regan, "how'd you like to fight on the same card with Mike?"

"What!"

"Sure. What do you say?"

"You must be crazy. I fight main-gos."

"Listen," said Regan, "this is a chance to show Mike up. I can get you a match with that Norsky bum that Mike almost picked. He needs the money. You can plaster him in one round and then give Mike the laugh."

Coke began to smile.

"Yeah?"

"Sure," said Regan. "Wainwright wired me from New York about it. Everybody down East wants to see you get a break. They're sick of Mike Shay."

"By God, I'll do it," said Coke.

"All right," said Regan.

They sat watching Speed and Dugan. Speed was giving the Irish boy a good lacing. When the bell rang, they shook hands and climbed through the ropes. Speed came over to Coke.

"Tough luck, old kid," he said. "You'll make it yet."

"Thanks," said Coke.

Coke and Regan sat for a long time without speaking. Regan began to watch Coke. He knew that when wrinkles appeared in his forehead he was doing some heavy thinking. Finally he inquired:

"What's on your mind, Coke?"

"You know," said Coke, slowly, "I was just thinking maybe the missus would be in New York. She always wanted to live there."

Regan rubbed his chin and stared at the floor.

"Yeah," said Coke. "Course I ain't gonna hunt her up, because she may be off of me for life. Only maybe I might see her or something."

"Yeah," said Regan, "New York's just a little place. You'll probably run into her at the main corner."

"You never know," said Coke.

VI

Regan talked at the door of the dressing-room with a New York reporter who had evidently never heard of Coke Mason. Regan, somewhat irritated, handed out one of his best cigars and gave the reporter the story of the Prince Pearl go with trimmings, and intimated that the young reporter, lately assigned to the sporting page, would see a fight tonight that would make his hair stand on end.

"Coming east," said Regan, "we had to take a stateroom so that boy of mine could work out. He's perfecting a punch that'll knock 'em silly and he won't let up for a minute. The boy's ambitious."

"Do you expect to get a match with Mike Shay?" asked the reporter.

"Yeah," said Regan, "unless he dies of fright after what he sees tonight."

The reporter laughed. Someone had told him that fight managers were great kidders.

"Well," said the reporter, "they tell me that Larsen's a comer."

"Well," said Regan, "you just keep your eyes open out there tonight and you'll see things."

Big Tim Morgan, the promoter, intercepted the reporter as he was leaving Regan and said:

"Before you print anything that bird says, kid, verify it, verify it!"

The reporter laughed and went back into The Coliseum. Big Tim offered Regan a cigar and leaned against the corridor wall for a talk. Regan put his hand on Tim's shoulder.

"Tim," he said, "that don't look like no capacity house to me."

"What do you care?" said Tim. "You ain't on percentage."

"No," said Regan, "but it's mighty funny a Grade A fixer like you, with all your ballyhoo, couldn't get a capacity house out for the champ."

"Mike's getting old," said Tim. "He's too smart for the comers, but the boys are getting sick of seeing him decision everybody. It's on the square, but they want decisive wins, see, knockouts."

"Sure," said Regan. "Well, they're gonna see one knockout tonight."

Big Tim laughed.

"Don't try to kid me about that boiler-maker of yours. Mike thinks he's all build-up. Anyway, I got it straight from Sleepy that Mandl said that Prince Pearl laid down."

Regan laughed.

"Mandl had his money on Prince, Tim. How about that?"

"I don't know," said Tim. "I'm just telling you what Sleepy said. Sleepy bet a hundred on Larsen tonight."

"Send him around," said Regan. "I still got two grand that ain't working."

Big Tim looked at Regan suspiciously.

"Regan," he said, "the only thing about you is, you got a hell of a reputation. I'd take that two grand if I was on the inside. But I don't know Larsen's manager from Adam. He can't speak hardly any English, anyway."

"Well," said Regan, laughing, "I can't speak Swedish, so there you are."

"Tell you what I'll do just to keep you honest," said Big Tim. "I'll take one grand of that two. Honor bet."

"O.K.," said Regan.

"If I was you, Regan," said Tim, "I'd chuck that Ohio kid and concentrate on that little Chicago wop you got."

"You mean Speed."

"Yeah," said Big Tim. "I got a good spot for him on my next card. He stood the customers on their heads in that first bout."

"That's his fourth straight knockout," said Regan.

Beyond the corridor the crowd began to boo and laugh.

"Somebody's getting razzed," said Regan.

"Yeah," said Big Tim, "and it's only the second round. I was afraid of that match."

"You leave it to me, Tim," said Regan. "I'll pep your show up for you. I'll show you smart New York hicks a fighter. A gong to gong fighter."

Tim gave Regan a push.

"A gong to gong set-up fighter," he said.

Speed came down the corridor in a big, blue sweater.

"Hello, boss," he said.

Big Tim offered his hand.

"Nice fight, kid."

"Thanks," said Speed. "That boy I fought was all right. But he couldn't stop that left hook Coke Mason taught me."

Tim laughed and shook his head.

"You got 'em all working for you, haven't you, Regan?"

Regan shrugged and said to Speed:

"Tim thinks Coke's all build-up."

"That so?" said Speed. "Wait."

"Aw, hell," said Big Tim. "Well, I'm going back and watch the massacre. Get your boy out in good time, Regan."

He nodded to the two of them, and went down the corridor and out into The Coliseum. When he opened the door Speed and Regan heard the crowd booing loudly.

"Speed," said Regan, "come in the dressing-room with me. I'll talk to you, see, for Coke's benefit, and all you got to do is say 'yeah?' and 'that so?' like you was surprised, see?"

"Sure, I got you."

When they went in Coke was sitting on the edge of the rubbing-table talking to McNeil and Jeff. He was all ready for the go, but seemed pepless. McNeil was begging him to take some exercises and loosen up. But Coke sat staring at the floor.

"Hello, Coke," said Regan. "All set?"

"Yeah," said Coke.

"He needs a shot in the arm," said McNeil. "He acts like he was out all night."

"Hell," said Regan, turning away, "I guess that boy Larsen ain't so far wrong in what he says."

Coke paid no attention.

"That so?" said Speed.

"Yeah," said Regan. "I was just over talking to Larsen and he told me that he thought Coke was yellow and couldn't take it."

"Yeah?" said Speed.

"He said that his manager told him the Prince Pearl go was fixed, but that Coke was so scared of the nigger in spite of that, that it took everybody in his corner to make him wade in."

"Is that a fact?" said Speed.

Jeff had got slowly to his feet and was standing listening to Regan with his mouth open. McNeil watched Coke, who was beginning to pay attention to what Regan was saying.

"Yeah," said Regan. "Larsen told me that he was gonna knock Coke flat in two rounds so he'd be sure to get a whirl at Mike Shay. Of course I stood up for Coke. But Larsen said if I was wise I'd tie a can to him. Larsen bet two grand of his own dough on a knockout."

"Is that a fact?" said Speed.

Coke stood up and stared at Regan.

"You wait," he said. "I'll flatten that Dutchman if it's the last thing I ever do."

"Well, you better do it quick," said Regan, "because he's aiming to plaster you all over the ring the first round."

"Yellow, am I!" said Coke. "Yeah, I'm yellow. That goddam hunky or whatever he is'll think he got hit by a truck."

"I don't know," said Regan. "Maybe we better fight cautious, Coke."

"Like hell we will," Coke shouted. "Not a chance. This is one time I'm gonna fight to suit myself, George Regan. I'm gonna murder that guy. I'm gonna hit him so hard the referee'll feel it. Yellow am I? I never seen a foreigner yet I couldn't lick."

"What do you think, Mac?" asked Regan.

"Well," said McNeil, "this Larsen's about the best puncher in the division.

If he lands one of them rights, it'll be about over."

One of the Coliseum employees put his head in the door.

"Aw, you guys make me sick," said Coke, dancing on his toes.

"All right, Mr. Regan," said the employee.

"Coke," said Regan, "if you're dead set on fighting from gong to gong catch him with that left hook as soon as he steps in."

Coke pushed him away.

"I'll do my own fighting," said Coke. "All you guys do is carry tales, like a bunch of old women. I'm sick of the whole bunch of you."

He pulled on his bathrobe over his sweater and went out, followed by McNeil and Jeff.

Larsen was already in his corner. A big, slim, pale Swedish boy with a lot of curly, light hair and a bland smile. Coke climbed through the ropes and sat glaring across the ring at Larsen. Larsen smiled at Coke, then, noticing the glare, looked over Coke's head, turned and stared at the crowd, and then talked to his handlers. During the preliminaries, Coke never took his eyes from Larsen's face. Larsen seemed uncomfortable.

When Coke was introduced there was a ripple of applause, but Larsen got quite a hand. Coke turned to McNeil.

"Wait," he said.

"I'm with you, Coke," said McNeil. "I don't like foreigners no better than you do. Sock him for me."

Coke was so anxious to get at it that they could hardly keep him on his stool. When the bell rang he bounded into the middle of the ring, met Larsen, who came in cautiously, with a two-handed attack and drove him to the ropes. Larsen maneuvered himself out of a bad place and started throwing rights at Coke, who took two on the head and a third on the chin. He staggered and went to his knees. The referee began to count, but Coke leapt to his feet, and, crouching and weaving, banged into Larsen, landed a left hook to the short ribs and upset him with a right. Larsen bounded up immediately, but, puzzled by Coke's wide open attack, he ducked to the left from a left hook and caught a jarring right on the head. This hurt him and he tried to cover up, but Coke was on top of him, wasting his breath swearing, and ripping rights and lefts into him. Toward the end of the round Larsen went down. The bell rang while the referee was counting.

Coke swaggered to his corner and sneered at the crowd.

"Bunch of bums," he said to McNeil, "thought they was gonna get a chance to boo me."

"Shut up," said McNeil. "You ain't as fresh as you think you are."

Jeff and McNeil worked over Coke, while the crowd continued to roar. Coke glared across at Larsen, who was pale and groggy. But Larsen's handlers were working on him fast and when the warning whistle blew, his head had cleared.

Coming up for the second round, Larsen was cautious, but Coke bounded into the ring, his left low, weaving and bobbing. Larsen back-pedaled, ducked, sidestepped, and covered up, but Coke was on top of him, pumping punches. Suddenly, Larsen, fighting frantically, missed a right swing, which Coke swayed away from, but landed a left uppercut. Coke nearly went down, and before he could regain his balance, Larsen was banging him with body punches that smacked all over The Coliseum.

"My God," yelled somebody, "look at him taking 'em."

Coke did take them. He took them without staggering and in a moment began to return them blow for blow. The ring side had gone crazy. Newspapers sailed down from the gallery and there was a continuous uproar. Larsen began to fade. The pace was too fast for him. His handlers watched the time-keeper, and one of them kept shouting commands in Swedish. Larsen was driven to his knees by a right cross. He staggered to his feet and tried to cover up, but a hard left hook followed by a jarring right sent him down again. The referee dragged Coke to a neutral corner, then took up the count with the time-keeper. Larsen tried to prop himself up, but he was out. He turned over on his back and his right leg began to twitch. The bell rang at the count of nine.

Coke's legs were giving out, but he swaggered over to his corner and said to McNeil:

"One more punch and it's all over."

But he was tired and lay back with his eyes closed while Jeff and McNeil worked over him. McNeil looked across at Larsen. The Swede was lolling his head.

"The fight's over, Coke," said McNeil. "Your boyfriend'll never come up for number three."

When the bell rang for the third round, Larsen was still on his stool, unable to get up. The referee came over to Coke and held up his hand. The crowd roared.

Larsen sat shaking his head, trying to smile.

"Coke," said McNeil, "go over and mit the Swede."

"What," said Coke, "after the way he talked about me!"

"Listen," said McNeil, "go mit him. He never said nothing about you. That was just some of George's bull."

Coke stared at McNeil, then got to his feet and went across to shake hands with Larsen, who was coming round.

"Good fight, kid," said Coke. "You almost had me in the first."

Larsen took the proffered hand, mumbled a few words in what he thought was English, and looked at the floor. The crowd applauded loudly.

"Atta boy, Coke," yelled the gallery.

When Coke climbed out of the ring Regan grabbed him and hugged him.

"That's the best fight you ever fought, Coke, old kid," he said.

"Yeah," said Coke, pleased.

"Listen, Mac," said Regan, "take Coke back, rub him down quick, dress him up warm, put that big white sweater on him, see, and send him out here. I got a seat for him."

"Yeah," said Coke, "I want to get a slant at Mike."

The crowd stood up to cheer Coke as he went out, followed by his handlers.

VII

Coke, in his big white sweater, flushed from his shower and rub, came out into The Coliseum, followed by Speed. Joe Savella was just climbing through the ropes. He got a fair hand. Coke started down an aisle, and Speed, standing in a dark entry-way, shouted:

"Yea! Coke Mason!"

Coke was greeted by a roar, and Joe Savella, thinking the applause was for him, got up and mitted the crowd again. By the time Coke reached his seat, nearly everyone in The Coliseum was standing, cheering.

Mike Shay, the champion, ready to enter The Coliseum from a far entry-way, turned to his manager and said: "Where do they get that stuff!" And went back to his dressing-room. His handlers followed him, remonstrating with him, but his manager, a fussy, little man, went to hunt for the promoter, Tim Morgan.

"I got some friends," said Coke, sitting down beside Regan.

"Yeah," said Regan.

Big Tim Morgan, flushed and puffing, rushed over to Regan.

"Say, Regan," he shouted, "what the hell kind of a side-show are you running?"

"Why, what's wrong with you, Tim?" Regan demanded. "I can't help it if the boy's popular, can I?"

"You're the damnedest crook I ever seen," said Big Tim. "Don't try to kid me."

"Well," said Regan, "you ain't in the game for your health, are you? Match Coke with the champ and they'll stick up a sold out sign ten days before the fight."

The champion's manager came rushing over to Morgan.

"Mike went back to his dressing-room, Tim," he said. "I can't do nothing with him."

Regan burst out laughing.

When Morgan and the champion's manager had gone, Coke asked:

"What you pulling off, George?"

"Me!" said Regan.

Joe Savella was forced to wait over five minutes for the champion. The crowd grew impatient and began to stamp and whistle. Finally the champion climbed through the ropes, mechanically mitted the crowd, and nodded toward Joe Savella.

"This'll be one sweet fight," said Regan.

"I could lick 'em both," said Coke.

The championship match was a great disappointment to the crowd. Savella was cautious and forgot he had a right hand. The champion was sluggish and slow. The first five rounds were fought at such a slow pace that some of the customers got up and went home. The same old thing! Mike Shay letting somebody stay the limit and shading them at the final gong.

"Good Lord," said Coke, when they were coming up for the seventh round, "how'd that guy ever get to be champ."

"Well," said Regan, "he caught Tuffy Munn on a bad night and knocked him out, and he's been stalling ever since. He's not as bad as he looks, Coke. He's a slicker."

"Hell," said Coke, "let's go. This ain't no fun."

"Let's wait till it's over," said Regan.

In the middle of the eighth round someone in the gallery began to yell:

"We want Coke Mason! We want Coke Mason!"

The cry was taken up and passed from aisle to aisle.

At the end of the eighth round Mike sat in his corner glaring at the crowd.

"There you are, Coke," said Regan, "he's got to fight you now."

The last rounds of the fight were not quite so slow, but they were just as even. Mike speeded up in the last round and batted Joe around a little, but Joe, a good counter fighter, began to land a left to the body and Mike changed his tactics. When the final bell rang, the crowd yelled:

"Draw! Draw!"

But the referee held up Mike's hand. Joe ran over and shook hands with the champion.

"Where you guys appearing next week!" somebody shouted, and there was a prolonged jeering.

"Well," said Regan, "that's that."

Coke and Regan started out, but Coke's path was blocked by a bunch of men who wanted to shake hands with him. Even Morgan offered his hand.

"You got a good boy here," Morgan said to Regan.

"Well," said Regan, "it cost you a thousand bucks to find it out."

"That's right," said Morgan. "I'll send you a check, George."

"Never mind," said Regan, "send me an I.O.U. and keep the money. That's a thousand I won't have to put up when Coke fights the champion."

VIII

Jeff tore the papers apart one by one and handed the sport sheets to Regan, who read them and passed them on to Coke. In every paper except one Mike Shay was severely criticized for his choice of opponent. One article started with the caption: "Mike used to dodge Prince Pearl. Now dodges Coke Mason. Color no longer excuse."

"Well," said Regan, "all we got to do now is promise Mike the Woolworth Building and the Statue of Liberty and maybe he'll fight you."

"He's got to fight now," said Jeff.

"I'll fight him winner take all," said Coke.

"Don't keep repeating that," said Regan. "You know that's just plain bunk. Anyway, I've given it out to the press. If they print it, Mike'll turn a back flip."

"Well, I mean it," said Coke.

"Smart boy," said Regan, getting up and stretching. "Listen, you might just as well pipe down about that winner-take-all stuff. It's gonna be Mike Shay take all win or lose."

"Well," said Jeff, "what's the difference? Coke'll lick him, and then Coke can grab the gravy."

"Oh, sure," said Regan, "all Coke has to do is walk into the ring and wave at Mike and it's all over. You bird's seem to forget that Mike Shay's the champion. If he wasn't champion he'd be bowling over a boy a week. Mike's no dub, he's a hell of a good fighter. But when a guy gets to be champion, he thinks in terms of dollars, not fights."

"I can lick him," said Coke.

The telephone rang and Regan went to answer it. It was Riley and he was excited. Regan listened to him with growing irritation and then, at the end of the conversation, he hung up the receiver with a bang.

"That's good," said Regan. "That's one I didn't figure on."

"What's wrong?" asked Coke.

"Why, that slippery Irishman has signed to fight an over-weight match with Ray Bluhm in California."

Nobody said anything.

"Jeff," said Regan, "get that little wop bell-boy to get you a quart of gin."

"Say," said Coke, "you lay off that stuff, George. It's poison to you. Ain't you got no sense?"

"Shut up," said Regan. "I got to get some fun out of life."

PART III

I

Since Coke's knockouts of Larsen and Bat Cahill and his ten round decision over old Joe Savella he had become the most written-about prizefighter, outside of the heavyweight division, in New York. Every time he
fought he filled The Coliseum, and Tim Morgan was as careful of his wel-
fare as he had once been of Mike Shay's. The Savella fight, a boxing match
which developed during the final rounds into a toe-to-toe slugfest had
reached the front page. Newspaper men in deploring the commercialized
atmosphere of the prize-ring always singled out Coke Mason as the one
honest-to-God fighter in the business.

But Mike Shay was still elusive. He had a busted rib, or his manager
thought that he ought to go south, or he was matched for an overweight
go. The truth of the matter was, that Mike was putting on weight and finding it difficult to stay in the division in which he was champion. He was
trying to get high in the lightheavy class before he took a chance on losing his title.

Riley, Regan and Morgan kept after Mike's manager and reported all
their doings to the sports writers, who had no love for Mike Shay. Boxing
commissions in several states demanded that Mike Shay defend his title by
a certain date or lose it. But Mike crossed them all by getting banged up in
an automobile accident.

This was a front page item and when Regan read it, he exclaimed:

"Now I'm gonna throw my rabbit's foot away and hit for home. It's all
over now. He won't fight nobody for a year."

"Some people have all the luck," said Jeff.

"Well," said Coke, "sign me up with some other boys like Cahill and
Larsen. Mike'll have to fight me some time."

"Yeah," said Regan. "Listen, boy, you ain't no wonder-man. Some night
you're gonna take a high-dive and land on the canvas, and then it'll all be
over."

"Hell," said Coke, "I've licked the best boys in my division. Who you figure can knock me out when I never been better in my life?"

"Well," said Regan, "how many guys figured you to beat Prince Pearl?"

"That's all right," said Coke, "but if you think I'm gonna sit around and wait
for Mike Shay to come out of the hospital you got another think coming."

"All right, Coke," said Regan.

II

Regan, who was just recovering from a three day jag, was feeling pretty low, so Jeff and Coke took him to a picture-show. On their way in the head-usher recognized Coke and rushed over to him, offering his hand.

"Will you shake hands with me, Mr. Mason?" he said.

"Sure thing," said Coke, giving him a grip that made his hand tingle.

"I seen you fight Bat Cahill and I yelled so much I couldn't talk for two days."

"Yeah," said Coke, "it was a good go. Cahill's a sweet fighter."

The theatre manager came out of his office under the stairway, recognized Coke, and came over.

"How do you do, Mr. Mason," he said.

Coke shook hands with him.

"Howdy," he said.

"Did you buy a ticket to get in?" the manager inquired.

"Yeah," said Coke, jerking his thumb toward Regan and Jeff, who were standing a few yards away. "My manager and one of my sparring partners is right over there. Nice place you got here."

"Listen, Mr. Mason," said the manager, "don't you ever buy another ticket to get in here. Just tell the ticket-taker who you are. I'll arrange it for you. Bring a party if you want to. If the place is crowded, send the doorman into my office and we'll take care of you."

"Much obliged," said Coke, "that's sure mighty nice of you."

"Not at all. Not at all," said the manager.

"Well," said Regan, when Coke came over to them, "you're getting as important as a big-time bootlegger. But, listen, Coke, don't be mitting everybody that way. Just grin at 'em or something, or tell 'em you got a bad hand. That right of yours ain't any too tough anyway."

"Give me your hand," said Coke.

"No," said Regan, pulling away, "don't try that strong arm stuff on me. Just listen to what I'm saying, or you'll ruin your mit."

"Sure," said Jeff. "You better do what the boss says, Coke. Once you get your hands on the bum and you're done."

"I guess you better get a keeper for me," said Coke.

"It's a good idea," said Regan.

"Anyway," said Coke, "I got free passes from now on for shaking hands."

"Ain't that good!" said Regan. "The more money you got, the less you have to spend."

The picture was on when the usher led them down the aisle. Regan

wanted to sit in the back, Jeff wanted to sit in the middle, and Coke wanted to sit up front. Coke was the most obstinate of the three, so the usher
seated them in the sixth row. Coke immediately fell into a daze, there were
but two things, excluding women, that interested him: fighting and the
movies. Jeff was capable of following only the simpler sort of movie, and
as this one was full of plots and counterplots and dukes and revolutionists,
he grew confused and began to fidget. Regan went to sleep with his head
on Jeff's shoulder.

At the climax of the picture, when the heroine, a baby-faced blond, was
being attacked by the bad revolutionist, Coke turned to Jeff and said:

"Look at that dirty bum, Jeff. I wish I was there. If I wouldn't paste him
one."

"What's his idea?" asked Jeff.

Coke didn't answer and sat tensely waiting for the inevitable last minute
appearance of the hero, a democratic grand duke. At last the hero
appeared, sent the bad revolutionist to the mat with a wild uppercut that
a blind man could have dodged, took the heroine in his arms and dried her
glycerine tears. Coke sighed and relaxed.

"That's a cute blond," he said to Jeff, "but you ought to see my wife."

The lights came on, and a big orchestra in the pit began to play.

Regan woke up.

"Is the picture over?" he inquired.

"Yeah," said Jeff.

"Peach of a picture," said Coke.

"If you think so, I'm glad I missed it," said Regan.

"I didn't think it was so good," said Jeff. "I like comedies."

Regan sat up when the outer curtain rose, revealing a jazz-band surrounded by scenery. The band leader, a Jew with sleek hair, came out smiling and was greeted by loud applause.

"That boy's in a good racket," said Regan. "He gets mash notes by the
ton."

"Yeah, the kike!" said Jeff.

"Yeah," said Coke, "he don't even play a horn or nothing. Just stands up
there and waves a stick. I could do that."

"Sure," said Regan, "but you ain't got nice, pretty hair, and when you
smile you look like a rhinoceros."

"There you go," said Coke.

The stage-show was good. There was a roughhouse comedian who made
all three of them laugh and the chorus had a bunch of pretty legs and could
dance. Regan cupped his hands and held them to his eyes.

"Coke," he said, "what about the third from the right? Suppose we could
make a connection?"

"She's got black hair," said Coke. "I like blonds."

"That shows how dumb you are," said Regan.

"I ain't got no choice," said Jeff, laughing. "They all look good to me."

When the show was over Jeff and Regan went down into the Men's Room, and Coke stood in the lobby waiting for them. The manager came over to him, handed him a slip of paper, and said:

"Here's a year round pass, good for everyday except Saturday, Sunday, and Holidays. I thought I better fix you up right."

"Say," said Coke, "that's mighty nice of you. Thanks."

The manager smiled and went back into his office. Coke stood waiting for Regan and Jeff, watching the crowd. Someone called:

"There's Coke Mason!"

A lot of people stared. Coke shifted, flushed, and turned his back to the crowd. In the outer lobby some of the theatre employees were pulling down the signs and pictures, and putting up new ones. Coke, embarrassed, watched them. He read the signs then looked at the pictures. In one picture the hero and heroine, well-known screen-lovers, were being married and were surrounded by a group of extras. There was a blond in the foreground that caught Coke's eye. It was Rose. Coke stood staring at the picture, stupefied, then, turning, he ran back into the inner lobby to hunt for Regan.

Jeff and Regan were coming up the stairs from the Men's Room.

"George," cried Coke, "I seen Rose. I seen her plain as day. She looks great."

He grabbed Regan by the arm and began to pull him toward the outer lobby.

"Say," said Regan, "calm yourself, you big sap. People'll think you're crazy."

"Is she outside?" asked Jeff.

"No, in a picture," cried Coke. "She's in the movies."

He guided them to the picture and pointed Rose out. Jeff stared at her, then turned to stare at Coke.

"Gee!" said Jeff. "She's a looker."

Coke stood staring at the picture.

"Come on," said Regan.

"Say," said Coke, "let's go west, George. I'd like to see her once and talk to her. She's off of me. I know that. But I'd just like to talk to her once."

"Go get a cab, Jeff," said Regan.

Jeff went out to get a cab. Coke stood staring at the picture of his wife. She was facing the camera, but not looking into it, her head was tilted up, and she was smiling.

"She makes that star look like a bum, George," said Coke. "I want to see

her. George, can't we pack up and go west? We can get matches out there
and I can kind of look around."

Regan stood looking at the picture for a long time, then he said:

"Listen, Coke, I got a better idea. We'll write to her in care of the company she's with. If she ain't off of you, you know what I mean, she'll
answer your letter. If she don't want to see you no more, you'll never hear
from her. No use chasing a woman that don't want you, see, Coke?"

Coke took hold of Regan's arm.

"Gonna help me, are you, George?"

"Sure," said Regan. "I'll help you. If you want to see her that bad, why,
I'm for you."

"That's fine, George," said Coke. "Sure. You got the right dope. If she
don't answer, why, I'll just forget about it, that's all."

"Sure," said Regan, "that's the talk. We won't take no chances, see? We'll
put her name before she was married on the envelope and your name too."

"Yeah," said Coke. "I'd've never thought of that."

Jeff came in to tell them that he had a cab, and they went out. All the
way to the hotel Coke sat staring out the window at the traffic. Regan and
Jeff said nothing. When they got out of the cab, Jeff said:

"You sure that was your wife, Coke?"

"Why, course I'm sure. Don't you think I know my own wife?"

"Boy," said Jeff, "she's sure a looker."

Jeff went to a gymnasium two blocks away from their hotel to see if any
of the pugs were still there, and Coke and Regan went up to Regan's room.
Regan went to his writing-desk, got out some stationery, and said:

"There you are, Coke. Go to it."

"No," said Coke, "you write it. Nobody can read my writing and I can't
spell good. Rose's hell on spelling and that stuff."

Regan sat down at the desk and Coke pulled up a chair beside him.

"Well," said Regan, "what do you want me to say?"

Coke leaned back in his chair and began to twist his forelock.

"Dear Rose," he said, "I seen your picture...."

"'Saw,'" said Regan.

"Well," said Coke.

"Go on. Go on."

"Dear Rose," said Coke, "I saw your picture out in front of a movie house
in New York and I just got to wondering whether you was all right or not.
I hope you are as I would be worried something fierce if you wasn't as you
know. I am getting along fine and if I can ever get a match with Mike Shay
I will be the next middleweight champion of the world as I told you I
would be when you said I never would. Well, Rose, I would like to see you
and talk over old times with you as I get lonesome...." Coke hesitated and

sat looking at the floor. "Say, George," he said, "maybe I better not say noth-ing about being lonesome in case she's off of me for good, see?"

"Good idea," said Regan.

"All right. Cut that out. Just say, 'I would like to see you and talk over old times with you. If you want to write to me and tell me how you are feel-ing bad or good you can write me at....' Put the address in, George, and then say, 'yours respectfully, William C. Mason.'"

"O.K.," said Regan.

Regan finished the letter, handed it to Coke, and began to address the envelope. Coke read the letter and said:

"That letter don't sound none too friendly to me."

"Friendly enough," said Regan. "If she writes to you then you can open up."

"That's right," said Coke.

"Have 'em send up a bell-boy and we'll mail this letter right away," said Regan.

Coke called for a bell-boy, then sat staring at the floor. Regan sealed the letter, and sat waiting.

"Say," said Coke, "much obliged for helping me out, George. I couldn't get along without you."

Regan looked slightly uncomfortable, rubbed his chin and said nothing. When the bell-boy came in Regan handed him the letter and a tip, and said:

"Get a special on that and an air mail stamp and see that it gets out."

"Yes sir," said the bell-boy.

He went out. But Regan called to him and followed him out into the hall.

"Don't get no more liquor, George," called Coke.

Regan handed the bell-boy a dollar bill and took the letter from him.

"You mailed that letter, son," he said.

"Yes sir," said the bell-boy.

Regan slipped the letter into his pocket and went back into the room.

"Was you after him for liquor?" Coke demanded.

"Yeah," said Regan, "but he said he couldn't get me none till tomorrow. Trying to shake me down, but I wouldn't shake."

"Why don't you let up on the liquor, George," said Coke. "It'll beat you sure. A guy as smart as you ought to have better sense."

"That's my weakness," said Regan.

Coke sat looking at the floor.

"Coke," said Regan, "go hit the hay. It's late."

"All right," said Coke.

He got up, stretched, and aimed a few lefts at the air, then he went over and put his hand on Regan's shoulder.

"Goodnight, George," he said. "You're sure a good pal."

"Don't get sentimental," said Regan. "Beat it."

Coke went out. Regan sat for a long time looking at the wall, then he got up, took Coke's letter from his pocket, read it over a couple of times, then burned it and threw the ashes out the window.

III

Coke went three times to see the show his wife was in. She only appeared for a few minutes in one scene toward the end of the picture, but Coke sat through the whole performance, waiting for that moment. The third day the manager stopped him in the lobby and said:

"Mr. Mason, the head-usher tells me you've been here three times this half-week. You sure must be crazy about that picture."

"Well," said Coke, grinning, "my wife's in that picture, and you know I don't get to see her very much so I thought...."

He stopped and stood shifting.

"Has she got a part?" asked the manager.

"No," said Coke, flushing, "she's only an extra in this picture, but she tells me, I mean in her letters, see, that she's gonna get a good part pretty soon."

"That's fine," said the manager. "When she does I'll get the picture if I can and we'll get up a little story about it, eh?"

"Well," said Coke, flushing, "it won't be for some time yet, I guess."

"You just let me know," said the manager.

"Sure. I'll do that," said Coke.

When Coke got back to the hotel he went to Regan's room. Regan was playing poker with McNeil, Riley, Tim Morgan and a couple of Riley's friends. Regan was winning and giving everybody the laugh. Coke sat down to watch the game. Finally he whispered to Regan:

"You didn't hear nothing yet, did you, George?"

"Good Lord!" said Regan. "She ain't had time to write."

"Well," said Coke, getting up and looking over Regan's shoulder, "I thought maybe she might telegraph."

Regan turned and pushed Coke away.

"Don't look over my shoulder, you sap," he said. "Don't you know you'll break my luck?"

"Good boy," said Riley, "he won't hit any in-betweens now."

Coke watched the game for a while, then he sent down for a couple of papers, and lay on the bed, reading.

IV

Coke was sitting in a chair by the window, staring down into the street. Jeff, who had come in to talk with Regan about a match, addressed several remarks to Coke but got no answer. Jeff went over to Regan and whispered:

"What's the matter with Coke?"

"Don't pay no attention to him," said Regan, "he's just feeling low."

"Ain't he heard from his wife yet?"

"No," said Regan, raising his voice, "and he ain't likely to. I told him he'd never hear from her."

"Say," said Coke, getting up, "maybe she never got my letter. Maybe she ain't out in Hollywood no more."

"Oh," said Regan, "don't always be alibi-ing her. I'm getting sick of it."

Coke went back to his chair and sat looking out the window. Jeff and Regan sat talking about Jeff's semi-windup match with Kid Green. Jeff was a veteran and had at one time fought a lot of good men, but his hands had gone bad. Regan had got him the match with Kid Green, a good welter, trying to break into the middleweight division. Jeff lived in a state of perpetual excitement and couldn't think of anything else. Coke turned from his contemplation of the street, listening to Regan and Jeff for a few minutes, then got up and put on his hat.

"I'm gonna take a walk, George," he said. "I may go down to the gymnasium and I may not."

"Go to a show," said Regan.

"Want me to go along?" asked Jeff.

"No," said Coke.

He went out. Regan sat shaking his head.

"I don't know what I'm gonna do with that bird," he said. "Listen, Jeff, what makes guys such damn fools? I mean guys like Coke. He ain't exactly dumb, he's been around. He's a good fighter and now he's got the money. But you think he gives a damn about his money and all the fun he can have?"

"Well," said Jeff, "he's crazy about that kid of his."

"Sure," said Regan, "but ain't there plenty of other women just as good looking? Better looking. I see fifty better looking than Coke's wife every day on the street. It's too deep for me. You know I sicked that blond kid from Martin's Revue on him. And did she go for him! But it didn't do no good. He took her around and got a play, but it didn't take. Let me tell you something, Jeff, if I don't get that bird straightened out pretty soon he's gonna get walloped the next time he fights. When he's feeling low, he ain't got nothing in his legs. And when your legs don't work, you might just as well throw in the towel."

"Aw, he'll snap out of it as soon as the bell rings," said Jeff.

"Maybe," said Regan. "But that guy's in pretty bad shape. And the funny part of it is, he'd be in worse shape if he found his wife. That's the hell of it. She makes him jump through, see? Maybe that's what he likes, I don't know. But, Jeff, you're smart enough to see that no guy can be a champion with a darn fool wife hanging on to him and telling him when to breathe."

"Well," said Jeff, "I don't know."

"Yeah," said Regan, "I used to get a big kick out of the missus. She had about as much use for me as she had for a rattlesnake. She knew I was on to her. Why, when Coke was fighting his most important fights—a semi-windup on a two-bit card was big stuff for him then, see?—why, she was out riding with one of her part-time boyfriends. I'm telling you straight, Jeff. She even tried to make me, and I'm no beauty as you can see by taking a good look. Yeah, she tried to make me and I wouldn't make. That cooked it. From then on I might just as well've been home when she was around."

"Good looking kid," said Jeff.

"Fair," said Regan.

"Well," said Jeff, "you can't tell nothing about what a guy'll do. I used to know a guy that got so nuts about a dame, he bumped himself off when she wouldn't play."

"Well," said Regan, "them kind of guys are better off dead."

"Yeah," said Jeff.

"You know, Jeff," Regan went on, "the funniest part about the whole thing is, Coke thinks she's as nice as pie. Even when she's trying to make a guy right in front of him, he don't tumble. It's too much for me. I've even spilled it to him, Jeff, told him the truth. What does he do? He says if I wasn't his pal, he'd sock me."

"It's too bad," said Jeff.

"Well," said Regan, "I got to do some tall figuring."

"He'll snap out of it," said Jeff.

Regan got up to get a cigar and while he was on his feet, the phone rang. It was Riley and he was so drunk that he could hardly talk, but Regan finally caught what he was saying and began to dance. Jeff sat watching him.

"Hurray!" cried Regan, hanging up the receiver. "We're all set, Jeff. You heard me shout. We're all set. Mike Shay's been passed by the doctors and he wants to sign for a go with Coke."

"Yeah?" said Jeff.

"Oh, what a break," said Regan. "Sunday morning I'm going to early Mass."

"Is it straight?" asked Jeff.

"You bet it's straight. You never heard Urban Riley talk through his hat, did you? Not a chance. That mick's a wise bird. And get this, Jeff, he's gonna lay his roll on Coke."

"I'll lay some too," said Jeff.

Regan sat down at his writing-desk and began to write a letter.

"Jeff," he said, "go see if you can find Coke. Call up the gymnasium and if he ain't there, have him paged at the theatre."

"O.K.," said Jeff.

V

Coke came in grinning and put his arms around Regan.

"Well, George," he said, "I heard the good news."

"We finally landed, Coke," said Regan.

"Yeah," said Coke, "great stuff!"

"The newspapers did it," said Regan. "They kept razzing Mike till he got sick and tired of it. Newspapers are good for something after all, I guess."

"Sure," said Coke.

Coke sat down beside Regan, who was still working at his letter.

"What're you doing?" asked Coke.

"Writing to Mike's manager. Putting it in black and white, see? I'm gonna get my bid in quick. We might as well try to grab all we can. You know Mike."

"Well," said Coke, "get the match. That's all I care about."

Regan didn't say anything, but went on with his writing. For the next half hour Coke was kept busy answering the telephone and verifying the report that Mike Shay had actually decided to give him a match. Toward evening a couple of sport writers appeared and were asked to dinner by Regan. The hotel chef fixed them up a good meal and sent it up. Coke sat silent, while Regan discussed the fight with the newspaper men.

When they had gone, Regan said:

"Coke, there's something I want to take up with you now."

"All right," said Coke.

"It's like this," said Regan. "We're on big time now, we're gonna make a lot of dough, especially if you can lick Mike Shay, and from now on we got to do things business-like."

"Sure," said Coke.

"Well," said Regan, "you know, Coke, I been managing you for God knows how long and there ain't a scrap of paper between us, see? That's not business."

Coke looked at Regan in surprise.

"Ain't you satisfied, George?" he asked. "Don't I give you a fair shake?"

"Sure," said Regan, "but you're gonna be champion maybe, Coke, and we ought to have a contract or something. I even got Speed on a contract. We been pals, Coke, and all that, and I never felt like we ought to have a legal agreement or nothing like that. But we got to now. Hell, it don't look right."

"Well," said Coke, "it's all right with me. Fix up a contract and I'll sign it."

"That's the talk," said Regan.

He took a document out of his desk and handed it to Coke.

"Read that over, Coke, and see if it's O.K."

Coke took the document, turned it over and over, and finally began to read it, but the language was so complicated that he gave it up.

"Hell," he said, "I wouldn't read that thing for fifty bucks. If you say it's O.K., George, I'll sign it. But I don't get the idea."

"Just a legal agreement, that's all," said Regan. "Like all other managers have, see? It protects us both."

"Hell," said Coke, "ain't we pals?"

"Sure," said Regan. "But it's just good business, that's all. I don't mean we'd gyp each other if we didn't have a contract or nothing like that, but it's just the right thing to do, see?"

Coke shrugged and picked up a pen.

"Well," he said, "it's all the same to me."

He signed his name, screwing up his mouth as he wrote, then he handed the contract back to Regan and got up.

"Fine," said Regan. "Now Coke, I got a nice place picked out for you where you can train. Out on Long Island. By the time you start to train the weather'll be nice, and you can do all the roadwork you want to."

"Sure," said Coke. "I want to take off about six pounds."

"All right," said Regan. "Mac's going with us, and Jeff'll be one of your sparring partners. But I got to pick up a good fast lightweight in place of Speed. No more of that stuff for Speed."

"No," said Coke, "Speed'll have to watch himself. He's a comer, and getting socked by a guy my weight ain't healthy for him."

"I got my eyes on an Irish kid," said Regan.

Coke didn't say anything and sat flexing his fingers and looking at the floor. Regan turned back to his desk and began to write another letter.

"George," Coke said finally, "I guess I ain't gonna hear from Rose."

"Looks that way," said Regan.

"Mighty funny," said Coke. "You'd think she'd write, anyway."

"Coke," said Regan, "don't you know that other people ain't like you?

They get over things. You probably don't mean no more to her right now than I do."

"That's about it," said Coke.

Regan went on with his letter and Coke sat flexing his fingers and staring.

"You know," said Coke, "I guess I'm a pretty dumb guy. I should've knowed that a kid like her couldn't stay stuck on an ugly mutt like me. Yeah, sometimes I look in the mirror at my mug and I think to myself, 'how'd she ever put up with a mug like that?'"

"You ain't no beauty, that's a fact," said Regan.

"Well," said Coke, "I guess I may as well forget all about the missus and get me a regular girl."

Regan got to his feet and said:

"Listen, Coke, I'll make you a proposition. Come on in here."

Coke followed Regan into the bathroom. Regan took a quart of whiskey from the medicine-cabinet.

"See that?"

"Sure," said Coke.

"You know how well I like liquor," said Regan, "and you know what this quart of Canadian cost me. All right. Here's my proposition. You forget the missus and quit moping around and get down there to the training camp and work your tail off, and I'll quit the booze."

"You mean it?" exclaimed Coke.

Regan took the cork out of the bottle and poured the whiskey into the bathtub.

"All right, George," said Coke, "you're on."

They shook hands.

VI

Regan, Coke, Mike Shay and Mike's manager Little O'Donnell, were sitting at a table in Tim Morgan's office. The papers for the fight were all signed and a dozen or more flashlights had been taken. But the office was still crowded with newspaper men, big shot gamblers, amateurs and pugs.

Mike Shay was a nervous little man with dark auburn hair and freckles. His legs were slightly bowed and his shoulders bulky. His clothes were always too tight for him, and he walked like a sailor. He was thirty-four years old. From time to time he glanced at Coke and measured him.

"Well," said Little O'Donnell, "it's gonna be one of the fights of the century, and I'll bet any of you guys from the press that it'll outdraw any heavyweight match you name, barring a championship go."

"It ought to," said a reporter, "with the bums that's fighting in the elephant class."

"All the same," said Tim Morgan, "it's gonna be a big match, and anybody that comes to this fight'll see a fight. Shay and Mason are the two toughest guys in the business."

"Sure," said someone on the edge of the crowd, "they're matched so even it'll be a draw."

There was a laugh.

"That must be one of them fight experts," said the champion.

"Let's break it up," said Regan, getting to his feet.

"Just what I was thinking," said O'Donnell, also getting up.

Mike came over to Coke and awkwardly offered his hand.

"Glad I met you, Mason," he said.

"Thanks," said Coke. "Same to you."

"I still got a kink in my leg from that automobile accident," said Mike, "but it's working out."

"Glad to hear it," said Coke, slightly embarrassed. "I been having some trouble with my legs myself."

"The legs go first," said Mike.

"Yeah," said Coke.

Two reporters followed Regan and Coke out to Coke's car.

"Say, Mason," said one of them, "I got a bet on you already."

"Well," said Regan, "start spending it right away."

The reporter laughed.

"Some guy give me two to one."

"Take all you can get at that," said Regan, "and you'll get rich."

Regan got into the driver's seat and Coke climbed in beside him.

"Well," said Coke, "all we got to do now is wait till June."

"Wait, hell!" said Regan. "You got to train hard for this fight, Coke. Mike's a limit fighter. Never been knocked out in his life."

"Well, have I?"

"No," said Regan, "but Mike ain't got no iron jaw like you got. He's clever."

"He don't look clever to me. He just looks like a little gashouse mick."

"The Irish are the best fighters in the world," said Regan. "My mind'd be a lot easier if you had a little Irish blood."

VII

Coke was sluggish and generally in a bad humor. Even the sport writers noticed this and commented on it. Coke worked with effort, seemed to get no pleasure out of it, and when he wasn't working he spent his time lolling around staring into space. As a rule he sparred indifferently with Jeff Davis, sometimes taking them on the side of the head or flush on the mark without attempting to counter. Buddy Dugan, the little Chicago lightweight, would rip into him and get away without a scratch, and Ruby Hall, the big negro middleweight, who at first was scared of Coke began to think that in a fair go he could lick him.

But one afternoon Regan brought a headgear out and made Coke put it on. Coke had never worn a headgear in training before and thought it was effeminate. Regan didn't want him to go into the ring against a slicker like Mike Shay with a cut over his eye, so he insisted that Coke put it on. Coke yielded and climbed through the ropes glaring. Ruby came out to meet him, grinning and shuffling, and immediately landed a left lead. But Coke stepped inside a right, sent a left hook to the body and banged Ruby on the side of the head with a right. Ruby was stunned.

"My God," said Ruby, "you got concrete in them gloves!"

After that he boxed cautiously and seldom led. Coke took it easy with Buddy Dugan, who circled around him, crouched, rushed in with rights and lefts and got away. But Coke was still surly, and when Jeff climbed through the ropes for the final rounds, he sailed into him and had him groggy at the end of two minutes.

Regan put his arm around Coke and led him into the dressing-room, where McNeil was waiting to give him a rub-down.

"You looked like a champion today," said Regan. "Keep it up. You scared that big shine stiff. He probably won't be no good to us from now on."

"I just pasted him a little," said Coke. "Some day I'll hit that shine with all I got and then watch."

"Well," said Regan, "all I want you to do is to keep going the way you are. You been soldiering on me, Coke. Don't you forget that I ain't touched a drop of liquor since we made our agreement."

"Well," said Coke, "a guy can't be his best every day. Sometimes I don't feel like doing nothing."

Coke got used to the headgear finally, and in a little while he was as sluggish as before. Several of the sport writers confided to Regan that they thought Coke's legs were giving out. Regan told Coke. But Coke shrugged. The same sport writers, friends of Regan, told him confidentially that

Mike Shay was in wonderful shape, never looked better in his life, and was already talking about what he intended to do after he beat Coke. The newspapers carried accounts of Mike's difficulty in rounding into shape due to his automobile accident, but the sport writers told Regan that this was all front. Mike didn't want to be a big favorite to win as he was going to bet heavily on himself. Regan told Coke that Mike said that he would win by a knockout in three rounds.

"He'll lose by one," said Coke, but didn't seem especially interested.

Regan, though worried about Coke, played the match up and got a lot of publicity. Coke had saved somebody from drowning, or Coke had knocked out two sparring partners in three minutes, or Coke was going to travel in Europe after his victory over the champion, or Coke was contemplating putting on weight and getting into the heavyweight tournament, or Coke had had an offer from the movies, or Coke had been visited by a committee of prominent citizens of Cleveland, Ohio, who wanted him to open their new coliseum, or Coke had been invited to make a tour of the world in the yacht of a millionaire, not named.

This last stunt was to offset Mike Shay's popularity with "Society." For some reason Mike Shay was backed by some of the so-called Four Hundred. They went to see him train, took him out to lunch, had their pictures taken with him, and made his training-camp a sort of social center. This was great publicity for Mike, and his manager, Little O'Donnell, made the most of it. Of course O'Donnell had some difficulty with his employees as they were not conversant with social usage and were apt to pick their noses in public and eat with their hats on. But Mike himself passed for "refined," principally because he hardly ever opened his mouth.

Coke's camp was quite the opposite. Bums from all over the world turned up there, ex-safe blowers, now prominent bootleggers, took rooms in a nearby hotel and scandalized the proprietor and his other guests. Gate-crashers, bunco men, small time and big shot gamblers, a noted gunman from Chicago, and a scattering of burlesque comedians of the old school could be seen sauntering through the village streets. "Society" was represented by the upper stratum of theatrical folk, who, though not in the Blue Book, were every bit as snobbish as the Park Avenue variety and deplored the atmosphere of Coke's training-camp. One movie actress got herself some free publicity by claiming that she had been insulted by one of Coke's henchmen. But the affair blew over.

Ten days before the fight, Tim Morgan ran an announcement in the paper that The Coliseum was nearly sold out. There was a scramble for tickets, a couple of scalpers, working from the inside, made a big haul, some outlaw scalpers were arrested and fined, Tim Morgan made the front page with a paragraph, and in four days The Coliseum was actually sold

out. Tim, relieved of all anxiety, now divided his time between the two
training-camps, getting in the way, giving unnecessary advice, and having
his picture taken with the two fighters, and, when he was lucky, with one
or another of the Four Hundred.

But the sell-out didn't seem to interest Coke, who sparred listlessly and
worked without interest. Regan tried dodge after dodge to no purpose.
Coke remained listless and bored.

One day Speed De Angelo, who was nursing a sprained wrist, turned up
and went into a conference with Regan behind closed doors. Coke got
curious and went over to the gymnasium to talk with McNeil. McNeil and
Jeff were sitting on the rubbing-table, talking.

"Say," said Coke, "what's Speed De Angelo doing here?"

"Talking business with the boss," said McNeil.

"Yeah," said Jeff. "Speed's climbing. If he wins his next two fights he's
gonna get a shot at the championship."

"Yeah," said McNeil, "Willy Strapp's willing to give him a go if he can lick
Red Stuart."

Coke sat swinging his feet.

"Coke," said McNeil, "you know what Regan said to me this morning?"

"About me?"

"Yeah. He said you was turning out to be just what Mike Shay said you
was. A flop."

"He did, hunh?" demanded Coke, getting to his feet.

"Yeah," said McNeil, "and that ain't all. He said he was losing interest in
you on account of the way you was training. He said he had a real boy now
and he didn't care whether you won or lost."

"What do you mean, a real boy?"

"Why," said McNeil, "Speed De Angelo. He's had six straight knockouts."

Coke went out of the dressing-room without speaking.

"Maybe that'll bring him to," said McNeil.

Jeff shrugged and got up.

"He ain't half what he used to be," he said. "I never seen a guy go back
so fast. His legs ain't no good."

"Good as they ever were," said McNeil. "It's in his head."

At four o'clock Regan came out of his office and began to hunt for Coke.
But nobody knew where he was. Regan drove into the village and went to
the hotel, but Coke hadn't been there. All the gamblers, begging for the
latest news, tried to detain Regan, but he pushed them away and went out.

At five o'clock Jeff found Coke sitting alone on the beach, drawing pictures in the sand.

"Hello, Jeff," he said.

Jeff sat down beside him.

"What you hiding for, Coke," he inquired.

Coke shrugged and sat staring at the water.

"I just got sick of that camp and all the bums hanging around and everything. I'll be goddam glad when this fight's over."

"Hell," said Jeff, "I wish I was in your shoes, I wouldn't be crabbing. Fight your best and you'll be the next middleweight champion."

"Sure," said Coke. "But you know I get low when I'm training."

"So does a lot of guys," said Jeff. "That ain't nothing."

Coke sat there mussing up the sand.

"Well," said Jeff, "it's time for the dinner-gong. Let's get going."

"All right," said Coke.

Getting to his feet, he followed Jeff back to the training-camp. The dinner-gong had just rung and the men at the camp, including Regan and Speed, were already seated. Speed looked sleek and prosperous. He had on a double-breasted, blue serge coat, gray trousers and spats. His black hair was plastered with pomade, and he was flashing a diamond ring. Regan and Speed sat together and paid no attention to Coke when he came in. Coke stared at them, then walked through the dining-room into the kitchen. Lasses, the cook, grinned when he saw Coke.

"Hello there, champ," he said.

"Hello, Lasses," said Coke. "Say, put my grub over here on the window-sill, will you? I think I'll eat out here."

"Sure," said Lasses, "but it's pretty hot up against that stove."

"That's all right," said Coke.

Lasses fixed his dinner, then began to fill the plates which Curly, the waiter, carried into the dining-room.

When Coke had finished his meal, he went out on the back-porch and sat on the steps. Far over the treetops he could see the ocean, dancing with light. He felt lonesome.

In about a half an hour Regan came out and sat down beside him.

"Why the lone-eagle stuff?" he inquired.

Coke turned and stared at Regan.

"Why," he said, "you guys was so damn busy you didn't see me come in. I didn't want to crowd you none."

"I thought you come in the back way," said Regan.

"Yeah," said Coke, "you were sure busy all right."

"Well," said Regan, "Speed and I have got a lot of stuff to talk over."

"Say," said Coke, "are you managing me, or ain't you?"

"I guess you're managing yourself," said Regan, getting up. "You're a pretty big guy now, I guess, and you ought to know your own business. But Speed wants my advice, see? He don't figure he can do the fighting and the managing at the same time."

Regan went in, slamming the door.

"George," called Coke, but Regan paid no attention.

VIII

Coke began to improve steadily. He not only went through his routine without a word of protest, but when he climbed into the ring for a round with Ruby Hall, or Dugan, or Jeff, he danced on his toes, couldn't get enough, and grinned all the time.

"He sure is a fighting man," said Ruby.

The sport writers noticed the change and wrote to their papers that Coke was in perfect condition for the fight, and that the odds of 8 to 5 with Mike Shay favored were paper odds and didn't mean a thing. Regan kept up his steady bombardment of the newspapers, and column after column were devoted to the doings of Coke Mason, contender. Mike Shay announced that he would win by a knockout, but very few believed him. The opinion of the majority of experts was that Mike Shay would shade Coke and retain his title. Seventy-five per cent of the wise money was bet that way. The hunch betters and the heart betters and the chronic short end betters were all on Coke. The only big shot gambler to bet a large amount on Coke was Urban Riley.

John Keen, the New York fight expert, wrote the following:

"The champion is an 8 to 5 favorite over the contender, and rightly. The champion is one of the cleverest fighters in the business and while he is not a hard puncher and will probably not upset the rugged Mason, he will win the fight on points. Mason is a hard puncher and a real gong-to-gong fighter, but, while he has shown occasional flashes of boxing, his style is such that the champion will outpoint him handily. Barring accidents, Mike Shay will retain his championship."

Regan read Keen's summing up to Coke, who grinned.

"That's about right I guess," said Coke. "Barring accidents, Mike ought to win."

"Yeah," said Regan, "but I'm afraid that Mike's gonna accidentally run into a left hook."

"Wouldn't that be too bad?" said Coke.

PART IV

I

When Jeff, who was sitting on the porch, saw Regan get out of the automobile, he jumped to his feet, ran down the steps, and grabbed him by the arm.

"I been watching for you," he said.

Regan glanced at Jeff, who seemed excited.

"Now what?" he demanded.

"Why," said Jeff, "Coke's gone nuts. Nobody can do nothing with him. He just dances around and yells and grins fit to kill."

Regan looked puzzled.

"Well," he said.

"He got a letter," said Jeff.

"Goddam it," shouted Regan, "didn't I tell you and Mac never to give that guy any mail till I looked it over?"

"Yeah," said Jeff, "I know what you're driving at, George. And at first Mac thought maybe it was from his wife. But...."

"Where'd he get it?" Regan demanded. "I got the morning mail myself, and it ain't time for the afternoon mail."

"A newspaper guy give it to him. He told me it was sent to Coke care of his office."

Regan took off his hat and mopped his forehead.

"Well," he said, "who's it from?"

"I don't know," said Jeff. "He won't tell us nothing."

Regan nodded his head and laughed sarcastically.

"Ain't that a break!" he said. "You guys must be dumb as hell. That letter's from his wife sure as we're here. I thought he'd hear from her soon as he got up in the A-one class."

Regan sat down on the porch in a rocking-chair and mopped his forehead. Jeff sat on the steps and looked out across the water.

"Did you see the postmark?" asked Regan.

"No."

"Well," said Regan, "I hope to God she's in California."

Coke came out on the porch, pulling on his coat. He had just washed and shaved, and his face shone. He was wearing a high stiff collar, which was punishing him, and he had put water on his hair in an attempt to plaster it down, but it stuck up in the back like a rooster's comb.

Regan took one look at him, then turned away in disgust.

"George," cried Coke, "I heard from the missus. She's right here in town. She was sick, poor kid. She had the flu, and she's still laid up, but she's getting all right. You hear me! She's getting all right, good as ever. And she wants to see me, George, ain't that great? She ain't off of me at all. She's sorry cause she went away, and she says she's missed me all the time, only she was too proud to write me. That's the missus for you."

"Well," said Regan, "take your checkbook along."

"Aw, George," said Coke, "don't talk that way. Read this letter."

He offered the letter to Regan, but Regan pushed it away.

"Keep your private business to yourself," he said.

Coke stuffed the letter back into his pocket and started down the stairs.

"Wait a minute," said Regan. "Where you going?"

"Why," said Coke, "I'm going after the missus. She's down in some God-awful rooming house. I'm gonna put her up in some swell hotel."

"Listen," said Regan, "why don't you let me take care of that? And you stick around here and meet people."

"Not a chance," said Coke. "Anyway, the missus wouldn't like it, George. Not after she swallowed her pride that way. She'd think I wasn't acting right."

"Yeah?" said Regan. "Well, she ought to've thought about that before she packed up and left you."

"Aw, George," said Coke.

"Yeah," said Regan, "if it was some guys they'd tear the letter up and forget about it."

"Not me!" said Coke.

"Right on top of this fight too! I suppose now you'll want to sleep with her and knock your training to hell."

"No," said Coke, flushing.

"Well," said Regan, "if you're dead set on going, why, I'm going with you. We'll fix her up at some downtown hotel, and leave her there. After the fight you do as you please."

Regan got up and Coke put his arm around him.

"All right, George," he said, "I'll do whatever you say. But you know, after getting that letter, I had to go see her, poor kid."

"Well," said Regan, "if it was me, she could go hang."

"Aw, George," said Coke, grinning, "don't talk that way. You're all steamed up over that fight, that's all. I'll do whatever you say, George. You boss the job, only I got to see the missus. Come on, let's go."

Regan turned to Jeff, who was sitting with his mouth slightly open.

"Jeff," he said, "tell McNeil to go right ahead with meals and everything.

I don't know when we'll be back. And another thing, no leaks to this. If this gets out, I'll skin somebody alive. You tell White that I got a big story for him. A big human interest story for him, see? But if you give him any idea what it is, I'll shoot you personally."

"You gonna write the missus up!" cried Coke.

"Sure," said Regan, "it'll get you a lot of good publicity, and all the girls'll say, 'God, ain't he the sweetest thing!' You sap!"

Coke climbed into the driver's seat but Regan said:

"Slide over, boy. I'll do the driving. You think I want you to climb a pole two days before the fight?"

Coke obeyed.

II

When Regan stopped at the address Coke's wife had given in her letter, Coke said:

"Boy, what a neighborhood!"

"Hell," said Regan, "this ain't so bad. Cheap boarding-houses. Don't try to kid me. You never seen the inside of a hotel till two years ago, and your missus used to live over a plumbing shop."

Coke laughed, jumped out of the car, ran up the steps and knocked at the door. Regan, muttering to himself, locked the car, climbed out wearily, and followed Coke. An old woman in a wrapper opened the door.

"I'm Coke Mason, the prizefighter," said Coke. "Is my wife here?"

The landlady smiled, very friendly, and nodded.

"Yes sir, Mr. Mason. I'll take you right up to her. We sure been hearing a lot about you, Mr. Mason."

"Yeah?" said Coke.

"Yes sir," said the landlady, leading the way up the stairs, "your little wife has been telling us all about you. How the two of you had an awful quarrel and busted up. Your wife's a mighty sweet little woman, Mr. Mason."

"You bet," said Coke.

Regan followed silently.

Rose's room was in the back of the house on the third floor. The halls were dark and dirty, and the windows hadn't been washed for years. The landlady apologized for the looks of the place, saying she couldn't afford enough help and her rheumatism kept her from doing very much work.

"Uh hunh!" said Regan, in a bad humor.

The landlady knocked at Rose's door.

"Come in," said a voice.

Coke turned to Regan.

"That's the missus!"

He hastily took out his bill-fold and handed the landlady a dollar bill.

"Thank you, thank you," said the landlady. "The missus'll tell you about the rent."

"You can bet on that," said Regan.

The landlady pushed open the door and Coke went in. Rose was sitting in a chair by a dark court window. She was wearing a faded red kimono, and she had a blanket across her knees. Her face was thin and there was a sickly pallor under her heavy make-up. But her blond hair was carefully waved and arranged, and her eyes were mascara-ed.

Coke turned, blinked, and stared at Regan, who said:

"Well, kid, here we are."

Rose looked at them without speaking, then her lips began to twitch, and, putting her hands over her face, she sobbed. Coke ran over to her, bent down, and put his arms around her.

"I been awful sick, Coke," she said. "I nearly died."

Coke just stood there with his arms around her.

Regan went out and shut the door behind him. The landlady was still in the hall. She looked slightly embarrassed when Regan came out.

"Say, sister," said Regan, "how much does the kid in there owe?"

The landlady wrinkled her brow.

"She owes me four weeks rent," she said, "that's forty-eight dollars. And for meals I give her, poor kid. About ten dollars for meals."

"Twelve bucks a week for that room!" said Regan.

"Private bath," said the landlady. "I've got more."

"All right," said Regan.

He took out his billfold, counted out fifty-eight dollars, and handed it to the landlady.

"Give me a receipt in full," he said.

"Yes sir," said the landlady. "When you come downstairs I'll have your receipt ready."

"Listen," said Regan, "does the kid owe any more bills that you know about?"

"Well," said the landlady, "she owes a doctor a big bill, and the drugstore over on the corner has been dunning her for a couple of weeks. I don't know of nothing else."

Regan took out a card, wrote an address on it, and handed it to the landlady.

"If anybody comes around here looking for her tell 'em to get in touch with me and I'll pay the bills. I'm Mason's manager."

"Yes sir," said the landlady, "thank you, sir."

She started down the stairs and Regan knocked at Rose's door and went in.

Coke was sitting on a chair facing his wife. When Regan came in Coke turned his back to him and blew his nose. Rose had been crying and the mascara had made streaks on her face.

"Well, kid," said Regan, "been coming tough, eh?"

"Yeah," said Rose. "I was getting along all right, but I got the flu."

"Show business?"

"Yeah. In a chorus."

"Only think," said Coke, "she never got my letter."

"I wish I had," said Rose. "You'd sure have heard from me."

"The career stuff ain't paying dividends," said Regan.

"You haven't got a chance in Hollywood unless you're on the inside," said Rose. "Same as here, only worse."

"Coke's been batting 'em over," said Regan.

"Yeah," said Rose, "so I see by the papers. I wasn't going to bother Coke till after his fight, but I got so lonesome I didn't know what to do."

"Me, too," said Coke.

"I fixed up all the bills," said Regan.

"Much obliged, George," said Rose.

"Hell!" said Coke. "Why didn't you leave that to me?"

"You got your hands full," said Regan.

Coke grinned, and, getting to his feet, he picked Rose up and sat down holding her on his lap.

"He ain't changed a bit," said Regan.

Rose put her arms around him.

"Still my sweet boy," she said.

"I bet you don't weigh a hundred pounds," said Coke.

"Well," said Rose, "you don't get fat on graham crackers and milk."

"You wait," said Coke, "I'll fatten you."

Regan got up and began to walk around. When his back was turned Rose kissed Coke.

"Honey, what did you want to run away for?" asked Coke.

"I was just a kid, Coke," said Rose. "I didn't know any better."

"Well," said Regan, "have you two screen-lovers made up your minds what you're gonna do yet?"

"Why, sure," said Coke. "I'm gonna take Rose down to the Touraine and get her a suite."

"Just a room," said Rose.

Regan rubbed his chin and stared at Rose.

"No sir," said Coke. "Coke Mason's wife is gonna have a suite. Hell, I got money. Let me spend it."

"No, big baby," said Rose. "A room's all I need. So that's settled."

Coke looked at Regan.

"You talk to her, George."

"Kid," said Regan, "if this guy wants to spend his money, let him spend it."

"No," said Rose.

"Well, what do you do in a case like that?" Regan asked Coke.

"The only thing is," said Coke, "I want her to be satisfied."

Rose laughed.

"Say," she said, "I been satisfied with a lot less for a long time. Yet let me do things my own way and it'll be all right."

"Good," said Regan. "Sounds to me like you've learned some sense."

"Well," said Rose, "I learned a lot of things I never knew before."

"Good," said Regan. "Now you two birds untangle for a minute and listen to me, because I'm running the show till the fight's over. We'll fix you up at the Touraine, kid, and see that you get everything you want. I'll get Coke's doctor to come down and give you the once over and see what you'd better do till you get on your feet again. We'll get you a maid and fix things so you can buy the clothes you need...."

"Don't I need them though," said Rose, smiling.

"Well, you don't buy no ermine on forty a week," said Regan.

"Thirty-five," said Rose.

"All right," said Regan. "But get this. Take a good look at your sweet boy because you ain't gonna see him no more till the doctor brings him to, after Mike Shay gets through pasting him."

Rose laughed and patted Coke's face.

"He'll never whip my boy," she said.

"You tell 'em," said Coke.

Regan turned his back and lit a cigar. Rose took Coke's face between her hands and kissed him repeatedly.

"Wait a minute," said Regan, turning. "You're putting bad ideas in that boy's head. I'll have to lock him up at night."

"Oh, no," said Rose. "I'm not feeling any too frisky."

Regan laughed loudly and hit Coke on the back.

"Well," said Regan, "do you feel strong enough to get your stuff packed up and go down town with us?"

"Do I!" exclaimed Rose, getting up. "I'd leave this place if I had to crawl."

"Don't blame you," said Coke.

"Well," said Regan, "I've lived in worse."

"So have I," said Coke, "but not lately."

"Coke," said Rose, "go over in the closet and get my bags."

"I'll tell you," said Coke. "Just leave all this stuff here. Bags and all. We'll get all new. Just put on a dress and take a toothbrush."

"All right," said Rose. "That's a notion. I can't get used to the idea that I got money. I'll give the landlady all my stuff."

"And snap it up," said Regan. "I want to get this bum back for a light workout before I put him to bed. Tomorrow he rests."

"First," said Rose, "I want a decent meal."

III

Regan lay back in his chair and lit a cigar. McNeil sat on the table, whittling, and Jeff was looking at the pictures in the Police Gazette. In an adjoining bedroom, Coke was snoring.

"Well," said Regan, "Mac, you know I don't talk wild, but, listen, tomorrow night you're gonna be the trainer of a world champion."

"Maybe," said McNeil.

"No maybe about it," said Jeff. "I never seen Coke in better shape."

"You said it," said Regan. "And tomorrow night he can fight his own way. I ain't gonna tell him a thing. He'll left hook that Irishman to death."

"Only thing I'm afraid of," said McNeil, "is that Mike'll be smart enough to keep away from him. He's the smartest fighter in the business. I've watched him fight twenty fights. He changes his pace, and that's tough to begin with. He fights slow the beginning of one round and speeds up at the end, then, the next round, he comes out of his corner a-boiling and slows down toward the end. He runs his fights to suit himself. He ain't been extended for over a year."

"Well," said Regan, "he didn't look very good against Joe Savella."

"Just what I been telling you," said McNeil. "He fought Joe to suit himself. He stalled through most of the fight and speeded up the last three rounds. All he wanted was a decision."

"That's all he wants tomorrow," said Regan, laughing. "Can you picture Mike Shay knocking Coke out?"

"No," said McNeil, "Coke's the toughest boy fighting. But don't forget that Larsen knocked him down."

"Yeah," said Regan, "but he bounced up and the Swede thought the roof fell on him."

"All right," said McNeil. "I got a little money on Coke, and I'm for him. But I don't want you guys to get disappointed. I've seen too many near champions get decisioned by Mike Shay."

Outside it began to blow, they could hear the waves on the beach, and in a little while it was raining, a steady, monotonous drumming on the roof.

"Tim Morgan's luck," laughed Regan. "Some of the newspaper guys couldn't find nothing else to kick about, so they started razzing Tim for holding an indoor show in June. There's the answer," he concluded, indicating the rain by a jerk of his thumb.

"Yeah," said Jeff, "cats and dogs."

"That reminds me," said Regan. "Speaking about newspapers, wait till you read the story about Coke and his missus that I gave White exclusive. It's a dandy."

"How about the missus, anyway?" McNeil inquired.

"Well," said Regan, "she's been a pretty sick girl and she's kind of tame right now. She acts like she's learned some sense. But you never know."

"She's a bear for looks," said Jeff. "I wish I had a wife like that."

McNeil and Regan laughed. Coke put his head in the door. His hair was standing on end and his face was swollen with sleep.

"Say," he said, "it's raining."

"Well, what of it?" Regan demanded.

"Nothing. How long have I been asleep?"

"About three hours."

Coke stood scratching his head.

"Say," he said, "I think I'll call up my wife. It's only about one o'clock, ain't it?"

"You go back to bed, Coke," said Regan. "The doctor said he wanted the missus to get a lot of sleep."

"Oh, yeah," said Coke, "I forgot."

Coke shut the door, then he opened it.

"George," he called, "I'm hungry. Can't you get Lasses to cook me something?"

"How about soup?" asked Regan. "We got some left. Mac'll get it for you."

"All right," said Coke.

Coke went back and put on a sweater and a bathrobe, then he came out to sit with them. Mac and Jeff went out to the kitchen to get Coke's soup.

"How you feeling, Coke?" asked Regan.

"A-one," said Coke. "I feel like a champion."

"That's just what you're gonna be."

"George," said Coke, "I want to thank you for being so nice to the missus when you don't like her. You're a good pal, George."

"Never mind," said Regan.

There was a screech of brakes on the lawn outside.

"Who the hell you suppose that is?" Coke demanded. "Maybe it's the missus."

He got to his feet. Someone knocked at the door and Regan went over to open it. Riley came in followed by Ben Mandl and Bat Cahill, the middleweight.

"Hello, Coke," said Riley. "What you doing up this hour of night?"

"I got hungry," said Coke. "I woke up hungry."

"What do you guys want?" asked Regan.

They all sat down at the table.

"Well," said Mandl, "we're all betting on your boy and we came out for a chin."

"You betting on Coke, Mandl?" asked Regan.

"Yeah," said Mandl, flourishing a cigar to display his big diamond ring, "I switched."

"Me, too," said Cahill, grinning at Coke.

McNeil and Jeff came in with Coke's soup and set it down on the table. Coke began to eat, paying no attention to the others.

"Well," said Regan, "what did you want to come out here at this time of night for?"

"We heard a rumor," said Mandl.

"I don't know what you mean," said Regan, "but get this: Coke's fighting on the square like he's always fought, and if Mike Shay wins it'll be because Coke ain't good enough to whip him."

"That's all right," said Mandl, "but how about his hands?"

Coke looked up.

"Whose hands?" he demanded.

"Your hands all right?" Riley inquired.

Coke held his hands up and smacked them together, then he doubled up his fists and said:

"Anybody want to see how good they are?"

Cahill came over and examined them, then he began to laugh.

"Can you beat it!" he said.

Mandl and Riley burst out laughing.

"Oh, what a break," said Mandl.

"Say," said Regan, "what's the idea of the vaudeville act? If you guys got any cracks to make, make 'em!"

"Well," said Riley, "the report's out that Coke busted one of his hands, but that he ain't gonna say nothing about it, but just favor it as much as he can on account of the money that's up."

"Which hand?" asked Regan, quickly.

"His right," said Mandl.

Regan turned to Coke.

"Things are sure coming our way," he said.

"Yeah," said Mandl, "some of the guys betting on Coke are panicky and have started hedging. Mike's two to one downtown."

Regan took out his checkbook, wrote a check and handed it to Riley.

"Bet all of that, Urban," he said.

"Sure," said Riley.

"Half of that's mine," said Coke.

"All right," said Regan.

"George," said Riley, "I'll cash this check for you and bet the money. We don't want a check this size with your name on it floating in."

"All right," said Regan.

Cahill got up and was followed by Riley and Mandl.

"We'll be going," said Cahill. "Much obliged for giving us the dope."

"Sure," said Regan, "but don't let it go no farther."

"Don't worry," said Mandl.

They went out. Regan turned to McNeil, who was smiling.

"Well, Mac," he said, "what do you think?"

"I think Coke's in."

Coke finished his soup and got up.

"Favor that right tomorrow night, Coke," said Regan, "and you'll have an ace in the hole."

"I got you," said Coke.

Coke went back to his bed and in a few minutes they heard him snoring.

IV

When Coke entered The Coliseum from the aisle near his dressing-room the crowd got to its feet and roared. The champion came in at the same time, in order, Regan said, to get in on the ovation. They climbed through the ropes together. The ring swarmed with officials, newspaper men, and cameramen.

"Looks like a convention," said Mike, smiling.

"Yeah," said Coke.

After the pictures had been taken, the fighters interviewed, and the announcements made, Leo Harness, the referee, climbed through the ropes, superintended the tying on of the gloves, then went into a neutral corner for a conference with the judges. Bud Shay, Mike's brother, and one of his seconds, said to Coke:

"Nice turn out, Mason."

"Yeah," said Coke.

When Coke went to his corner, McNeil said: "Kind of hobnobbing with the opposition, ain't you?"

"Well," said Coke, "they're just friendly, that's all."

"Yeah," said McNeil, "too damn friendly. That's just some of Mike's bunk. He wants you to enter the ring feeling nice and friendly and brotherly so he can give you a good socking."

"I don't fight that way," said Coke.

"Well," said McNeil, "I'm just telling you."

Coke turned to Jeff.

"They tell me you got decisioned, Jeff."

"Yeah," said Jeff. "I fought that O'Keefe kid I got a draw with in Chi. He ain't so much, Coke, but he's hardboiled and he's got a funny stance. It bothered me. I'm gonna get a return with him."

"The boss is gonna get the kid on a contract," said McNeil.

"O'Keefe?" Coke demanded.

"Yeah," said McNeil, "he's managing himself. Can you beat it?"

Coke laughed.

"What's wrong with George?"

"Oh," said Jeff, "the kid'll come in handy. He'll lick a mess of second raters. It'd take a pretty good boy to lick him in six rounds. You can't dope him out. I'd've decisioned him if the fight had gone four more rounds."

"Don't you worry about George," said McNeil to Coke. "He always knows what he's doing."

"It's all right with me," said Coke. "He can sign up fifty palookas if he wants to."

The referee called the fighters to the center of the ring for instructions. When he had finished, he ordered the ring cleared.

"Well," said Mike, smiling, "here we go."

"Yeah," said Coke.

Coke went to his corner. Regan put his head through the ropes and took Coke by the arm.

"Favor that right, kid," he said.

Coke nodded.

The bell rang. Coke shuffled into the center of the ring, carrying his right low. Mike circled around him, trying to draw him. Coke led with his left, missed and took a series of light body punches. He clinched. The referee broke them, and Mike stepped back slowly, feinted, then rushed Coke, beating him about the body. Coke landed a light left and clinched. Mike repeated his former tactics, landing three blows to Coke's one. Mike's blows were light and Coke hardly felt them, but Mike was taking no chances and was piling up points. Coke, hampered by favoring his right, fought awkwardly, and frequently clinched. The crowd didn't like it, and shouted for Mike to straighten him up. Before the first round was over, the crowd was for Mike. But Coke grinned. When the bell rang Coke shuffled to his corner.

"It's O.K.," said McNeil. "I seen him watching your right."

"Yeah," said Coke, "but I can't keep it up. I can't seem to hit hard with my left when I'm stalling with my right."

"All right," said McNeil. "Don't talk."

In the middle of the second round Mike landed a vicious left to Coke's mouth, drawing blood, and Coke, forgetting himself, swung with his right, hitting Mike on the shoulder. The punch was a hard one and Mike was momentarily thrown off balance.

"Better watch that mit," said Mike, smiling.

Coke said nothing, but fell into a clinch. The referee separated them. Mike backed toward the ropes on his toes, watching for an opening. Coke led with his left and Mike bounded off the ropes, landing a hard left to the body, followed by a right to the head. Coke fell into a clinch and the crowd booed. When the bell rang, Coke shuffled to his corner shaking his head.

"Bring on the Iron Man," somebody shouted.

Pieces of newspaper began to sail down from the gallery. Mike sat in his corner, nodding, while his brother talked to him.

The radio-man, a fight expert, was telling his audience that it looked very much as if the Ohio Iron Man was going to get a good lacing.

Mandl, who was sitting with Riley and Regan, said:

"Well, that's two rounds for Mike."

"That ain't nothing," said Riley. "When he fought Prince Pearl he lost the first five rounds."

Coke wasn't even winded and sat leaning on the ropes with his legs crossed.

"He can't hit worth a damn," said Coke. "I can't even feel that left."

"No," said McNeil, "and he's getting careless."

Coke grinned.

The third, fourth and fifth rounds were duplicates of the first two, except that round five was faster and more even. Coke wasn't landing heavily, as Mike was going with the punches, but he was landing, in spite of stalling with his right, and at the end of the fifth Mike looked worried. The crowd was quiet, and even a flurry of infighting in the middle of the fifth round failed to rouse them. They had come to see Mason, the heavy puncher, upset Mike, whom they had never seen on the canvas. As far as the crowd was concerned, this was just another Mike Shay circus, another waltz-me-around-again bout with Mike Shay getting the decision at the end of the fight. When the bell rang for the sixth round, somebody yelled:

"Well, go into your dance!"

There was a prolonged jeering.

The radio-man informed his listeners that the crowd was kidding the fighters and that this was probably the worst championship fight he had ever seen.

"Mason," he said, "lumbers around like a brewery horse and doesn't seem to know that he's got a right hand. Little Mike is landing repeatedly but Mason doesn't even know he's been hit. If Mason could fight like he can take them, he'd be in a class by himself. Wait a minute," cried the radio-man, interrupting himself, "they are actually fighting, friends, actually fighting. Just now Coke Mason nearly fell on top of me. He stepped on one of his own feet and tripped himself."

Mike, who was no longer smiling, took advantage of Coke's accident, which was due to faulty footwork, and kept him on the ropes beating him about the body. Coke covered up and took them on the biceps. The crowd cheered. Mike kept peppering Coke, who remained covered up.

"Peek-a-boo!" yelled somebody.

Mike was giving Coke a bad beating and Coke was really in trouble. He tried to maneuver himself out of the corner, but Mike rushed him, beating him with both hands.

"My God," groaned Mandl, "he's got him licked. Smart boy, that Irishman."

Suddenly Coke straightened up, took a left hook flush on the jaw, and a right on the side of the head, and swung his right which landed squarely on Mike's ribs and sent him spinning. The crowd got to its feet and roared. Mason was living up to expectations. Mike, with a surprised look on his face, back-pedaled, but Coke was on top of him with both hands. Mike fought gamely, throwing his punches faster than Prince Pearl had thrown them. But Coke took them and came in for more. Feinting with his right, he shot his left to Mike's midsection and Mike went down. The bell rang. Mike sprang to his feet and danced to his corner, but he was hurt.

"I had to do it," Coke said to McNeil. "I was in a tight place."

"Shut up," said McNeil, working over him. "You'll need your breath before this fight's over. Listen, now, don't think you got Mike licked cause you floored him. He's a shifty boy, and you've got to watch your step."

"Well," the radio-man was saying, "this Mason boy's as tough as they make them, but you've got to get him sore before he'll fight. He worked himself out of a bad place, took all Mike Shay had, and floored the champion for the first time in his career."

When the bell rang for round number seven, part of the crowd got to its feet and yelled. Coke bounded into the ring, his chin on his chest, crouching, bobbing and weaving, his left low and his right cocked. Mike, who looked determined, met him and they swapped punches, but the going got too rough for Mike. He clinched. The referee separated them.

"Stalling bastard!" said Mike.

But Coke paid no attention and rushed Mike, landing on his shoulders and biceps but unable to penetrate his defense. Mike danced away, circled around Coke and made him lead and miss, then landed a hard left to the head. Coke rushed him again, carried him to the ropes, and Mike clinched. The referee separated them, and Mike danced away, sidestepped a rush, and landed a light left and then a right swing full on the point of the jaw. Coke's legs wavered. The crowd roared for a knockout. Mike was on top of

Coke, hitting him at will. Coke fell into the ropes and slid to the floor. Hats sailed through the air and men in the ringside section climbed on their chairs to get a better view of the fallen fighter. But at "nine" Coke got to his feet, met Mike in the center of the ring and traded punches with him. Again the going got too rough for Mike and he clinched, but Coke got a hand free and clubbed him. The referee pulled them apart. Mike circled Coke, looking for an opportunity for a right swing, but Coke crossed him by suddenly straightening up out of his crouch and rushing Mike. Mike swayed away from a right swing, but got a left hook in the short ribs. He was hurt and back-pedaled, Coke shuffling after him. The bell rang.

"Boy, what a fight," said the radio-man.

"Take it easy now," said McNeil, working over Coke. "I think you got him, Coke. Land that left hook square at the beginning of the next round and you got him."

Mandl tapped Regan on the arm.

"I thought you said Mike Shay couldn't hit."

"Why," said Regan, "he caught Coke on the button. Any other guy'd be laying there yet."

When the bell rang for the eighth round, Mike leapt into the ring, caught Coke slightly off balance and punished him about the body.

"I got you measured," said Mike.

Coke said nothing, and backed away, but Mike was on top of him again, so Coke clinched. There was a continuous roar from the crowd, who sensed the fact that the fight could not last at the pace it was going. Mike was giving Coke a bad beating, and Coke seemed unable to evade the body blows that threw him off balance and put him on the defensive. But the fight ended abruptly at the very moment the crowd was certain that Coke was licked. Mike, in getting away, missed his footing and got off balance for a second. Coke leapt in, sent a left hook to the body and followed up with a solid right to the jaw, the hardest blow of the fight. Mike went down. Coke, whose hair was bristling, was dragged to a neutral corner. At the count of nine Mike struggled to his feet, but stood weaving with his hands at his side. Coke glanced at the referee. Bud Shay threw in a towel.

In a moment the ring was full. Coke was dragged through the crowd to his corner.

"Well," said McNeil, "how do you feel, champ?"

Coke grinned.

"That boy's tough," he said.

The crowd parted violently and Mike Shay, dragging his brother after him, confronted Coke.

"You got to give me a return, Mason," he cried. "I can lick you any day in the week."

Coke got to his feet, uncertainly. A crowd surrounded them.

"Well," said Coke, "you got to see my manager about that."

"Hell," said Mike, "don't try to stall like you did all through the fight."

"What's the use of getting sore, Mike," said Coke. "I ain't fighting nobody for a while yet."

"Yellow!" said Mike, and turning on his heel he disappeared into the crowd.

"Yellow, am I!" cried Coke, leaping after Mike.

But McNeil, Jeff and Regan grabbed him.

"Don't pay no attention to that Irishman," said Regan. "He always was a sore head."

The radio-man took Coke by the arm as he climbed through the ropes.

"Say something, will you, champ?"

Coke stepped to the microphone.

"Hello, folks," he said. "It was a tough go and I'm glad it's over. Good night."

On the way to the dressing-room Coke was surrounded by a crowd of men, who insisted on shaking hands with him. Regan was as diplomatic as possible, but he knew how tired Coke was and hurried him along. Aided by McNeil and Speed De Angelo, he squeezed Coke through the crowd and into the dressing-room. He put Jeff on guard at the door.

"Say," said Coke, lying down wearily, "if anybody ever tells you Mike Shay can't hit, you tell him to put his jaw out once." Then he sat up suddenly. "Did anybody telephone the missus?"

"Lay down," said Regan. "She's got a radio, ain't she?"

"Sure," said Coke, "I forgot."

He lay quiet while McNeil looked him over.

"Funny for Mike to act like he did," said Speed. "What did he want to make a show of himself for?"

"His head was buzzing from that right," said Regan.

"If I was Coke," said Speed, "I wouldn't give him no return till I got good and ready."

"Don't worry," said Regan.

They sat silent, and watched McNeil work on Coke. There was a hubbub in the corridor and they could hear Jeff talking to the crowd. Finally Coke said:

"Well, boys, I'm champion."

"How does it feel?" asked Speed.

"I can't notice nothing different," said Coke, "except I got a nice headache."

V

"I'll go up as far as the door with you," said Regan. "Then I'm leaving."
They got into the elevator.

"You're gonna say hello to the missus, ain't you?" asked Coke.

"Well," said Regan, "I'll say hello, but that's all. I got a date with Riley and Mandl. I'm gonna break training."

"You better lay off that stuff, George," said Coke. "You been looking a lot better since you quit it. Why don't you lay off?"

"Say, pastor," said Regan, "why don't you speak from the pulpit?"

"All right," said Coke, "but liquor don't do you no good, George. It don't hurt some people, but it's poison to you."

The elevator-boy had been staring at Coke and missed their floor.

"I said five, buddy," said Coke.

"Yes sir," said the elevator-boy. "I heard part of the fight over the radio, Mr. Mason. We thought you was licked."

"I thought so myself," said Coke, laughing.

He took a dollar bill out of his pocket and when the elevator-boy opened the door for them, he gave it to him.

"Thank you, Mr. Mason," said the elevator-boy. "We was all pulling for you."

They left the elevator and Coke, motioning for Regan to be quiet, tiptoed to the door of Rose's room and turned the knob. But the door was locked. He knocked. A man opened the door. Regan stared at Coke. The man smiled.

"I suppose you're Mr. Mason," he said. "My wife and I were keeping your wife company."

"Oh," said Coke, "glad to hear it. What's the name?"

"Lewis," said the man. "Paul Lewis."

He took out a card and handed it to Coke, who gave it to Regan, and hurried into the room. Rose was sitting in a big chair with her feet on an ottoman. She was wearing a black silk kimono, trimmed with gold. Her hair was marcelled and her face was carefully made up. Mrs. Lewis, a big woman with black hair, was sitting across from her. Coke went over to Rose, put his arms around her and kissed her.

"Well," he said, "I'm champion."

"We heard it over the radio," said Rose. "I got so nervous when he had you on the floor that Mr. Lewis turned it off, but I made him turn it on again."

"Yeah," said Coke. "He hit me so hard I bounced off the ropes. But you should've seen me flatten him in the eighth. He got sore and made a row after the fight. But what's the use?"

"This is Mrs. Lewis, Coke," said Rose. "I used to know her out in Hollywood. Her husband used to manage Willy Strapp."

"Pleased to meet you," said Coke.

"Thank you, Mr. Mason," said Mrs. Lewis. "I was just telling your wife that the game got too rough for Paul. He gave it up. He's in the theatrical business now."

"Yeah," said Coke, "the game's pretty rough, but I like it."

"Coke's making a lot of money at it," said Rose.

"Well," said Mrs. Lewis, "as long as you're making money at it, it's all right. Anything is."

"But I like it, anyway," said Coke. "I liked it when I was getting fifty dollars a bout. Remember, Rose, when we was living over the grocery store?"

Rose didn't answer him, and turned to shake hands with Regan, who had been talking with Lewis.

"Hello, George," said Rose. "They tell me you're managing a champion now."

"That's right," said Regan. "How you feeling?"

"I'm still weak."

"Coke," said Regan, "Lewis here used to manage Willy Strapp before he was champion."

"Yes," said Lewis, "but I didn't like the game. Too crooked."

"Yeah," said Regan, "it's pretty crooked and getting worse, but we always been on the square."

"Sure," said Coke. "I wouldn't fight in no crooked fights."

He sat watching Lewis, who was his idea of a goodlooking man. Lewis was tall and slim, about forty years old, and very carefully dressed. His hair was black and lustrous, and he wore it rather long. His nose was straight and well-cut, and his eyes were blue with heavy lashes like a woman's. His hands were long and slim, the nails well-manicured, and he was wearing three rings, one of which was a big diamond mounted in a circlet of rubies. He had a long amber cigarette holder and he wore spats.

"That's the way to talk," said Lewis. "If there were more fighters like you the game would be a real game."

Lewis smiled blandly at Coke, who was flattered.

"There's more than you think," said Regan. "It ain't the fighters that make the game crooked, it's the hangers-on, the gamblers. Over half of the boys that go into the game, go in because they like it. Coke would rather fight than eat and he ain't the only one. But fighters are human same as anybody else, and when fixers begin to talk in four figures, well, use your imagination. To hear some people talk you'd think everything was straight but the fight game. Bunk!"

"Maybe you're right," said Lewis, smiling. "I guess I happened to run into a lot of crookedness all at once, and got a wrong slant."

"Sure," said Coke.

"Well," said Mrs. Lewis, "personally I don't like the fight game, and never will. I never had a peaceful moment while Paul was in it."

"Now, Louise!" said Lewis, frowning at her.

Mrs. Lewis looked very uncomfortable and tried to smile. Regan got up.

"Well," he said, "I'll be traveling. I got a heavy date with a couple of big shots. Coke, if I was you, I'd get to bed and get some sleep. How do you feel?"

Coke grinned.

"Tired," he said.

"It's no wonder," said Regan, "the socking you took. You should've seen him, Rose. Mike hit him with everything but the water-bucket."

"Yeah," said Coke, "but it didn't do him no good."

"Don't get up, none of you," said Regan, waving Coke and Lewis back into their chairs. "If that story's out yet, Coke, I'll send you up a paper. So long, everybody."

"Goodbye, George," said Rose. "Much obliged for taking such good care of the child here."

"Goodnight, Mr. Regan," said Lewis. "You've got my card. Look me up some time."

Regan went out.

"Well," said Lewis, "so that's your manager."

"Yeah," said Rose. "George and Coke've been friends for years. They was born right across the street from each other, only George is five years older."

"He looks older than that," said Lewis. "Mason here looks like a college boy. By the way, how old are you, Mason?"

"I'll be twenty-nine next September," said Coke.

"You don't look it," said Lewis. "And your wife here must be much younger."

"No," said Coke, "she..."

"I'm a couple of years younger," said Rose hurriedly.

"That would make you about twenty-six," said Lewis, smiling, "but you don't look it."

"Why, Paul," said Mrs. Lewis, "I think she does. She looks about the same age as Ada. Ada," she explained, "is in Paul's new roof show. She's a dear. She must be at least twenty-six."

"Oh, you're in the show business," said Coke.

"Well," said Lewis, "not very heavily. I train Martin's choruses for him. I'm getting a roof show ready for him now. We open in July."

"Well!" said Coke.

"You haven't got a front row job for me, have you?" asked Rose, laughing.

"Might be such a thing," said Lewis.

Coke looked from one to the other.

"Are you two kidding?"

Lewis glanced at Rose and said:

"Certainly."

"Well," said Coke, "I thought you was. Because Rose is out of that business. She's gonna have it soft from now on. She's had it tough and she's been sick. None of that for her. I got money and she don't never have to worry again."

"Lucky girl," said Mrs. Lewis.

"We was joking, Coke," said Rose.

"Sure," said Coke.

Someone knocked at the door. Coke started to get up, but Lewis waved him back.

"I'll go, Mason," he said. "You're tired."

Lewis opened the door and a bell-boy gave him a newspaper. He took the newspaper with a flourish and handed the boy a dollar bill.

"Mr. Regan sent that up to Mr. Mason," said the bell-boy.

Lewis closed the door and handed the paper to Coke. On the front page there were three fight pictures, one of Mike and Coke shaking hands, one of Mike on the floor in the eighth, and one of Coke after the fight. The round by round account of the fight was headed:

MIKE SHAY FIGHTS BEST FIGHT OF CAREER
AND IS DEFEATED

Coke turned to page two. There was an article topped by a young picture of Rose, headed:

MASON AND WIFE STAGE RECONCILIATION

"Here you are, honey," said Coke. "Here's a surprise for you."

He gave Rose the paper and looked over her shoulder. Lewis and his wife exchanged a glance, then they went to look at the picture.

"It's me!" cried Rose, hurriedly reading the article.

"Yeah," said Coke. "Ain't that a nice surprise? George done it."

"Oh, that's wonderful," said Rose.

"Is that an old picture?" Mrs. Lewis inquired.

"Yeah," said Coke, "that's the one I always carry in my pocket."

"It's not so very old," said Rose.

"Well," said Lewis, "all I can say is, that's wonderful publicity if you ever think about going back in the show business."

Coke turned and stared at Lewis.

"Say, Mr. Lewis," he said, "my wife don't have to go back in no show business. If I never fight another fight I got money enough to get by on."

"'Tisn't always a question of money," said Lewis.

"No, of course not," said Rose. "But I wouldn't do it if Coke didn't want me to."

"That's the talk, honey," said Coke, putting his arm around Rose.

"Paul," said Mrs. Lewis, "don't you think we better be going."

"Why, yes," said Lewis, "come to think of it."

"Don't rush off," said Rose.

But Coke said nothing.

"I think we'll be going," said Lewis. "I bet you two have got a lot to talk about."

"We sure have," said Coke, laughing.

"Call us up, won't you?" said Rose. "Coke won't be busy now for a while I don't suppose, and we can go places."

"That'll be fine," said Lewis. "Why don't you and your illustrious husband come down some afternoon to rehearsal and watch the girls work out?"

"Maybe we will," said Rose.

"Sure," said Coke.

"Goodnight, dear," said Mrs. Lewis. "Don't get up, please, on my account. Just stay comfy. Goodnight, Mr. Mason. So glad you won your fight."

"Thanks," said Coke.

Lewis offered his hand to Coke and bowed slightly.

"Mason," he said, "now I can tell people that I've shaken hands with the middleweight champion of the world."

Coke grinned and shifted his feet.

When they had gone, Coke said: "Nice guy, that Lewis."

"Yeah," said Rose, "he's all right. I never knew him very well. But I knew his wife out in Hollywood. She used to be in the scenario department at one of the studios. I don't know what she done. She hasn't got brains enough to write movies."

"No," said Coke, "she don't look it. That takes brains."

"Coke," said Rose, "come over here and give mama a big kiss."

Coke put his arms around Rose and kissed her.

"Not so rough, honey," she said. "I ain't up to par yet."

"Course you're not," said Coke. "How'd you like the story, honey?"

"Great," said Rose. "I'll have to give George a couple of hugs for that."

"You better not," said Coke.

Coke sat on the ottoman at Rose's feet. She bent over and ran her fingers through his hair, curling it, making it stand up in isolated strands.

"Oh, you look funny," she cried, laughing.

"Say," said Coke, "ain't it bad enough without you making it worse?"

Rose leaned over and kissed him.

"You got a cute face, Coke," she said.

"Yeah," said Coke, "like a nice bulldog."

Rose sat looking at Coke, then she said:

"Wasn't it funny for me to run into the Lewises?"

"Yeah," said Coke.

"I got sick of sitting up here all by myself," said Rose, "so I thought I'd go over to the restaurant across the street and get my dinner. Well, who should I bump into but Mrs. Lewis. She nearly dropped over. 'Why, Rose Mason,' she said, 'what are you doing here?' So I told her. I had dinner with them and they come up here with me."

"Well," said Coke, "if you was lonesome, I'm glad they did. It ain't much fun being lonesome."

"I'll say not," said Rose. "They was just lovely to me. They're nice people, Coke."

"Yeah," said Coke. "Lewis is sure a good looking guy. I don't see why he don't get in the movies or something."

"He's just fair," said Rose. "He uses perfume and if there's anything I hate, it's perfume on a man."

Coke grinned.

"Never ketch me with no perfume on," he said.

PART V

I

Two days after his defeat of Soldier Bayliss, a slugging match that great-
ly increased his popularity, Coke appeared at Kid Halloran's gymnasium in
a formfitting overcoat, a derby, and spats. He was wearing a big diamond
ring and was carrying a cane. Jeff Davis came over to shake hands with
him.

"Hello, champ," he said. "How you feeling?"

"Good," said Coke, "only I got a bad hand from hitting the Soldier."

"Some go," said Jeff.

Coke saw that Jeff was looking him over.

"Well," he said, "what do you think of the get-up?"

"It don't look natural," said Jeff. "I'd rather see you in an old pair of pants
and a sweater."

Coke grinned.

"Sure," he said. "I'd feel more comfortable. But I got to dress up now on
account of the missus."

"Yeah," said Jeff.

In a moment Coke was surrounded, hands were shoved at him, and
everybody talked at once. Across the gymnasium, beyond the noon business men's class, Rattler O'Keefe was working out with Ruby Hall, and
Regan was watching him. Coke went over to see Regan, followed by the
crowd. Just as Coke came up Ruby Hall sent a left to O'Keefe's ribs and
doubled him up, but O'Keefe crouched and came in for more, shuffling
awkwardly.

"That boy's tough," said Jeff. "You should've seen him lay Kid Green flat."

"Hell," said Coke, "the Kid must've run into one."

Regan clapped his hands for the fighters to stop.

"Rattler," he said, "go take a shower."

"Yes sir," said O'Keefe.

Regan saw Coke and called:

"Say, Jeff, introduce me to the Prince of Wales, will you?"

"Hello, champ," said O'Keefe.

"Hello," said Coke. "How they coming?"

"Fine, champ. When you gonna work out with me?"

"I'd do it right now if I didn't have a bad hand," said Coke, smiling.

"All right, Rattler," said Regan, "beat it."

"Yes sir," said O'Keefe and went toward the showers.

"There's a boy that's gonna knock your block off some day," said Regan, taking Coke by the lapels. Coke pulled away.

"Cut it out," he said. "Quit showing off in public."

Regan rubbed his chin and stared at Coke. Then he shrugged his shoulders.

"Excuse me," he said. "I forgot you was the champ."

Coke laughed.

"All right, George," he said, "only lay off me in public, see? It don't look right."

"I'll bet the missus taught you that song," said Regan, walking away.

"What's the matter with him?" Coke inquired of Jeff.

"You got me," said Jeff.

Kid Halloran came over to introduce somebody to Coke.

"Mr. Mason," said the Kid, "I want you to meet a friend of mine. Mr. H. W. Coon."

Coke turned. It was one of the fat business men, who worked out feebly every noon in the Kid's gymnasium. He had on a track suit and he looked embarrassed. Coke shook hands with him.

"Glad to meet you, Mr. Coon," he said.

"Thank you, champ," said Mr. Coon. "I always did want to shake your hand ever since you licked Prince Pearl. It took you to do it."

"Thanks," said Coke.

"I was just wondering," said Mr. Coon, "if you and your wife wouldn't take lunch with me some day. Any day will do."

Coke looked at Kid Halloran, who winked at him.

"Well," said Coke, "I don't have much time, you know. I'm not downtown much, but I'm gonna meet my wife at The Commander today, so...."

"Enough said," Mr. Coon put in. "Make it today. How about two o'clock."

"Well," said Coke, "the only thing is, I was gonna take my manager out to lunch today."

"Oh, you mean Regan," said Mr. Coon. "Well, bring him along. That'll be fine."

"Thanks, Mr. Coon," said Coke.

"I'll see you then," said Mr. Coon.

When he had gone back to his class, the Kid said: "Cultivate that boy, champ. He's got so much money he don't know what to do with it."

"Yeah?"

"He's rich, that guy," the Kid went on, "and he works every day. He's got a brokerage office or something. Swell guy. That's the kind of people we want to get interested in the game, champ."

"Sure," said Coke.

Regan, who was standing across the ring watching Coke, took a flask out of his pocket and drank, then he put the flask away and came over to him.

"George," said the Kid, "I wish to God you wouldn't do that right out in public. I got to be careful. When you want a drink, go back in the washroom."

"You pugs make me sick," said Regan. "You're getting so damn nice pretty soon you'll be carrying handkerchiefs."

"Give the Kid a break, George," said Coke.

"Yes sir, champion," said Regan, bowing. "I'll also give him a punch in the nose if he gets fresh with me."

Halloran walked away. Coke saw that Regan was beginning to get drunk. He took him by the arm.

"George," he said, "can't you leave that poison alone? It's gonna get you, George."

"Well," said Regan.

"Listen," said Coke, "how about Richy Kelleher? Remember the night he went bugs out in Omaha and a cop had to slug him? Yeah, and remember when we went out to the sanitarium to see him and they wouldn't let us in he was so bad?"

"Yeah, and I remember his funeral," said Regan. "What about it?"

"Well," said Coke, "that's what happens to a guy that can't leave the stuff alone."

"All right," said Regan. "Now I'll tell you one. What happens to a guy that used to be a mechanic's helper that gets up in the world and gets the swellhead?"

"There you go," said Coke. "What makes you think I got the swellhead?"

"Look at them clothes you got on," said Regan, "and look at your nails manicured to the quick. And look at your hair with the grease on it. Even old dumb Jeff says you ain't like you used to be. And if he knows it, everybody knows it."

"Well," said Coke, "that's the missus."

"Everything's the missus!"

"George," said Coke, "you know I got a mighty nice little wife. Now how come I can't do a few things to please her. It don't hurt me none."

"All right," said Regan.

O'Keefe came out of the dressing-room in a navy blue turtle-neck sweater and an old cap.

"What's on for tomorrow, boss?" he asked.

"Take it easy," said Regan, "and remember what I told you about that left. Practice it tonight in front of a mirror. Tomorrow night we'll give Willis a surprise."

"Gonna come over and see me fight, champ?" O'Keefe inquired.

"Don't think I can make it," said Coke, "but I hope you win."

"Thanks," said O'Keefe, then he turned to go. "Well, I'll be seeing you."

Before he could reach the door he was stopped by half a dozen men, who wanted to exchange a few words with him.

"That kid's gonna be a top-notcher some day," said Regan. "He's got everything but science and I'm learning him that. Best disposition I ever seen."

"He's got too many feet," said Coke.

"Well," said Regan, "you ain't no toe-dancer yourself."

Coke took out a cigar-case. It was leather and had gold and green arabesques on it.

"Take a look at this," he said. "Lewis give it to me."

"Doggy," said Regan.

"Yeah," said Coke. "It's Italian. It was made in some Italian city. I forget which."

"Well, well," said Regan selecting a cigar.

"Say," said Coke, "that reminds me. We got a date to eat lunch with Mr. Coon, George. Me and the wife and you."

"Yeah? Who's the new boyfriend?"

"He's a rich guy," said Coke. "He's got a big brokerage office or something."

Regan laughed.

"You're getting in Mike Shay's class," he said. "Before long you'll be training at Newport and having tea with Mrs. Whatzerbilt."

Coke grinned.

"Well," he said, "that's all right, ain't it?"

"Yeah," said Regan, "that's fine. But I don't know what you'd do with all the fast ramblers and panhandlers that usually hang around your camp. Course they're gentlemen of leisure, but they don't wash."

II

When Regan and Coke got to The Commander they found Mr. Coon waiting for them, but Rose hadn't arrived yet.

"Hello, Mason," said Coon. "You're on the dot. How are you, Regan? I don't think we've ever been introduced, exactly, but I've seen you quite frequently at Halloran's."

"Yeah," said Regan, shaking hands, "I remember you."

"Well," said Coon, "shall we sit down?"

They all sat on a big lounge overlooking the lobby.

"My wife's always late," said Coke.

"It's a woman's privilege," said Coon.

"One of 'em," Regan put in.

Coon laughed and glanced at Regan.

"You talk as if you didn't like women, Regan," he said.

"They're all right in their place," said Regan, unpleasantly.

Coon flushed slightly and looked at Coke.

"Don't pay no attention to George," said Coke. "That's just his way."

"Yeah," said Regan.

"Well," said Coon, "let's change the subject. Have you picked out your next opponent, Mason?"

"No," said Coke. "I'm gonna take it easy for a while. I might fight Larsen in the summer."

"He's champion now," said Regan, "and he's looking for soft spots."

Coon, disconcerted by Regan's manner, tried to laugh.

"You're way off, George," said Coke. "I never dodged a fight in my life, and I never will."

"Yeah," said Regan. Then he got up. "I'm gonna take a walk. I'll be back in a minute."

When Regan was out of earshot, Coon said:

"He's been drinking, hasn't he?"

"Yeah," said Coke. "He drinks too much. I try to tell him but he won't listen to me."

"Well," said Coon, "liquor's all right, it's the people that use it. Same as religion. I don't go to church myself, but it isn't because I don't think religion's a good thing, it's on account of most of the people I see practicing it."

"Yeah," said Coke, "that's right."

"You're not a religious man are you, Mason?"

"No," said Coke. "I suppose I ought to go to church once in a while. When I was a kid I used to go to Sunday School. George's a Catholic."

"I thought he was, being an Irishman. Well, one religion's as good as another. I haven't any quarrel with any of them. It's the people, that's all. They're not consistent."

Coke said nothing, but nodded and tried to look wise. Turning, he saw Rose coming toward them across the long lobby. She was wearing a leopard coat and a small black hat.

"Here comes the missus," said Coke, jumping to his feet. "Ain't she got the prettiest pair of legs you ever seen?"

Coon laughed.

"Maybe I better not express myself on that subject."

"Hello, Coke," said Rose, coming up to them. "Sorry I'm late."

"That's all right, honey," said Coke. "Me and Mr. Coon here have just been having a talk. This is Mr. Coon. Meet the wife."

"I've heard a lot about you, Mrs. Mason," said Coon, affably, "and I saw your picture in the paper, too. It didn't do you justice."

"Oh, thanks," said Rose. "Are you the Mr. Coon who owns all the horses?"

"Yes," said Coon. "I've got a few runners."

"Well," said Rose, putting her hand on his arm, "I don't know if I'm glad to meet you or not. I lost two dollars on your Flying Cloud yesterday."

"Your husband'll never be able to stand a loss like that," said Coon.

They all laughed. Regan came up to them and said to Rose:

"Well, you finally got here."

Rose looked slightly annoyed.

"Finally," she said.

"I got so tired of waiting," said Regan, "I went downstairs to take a drink and dropped my flask. Can you beat it! I lost a half pint of good liquor just on your account, Rose Mason. Women make me sick."

"I guess you got some of it down your throat," said Rose, drawing away from Regan.

Coon, embarrassed, glanced over the lobby to see if they were being observed.

"Don't high-hat me," said Regan.

"Don't you think we better go in and eat," said Coon.

"No," said Regan, "I lost my appetite now."

"George," said Coke, "snap out of it. You want to spoil our party?"

"Well," said Regan, "it gives me a pain in the neck to stand around and wait for people."

"Can you imagine such manners!" said Rose.

"You've said enough now, George," said Coke flushing. "That'll do."

Regan laughed, turned on his heel and walked away. Coke went after him and took him by the arm, but Regan turned and gave him a push.

"Go on and eat with the big shot," he said. "I'm going over to Mexican Joe's where I can eat with my knife."

"You're drunk, George," said Coke. "You better let me get you a cab."

"Nothing doing," said Regan, walking away.

Coke went back to Coon and Rose.

"I wouldn't stand for that, Coke," said Rose. "If it wasn't for you he'd still be running a pool-room out in the sticks."

Coke stood looking at the floor.

"That's just what I was saying," said Coon. "I was just telling Mr. Mason that liquor's all right, it's the people who use it."

"That's right," said Rose. "I take a drink myself once in a while, but I never had one too many in my life."

"You know," said Coke, "sometimes I think George can't help it. His old man was a periodical drinker."

"It's just lack of backbone," said Coon. "If you want to quit, and will it, you can quit. I stopped smoking over night once, and for six months I never touched tobacco."

"George worries me," said Coke.

"You're not his nurse," said Rose. "If he can't act like a gentleman, that's his tough luck."

"Well," said Coon, "shall we eat?"

"Yes," said Rose, "I'm starved."

Rose took Coon's arm and walked toward the dining room. Coke followed them reluctantly.

III

"No," said Coke, trying to keep his temper. "I told you I was going down and look after George."

"Well," said Rose, "you're a fine husband, I must say. Rather go look after some bum than go out with your wife."

"George's sick, ain't I been telling you?" said Coke, putting on his overcoat. "We can go over to The Viennese any time. It runs every night. You call the Lewises and tell 'em."

"I'll be damned if I will," said Rose.

"Well," said Coke, "let 'em go to the devil then. I'm looking after George. That guy looked after me when you was out running around the country God knows where."

"Yeah," said Rose, "that ain't all he did. He took you for half of everything you brought in without a contract and then when it looked like you was gonna be champion, he got your name on the dotted line. Don't you worry, old boy. Lewis knows all about it. Everybody does but you."

"Bunk," said Coke. "That's Lewis's story. He forgot to tell you how George loaned me money so I wouldn't have to work in the factory and could train."

"He knew how good you was, Coke," said Rose, moderating her voice, surprised by Coke's obstinance.

"Maybe," said Coke, "but nobody else did. By God, I guess you forget how you used to tell me what a bum I was."

"I was only trying to get you to make something out of yourself," said Rose. "Did you think I wanted to see a guy like you, with stuff in him, working in a factory?"

Coke stood looking at the floor. Rose began to cry.

"I thought you was gonna treat me nice," said Rose. "You get me all upset acting this way, Coke. You know my nerves are bad on account of the flu." She threw herself into a chair and sobbed.

"Listen, honey," said Coke, "I got to go see George. Mac says nobody can do nothing with him. He's all shot."

"Well, how about me?" Rose demanded. "To hear you tell it, you'd think I was in perfect health. Ain't I as important as George Regan?"

"Course you are, honey."

"Coke," said Rose, looking up through her lashes, "ain't I more important?"

"Course you are," said Coke, bending down and kissing her.

"Well, then," said Rose, pouting.

Coke, badgered beyond endurance, burst out:

"But I tell you it's different! We can go to night clubs any night. See what I mean? We can go any night, and it won't hurt you none to stay home one night, will it? I got to see George, Rose. I just got to."

Rose got up and went into the bedroom, slamming the door. The phone rang. It was McNeil. He told Coke that George was worse and wanted to see him.

"It ain't nothing serious, is it?" asked Coke.

"I don't hardly think so," said McNeil. "But he don't seem like George Regan. He just don't give a damn for nothing. He's been on a four day jag and he can't stand it like he used to."

"I'll be right over," said Coke, hanging up the receiver.

Rose opened the bedroom door.

"I heard you," she said.

"He's worse," said Coke. "I'm going down and get a taxi." He hesitated. "Say, Rose, why don't you and the Lewises go on over to The Viennese? I'll get there as soon as I can."

Rose didn't say anything.

"Yeah," said Coke, "I'll get the porter to have the garage man send the car over, see? He'll send somebody to drive it for you."

"Coke," said Rose, putting her hands on his shoulders, "we ought to have a chauffeur. But you'll never listen to me."

"Well," said Coke, "I'll see what I can do about that tomorrow."

"Will you, honey?" said Rose.

"Yeah, cross my heart," said Coke.

Rose kissed him.

"Mama's sorry," she said, "but mama didn't want her boy to run away and leave her all alone."

"I know," said Coke. "You get the Lewises and go on now, honey, and I'll be there just as soon as I can get there."

"Maybe I better invite Mr. Coon too," said Rose, "he's such a nice fellow."

"Sure," said Coke, "that's fine."

He kissed Rose and then started for the door.

"Goodbye, honey," he said.

"Goodbye, Coke," said Rose. "Sorry we had to have a row like that."

IV

When Coke came in Regan was lying on the bed fully dressed. His face, usually swarthy, was pale, and his hands shook. Jeff was sitting at the head of the bed looking at the pictures in a magazine, and McNeil was stretched out on a lounge.

"Hello, Coke," said Regan.

"Hello," said Coke, sitting down on the edge of the bed. "They tell me you ain't feeling so good."

"Too much gin," said Regan, trying to laugh.

"Did you get a doctor, Mac?" asked Coke.

"Yeah," said McNeil, "and he read George the riot act. If he puts any more of that poison in him, the doctor gives him up."

"Yeah," said Regan, "I tried to drink with Riley, but it can't be done. We was going to take a train for Frisco, but I passed out in the station."

"Why Frisco?" Coke inquired.

"Well," said Regan, "I don't know. I wanted to go to Mexico, but Riley was set on Frisco and I didn't want to bust up the party."

Coke glanced at McNeil, who shook his head slightly.

"Yeah," said Coke. "Say, George, don't you think you better get your clothes off and go to bed?"

"No," said Regan, "if I take my clothes off I'll go to sleep and I don't want to go to sleep, I get nightmares."

"Hell," said Coke.

"Straight," said Regan. "I see things."

"Well," said McNeil, "you ought to be glad you don't see 'em with your eyes open."

Jeff looked at his watch.

"Time for your medicine, boss," he said.

Regan shook his head.

"I won't take that stuff. It tastes like hell."

Jeff got the bottle and spoon, and handed them to Coke. Coke read the instructions and poured out a dose.

"George," he said, "you mean to tell me you ain't got guts enough to take a little medicine?"

"Who says I ain't!" cried Regan.

"Well," said Coke, "here you are."

Regan swallowed the medicine and made a face. "Boy!" he said, "that's powerful stuff."

Coke gave him a drink of water, then he said:

"Now, George, I'm gonna help you off with your clothes. You don't need to go to sleep. Just rest. I'll sit here and talk to you."

"All right," said Regan.

Jeff and Coke undressed him and got him into his pajamas. Regan, sweating from weakness, lay down and closed his eyes for a moment, then he asked for a cigar. Coke took out his case and handed him one.

"Still got the pretty case, have you?" said Regan. "Coke Mason, the fashion-plate champion."

"That sounds more like it," said McNeil. "You're beginning to talk like George Regan."

Coke grinned and lit Regan's cigar for him. Regan could hardly keep his eyes open, but he propped himself up to fight off his drowsiness.

"George," said Coke, "who do you think's gonna win the big heavyweight match?"

"What does it matter?" said Regan. "They're just a couple of bums getting money under false pretences. You could lick either one of them. Say, that reminds me, Mike Shay can't make the middleweight grade no more. I got it straight. Riley told me."

"A good lightheavy'll kill him," said Coke.

"It depends," said Regan.

McNeil and Jeff sat watching Regan, whose eyes were closing. Coke went on talking in low tones about fights, about Prince Pearl, about anything he could think of. In half an hour, Regan was asleep, snoring.

"Poor devil," said McNeil. "When he lays off the booze, there ain't a smarter guy in the game. But when he's drinking, he's no good on earth."

"It'll get him," said Jeff.

"Yeah," said McNeil. "That doctor give him a good scaring, but it won't last. He'll lay off for a while, then he'll start all over."

Coke sat looking at Regan, whose face was pale and drawn.

"This is the worst I ever seen him," said Jeff.

"Yeah," said McNeil, "and every time from now on it'll be worse. There ain't no hope for them periodical drinkers."

Coke got up and put on his hat.

"I got to be moving," he said. "We got a table over at The Viennese. The missus is already there. If anything happens, you know where to get me, Mac."

"All right," said Mac.

"One of you guys better stay right here with him all night."

"I'll stay," said Jeff.

Coke went out. The doorman got a taxi for him. On the way to The Viennese Coke sat looking out the taxi window. He thought how he and George used to shoot pool till midnight and then go and get a hotdog and a cup of coffee at the Greek's next door. He remembered how they used to go fishing and sit under big straw hats and pull in catfish and drink beer. He remembered the Sunday excursions to Cleveland and the moonlight boat trips to Detroit. George was always good company.

"Well," said Coke, "I don't know."

V

While Coke was taking off his coat one of the checkgirls whispered to the other:

"Coke Mason!"

Coke heard her and turned around, smiling.

"You girls fight fans?"

"No, sir," said one of them, "but we seen your picture in the papers."

"Yeah," said the other. "My brother seen you fight at The Coliseum."

"Yeah?" said Coke, smiling. "I'll see you girls on my way out."

The headwaiter came up to him.

"One, sir?"

"No, I got a party here. I'm Coke Mason."

"Yes sir, yes sir," said the headwaiter, bowing, "right this way, Mr. Mason."

He led Coke through the crowded nightclub to a round table near the dancefloor. Coon, in evening clothes, was talking very earnestly to Rose, who was sitting with her elbows on the table. Lewis and his wife were leaning back in their chairs watching a negro entertainer on the dancefloor.

"Well," said Coke, "here I am."

Coon and Lewis both got up to shake hands with him.

"How's George?" Rose inquired.

"He'll be all right," said Coke. "I got him to bed finally. He looks bad though."

"Your wife was telling us," said Coon.

They all sat down.

"I think it's awful the way some men drink," said Mrs. Lewis.

"Isn't it!" said Coon. "I always say that liquor's all right, it's the people that use it."

"My sentiments exactly," said Lewis.

The Master of Ceremonies came over to their table and put his hand on the back of Coke's chair.

"Mason," he said, "I'd like to introduce you from the floor."

"What?" exclaimed Coke, glancing up.

"We always introduce the celebrities, Mr. Mason," said the Master of Ceremonies, "it's one of our customs."

"Go ahead, Mason," said Coon, who applauded loudly.

"Listen," said Coke, "it's all right with me, but don't expect me to make no speech."

"Oh, no," said the Master of Ceremonies, "just come out on the dancefloor when I signal you, and sort of bow."

"I'll mit 'em," said Coke.

The Master of Ceremonies looked puzzled, but nodded.

"Great to be famous, eh Lewis?" said Coon.

Rose smiled across at Coke and said:

"He's just my big boy."

"Sure," said Coke.

The Master of Ceremonies walked to the center of the dancefloor, held up his hands for silence, and said:

"Friends, I want you to meet a man who is at present the most popular pugilistic figure in New York. Many of you saw him on that historic night when he defeated one of the greatest fighters of all time, Mr. Mike Shay, for the middleweight championship of the world." The Master of Ceremonies motioned for Coke to come to the dancefloor. "Let me introduce Mr. Coke Mason!"

Coke shuffled out onto the floor grinning. They turned the spotlight on him and he blinked. The crowd laughed and applauded. Coke mitted them, bowing slightly.

"Speech! Speech! Speech!" they shouted.

Coke grinned and shook his head.

"No," he cried. "I make my speeches with these." He held up his hands.

There was much laughter and prolonged applause. Coke shook hands with the Master of Ceremonies, and went back to his table.

"Well," said Lewis, "didn't he rise to the occasion, though! Good work, Mason."

"Mama's proud," said Rose.

"You should be," said Coon. "You chose just the right words, Mason. Leave speech making to Senators and other bores. Hurray for Coke Mason."

Coke glanced at Coon, puzzled. Coon's face was red and his eyes bulged. He was drunk.

"If it had been Paul," said Mrs. Lewis, "he'd've talked till they stopped him."

"Now, my dear!" said Lewis.

Lewis was always suave, never raised his voice, was almost always smiling, or nearly smiling, but sometimes the look in his eyes chilled Coke. Mrs. Lewis, when reproved, usually quailed, but this time she returned the stare.

"Folks," she said, "before I forget about it, I'd like to announce something."

"Announce it from the dancefloor," said Coon.

"Why, Harold!" exclaimed Rose, hitting him on the shoulder.

"Don't remind me," said Coon, then apologetically to Coke: "I must be a little drunk. Am I becoming noticeable?"

"No," said Coke.

"Go on with your announcement, dear," said Rose.

"Well," said Mrs. Lewis, "Paul and I are going to separate."

"What!" exclaimed Rose. "Really?"

"Not permanently," said Lewis, taking a drink and glancing at his wife. "Louise has got an offer to come back to Hollywood, you see. My business keeps me here."

"Exactly," said Mrs. Lewis. "I ran short of money in New York, so I have to go back to work."

Coke looked from one to the other, puzzled.

"What's the matter, Lewis," said Coke, "are you flat?"

"He's not," said Mrs. Lewis. "But I am."

"But..." said Coke.

"I don't see why you had to bring this up, Louise," said Lewis. "But a little liquor always makes you talkative."

"Now, now," said Coon. "I won't have quarrelling."

"Well," said Mrs. Lewis, "I'm going away at the end of the week and I want my friends to know it."

"You see," said Lewis, "our marriage is on a purely business basis. We both contribute to the upkeep of everything."

Coke laughed.

"That's a good one," he said.

"Coke," Rose put in, "you mustn't laugh."

"It's quite all right," said Lewis.

"Yes," said Mrs. Lewis, "it's a good joke on me, after the way I spent my money."

"Louise," said Lewis, "you've said plenty. If you go on talking like that, I'm going home."

The jazzband began to play. Coon waved his arms.

"Forget your troubles," he cried. "On with the dance."

Rose leaned over and whispered to Coke:

"Dance with Mrs. Lewis, honey. It'll cheer her up."

"Sure," said Coke. He got up and stood behind Mrs. Lewis's chair. "Can I have this dance?"

"Certainly," said Mrs. Lewis, getting up.

They stepped out onto the crowded dancefloor and began to dance. Mrs. Lewis was heavy and hard to lead, Coke was a very poor dancer, but as the floor was jammed this didn't matter much. Coke looked back at the table and saw that Rose, Coon, and Lewis, all standing, were having an argument of some sort. He paid no attention to the men, but stared at Rose. She was wearing a yellow evening-gown, which clung snugly to her slender body, and she was perched on extremely high heels.

"Ain't my wife got the littlest feet you ever seen?" Coke demanded.

"She's very small," said Mrs. Lewis.

Coke laughed.

"She puts my shoes on over hers and walks all over the apartment. It looks awful funny."

Mrs. Lewis said nothing.

"Yeah," said Coke, "I can't even get my hands in her shoes."

"Mr. Coon thinks your wife's quite a beauty," said Mrs. Lewis.

"Well, she is," said Coke.

"Mr. Coon's trying to persuade her to go back on the stage in Paul's new show."

"I won't let her," said Coke. "They better not say nothing to me about it."

"Maybe you'll change your mind," said Mrs. Lewis.

A couple collided violently with them. When the man saw who he had run into, he ducked behind the girl's shoulder in mock fright.

"Don't hit me, Mason," he said.

Coke grinned.

"Nice bunch of people here," said Coke.

"I'm sick of nightclubs," said Mrs. Lewis.

"I like 'em," said Coke. "Course I ain't a drinker, or nothing like that. I drink beer once in a while. But I like the music and seeing people."

The music stopped. Coke saw Rose and Coon at the far end of the dancefloor. Before the music started up again, Lewis left the table and took Rose from Coon.

"Them two guys are playing tag with my wife," said Coke.

"They've been doing it all evening," said Mrs. Lewis.

"That's the way she always was," said Coke. "When she was a kid about thirteen the boys used to be always hanging after her."

"No doubt," said Mrs. Lewis.

When the dance was over Coon, who had danced the final encore with Rose, led her back to the table, leaning over her, talking earnestly. Lewis sat at the table watching them, and he was so absorbed that he forgot to get up when Coke seated his wife.

"What's the matter, Paul?" Mrs. Lewis inquired. "Preoccupied?"

Lewis got to his feet.

"Didn't see you, Louise," he said.

"I noticed," said Mrs. Lewis.

"My God," said Coke, falling into his chair, "look at me sweating! I can sure pare my weight down dancing."

"Isn't it the truth!" said Coon. "By the way, Mason, when're you going to box with me? Listen, folks, Mason has promised to box with me down at Halloran's gymnasium."

"I'd like to see that," said Lewis, smiling.

"Oh, he'll be gentle with me, won't you, Mason?"

"Sure," said Coke.

"We'll make a party of it," said Lewis, "we'll all go down and watch."

"No," said Coon, "I refuse to fight before ladies. I'm much too brutal."

Rose burst out laughing.

"Oh, Harold!" she cried.

VI

Coke took his clothes off and put on pajamas and a bathrobe. Rose was lying on a lounge in her black kimono, smoking a cigarette and watching Coke.

"You sure got a build, big boy," she said. "Where'd you get all that muscle?"

"Training," said Coke. "When I first started out I used to train with Jimmy Pappas, the wrestler, and it sure put the muscle on me. I got too much in the shoulders for a good boxer. I'm damn near muscle-bound. But that's what puts 'em down when I hit 'em with that left hook."

"I'd hate to get hit with that," said Rose. "That'd be the end of me."

"Don't you never worry, honey," said Coke, grinning.

Someone knocked at the door.

"Who do you suppose that is!" exclaimed Rose, impatiently.

"Who's there?" called Coke.

"Bell-boy."

Coke went over and opened the door. The bell-boy handed Coke a magazine.

"The manager sent this up, Mr. Mason," said the bell-boy. "He thought maybe it might interest you."

"Yeah?" said Coke. "Thanks, buddy."

The bell-boy turned to go, but Coke told him to wait and went over to his trousers and took out a handful of change, which he gave to the bell-boy. The bell-boy thanked him and closed the door.

"What's the idea!" said Rose.

"You got me," said Coke.

He turned the pages of the magazine till he came to an article headed: When He Fights Something Always Happens. There he was with his hair on end and a grin spread over his face.

"Listen, kid," he said, excitedly. "Coke (Iron Man) Mason, the idol of the fistic fans. A fighter of the old school who would be as much at home with bare knuckles as he is with five ounce gloves. Conqueror of Prince Pearl, Larsen, Bat Cahill, Joe Savella, Mike Shay and Soldier Bayliss. He has cleaned up the Middleweight ranks and now, like Alexander, is looking for new worlds to conquer."

Coke scratched his head.

"Who's Alexander?" he said. "I never heard of him."

"He's a general or something," said Rose. "My God, you're dumb!"

"Well," said Coke, "what they want to put his name in here for?"

Rose burst out laughing, and getting to her feet she took the magazine away from Coke and lay down again.

"Give me that," said Coke. "I ain't finished it yet."

"No," said Rose, pushing him away, "I want to read all about my big, strong, cute, dumb papa."

"Sure I'm dumb," said Coke. "I never had no education. I can't help it."

"Mama was just kidding," said Rose, putting the magazine down and holding out her arms to him. "You're smart enough to make lots of money, and that's plenty smart."

"Sure," said Coke, grinning.

He lay down on the lounge with Rose.

"Ooch over," he said.

"God, do you want all the room," said Rose. "I'm glad we got twin beds, even if we don't use 'em much."

VII

Coke was sitting in an armchair by the window, and Rose was pacing up and down. They had just returned from seeing Mrs. Lewis off. Coon and Lewis were waiting downstairs for them. But Coke was tired.

"Can't we call this off?" said Coke. "You know I ain't used to this staying up till three o'clock every night. I feel stale."

"All you do is crab parties," said Rose. "You suggested this yourself."

"Yeah," said Coke, "but I was full of beer then. Now I don't feel like going. For God's sake, Rose, can't you stay home one night."

"If you had your way," said Rose, "you'd plant me here so I couldn't do nothing but read magazines, then you'd go running after your bum friends. Let me tell you something, if you bring that Jeff Davis up here again, I'm gonna get an apartment of my own."

"Say, what's wrong with Jeff?"

"He looks like a cross between a gunman and a what-is-it!"

"Well," said Coke, "I ain't no beauty myself."

"You look all right," said Rose. "You look like other people, but Jeff's got a cauliflower ear and how he dresses!"

The phone rang. Rose ran to answer it. It was Coon. He told her that Marty Wills, the comedian, and his wife had joined the party and they were all patiently waiting. Rose was so excited and talked so rapidly that Coke could hardly make out what she was saying.

"Marty Wills is a big shot, Coke," she said. "When you travel with him, you're traveling."

"No," said Coke, flushing. "I'm not going, goddam it! I guess I ought to know what I want to do, oughtn't I? I don't care if President Coolidge is down there."

"All you think about is yourself," said Rose. "I never seen such a selfish guy."

"I'm not selfish," said Coke. "But I guess I can do what I want to once in a while, can't I?"

"Do what you please," said Rose. "Only why don't you let me do what I please?"

"You want to go without me?" Coke inquired.

"Yes," said Rose.

"Well, go then," said Coke.

Rose hastily wrapped a cloak around her and went out. Coke got up, took a magazine from a table, and threw it against the wall. Then he lay down on the lounge, put his hands under his head, and stared at the ceiling.

"Maybe I better go," he thought. "It won't look right."

The phone rang. It was Coon, who politely requested that he go with them.

"No," said Coke, "I'm tired. I'm gonna get a rest."

He slammed up the receiver.

"Think they can tell me what to do!" he said.

He lay down on the lounge again and stared at the ceiling. Little by little his resentment left him and he fell asleep. When he woke up the clock was just striking twelve. He got to his feet and started to undress, but stopped and stood looking at himself in a mirror. He smiled, showing his teeth, he took a brush and tried to brush his hair flat, he pulled his collar low and tightened his tie, in imitation of Lewis.

"No use," he said to his image in the mirror, "you'd look better in a sweater."

He walked about the room, not knowing what to do with himself, then, finally, whistling out of boredom, he sat down and picked up a newspaper. He read the fight news with slight interest and threw the paper on the floor. He tried a magazine, but could find nothing to hold his attention. He walked over to the radio and tentatively fiddled with the dial, but, shrugging his shoulders, he turned off the current before he had located a station. Finally he put on his coat and hat and went out. There were vacant taxis standing in front of the hotel, but he started out on foot. It was nine blocks to the hotel where Regan lived, and before Coke reached it, he felt better.

"By God," he thought, "I need exercise. I'm gonna get myself in shape."

Jeff opened the door to let him in. Riley, Regan, Mandl and Cahill were playing poker. Regan was the big winner, Mandl the big loser.

"There's my jinx," said Regan. "Who asked for you, anyway?"

"Just thought I'd drop in and see how you was," said Coke, sitting down.

"Pretty fair," said Regan, "and laying off the booze. Say, Coke, are you getting fat?"

"Yeah," said Coke, "I put on ten or twelve pounds."

"Better cut it out," said Regan.

"I can take it off," said Coke.

"Calling," said Mandl.

Regan laid down three aces.

"My God!" cried Mandl, slamming down his cards. "Where do you keep 'em, up your sleeve?"

"You can stay, Coke," said Regan. "I guess you ain't gonna jinx me tonight. Where's the missus?"

Coke hesitated.

"She's home," he said.

"Getting her trained, are you, boy?" Cahill put in.

"Mighty sweet kid," said Riley. "If I had a kid like that I'd be home with her."

"Seen her the other day," said Mandl. "Down at The Commander with some big fat guy."

Regan kicked Mandl under the table.

"Yeah?" said Coke.

"That is, I thought it was her," said Mandl. "Has she got a big black fur coat?"

"No," said Coke.

"Well, it wasn't then," said Mandl.

Coke laughed.

"I thought you was way off," he said.

The cards were dealt again. Regan opened and Cahill stayed. Regan bet.

"Up one," said Cahill. "I'm gonna keep you honest, George."

"All right," said Regan. "Up five more."

"I ain't curious," said Cahill.

Regan showed his openers and threw the rest of his hand into the discard.

"Come on, Coke," said Regan. "Pull up a chair and get a stack."

"No," said Coke. "I might just as well hand you guys my money. You're too smart for me."

"Too smart for me, too," said Mandl, "but I ain't got such good sense as you got."

But the next hand, Mandl drew to a pair of aces and caught an ace full. Regan was out, both Cahill and Riley had fair hands and stayed. Mandl won a big pot. He reached over and put his hand on Coke's shoulder.

"Stick around, champ," he said. "Maybe I can get even before the winners want to quit."

"Did you hear me make any crack about quitting?" Regan inquired.

Jeff came over and sat down beside Coke.

"Champ," he said, "you missed something when you missed the O'Keefe-Willis go. I never seen such a battle. Just like Firpo and Dempsey."

"I read about it," said Coke.

"I won a hundred bucks on that bum," said Mandl.

"You plunger," said Riley.

"Well," said Mandl, "you don't expect me to bet my roll on a guy that tramps on his own feet, do you?"

"You wait," said Regan. "When our friend William Coke Mason retires, O'Keefe's gonna fill his shoes."

"That's the only way he will," said Coke.

"All right," said Regan. "But anyway Joe Savella thinks he's good enough."

"You gonna match him with Joe?" asked Coke.

"We'll sign up this week," said Regan. "And if he licks old Joe, Bat's gonna give him a match."

"Well," said Riley, "I'll say one thing for the Rattler, it'll take a damn good man to knock him out. That guy Willis hit him on the jaw so many times he sprained his wrist."

"He's tough," said Jeff.

"Some day I'll hit him with a left hook just to show you guys how tough he is," said Coke.

He got up and put on his coat.

"Well," said Regan, "he wants to work out with you, Coke."

"I'll drop down to the gym some time," said Coke, "and we'll go a couple of rounds."

He put on his hat.

"Remember me to the missus," said Regan.

"All right," said Coke, then: "Say, George, why don't you never drop around and see us?"

"I'm waiting to be invited," said Regan.

"Say," said Coke, "don't I come to see you without being invited?"

"Sure," said Regan, "but I ain't got no frau. Anyway, I might run into some of your Four Hundred friends and I'd shock 'em to death."

Everybody laughed.

"None of you guys ever look me up any more," said Coke. "None of you guys ever drop around to see me except Jeff."

Jeff grinned and shifted.

"Well," said Regan, "you're the champion now, my boy, and champions are exclusive."

"Don't let him kid you," said Cahill.

Coke smiled and stood silent, looking at the floor.

The players went on with their game.

"Well," said Coke, "so long."

He went out. The wind was cold now and he took a taxi. It was about one thirty when he got up to his room. He undressed and put on his pajamas, then he lay down and began reading a magazine. He was asleep when the clock struck two.

At two-thirty Rose came in. Coke opened his eyes and sat up.

"Well," he said, "sure is time you was coming home."

"Coke," cried Rose, running over to him and putting her arms around him, "listen, I got the best news."

"All right," said Coke. "What is it?"

"You love your mama, don't you, honey?" said Rose, kissing him. "You ain't mad cause mama went and left you, are you?"

"No," said Coke.

"You want your mama to have a good time, don't you, Coke? You want her to be happy and contented, don't you?"

"Sure."

"Well," said Rose, cuddling up to him, "I got good news. Ivor Martin was down to The Viennese, and he came over to our table. When Paul told him who I was, he asked me why I didn't go back in the show business. But I said, 'Because my papa don't want me to.' But he kept insisting, Coke, and so finally we all went to a back room and he gave me a try-out."

"Yeah?"

"Well," said Rose, "I sang a couple of songs for him and danced. Did he

like it? Ask Marty Wills. He said he had a spot for me in his big show. Not
a chorus job, but a spot, Coke, a spot. But I told him I couldn't do nothing
till I saw my papa."

"That's right," said Coke, scratching his head. "You don't need to go back
in the business, Rose. Ain't I got plenty of money? Don't I give you everything you want?"

"Oh, but I want to," said Rose. "'Tain't every girl that gets a chance to be
in one of Ivor Martin's shows. It'd be great, Coke. Just think: little Rose
with a spot in one of Ivor Martin's big shows. Only one season, Coke,
that'd be enough. Just for the fun of it."

"I don't like it," said Coke. "I never would see you, honey."

"Course you would, Coke. You could meet me every night, and we'd have
every day together. Be a sport, Coke!"

"I don't get the idea," said Coke, getting up and walking back and forth.
"You got wonderful clothes, and a nice apartment and a big car and a
chauffeur. What's the idea?"

"Let me ask you something," said Rose. "Remember that magazine the
manager sent up here for you with your picture in it and all that?"

"Yeah," said Coke.

"Well," said Rose, "did you get a kick out of it, or didn't you?"

"Sure I did," said Coke. "I like to read articles about myself."

"Well," said Rose, "so do I. Everybody does, see? I want to be doing something for myself, Coke, so I won't feel like I don't amount to nothing. As it
is, I'm just the champion's wife, that's all."

"Ain't that something?" asked Coke.

"Yeah, but it ain't to my credit. Anybody could be that."

"Oh no they couldn't."

"Well, in a way they could. Don't be so stubborn, Coke. Lots of husbands
would be tickled to death to see their wives picked out like I was without
trying or nothing."

"I bet Lewis done it," said Coke. "He and Coon are always talking about
you going back on the stage. Lewis works for Martin, don't he? I bet he
pulled the whole thing."

"Well, you just call him up and ask him if he did," said Rose.

Coke didn't say anything.

"Just call him up and ask him."

Coke sat down and stared at the floor. He didn't know what to do.

Rose went into the bedroom, took off her dress, and put on a kimono.
When she came back into the livingroom, Coke was still sitting with his
elbows on his knees, looking at the floor.

"Coke," she said, "suppose I said to you, 'Don't fight no more. I don't want
you fighting. I want you to stick around home all the time.'"

Coke just looked at her.

"You got money enough, Coke," she went on. "You got enough money out of that fight with Bayliss to last you the rest of your life, and you know it. What's the idea, then? Why don't you quit fighting?"

"I like it," said Coke. "I wouldn't know what to do with myself."

"Don't you suppose other people feel that way? It ain't just the money, and you know it."

"No," said Coke, "it ain't. But women are different. When they get married, they ought to settle down and let their husbands look after 'em. That's what I say."

"You're behind the times, honey," said Rose, going over to him and putting her arms around him. "That's old fashioned."

"I'm old fashioned," said Coke. "I don't like the way people do things now. You'd never ketch my mother talking like you talk."

"Times have changed, honey," said Rose, kissing him. "Women don't take a back seat nowadays."

"No," said Coke, "you said a mouthful."

He pushed Rose away, got up and stood looking down into the empty street. Rose lit a cigarette and watched him.

"Well," said Coke, "I always wanted you just to have nice things and take it easy and have women friends and play bridge and stuff like that, like women do. I thought since I made a pile of money that everything'd go along smooth and we'd just kind of have a good time. But I guess you don't see things that way."

He rubbed his hands over his face.

"Listen, Rose," he went on, "I don't want you moping around here saying I won't let you do nothing. If you want to go back on the stage, go!"

He went into the bedroom and closed the door. But Rose followed him and called:

"Honey, come here. I want to show you something."

Coke came back.

"Sit over there," said Rose, pointing to the lounge.

Coke obeyed. Rose twisted the dial of the radio till she found some jazz music, then she took off her kimono and began to dance. Coke sat watching her sullenly for a moment, then little by little his face lit up and he began to grin. When she had finished, he got up and applauded loudly.

"You'll knock 'em dead, kid," he cried. "Just as sure as shooting, you'll knock 'em dead."

"Ketch me," said Rose.

Coke spread his feet apart and set himself. Rose ran across the room and flung herself into his arms.

"Alley-up!" cried Rose.

VIII

When Coke came in Rose, Lewis, Ada Berger, one of Martin's stars, Coon, and Marty Wills and his wife were all sitting in the living-room.

"Hail the champion!" said Marty Wills, jumping to attention and saluting.

Coke was received with shouts and laughter. But Rose seemed sullen. Lewis took Coke by the arm and said:

"Your wife just had a very unpleasant experience."

"Yeah?" said Coke.

"We were all standing down in the lobby," Lewis went on, "when Regan and Urban Riley came in. They were looking for you. Rose told them that you'd be here in a few minutes, to wait."

"Yeah," said Coke.

"Well, Regan was slightly drunk, and you know how he is. Good fellow otherwise, but unpleasant when he's drunk. Rose was nice to him, but he proceeded to wisecrack everybody and make a show of himself. Riley tried to make him behave. But it wasn't any use. Pretty soon Rose told him to come upstairs with the rest of the party and wait, but he said, 'No, too damn many ham actors to suit me.'"

Coke stood looking at the floor. Rose came over to them.

"What did you want to tell him for!" she demanded. "He swears by George Regan."

"He ought to know it," said Lewis.

"Yeah," said Coke, "much obliged."

"I wasn't going to tell you, Coke," said Rose.

Coke said nothing but went into the bedroom, took off his coat, and sat down in a chair beside the window. In the living-room somebody turned on the radio and they all began to dance. Coke sat looking down into the street. Gradually the noise from the next room became blurred and faint, it seemed far away, he closed his eyes and began to nod. He saw Lake Erie with the sun on it: he and George were sitting in a battered rowboat drinking beer. In a moment he was asleep.

Rose was shaking him. He rubbed his eyes and looked up at her.

"Old man," she said, "you been sleeping for one solid hour."

"I was tired," said Coke.

"We're all going down to rehearsal," said Rose. "If you're tired you can stay here."

"All right," said Coke.

"Listen, Coke," said Rose. "Don't say nothing to George. He was drunk."

"I wish he wouldn't act that way," said Coke.

Rose made up her face and wrapped a cloak around her.

"Good-bye, papa," she said.

"Good-bye," said Coke.

She went out. Coke sat listening. When the hubbub of voices had ceased, he pulled himself to his feet yawning and stretching, and opened the door into the living-room. Everybody had gone but Coon and Lewis. Coon was standing with his back to the wall and Lewis had him by the arms, shaking him. Coon's face was pasty and pale.

"Hey," said Coke, "what's going on here?"

Coon started and stood with his mouth open, but Lewis released Coon, turned and smiled blandly.

"Just a little argument, Mason," he said.

"Yeah?" said Coke looking from one to the other.

"Just a little argument," said Coon.

"I gave Coon some money to bet for me," said Lewis, "quite a bit, and due to a misunderstanding, I guess, he put it on the wrong horse."

"Yes," said Coon, "that's it. Just a misunderstanding."

Coke grinned.

"I'm surprised at you guys fighting over money," he said.

PART VI

I

The main-go was on when Lewis and Coke took their seats. O'Keefe was shuffling around the ring trying to catch up with old Joe Savella, who eluded him, rushed him when he wasn't looking for it, and hit him with a left so many times that at the end of the round O'Keefe's face was beefy. Regan saw Coke and waved to him. McNeil and Jeff were working on O'Keefe, who was grinning and seemed fresh.

"Joe'll lick him sure," said Coke.

"He's made for him," said Lewis.

The second round was the same as the first, except that O'Keefe took more lefts in the face. But the lefts didn't stop him and he hounded old Joe from corner to corner, shuffling, throwing rights, and wading in wide open.

"Stamina's all he's got," said Lewis.

"Yeah," said Coke. "But if Joe could hit the fight'd be over."

During the third and fourth rounds O'Keefe continued to take lefts, but he was increasing the pace and Savella was tiring. In the fifth Savella showed unmistakable signs of weariness, but O'Keefe seemed fresher than ever and shuffled after Joe and drove him against the ropes time after time. Joe clinched and rested, but his arms were weary and his legs were wavering. In the sixth Joe spurted and upset O'Keefe with a series of perfect body punches, but O'Keefe, without waiting for a count, leapt up and mauled Joe all over the ring.

Coke sat biting his lips.

"That Irish boy's going to win," said Lewis.

"Yeah," said Coke, "old Joe's about through, I guess."

In the seventh and eighth rounds Joe gave a wonderful exhibition of emergency fighting, staying in close to O'Keefe, tying him up, making him miss. Toward the end of the eighth round, O'Keefe, trying for a knockout, missed a wild right swing and fell head first through the ropes, nearly falling into the crowd. For the rest of the round, Savella kept him on the ropes, pummelling him. But it was no use. O'Keefe seemed as fresh as at the beginning, fresher even, and Savella was nearly through. In the ninth, O'Keefe landed three or four hard body punches, followed by a right uppercut to the jaw, and Savella went down for the count.

"Well," said Lewis.

"I'll have to work out with that kid," said Coke.

He glanced up. There was O'Keefe, twenty-three years old, freckled and homely, with big shoulders and small legs—Young Fitz, the papers called him—grinning from ear to ear, calm and fresh. Coke clenched his hands.

"Yeah," he said, "I'll have to work out with that boy."

"Well, champ," he said, "what do you think of the kid?"

"Well," said Coke, "stamina's about all he's got. Wait till Cahill gets through with him."

"You must admit though," said the writer, "that Joe Savella is one of the best fighters in the business."

"Yeah," said Coke, "but he's about through now. He's getting old."

Regan came over and put his hand on Coke's shoulder.

"Well," he said, "you and your boy-friend here saw a real fighter tonight. A near champion."

"He wouldn't last one round with Coke," said Lewis.

"No, he's meat for me," said Coke.

"I ain't so sure," said Regan. "Not with that belly on you."

"I'll show you," said Coke.

II

Everybody who heard about the exhibition match between young O'Keefe and the champion turned up at Halloran's gymnasium: admission fifty cents.

Coke came in with Lewis and went straight to his dressing-room. Regan followed him.

"Take it easy with the kid, Coke," said Regan. "Don't try to show off, just because you got a crowd."

"I can't pull punches," said Coke. "We'll have the big mits on, won't we?"

"Sure," said Regan, "but you got dynamite in that left and I don't want the kid hurt."

"Hell," said Coke, "I won't hurt him."

Regan went out.

"It's funny," said Lewis.

"What's funny," demanded Coke.

"Why," said Lewis, hitting at one of his spats with his cane, "you'd think to hear Regan talk, that O'Keefe was the champion and you were just some tough pug. If I was Regan I'd be worrying about you, not O'Keefe. Not that you can't lick this kid, but people do get hurt in the ring, you know. Foul blows and spills."

Coke didn't say anything, but he sat thinking.

When Lewis and Coke came out of the dressing-room, O'Keefe was already in the ring, waiting. Coke, looking over the crowd, saw Coon sitting near his corner.

"There's Coon," said Coke

"I see him," said Lewis.

"Say," said Coke, "what's wrong between you two guys? You act awful funny lately."

"We don't get along, that's all."

"Why, I think Coon's a pretty nice fellow," said Coke.

"We don't hit it off," said Lewis, sitting down.

Coke went over and shook hands with Coon.

"I'm waiting to see something, champ," said Coon.

When Coke climbed through the ropes, O'Keefe got up, ran across the ring and shook hands with him.

"Hello, champ," he said. "Mighty nice of you to come down and work out with me."

Coke couldn't resist O'Keefe's genuine friendliness. He put his arm around O'Keefe.

"Nice fight you fought the other night, kid," he said. "I had you on the short end sure."

"Well," said O'Keefe, "Joe's a great fighter, but I'm a lot younger."

"Yeah," said Coke, "that counts."

The crowd around the ring gave them a big hand and they both grinned and mitted the crowd. Regan stepped into the ring and held up his hands for silence.

"Folks," he said, "this is more than just an ordinary work-out. As you all know I'm managing both these boys, and they're both mighty good boys, if anybody should ask you, and we decided it'd be pretty nice if the champ would work out with the kid, over here. The champ's O.K. as you all know, and he's for giving a comer a break. So here we are, folks, just a little exhibition with the big mitts. Two two-minute rounds."

McNeil refereed. The bell rang and the fighters shook hands. Coke rushed O'Keefe and landed a few light body blows. O'Keefe took them without a return. Coke backed away and circled around O'Keefe, who grinned and shuffled. Coke rushed in again and landed a left to the body followed by a right to the head, both light, but he got a stiff left in return. O'Keefe was a natural lefthander but fought with the orthodox stance, and his straight left was a wallop. Coke looked surprised. Before the end of the round he got that left on the forehead again and it hurt. But he went to his corner grinning. Lewis leaned through the ropes.

"He certainly is careless with that left," he said.

"If he hits me hard with that left again," said Coke, "I'll hook him, and then watch."

The first part of the second round was very tame. Coke landed light blows at will and clubbed O'Keefe in the clinches, but not hard. O'Keefe, grinning and shuffling, couldn't elude Coke, who looked fast compared with him. But toward the end of the round, as much through clumsiness as anything else, O'Keefe hit Coke a terrific wallop with his left. Coke went back on his heels. There was a roar from the crowd. Coke glanced at O'Keefe. O'Keefe was grinning. Coke misinterpreted the grin, maneuvered him into a corner, feinted him into a right swing and lifted him off his feet with a left hook. But O'Keefe grinned. So Coke hit him with the left hook again and banged him on the jaw with a right. The grin faded.

Regan leapt through the ropes and gave Coke a push.

"Say," he said, "what you trying to do, kill this kid! He's out on his feet."

"Well," said Coke, flushing, "let him watch that left."

"I'm all right," said O'Keefe. "Boy, what a punch you got!"

"It's all over," Regan shouted to the crowd. "The champion lost his temper."

A few people in the rear booed Coke.

McNeil and Jeff took O'Keefe to his corner and worked on him. Regan stood in the center of the ring, mumbling:

"Goddam swellhead!"

"Shut up!" said Coke, "or I'll hook you one."

"Try it," said Regan, reaching toward his hip pocket where he always carried a blackjack.

Lewis jumped through the ropes and grabbed Coke from behind.

"Never mind, Coke," he said. "It was all a frame-up to make you look cheap."

Regan turned on his heel and climbed out of the ring. A fight started on the edge of the crowd and a small riot was averted by the quick thinking of Kid Halloran, who shouted:

"Police! Police!"

Coke climbed through the ropes and, glaring at the crowd, went to his dressing-room, followed by Lewis. Before he got his clothes on O'Keefe came in.

"Champ," he said, "they tell me you think I was trying to show you up. That's a lie. I just wanted to work out with you, that's all."

"All right," said Coke. "But the next time you work out with me, it'll be in The Coliseum and you'll find out how a left hook feels with a five ounce glove."

"You gonna give me a match, champ?" cried O'Keefe.

"Soon as you get a reputation," said Coke. "Now beat it."

O'Keefe stood shifting.

"What's the use of us being sore, champ," he said. "I'm for you."

"Yeah," said Coke.

"Let's shake hands," said O'Keefe.

Coke held out his hand but shook hands limply. O'Keefe looked at him for a moment, then went out.

"You're foolish if you think this was an accident, Mason," said Lewis. "It was just one of Regan's smart tricks."

"I don't know," said Coke.

As soon as he got dressed, he and Lewis went out into the gymnasium. One of the pugs took Coke by the arm.

"It takes you to do it, champ," he said.

Regan was standing at the door talking to Coon and Halloran. When Coon saw Lewis, he said goodbye to Halloran hastily and went out.

"George," Coke called.

Regan came over and glanced at Lewis, who was standing with Coke.

"Coke," said Regan, "let me give you a straight tip. Lay off these dressed up theatrical boys. They're fixing to take you."

Lewis laughed.

"What are you sore about, Regan?"

"Never mind," said Coke, cutting in. "Listen, George, did you try to frame me? If you did, all I can say is that you're as rotten a friend as you are a manager."

"Well," said Regan, "your name's on the dotted line and you're working for me. Get the idea?"

"Sure," said Coke.

"All right," said Regan. "You get funny with me and I'll tie you up so you won't fight for a good long while."

"What did I tell you!" Lewis put in.

"You better keep out of this, you damn crook," said Regan. "I might tell some funny stories about you."

"I been expecting you to," said Lewis, "but I think Coke knows just about how much dependence to put on what you say."

"Wait a minute," said Coke. "I'm gonna do the talking. George, if you try to tie me up, I'll retire and then where'll you be. I got plenty of money. If I never fight again, I won't die in the poor house."

Regan stared at Coke, then walked away.

III

About eight o'clock one night Coke went up to Regan's room unannounced and knocked at the door. Regan let him in, but said nothing. Coke took off his overcoat and hat, and picked himself out a chair, then he took out his cigar case.

"Cigar, George?"

"Yeah, thanks," said Regan, selecting one and sitting opposite Coke.

"Well, George," said Coke, "how's things?"

"All right," said Regan. "Where you been keeping yourself?"

"Oh, I been kind of sticking around since the wife went back on the stage," said Coke. "I'm going down to the gymnasium tomorrow."

"You better," said Regan, "and get some of that belly off."

"Yeah," said Coke.

"I bet you put on fifteen pounds."

"Yeah. I wear a sixteen and a half collar now."

"Horse collar," said Regan, "and me with a fourteen."

"Say," said Coke, "why don't you never look me up no more...?"

"I don't like your gang," said Regan, "and while we're on the subject, I want to have a little talk with you."

"That's what I came down for, George."

"Yeah?" said Regan. "Well, here's the way it is, Coke. I'll be frank with you. It don't look to me like we're ever gonna get along together again."

"Aw, hell," said Coke, laughing.

"All right," said Regan, "laugh your head off. But a guy can't work for two bosses. The missus has got you roped and hogtied, and you won't listen to me no more. Now here's the thing: either I'm your manager or I'm not. As it is, I'm not. I'm just a kind of junior partner that's in the way. Get the idea? You never ask me about nothing. You never pay no attention to what I say. All you can see is the missus and her prompter."

"What do you mean, her prompter?" Coke demanded.

"I mean Lewis," said Regan, "and a dirtier crook never lived."

"Now wait, George," said Coke. "Lewis is a good friend of mine. You think he's a crook, but I don't. So let it go at that."

"They sure got you hooked," said Regan, meditatively.

Coke sighed and sat looking at the ash on his cigar.

"Yeah," said Regan. "Just like I said. It's hopeless."

"Hell," said Coke, "to hear you talk you'd think I didn't have good sense."

"I wouldn't go that far," said Regan.

Coke got up and stood looking out the window.

Regan leaned back in his chair and stared at the ceiling.

"Coke," said Regan, "Cahill's ready to fight O'Keefe."

"Yeah?"

"Yeah. And I'm going to bet two grand on O'Keefe."

"Kiss that good-bye," said Coke. "Bat'll left jab him to death."

"Maybe," said Regan, "but you ain't seen the Rattler lately. He's a hundred per cent better than when he fought Joe Savella."

"He'll have to be, unless Cahill takes it easy with him."

Regan laughed.

"The only thing that worries me about the Rattler," he said, "is his weight. He'll be a heavy some day, but I want him to make his mark in the middleweight division before he takes on weight."

"Listen, George," said Coke, "a lot of people think that if you paid more attention to me and less to O'Keefe, you'd be a lot better off. 'Tain't every guy that gets to manage a champion."

"Well," said Regan, "I'll admit I've got more breaks than a guy is entitled to. Because if anything happens to my champion, I got two more boys that'll both make a bid for it."

"What do you mean?"

"Well," said Regan, "with you out of the way, who do you think can lick O'Keefe? Nobody, that's the answer. All right, that's one. Now what do you suppose would happen if Willy Strapp'd get big-hearted and give Speed a bout? Speed'd lick him. So you see, Coke, I'm fixed."

"Meaning," said Coke, "that you can get along without me, I guess, now since I made you a pile of jack. That's what the wife says. She don't think you're giving me a square deal. Neither does Lewis or Coon."

"Well, well," said Regan. "By the way, Coke, they tell me that Coon's leaving for Europe this week."

"Yeah," said Coke, "he's taking a trip around the world or something. That's one reason I come down to see you, George. The missus and I are giving a party for him down at The Viennese. We got a private room with all the fixings. I want you to come."

"Do I have to wear a monkey suit?"

"Well...."

"You said enough."

"No, George," said Coke, "you don't have to. The missus likes that kind of stuff, you know, that dressing up. But I don't, see? I just do it to please her. Look, George, all the other guys are gonna wear dress suits, but you don't need to, and I won't."

"I'm not much on parties."

"Be a sport, George."

"Well," said Regan, "I'll go."

Coke hit him on the back.

"That's good. Glad to hear it," he cried, then he looked at his watch. "Say, George, are you going any place tonight?"

"No," said Regan. "Why?"

"Let's get a taxi and go down and see the missus," said Coke. "You ain't seen her in the show yet, have you?"

"No."

"All right," said Coke, "come on. If we step on it, we'll just get there in time to see her."

"It's all right with me," said Regan.

They sat silent in the taxi, Regan smoking and Coke looking out at the traffic. It was a chilly night and a heavy fog had come in from the Atlantic. Wet pavements shone under the white headlights. When they got to the theatre, Coke pointed to the sign.

IVOR MARTIN PRESENTS
Señor Caballero
with
Marty Wills, Ada Berger
Ann Hogarth and Rose Mason

"Pretty nice, eh, George?" Coke demanded.

"Yeah," said Regan, "but the 'Mason' don't hurt that sign none."

Coke laughed.

They were led to a box by an usher who seemed overwhelmed by the presence of the middleweight champion. They sat down. The house was dark except for the footlights, a great maroon curtain ornamented with designs in silver had just fallen, and the orchestra was playing a lazy nigger tune.

"Just in time," said Coke, "the missus does her first stunt in front of that big curtain. Ain't it a dandy? Lewis designed it."

"I didn't know he was that kind of a boy," said Regan. "Does he crochet?"

"There you go," said Coke laughing.

The orchestra reiterated the slow nigger tune, then a little cabaret piano was wheeled out on the stage by one of Rose's helpers: a slim little fellow in a Tuxedo with his face blacked up. The pianist, another blackface, was already seated at the piano playing, and Rose, in a hoop skirt, made up as a high yellow, was perched on the top of the piano. The orchestra crashed out a series of consecutive ninths, and subsided, then the piano was heard in syncopated arpeggioes. In a somewhat husky soprano Rose began to sing a nigger blues called "Old New Orleans," and the little black boy, standing beside her, looking up at her, furnished the breaks in a high-pitched, syncopated chant.

A verse and two choruses were sung, then the time was suddenly speeded up by the pianist, the orchestra joined in, and Rose, leaping down from the piano, snatched off her hoopskirt and appeared in a brassiere and tight yellow shorts. She and the little black boy began to dance, a fast syncopated nigger dance, built on the blackbottom.

"Say," said Regan, leaning over and putting his hand on Coke's shoulder, "the missus is really good."

"Sure," said Coke. "All she needed was a chance."

Toward the end of a second repetition of the chorus, the time was retarded, the orchestra subsided, Rose jumped up on the piano and was wheeled out by the little black boy, who shuffled with the music and was still taking the breaks. The act seemed so spontaneous that the audience roared for an encore, but Ivor Martin allowed no one to interfere with the pace of his Revues, so the show went on.

Marty Wills came out in an exaggerated Spanish costume and convulsed the house by tangoing with Ann Hogarth, a good clown.

"Some show," said Regan.

"Yeah," said Coke.

Rose made another appearance at the beginning of the second act. This time, supported by the two black boys, now Argentinians with baggy trousers and whips on their wrists, she danced a jazzed up version of the tango, and sang a pseudo-Spanish song in Spanish.

Coke took Regan by the arm.

"That kid can do anything," he said. "She picked up that lingo in no time."

"She's O.K.," said Regan, impressed.

Then toward the end of the show, Rose made another appearance. This time she danced and sang in front of a chorus of girls in black and rhinestone, wearing blond wigs. The applause was long and loud, but the show went on.

At the finale the big spotlight was suddenly shifted from the stage to the box where Regan and Coke were sitting. Marty Wills stepped to the footlights and cried:

"Friends, Coke Mason, the champion."

"God, they spotted us," said Coke.

Regan, blinded by the glare, drew back into a corner, but Coke stood up and bowed to the audience.

When the show was over, Regan wanted to get a taxi and go home, but Coke led him back to the stage entrance. Coke's chauffeur had the car parked in the alleyway and was walking up and down, smoking a cigarette.

"Hello, boss," he said.

"Hello, Harry," said Coke. "Is she coming right out?"

"Yeah," said the chauffeur, "but I think she's got a load."

"That's all right," said Coke.

Regan and Coke lit cigars and stood talking. The fog had lifted, it had got cooler, and the stars were shining.

"Nice night," said Coke in a good humor. "Say, George, remember when we used to go fishing?"

"Yeah," said Regan.

"Remember when we used to take them moonlight excursions to Detroit and Put-In-Bay?"

"Yeah," said Regan.

The chauffeur stood listening. Pretty soon he said:

"You guys must've known each other for a long time."

"We sure did," said Coke. "George used to black my eye when we was kids."

"I'd like to see him do it now," said the chauffeur.

They went on talking about Lake Erie and the summer resorts. The chauffeur, who was from Clyde, Ohio, knew that part of the country himself and joined in the conversation. When Rose came out the three of them were standing smoking cigars, laughing and talking.

"Harry," called Rose, "don't you see me? Open that door."

"Yes, ma'am," said Harry, throwing away his cigar and leaping to attention.

Rose came over to Coke, nodded to Regan, and said:

"Coke, how many times do I have to tell you not to be so familiar with Harry. If you had your way he'd be eating with us. Won't you ever learn anything?"

"Aw, Rose," said Coke.

Regan stiffened.

"No, Coke," he said, "you mustn't get contaminated by the hoi polloi."

Ann Hogarth, Marty Wills, Coon and Ada Berger came out in a group, followed at a little distance by Lewis.

"Well," said Regan, "here comes your playmates, so I'm fading."

"Stick around, George," said Coke. "I'll take you home."

"Take him in a taxi, dear," said Rose. "I've got a load."

"Good Lord," said Coke, "why can't some of them other people ever bring their cars. I get sick of taxis."

"But I promised," said Rose. "We're going out to Coon's place. Everything's arranged."

"I guess I ain't invited," said Coke.

"Don't be silly," said Rose. "Get a taxi and follow us out."

"Sure," said Regan, "don't mind me. I'll get home."

Coke stood looking at the ground. Regan took his hand and shook it.

"Much obliged for the evening, kid," he said. "I'll be seeing you."

Coke nodded. Regan climbed into a taxi and slammed the door.

"You follow us, Coke," said Rose, turning, she cried: "Pile in everybody."

Coke just stood there.

"Get a cab, dear," said Rose, "so you can follow us right out."

Rose got into the car. Everybody in the car began to laugh.

"I guess you'll have to sit on my lap," cried Coon.

Lewis tried to climb in, but Rose pushed him out and said:

"Up front, Paul."

Lewis climbed in with the chauffeur. Coke stood watching them for a moment, then he went over to the car.

"Ooch over, Lewis," he said.

"There isn't much room here," said Lewis.

"Well," said Coke, "ooch over anyway."

He got in beside Lewis and the three of them sat wedged together, very uncomfortable. Nobody had anything to say.

IV

Regan took off his coat and hat, and handed them to the checkgirl. He was in evening clothes and already drunk. He took a silver dollar from his pocket and spun it on the counter.

"Heads it's yours and tails it's mine," he said.

The girl laughed. The dollar came tails.

"Tough break," said Regan putting it back in his pocket.

The headwaiter came over to him, followed by Coke, who was wearing a Tuxedo.

"Just what I thought," said Regan. "Boy, I'm too smart for you, that's all. I thought you'd cross me and put on a monkey-suit, so I rented one."

"You look fine, George," said Coke.

The headwaiter stood smiling. Finally he inquired if he should have the dinner served.

"Yeah," said Coke, "we're all set now."

Regan took the dollar out of his pocket and spun it on the counter.

"Sister," he called, "I'll give you another break."

The checkgirl watched the dollar, it came heads and she picked it up.

"All right," said Regan, "it's yours. I could hold out for two out of three, but I won't. Coke, old boy, if you don't look like a straight man in a burlesque show, I'll pay your way to Alaska."

"This collar's sawing my neck," said Coke.

Regan followed Coke back through the crowded nightclub into a big private room beyond. Ada Berger, Ann Hogarth, Marty Wills and his wife, Coon, Rose and Lewis were all seated at a big, round table. Regan sat down beside Ada Berger and immediately began to talk to her.

"I suppose you all know my manager George Regan," said Coke.

"What does it matter!" cried Regan, taking a silver flask out of his pocket and offering it to Ada.

"I can't take mine straight," said Ada.

"How come I picked you out!" said Regan.

"I'll take a drink, George," said Rose.

Regan got up and went to sit beside her. She drank from his flask, and when the jazzband began to play, he brushed aside Coon and Lewis, who both wanted to dance with her, and led her out to the dance floor. The rest of them paired off gradually. Coke, pleased by the way Regan was acting, sat alone with his stein of beer. A waiter entered with the soup.

"Left you all by yourself, did they, champ?" said the waiter.

"Yeah," said Coke, smiling. "I'd rather drink beer anyway."

"Don't blame you," said the waiter. "I see 'em dancing every night and I often wonder what they do it for. I don't see no fun in shoving each other around in a mob like that. If they had to earn their living that way they'd put up an awful howl."

"Yeah," said Coke. "I'd rather swap punches any day."

"Sure you would," said the waiter, "and I'd rather swing a tray."

Coke took out a cigar and gave it to the waiter.

"I'll see you when we bust up," he said.

"O.K.," said the waiter.

He went out.

At the end of the first encore, they all came back to eat their soup, Regan and Rose arm in arm. Lewis was with Ada Berger, Coon with Mrs. Wills, and Marty with Ann Hogarth.

Two waiters came in carrying the champagne and everybody stood up and cheered. As soon as the champagne was poured, Lewis got up with his glass and said:

"Folks, let's all drink a little toast to the greatest fighter in the business, Mr. Coke Mason."

The toast was drunk and Coke bowed and shouted: "Thanks! Thanks!"

Regan got up and waved his flask.

"'Tain't right, folks. You hear me! Ladies first is what I say. So just forget you've drunk that one and we'll start off with a toast to one of the hottest little hoofers on Broadway. A small town girl who made good. Rose Mason."

There was a prolonged clamor.

"Good for you, George," cried Coke.

The soup was eaten and the first round of champagne consumed, then there was a rush for the dance floor, and again Coke was left alone. The friendly waiter came in with another stein for Coke. He drank it thoughtfully. Then two waiters came in with the second course, and in a moment were followed by the party. Regan and Rose were still arm in arm, and Lewis, ignoring his partner, was trying to get a word with Rose. They all sat down, more champagne was brought in, and Coke got to his feet and said:

"Folks, before you get too soused to know what I'm talking about, I want to tell you that we have with us tonight a man you all know, who is going away on a long trip and won't be back for six months. Mr. Harold Coon."

"Speech! Speech! Speech!" yelled Marty Wills.

Coon got uncertainly to his feet.

"Well," he said, "I'm not going to interrupt this nice party by holding forth at length, but I do want to say that I'm sorry to leave you all and certainly hope that when I come back you'll all be as glad to see me as I am to see you. As a matter of fact, I wouldn't go at all if my doctor hadn't insisted. He thinks ocean air will be good for me, also a change of regimen, what ever that is. I'm quoting him. He says I drink too much, eat too much, sleep too much, and there are other accusations I won't bother you with...."

He was drowned out by shouts of laughter, and Ada Berger pulled him back into his seat. In the club proper the jazzband began to play and in a moment one of the entertainers came into the room and stood beside Coke, singing to him. At the conclusion of her song, she kissed him on the forehead and ran out. Coke jumped up and ran after her with a five dollar bill in his hand.

"Look at that," shouted Regan. "And right in front of his wife."

"That's all right," said Rose. "It looks bad, I'll admit. But you know Coke."

"His intentions are pure," said Ann Hogarth. "He's the only decent man I ever met in my life."

"That's an insult," cried Regan, then he pulled out his flask and drank from it. "You met me, didn't you? Well, you still got your virginity as far as I'm concerned."

"Whoa!" said Lewis.

They all stared at Regan.

"What's the matter?" Regan demanded. "Didn't none of you ever hear that word before?" He stared at them. "Maybe not," he concluded.

Coke came back, grinning.

"I had to chase her all over hell and back," he said.

"Did you force the nasty money on her?" asked Regan.

"Yeah," said Coke, "but the manager says I shouldn't do it no more."

"He wants a cut himself," said Regan.

Lewis pushed himself between Regan and Rose, and asked her to dance with him.

"I'm dancing with Harold this time," she said.

Regan laughed and gave Lewis a shove.

"Be patient," he said, "your turn'll come. You'll have almost a clear field after tonight."

"Hey, George," called Coke, noticing the expression on Lewis's face, "not so rough."

Lewis got very pale and stood staring at Regan.

"Yes," said Lewis, "try to act like a gentleman."

Regan took Lewis by the lapels, put his face close to Lewis's and whispered:

"Don't try to kid me, big boy. You can kid the mister all you please, but don't try to kid me."

Lewis jerked away and asked Ada Berger to dance with him. Rose and Coon went out, followed by Marty Wills and his wife. Ann Hogarth went to sit beside Coke, who was drinking another big stein. Regan emptied his flask and put it back in his pocket.

"Want to dance with me, baby?" he said.

"No, thanks," said Ann. "Me and the champ here are going to sit this one out."

She ran her fingers through Coke's hair and patted his cheek.

"Well," said Regan, getting up, "I think I'll go out and see a gentleman friend. That champagne sure does go through you."

Coke laughed, but checked himself when he saw the expression on Ann's face. Regan went out.

"What's wrong, honey?" Coke inquired.

"I don't like that man," she said, pouting.

"Aw, he's all right," said Coke. "Just kind of rough, but he's got a good heart."

"I wish he wouldn't talk like he does," said Ann. "He embarrasses me."

Ann was small and slender and childish-looking. Her hair was cut short, a crock-cut Coke's father would have said, and in certain attitudes she didn't look over thirteen years old. She made Coke feel very protective and masculine.

"Well," said Coke, "he didn't mean nothing by the way he talks. It's just his way."

"Uh hunh," said Ann, pouting. Then she pointed to his stein. "Give baby drink."

Coke tipped the stein up for her and roared with laughter when she emerged from it with foam on her eyelashes.

"Boy, you sure took a high dive," he said.

Ann put her head on Coke's shoulder.

"I like beer," she said. "My mama says beer is vulgar, but I like it. I like corned beef, too, and I like cabbage. I'm so vulgar."

"Hell," said Coke, "that's real food."

"Mama likes croquettes," said Ann, "and duck and avacadoes and all that stuff you're supposed to like, but I don't. Mama used to like corned beef when we had a kitchenette in the Bronx. But that was before I got going. Now it takes half of what I make to feed her."

"That's the way it goes," said Coke. "That's the way Rose is, sort of."

He tipped up his stein and emptied it.

"You know," said Ann, "you and Rose are just an ideal couple. You both got your own work and you seem to get along so good. Gee, I wish I could find a man like you."

"Aw!" said Coke, embarrassed.

Ann ran her fingers through his hair.

"Did you know I went to see you fight for the championship?" she inquired.

"Did you?"

"I sure did. And when that little mick had you on the floor I jumped up and yelled, 'Stop that! Stop that!' and mama like to killed me."

Coke burst out laughing.

"That was before I ever knew you," she said.

"Yeah," said Coke, "that's right."

Regan came in followed, almost immediately, by the rest of the party. Rose stopped in the doorway when she saw Ann sitting with her head on Coke's shoulder.

"Well," she said, "ain't that cute!"

Coke grinned and Ann sat up.

"Atta boy, Coke," cried Regan, who was quite drunk now. "Give 'em what they send, kid."

"Say," said Lewis, sharply, "wouldn't it be a good idea for you to go home and go to bed? You're drunk!"

Regan turned, stared at Lewis for a moment, then without a word, he took a blackjack from his hip-pocket and struck at Lewis, who, white as chalk, ran out of the room. Regan started after him, but Coke, leaping from his chair, seized him from behind and held him.

"My God, George," he said, "where do you think you're at?"

"You wouldn't listen to me, would you!" said Rose. "I told you you couldn't invite that dirty mick with decent people."

Regan's face was red and congested. He shook Coke off, put his blackjack away, and said:

"Listen, blondy, when I came up here I made up my mind to be nice to you, but it can't be done, see, it can't be done. You ought to be ashamed of yourself, pulling the stuff you do, and then raising hell with Coke because a little kid sits with her head on his shoulder. If I was him, I'd have her out in the back room."

"Oh, would you!" cried Ann. "Coke are you gonna stand for that?"

"Yeah," said Rose. "You're a fine man!"

Coon and Ada Berger slipped out the door unnoticed, followed by Marty Wills and his wife.

"You're damn right he's gonna stand for it," said Regan. "There ain't a guy in the world that can keep me from saying my piece, when I start to say it."

Coke stood staring at Regan, not knowing what to do.

"Yeah," said Regan, "all you damn hypocrites get all excited when I say a naughty word, but there ain't one of you decent enough to appreciate a good guy when you see one. I mean Coke. He's a damn dummy and all that, but he's straight and that's more than I can say for any of the rest of you. This little kid here with all her nicey-nice talk, this cute little Ann Hogarth. Why don't somebody ask her who got her a chance in Martin's show. I'll tell you. A guy seventy years old, and he ain't her grandpa!"

Ann put her hands over her face and began to cry.

"George," Coke implored.

"Yeah," said Regan, "and who put you in the show for that matter, blondy?"

"Coke," cried Rose, "are you gonna let that dirty pool-room bum insult me?"

"George, cut it out," said Coke, flushing.

"You're gonna listen," said Regan. "I'm done with the whole damn bunch of you, see? So you're gonna listen. Yeah, blondy, why don't you speak up and tell the mister who put you in the show? Lewis put her in, Coke. You heard me. Lewis put her in the show, and his own wife knew what was going on and left him. If you don't believe me, write and ask her."

"Coke," said Rose, "hear what he's saying about me?"

"Take it back, George," said Coke. "You can't talk about my wife like that."

Regan laughed. Coke's biceps swelled under his coat and tears started from his eyes.

"Sock him, Coke," said Rose. "You gonna stand there and let him call me a whore?"

Regan saw Coke coming and reached for his blackjack, but too late. Coke sent a swift, hard right to the side of his head and followed it with a left to the body. Regan was flung back against the wall.

"Sock him again, Coke," cried Rose, screaming with excitement.

But Ann grabbed Coke's arm.

"That's enough! That's enough!" she cried.

Coke stood with his hands at his side, staring at Regan, who leaned against the wall for a moment, then slid to the floor.

"Let's go, Coke," said Rose. "The party's all busted up now."

"Yeah," said Ann. "Let's go."

They tried to drag Coke out, but he shook them off, went over to Regan, picked him up and carried him to a chair. Regan put both his hands on the table and sat staring into space, groggy.

"George," said Coke, "I had to do it. I couldn't stand for you shooting off your mouth that way."

"Get out of here and leave me alone," said Regan.

Coke stared at Regan, then turned and went out followed by Ann and Rose. Coon, Ada Berger and Mr. and Mrs. Wills were waiting at the check-room. Lewis was downstairs in the car. No one in the club proper knew that anything had happened.

Coke put on his coat and hat, tipped the checkgirls and the waiters, then he went to find the headwaiter, who was totaling up the bill. The head-waiter presented the bill and Coke paid it. Then he said:

"Mr. Regan is still back in the room. He ain't feeling so good, so he don't want to go along with us. If he wants anything give it to him and charge it to me."

"Yes sir," said the headwaiter. "Good night, Mr. Mason."

V

Lewis, Rose and Coke sat waiting for Regan, who had telephoned that he'd be down to see Coke on important business, to have Lewis there. Coke was puzzled, Lewis uneasy. But Rose was calm and sat smoking and humming to herself. Lewis had just been reading aloud some of her press notices, they were uniformly favorable.

"Mighty nice," said Coke. "I always said all you needed was a chance."

"Yes," said Lewis, "that's all she needed."

"Well," said Rose to Coke, "you held out long enough."

"I didn't want you working," said Coke.

"I know just how you feel," said Lewis. "My wife insists on working, too. It makes you feel like you aren't man enough to do the right thing, you know. I mean a man feels like he ought to support his wife."

"Yeah," said Coke, "but since Rose is doing so well and having so much fun, why, I kind of feel different about it."

"That's only natural," said Lewis.

"Yeah," said Coke, "but I don't see her much. That's the thing I don't like about it."

"The less you see of me," said Rose, "the more you'll enjoy seeing me when you do."

"That's a fact," said Lewis.

"I don't know," said Coke.

They sat in silence. Pretty soon the telephone rang. Coke answered it. It was the clerk, he told Coke that Regan and another man were on their way up.

"Coke," said Lewis, "maybe I better go in the bedroom. I don't want any trouble with Regan. He was just drunk, that's all. But you know him! He holds a grudge."

"Hell," said Coke, "you leave me handle him."

"Sure," said Rose, laughing. "He won't bite you, Paul."

Lewis flushed and stared at Rose.

There was a knock at the door and Coke opened it. Regan came in followed by McNeil. Regan was pale and there was a purplish bruise on his right cheekbone. McNeil didn't look at Coke, but took off his cap and stood twisting it.

"Sit down, you guys," said Coke. "Want a drink?"

"No," said Regan. "Don't bother trying to be friendly. I don't feel friendly. This is just a matter of business, that's all, and the sooner we get it over with the better."

"That goes for me," said McNeil.

They sat down.

"Well," said Coke, "let's have it then, if that's the way you feel about it."

"All right," said Regan. He took a document out of his pocket and showed it to Coke. "There's the contract you signed to fight for me, Coke, and it's got a year to run. According to some of the clauses in it, that you were too dumb to understand, you got to fight who I tell you, when I tell you."

"You dummy," said Rose, "signing a contract like that!"

"Just a minute," said Regan. "Now, Coke, we're through, see? I'm done with you for good. I knew just as soon as you found the missus again that we was through. I did the best I could, but let that pass. The point is, we're done. According to this contract, I could tie you up for a year. Of course you could cross me by retiring, like you said. Well, you don't have to. I'm gonna tear this contract up."

"Fair enough," said Lewis.

"Just a minute," said Regan. "But I ain't gonna tear this contract up just for fun. That ain't my way and that ain't business. I've spent a lot of time on you, Coke, making a champion out of you, and I figure I got something coming. Well, all you got to do is sign a little paper I got here and you're free."

He took the paper from his pocket and handed it to Lewis.

"Let me see that," said Coke.

"Let Lewis read it," said Regan. "He'll probably be your next manager and he might just as well get in on the ground floor."

Coke sat staring at the wall, avoiding Regan's eyes.

Lewis read the paper, then said:

"This sounds O.K. to me, Coke. All you got to do is agree to give O'Keefe a shot at the championship within four months."

"Providing he licks Cahill," McNeil put in.

"That's a mere detail," said Lewis. "Regan'll see to that with a championship go at stake."

"I don't have to fix no fights for O'Keefe," said Regan. "He fixes them with lefts."

"Is it all O.K., Paul?" Rose inquired.

"Yes," said Lewis, "except this twenty-five per cent gate. That'll have to be settled later."

"Let it stand," said Coke.

"But good Lord, champ," said Lewis, "O'Keefe's lucky you're giving him a match at all."

"We won't fight about that," said Regan. "We can settle that later."

"I should think so," said Rose.

"We'll scratch that out then," said Lewis.

"Tim Morgan's willing to make you a record guarantee for the match, Coke," said Regan.

"All right with me," said Coke.

Lewis scratched out the clause dealing with the gate guarantee and Coke signed the paper. Then Regan took the old contract Coke had signed and tore it up.

"Now," said Regan, "we're all set except I want to see your duplicate torn up."

"I don't even know where it is," said Coke, scratching his head.

"I got it," said Rose.

She unlocked a drawer in the writing-desk and took out the contract. Coke took it from her and tore it up.

"Well, that's that," said Regan.

He got to his feet and so did McNeil.

"Going with George, are you, Mac?" Coke inquired.

"Yeah," said Mac. "I ain't got no use for people that go back on their friends."

Coke didn't say anything. Regan and McNeil went out.

"Well," said Rose, "I'm sure glad to see the last of George Regan."

"Yes," said Lewis, "he's a bad one."

"He's bossed Coke around since Coke was a kid," said Rose.

Coke went into the bedroom and shut the door.

VI

Lewis and Coke came in just as the main-go was starting. O'Keefe was lumbering around with his left stuck out as far as it would go, and Cahill, with his hands at his sides, was trying to draw him. Coke saw Regan at the ringside, but Regan avoided his eyes.

"O'Keefe'll lick him," said Coke. "Cahill's as thick as ten in a bed with Regan."

"Certainly," said Lewis. "It's all set."

The first round was slow, both fighters cautious, and when the bell rang somebody shouted: "Wait till Coke Mason starts socking you, Red Head!" This started a laugh and quite a few people at ringside turned to look for the speaker. A man behind Coke leaned forward and patted him on the back.

"You can lick 'em both, Coke," said the man.

"I have," said Coke.

At the beginning of the second round Cahill leapt out of his corner and began to hammer O'Keefe with body punches, some of which looked low. The referee warned him. O'Keefe stalled around, occasionally landing a long-range left, but Cahill was all over him, hitting him with body punches which he ripped up from his knees. O'Keefe grinned and stalled and shot out his long left. Once he caught Cahill coming in with that left, and Cahill went back on his heels. At the end of the round Cahill had a cut over his left eye, and O'Keefe's body looked as if it had been beaten with a paddle.

"Well," said Lewis, "O'Keefe better wake up if he's gonna win this fight."

"Yeah," said Coke, "that was Bat's round all right."

Coke itched to be in the ring.

The third and fourth rounds were Cahill's. He was landing body blows at will, and O'Keefe, who seemed very much puzzled by his attack, kept missing rights. Once or twice he shot out his left and landed. Once a glancing left sent Cahill into the ropes, but he leapt in immediately and drove O'Keefe across the ring with short jolts to the body. O'Keefe clinched.

"You know, Paul," said Coke, "I think this fight is straight. I know just what O'Keefe's up against. Bat's hell when he's in close."

"Maybe you're right," said Lewis. "But I thought Regan had more sense than to take a chance on this fight. Cahill's no cinch for anybody."

Coke glanced at Regan, who sat chewing on a cold cigar. He seemed calm enough. But in the ring, while Jeff worked over O'Keefe, McNeil was talking to him. From time to time O'Keefe nodded.

At the beginning of the fifth round Cahill used his usual tactics, rushing in immediately to get at O'Keefe's body and offset his long left, but this time, the left, a hard wallop, met him coming in. O'Keefe had shot it at a slightly different angle and connected. Cahill was thrown off balance, and before he could get back on his stride, O'Keefe hit him with a right followed by another left, good solid punches. Cahill went down. It was a clean knockdown, but Cahill wasn't groggy, and at the count of nine he leapt to his feet and weathered a terrific fusilade of punches. Then suddenly he landed a hard right to the body. O'Keefe arched his body as if it had stung him, but he didn't back up and continued his attack. Seeing that he had hurt his opponent, Cahill opened up and stood toe to toe slugging with O'Keefe. Toward the end of the round, Cahill, ripping his body punches up from his knees, fouled O'Keefe and O'Keefe fell to the floor, writhing.

"Hell," said Coke.

"Foul sure enough," said Lewis.

Cahill stood in the middle of the ring, shaking his head from side to side. O'Keefe was carried to his corner.

The fight was awarded to O'Keefe on a foul. The crowd was disgusted. They booed and stamped. Someone started the story that Cahill had fouled O'Keefe on purpose, that he was sore at him. Someone else said that O'Keefe hadn't been fouled at all, that it was just a stall so he would be sure to get his match with the champion. Regan, known as a slicker, was accused of all sorts of things.

Coke and Lewis went back to see Cahill. Cahill was lying on the rubbing-table.

"Too bad, Bat," said Coke.

"Yeah," said Bat. "That's the only fight I ever lost on a foul."

"Tough," said Coke.

"Yeah," said Bat. "He crowded me just as I was pulling one up. He ran right into it. It was a foul all right."

Bat's trainer started to work on him.

"He ain't hard to hit, champ," said Bat. "But watch that left. Boy, what a wallop."

"He's a natural lefthander," said Coke.

"Well," said Lewis, "he won't cause you much trouble."

"No," said Coke.

PART VII

I

Coke had just got out of bed. It was eleven o'clock in the morning. He put on a bathrobe and went into the bathroom to shave. Rose came in with a stack of letters.

"Look," she said, holding out one of the letters, "from Calcutta."

"Calcutta!" Coke exclaimed. "Who the hell's he?"

"Oh, Lord," said Rose, laughing. "It ain't a he, it's a town away over in Europe some place. Haven't you ever heard of Calcutta?"

"I don't remember," said Coke. "Is it from Coon?"

"Yeah," said Rose.

"Did you read it yet?"

"No," said Rose. "It's yours."

"Mine!" said Coke. "Well, that's mighty nice of old Coon to remember me that way."

He took the letter, tore it open and started to read it. Then he shrugged his shoulders and handed it to Rose.

"He writes funny," he said. "Anyway, what does he want to tell me all about them places for. I ain't got no interest in foreign countries."

"Well, you ought to have," said Rose. "Everybody that is anybody travels."

"Hell," said Coke, "ain't I traveled? I been every place from Frisco to New York and from New Orleans to Detroit."

"That don't count," said Rose. "Nobody travels in America. When you travel, you ought to travel in Europe."

"How come?"

"Because," said Rose, and she went on reading Coon's letter.

"Well," said Coke, "I notice one thing. Them foreigners are mighty glad to get over here. Yeah, they come by the boatload. If Europe's such a hell of a place why don't they stay there...?"

"Don't bother me," said Rose. "I'm reading."

"Yeah," said Coke, "that's what I want to know. One time I asked Speed De Angelo why his old man left Italy and he said 'to make money.' Try and get Speed to go back to Italy. Yeah, he'd give you the horse-laugh."

"Don't talk so ignorant," said Rose.

Coke lathered his face and began to shave. Rose sat on the edge of the bathtub and went on reading.

"Gee, Coke," said Rose, "Harold says he nearly got mobbed in Calcutta because he went in some place where he wasn't supposed to go. Gee, this is exciting."

"I'd like to see some of them foreigners mob me," said Coke.

II

Coke was lonesome. He sat at the window looking down into the street. He had tried to read. He had even stripped off his clothes and shadow-boxed for three minutes, following this with a shower and a good rub-down. But it didn't help any. He felt stale and tired and lonesome, and sat staring down at the unending procession of cars in the street. When the clock struck eight, he got up, put on his Tuxedo, and went out.

It was the beginning of May, but a cold March wind was sweeping up the street. Coke walked for a block or two, but, changing his mind, got into a taxi and instructed the driver to take him to the Ivor Martin Theatre.

He got in just as the big maroon curtain was descending. The piano was wheeled out by the dapper little black boy, the orchestra played its series of consecutive ninths and subsided, the piano was heard in syncopated arpeggioes, then Rose began to sing her song about New Orleans, the lit-tle black boy taking the breaks. The orchestra began to play, the time was speeded up, and Rose leapt down, snatching off her hoopskirt, and began to dance, accompanied by the dapper little black boy. When the act was over, Coke went backstage to see Rose. She was in her dressing-room with her negro maid.

"Well," said Rose, "here's papa."

"Yeah," said Coke. "I got lonesome."

"I thought you was going to bed early tonight," said Rose, shaking her finger at him, "you got to begin to get yourself in shape."

"Yeah, I know," said Coke. "But I just kind of got lonesome."

"That's all right," said Rose, "but you got to start taking hold of yourself, Coke. Mama spank."

"I wish to God you'd give up this damn show business, so I could get set-tled down," said Coke.

"Naughty, naughty," said Rose. "Mustn't interfere with mama."

Coke sat looking at the floor. Someone knocked and the maid opened the door. It was Lewis. When he saw Coke a shadow of annoyance crossed his face, then he smiled and drew back.

"Didn't know you were here, champ," he said. "I won't bother you. I just wanted to see Rose about a bit of business for our new show."

"Come on in, Paul," said Rose. "You're not bothering anybody."

But Coke didn't say anything, so Lewis said:

"No. There's no hurry about this. It can wait. See you later on."

He went out.

"Say," said Coke, "get your dress on and lets go over to Mike's and get a stein of beer between the acts."

"All right," said Rose.

Mike's was in the alley straight across from the stage entrance of the theatre. When Coke and Rose came in there was a crowd around the bar and somebody said:

"There's Coke Mason."

Coke shook all the hands shoved at him and guided Rose to a stall in the rear, where they wouldn't be bothered. A waiter brought them two big steins. They drank in silence.

"Looking mighty sweet tonight," said Coke, finally.

"Yeah," said Rose, "I feel pretty good. I'm beginning to get my strength back. I sure had the flu like nobody else."

"I never have nothing," said Coke. "I never been sick in my life."

"Brute," said Rose.

"Well," said Coke, "I always took pretty good care of myself."

"It's a wonder," said Rose, "associating with that no-account George Regan."

Coke stared at his stein.

"Yeah," said Rose, "it's a wonder you haven't got the D.T.'s and other things."

Coke said nothing. Rose took a mirror out of her handbag and began to rearrange her hair. Coke ordered two more steins.

"Rose," he said, "I think I'll stick around and wait for you, tonight. I don't feel like sleeping."

"But I'm not going home after the show," said Rose. "We're all going out to Ivor Martin's."

"Well," said Coke, "can't I go?"

"No," said Rose, "it's just for the people in the show. It'll be a nice party. Mrs. Martin's gonna be there."

"Damn funny I can't go," said Coke, sulking.

"Well," said Rose, "Mrs. Wills isn't going, and neither is Ada Berger's boyfriend, you know, the one she says is going to marry her."

Coke emptied his second stein, and leaned back in his seat, looking at Rose.

"I bet Lewis is going," he said.

"I don't know whether he is or not," said Rose. "I haven't talked to him for a couple of days."

"I bet he is."

Rose thought for a moment, then she said:

"Coke, I got a good one to tell you about Lewis. But you got to promise not to say anything. Promise?"

"Sure."

"Don't kid me now, because Lewis would be sore at me if he knew I told you."

"All right," said Coke, "I won't say nothing."

"Well," said Rose, "he's in love with some married woman, and she's got him down good and plenty. I don't know who she is yet, but I've got my suspicions."

Coke smiled, relieved.

"Ain't that good!" said Rose, laughing. "The other day down at the theatre when we was rehearsing a new gag for the last act, he got so absentminded he started to walk around the stage and fell over a chair. Did we laugh!"

Coke leaned back in his chair and roared. Lewis was always so dignified. The picture of him falling over a chair made Coke laugh.

"Yeah," said Rose, "I'm not telling anybody what I think, see? But I got my suspicions."

"Tell me," said Coke.

"Cross your heart and hope to die you won't tell?"

"Hell," said Coke, "I don't go around blabbing things."

"All right," said Rose. "I think it's Mrs. Wills."

"What!" cried Coke. "Why, she seems like such a nice little woman."

"You can't never tell," said Rose.

"No," said Coke, "that's a fact."

"That's why I don't know whether he'll be at the party or not. Marty's going but Mrs. Wills isn't, see? So my guess is, that he won't."

"Well, I'll be damned," said Coke.

Rose glanced at her wrist-watch.

"We better be going, Coke," she said.

They got up and Coke went over to pay his bill.

"On the house, champ," said Mike. "Your money ain't no good in here."

"All right," said Coke, "if that's the way you feel about it. But I'm gonna bring you down two ringside seats for the big match."

"Thank you, champ," said Mike. "I'll be there pulling for you."

Coke shook hands with a new bunch of Mike's patrons, then he and Rose went out. Mike put his elbows on the counter and whispered to one of his patrons.

"The champ's O.K.," he said, "but that wife of his ain't worth the powder to blow her up. Damn near every night she's in here with that dressed-up manager of Coke's."

"That ain't none of our business, Mike," said the man.

"No," said Mike, "but I like to see a guy like him get a straight deal."

"Well," said the man, "you don't know the inside, Mike, so you better keep out of it."

"I'm keeping out," said Mike.

Rose stopped at the stage entrance, put her arms around Coke, and kissed him.

"Better run on home, honey," she said, "and get a good sleep."

"Yeah," said Coke, "I guess I better."

"Don't worry about mama," she said. "I'll probably come home with Marty Wills and you know he's O.K."

"Yeah," said Coke, "Marty's O.K. But somebody ought to tell him about Lewis. That ain't no way to do." He stood thinking, then he laughed and went on: "But it's funny all the same."

"Well," said Rose, "it's none of our business."

"No," said Coke, "that's a fact."

"I'm going, honey," she said. "I got to get dressed."

"All right," said Coke, kissing her. "Good-bye, baby. Don't stay too late."

When she had gone, he stood in the alley for a little while, looking at the ground, then he climbed into a taxi. Sitting with Rose in Mike's had made him feel better, but now that she was gone the old feeling of loneliness returned. He sat looking out at the rows of brilliantly-lighted shops, hardly seeing them. The wind was still blowing strong and now a mist had begun to cloud the windows.

"Ain't much like summer," said Coke, sighing.

He didn't want to go home. Reading didn't interest him, he was sick of the radio, and he didn't feel like sleeping. What could he do? He'd get out and walk. He ordered the taxi-driver to draw up at the curb, and he got out. The taxi-driver looked at him suspiciously, then he grinned, recognizing him.

"Hello, champ," he said.

"Hello," said Coke, giving him a big tip. "I just kind of thought I'd better walk and get some of this belly off of me."

"That's O.K.," said the driver, "if it don't blow up a rain. Gonna walk straight out this way? I can keep an eye on you if you are."

"No," said Coke, "that's all right. I don't mind a little rain."

"Good-night, champ," said the driver, getting back into his seat.

"So long," said Coke.

Before Coke had gone two blocks it began to drizzle. He turned up the collar of his topcoat and leaned against the wind. The exercise made him feel better, but he was still lonesome.

"Funny!" he thought. "When I didn't have Rose I figured if I could find her, I'd never be lonesome no more. Funny! Yeah, and when I was a kid I thought if I could ever be champion I'd be the happiest guy on earth. Funny, how things are!"

It began to rain, slowly at first, big drops which splattered on the pavement, then more heavily, hissing and splashing, and filling the gutters. The wind caught up the rain and flung it in Coke's face. He swore at himself for being such a fool and made for a cafe, whose sign was reflected upside down on the wet pavement.

A one-legged beggar was crouched in the entryway. His coat was soaked with rain and water dripped from his battered hat.

"Buy a pencil mister," he said.

Coke studied him.

"Hell of a night, ain't it?" he said.

The beggar looked up at him.

"I been out in worse than this."

"Yeah?"

"Yeah," said the beggar, "I been out on winter nights when the snot froze on your nose."

Coke rubbed his chin and looked at him. Then he took out his billfold and gave him a five dollar bill. The man looked up at him.

"That's a five, kid," he said.

"I know," said Coke.

"Ever been on the rocks yourself?" asked the beggar, putting away the money.

"Sure," said Coke. "I've hit the grit."

"Well," said the beggar, "them's the kind of guys that knows what it means to be hungry. They ain't got no strings on their pocketbooks, when they got pocketbooks."

"You said a mouthful," said Coke.

A waiter glanced out of the window of the cafe, then opened the door and came out.

"Say," he said to the beggar, "you want me to call a cop! What you mean bothering our patrons. You get the hell out of here and be quick about it."

The beggar shrugged and pulled himself up on his crutch.

"Say," said Coke to the waiter, "it's raining cats and dogs out there. Give the guy a break."

The beggar laughed.

"Hell," he said, "I'm used to this."

"Yeah," said the waiter, "you damn bums are all alike. Every time it rains we got to kick one of you bums out of this entryway."

"I'm going," said the beggar.

He put his box of pencils into his pocket and hobbled out into the rain.

"So long," said Coke.

"So long," said the beggar.

The waiter held the door open for Coke, smiling.

"Step right in, sir."

Coke was ushered to a table near the orchestra and the headwaiter came over to him.

"Excuse me," he said, "but aren't you Mr. Mason?"

"Yeah," said Coke.

"Well," said the headwaiter. "We're certainly glad to see you here, sir. If you don't get the proper attention from your waiter please tell me."

He bowed and went away. Then the waiter who had ejected the beggar came to wait on Coke.

"You handle them guys pretty rough, don't you?" said Coke.

"Well," said the waiter, "we got our orders. If we let 'em alone they wouldn't give us no peace. They'd hurt the business. Personally I don't care. But people don't like to be bothered with beggars when they're out for a good time."

The waiter took Coke's order and went away. Coke sat drumming on the table, listening to the braying of the trombone and the moaning of the saxophone. He watched the dancers in the little roped-off dance floor.

"Funny," he said.

III

Although Lewis had signed to manage Coke, he paid very little attention to him. In the first place he was busy with the show business, in the second place he didn't know a great deal about the fight game and figured that a champion ought to be able to look after himself. But he was interested in one side of it, he looked after the money. He saw that Coke gave proper testimonials to various manufacturers of nostrums, bargained for hours with advertising men, and in general made Coke's position as champion a very lucrative one. Where money was concerned he was hard as iron. In spite of his dignity, he could drive a shrewd bargain, and many men who visited him with the idea of robbing him, came away feeling that they had got the worst of it. But outside of that, he wasn't much help to Coke.

Coke had no very deep feeling of friendship for Lewis. Lewis wasn't his kind. There was something distant about him, something withdrawn, even when he was laughing and seemingly all attention. He just didn't mix. As far as Coke knew, Lewis hadn't a close friend in the world. He seemed stiff and formal to Coke even when they had their coats off, drinking beer. He couldn't unbend. With strangers he was silent and dignified. With people he knew he was affable, but even to Coke the affability seemed forced. Sometimes Coke would sit and look at him, noting the clear, pale complexion, the carefully-kept black sideburns, the long womanish eyelashes. Lewis talked without gestures and without opening his lips very far. He stared intently at you with his pale eyes while he was talking, but when you talked, he looked away, avoiding your eyes. Often Coke felt uncomfortable with Lewis, but he didn't know why. Rose said that Lewis was very "refined" and came from a very "old" family. Coke turned this over in his mind and eventually came to the conclusion that that was the reason he felt slightly uneasy with Lewis. Lewis was educated and refined, he wasn't.

Coke's loneliness increased. Trying to get himself into some kind of shape before he started his actual training, he got up at six o'clock, walked, skipped the rope, and took various exercises, at ten o'clock he was in bed. This schedule exactly suited Rose and when she talked with Coke, seldom now, she was careful to praise him for his self-discipline and to assure him that only a man of very strong character could make such an abrupt change in his way of living. Coke was pleased when Rose praised him, but the pleasure didn't last, and as soon as he was by himself again he was as unhappy as before. Often, in spite of the promises he had made, he would beg Rose to leave the stage and just stay with him and help him out. But Rose would tell him that he wasn't keeping his promises, was acting like a kid, and in a few minutes had him feeling ashamed of himself.

Coke fell back on Jeff. Rose was rehearsing a new show and was away from home most every afternoon. As soon as she was gone, Coke would call Jeff up and have him come over, or else he would take a taxi and go after Jeff. Jeff helped him train and they went to shows together. But even Jeff had changed. He was less talkative than he had ever been and he never seemed to understand what Coke was saying, unless they were talking "fight." Sometimes he would say:

"You talk funny, Coke."

Coke would stare at him, not knowing that his contact with Lewis and Rose, his semi-isolation from his old friends had made a deep impression on him, modified his mode of thought, and he was also unable to understand that his loneliness had made him think, had made him discover things about himself and the world that had never occurred to him before. Jeff seemed stupider than he used to be.

A week before the start of the actual training, Coke sent a telegram to Jimmy Pappas, the Greek middleweight wrestler, who used to train with him when he was a palooka in Sandusky, Ohio, and asked him to come to New York to act as assistant trainer. The newspapers made quite a story of it, a human interest story. Jimmy accepted the offer.

A few nights before Coke was to leave for Ash Harbor, Long Island, where he was to train, he woke from a sound sleep, laughing, and sat up. Rose heard him, climbed out of her bed, and shook him.

"What's wrong with you, Coke?" she demanded.

"Wrong with who?" said Coke, befuddled. "I'm all right."

"Why ain't you sleeping?" said Rose. "You know you got to get back in shape."

She was afraid he had heard her come in.

"I been sleeping," said Coke. "What time is it?"

"About four o'clock," said Rose.

"You just getting in?"

"Lord, no. I been in since one o'clock, or maybe a little later. What were you laughing at? You been laying awake...?"

"No," said Coke, "I been sleeping like a log. I come to bed at ten-thirty. I guess I was dreaming. Climb in here with me."

Rose leaned across the bed and kissed him.

"No, honey," she said, "mama's got a bad headache."

Coke didn't say anything.

"Yeah," said Rose, "I think I'll go take some of my pills."

"You always got something the matter with you," said Coke.

"Well, I like that!" said Rose switching on the lamp. "That's a fine way for you to talk. You know I ain't never got over that flu yet."

"That's all right," said Coke. "But every time I want you to be nice to me, you got a headache or something."

"I can't help it, Coke," said Rose. "You better get yourself another girl."

"Aw, hell!" said Coke, lying down and settling himself for sleep.

"Besides," said Rose, "you're in training, or ought to be."

"That's all I hear from morning till night," said Coke. "If it ain't you, it's Lewis. I'm getting sick of it."

"Now, now," said Rose. "You know you always get all upset when you're training. All the real fighters do."

Coke snorted and turned over irritably.

"I guess your mama'll have to look after you," Rose went on. "Such a big, bad boy! Such an awful, spoiled child! Mama spank."

"All right," said Coke. "Get your pills and go to bed."

Rose burst out laughing and pulled his hair. Coke grabbed her, jerked her across the bed and spanked her, then he stood her on her feet.

"If I can do that laying down," he said, "just think what I could do standing up."

"You must never, never strike a lady," said Rose.

She went into the bathroom and shut the door. Coke began to doze. He heard Rose come back into the room, turn off the light, and get into bed, but it seemed like a part of the dream he had had a moment ago. He and Regan were in Regan's poolroom. One of the town bullies was playing pool with a hustler and losing. When they were through playing, the bully settled with the hustler, but didn't have enough money to pay Regan what was due for the use of the table. Regan insisted that he pay and the bully laughed at him. "Take it out of my hide," he said. Regan said "All right!" and picked up a sawed-off pool cue. The bully took one look at him, made a dive for the door, and started down the middle of the street with Regan after him, flourishing the sawed-off pool cue.

"Rose," Coke called, "I just figured out what I was laughing at. I was dreaming about one time when George chased a guy with a pool cue."

"Coke," said Rose, "I'm gonna hunt something up to hit you with. I was just falling asleep."

Coke said nothing. He turned over on his back and lay thinking about all the fun he used to have in Regan's poolroom.

The next afternoon Coke went down to Kid Halloran's gymnasium, and sat in the Kid's office talking to Bat Cahill and Ben Mandl. Mandl thought Coke was a sure thing to win the match with O'Keefe, but Cahill didn't seem to have much to say. Finally, he said:

"They tell me Riley likes the Rattler."

"He wants the short end," said Mandl, laughing.

"He's kidding," said Coke.

"Maybe," said Cahill.

Halloran came in and told them that Regan had just arrived, that he wanted to see Mandl.

"Me?" said Mandl. "I wonder what his song is today! He's always got one."

Mandl went out.

"That's a fact," said Cahill. "Regan's the damnedest guy I ever seen. Never got a cent."

"Is he borrowing from Mandl?" Coke inquired.

"Trying to," said Cahill.

"That's funny," said Coke. "When George and me was working together he always had plenty of money."

"Plenty, hell," said Cahill. "That guy never had plenty. Riley signed his note for two grand the other day."

"What does he do with his money?" asked Coke.

"Well," said Cahill, "he drops a lot of it to the bookies."

"That's a new stunt," said Coke.

"That ain't all," said Cahill. "He's got a yen for faro. Crazy man's game."

"George never used to gamble," said Coke. "Except poker."

Cahill sat looking at Coke, wondering what was on his mind. Coke always struck him as being smarter than he acted. This was probably due to the fact that he had always associated Coke with Regan, who had the reputation of being a slicker.

"George is going to hell just as fast as he can get there," Halloran put in.

"I wouldn't say that," said Cahill. "Course he drinks a lot, but he always did, long as I've known him."

"All right," said Halloran. "But he don't seem like the same George to me."

Coke sat looking at the floor, very uncomfortable. He wanted to go out and see Regan but he was afraid Regan would make fun of him.

"Well," said Cahill, "I'll say one thing for him. He don't need nobody to show him around. He's always got a meal-ticket. First it was Coke here, now it's O'Keefe and Speed De Angelo. I wouldn't waste no sympathy on a guy that smart."

"You mark what I say," said Halloran. "If George Regan don't slow down on the pace he's going he won't be with us next summer."

"He looks bad, that's a fact," said Cahill.

Coke got up.

"Well," he said, "I guess I'll be going. Drop out to the camp, Bat. Always glad to see you."

"Does that go for me too, champ?" Halloran asked.

"Sure," said Coke. "Just drop out."

When Coke had gone, Cahill said:

"Kid, I wonder what the straight story about them two is?"

"You got me," said Halloran.

"Funny thing," said Cahill. "Regan's dead sure O'Keefe'll win."

"That's a pipe dream," said Halloran. "Coke'll left hook that guy out of the ring."

"I ain't so sure," said Cahill. "Coke's had a long layoff and O'Keefe's as strong as an ox. If the odds are right I'm gonna put one grand on the Rattler for luck."

"Say," said Halloran, "I'm a poor man. Just hand me that grand now and it'll save you the trouble of getting it up."

"Funny," said Cahill, "everybody always thinks a champion's a lot better than he is."

"Kiss that grand good-bye," said Halloran.

When Coke went out into the gymnasium, he saw Regan leaning against the wall, his hat on the back of his head, talking to Mandl. A strong light was streaming in through one of the big front windows and it fell full on Regan. Coke was startled. Regan looked so frail. He had always been skinny, of course. Coke's father said he had to stand twice to make a shadow. But his face had always had a healthy, swarthy color, except when he was recuperating from a drunk, and his clothes had never actually hung on him. Now he looked like a convalescent.

Coke walked over to watch a couple of amateurs, who were pounding away at one another. He heard Mandl say, "No, no, nothing doing." He heard Regan's retort. "I never seen a kike yet who could see farther than his nose." He saw Mandl turn on his heel and walk away, then he went over to Regan.

Regan pulled his hat down over his eyes and took out a cigar.

"Smoke," he said.

"No, thanks," said Coke. "I ain't smoking."

"Getting all set, are you?"

Regan put the cigar back into his pocket and stood with his legs crossed, looking at Coke.

"Yeah," said Coke.

"You're fat as a hog," said Regan. "You're gonna have trouble with your weight for the first time in your life."

"That's about it," said Coke.

He wanted to ask Regan how much money he needed, but he was afraid to.

"Yeah," said Regan, "I figure you won't be in such good shape. O'Keefe'll be prime. He's gonna give you a lacing, Coke."

Coke didn't say anything.

"But course you don't think so," said Regan.

"No," said Coke.

Regan started drumming on the wall, looking at Coke.

"How're you and the missus coming along?"

"All right," said Coke. "She's got a good part in Ivor Martin's new show."

"So I hear," said Regan. "Well, she'll be able to get along without you pretty soon, Coke, so get set to kiss her good-bye."

"There you go," said Coke.

"Dumb as ever," said Regan, then he stood away from the wall and nodded to Coke. "I got a heavy poker date for this afternoon, kid, so I'll be leaving you."

He started to walk away, but Coke called to him.

"George," he said, "I want to see you a minute."

Regan turned and came back.

"All right. Spill it."

"Say, George," said Coke, flushing, "don't get sore at me, but was you trying to borrow some money from Mandl?"

Regan stiffened. Coke knew he had said the wrong thing.

"What's it to you!" Regan exclaimed. "You tend to your business and I'll tend to mine."

He walked away. Coke saw him cross the long gymnasium and go into Halloran's office.

"Well," Coke told himself, "if that's the way he wants to act, he can go to hell!"

When Coke got home the clerk gave him a letter. It was from Coon and had a Japanese stamp on it. Coke went up to his apartment and sat down to read it. It was all about a mountain called Fuji and a seaport called Nagasaki and how cute Japanese children were and how much Coon had paid for a meal in Tokyo, etc. Ordinarily, Coke wouldn't have been interested, but now he was lonesome and the tone of the letter was so friendly. He read it three times. "Mighty nice of Coon writing me," he said.

IV

Coke was having trouble getting into shape. Jimmy Pappas and Jeff kept insisting that he double his roadwork, but he wouldn't listen to them. As fast as he sweat the weight off, it came back. One day he lost six pounds, the next day before taking to the road, he was weighed and he had gained it all back.

"Hell!" said Coke.

Jimmy Pappas and Jeff urged him to try drying-out, for a while, at least, just to see if he could lose a lot of weight that way, but Coke wouldn't listen to them. When he was thirsty, he wanted water. He wasn't going to go around thirsty all the time. What was the fun? Pappas conferred with Lewis, who smiled and shrugged, and put the full responsibility on Coke. Ruby Hall had one theory, Jimmy another, and Jeff another, they spent half of their time arguing, while Coke sat listening to them, trying to make up his mind what to do.

Finally one day, he showed a loss of five pounds, after drinking plenty of water and eating a big meal.

"O.K.," said Ruby Hall. "Now we're getting some place. You just listen to me, champ, and you'll be in shape in no time."

Coke said nothing, but Jimmy and Jeff began to argue with Ruby, who defended himself loudly.

"My God!" yelled Coke. "Shut up, you guys. I can't hear myself think."

The next day Coke hurt his wrist sparring with Jeff. Jimmy Pappas bandaged it for him and they all held a conference in the rubbing-room. Coke listened for a while, then he got up and took a walk. He began to be worried. He was jinxed. Donaldson, the trainer he had hired, had got banged up in an automobile accident the second day at the camp. Buddy Dugan, his lightweight sparring partner, had been taken to the hospital for an appendicitis operation, and three days ago Ruby Hall had nearly drowned swimming in the bay.

"I got a jinx on me sure," Coke said.

Things were going very badly at the camp. The place was overrun with visitors and there was hardly a private spot to be found. Coke was always being followed and asked for his autograph, or for money, or wouldn't he please give some wonderful amateur a chance to show him what he could do. The newspaper men thought they owned the camp and did as they pleased. The cook would get drunk and forget to come back from town, and Coke would have to wait two hours for his supper, or something would happen to the lights just when Coke wanted to read and relax. Jimmy Pappas was a willing worker and he did his best to fill Donaldson's shoes, but he was erratic and pigheaded. Ruby Hall had to be kept well in hand or he became dictatorial. Even Jeff joined in the clamor.

"Some day I'm gonna slap them guys to sleep," said Coke.

V

Jimmy Pappas, Jeff, Ruby Hall and Coke were sitting on the porch. It was about eight o'clock in the evening, but it was not yet dark, and a few birds were still singing in the trees on the lawn. The day had been hot with a blinding sun, and during the afternoon the thermometer had climbed to ninety-three, and the wind had been blowing off shore. But now the wind had shifted and it had begun to get cool. Coke sat looking off over the tree-tops. Between two poplars there was a green line of sea visible.

Jimmy Pappas took out his mouth organ and began to play. Joe Rogers, the lightweight, came running out of the living-room and sat down on the steps.

"Atta boy, Jimmy," he said.

Ruby Hall started to sing in a deep, rich baritone, and presently Joe and Jeff joined in. Jeff's bass was uncertain, but he sang so softly that his flatting didn't spoil the two-part harmony of Ruby and Joe. Coke sat listening. The song was doleful, all about unrequited love and how terrible it was to be left alone in the world. Coke felt sad. When the song came to an end, he said:

"For God's sake play something lively, Jimmy."

Jimmy grinned, shook the saliva out of his mouth organ, and started again.

"Hot dog!" said Ruby, getting to his feet and slapping his thighs.

Coke and Jeff beat time with their hands, while Ruby, rolling his eyes and grinning, did a slow nigger dance, shuffling. Joe began to sing.

"I left Frisco Kate
Swinging on the Golden Gate,
When Kansas City Kitty
Smiled at me...."

A taxi-cab lurched up over the steep grade at the end of the porch and stopped. Jimmy Pappas went right on playing.

"Wait a minute," said Coke.

Mandl and Cahill got out of the cab and Cahill told the driver to wait. The music stopped and Ruby Hall went inside. He didn't like Cahill, who had given him a bad beating the last time they fought.

"Well, champ," said Mandl, "how's things?"

"All right," said Coke. "Sit down. Hello, Bat."

"Hi, champ," said Cahill. "We just come out for a little visit. Thought we'd get cooled off out here."

They sat down on the steps.

"Well," said Mandl, "they're still quoting you at 3 to 1. A man can't make no money betting that way."

"Them odds are about right," said Joe Rogers.

"Tough on me, though," said Mandl. "I can't bet much with odds like that. I'm superstitious since that hundred-to-one shot beat Gustavus at Louisville. Did they take me!"

"Yeah," said Cahill. "Who took me? You did, Ben. I put three centuries on his hot tip, Coke."

"Three hundred!" said Mandl. "I wish that was all I had up."

"How's the legs, Coke?" Cahill inquired. "Heard you was having trouble."

"You heard wrong," said Coke. "The only trouble I had was with my weight. But that's all right now. The newspaper guys ain't giving me a square deal. To hear them talk you'd think I was as old as Jim Corbett."

"That's the way they always talk about a champion," said Mandl. "Just filling space. Giving their readers something they can understand. If you win they'll say you did pretty well for a man your age, if you lose they'll say it was youth that done it. Like Dempsey. Tunney was about six months younger, I think."

"I ain't figuring to lose," said Coke, gloomily.

"Course you ain't, champ," said Cahill.

"But I wish we could knock them odds down," said Mandl. "Couldn't you and Lewis pull something?"

"Listen, Ben," said Coke, flying up suddenly, "nothing doing! I wish to God you guys would let me alone. I got enough on my mind without thinking about odds and that kind of stuff. Everything's on me. I can't get nobody to do nothing around here. I got them newspaper guys on my trail from morning till night. And if it ain't them, it's some of you guys. It's enough to drive a guy crazy."

"But, champ..." Mandl began.

Jeff kicked him on the shins.

"Yeah," said Coke, paying no attention to the interruption, "I ain't seen Lewis for two days, and Tim Morgan's only been out here twice since I started to train. Yeah! No matter what comes up, they say, 'See Coke!' By God, I got to be the manager and the promoter, besides the main attraction. By God, I'll bet you they'll want me to take tickets at the gate the night of the fight."

He got to his feet and began to pace up and down.

"Never mind, champ," said Mandl. "Forget it. We won't bother you no more."

Coke went inside without saying another word.

"Lord!" said Cahill, "he sure is on edge. They got him worried. Well, it's a tough break, but it's his own fault. What did he want to team up with a guy like Lewis for? Damn dressed-up highhatter!"

"His wife," said Jeff.

"Less said about that the better," Mandl put in.

"I ain't talking," said Jeff.

"Well, somebody ought to," said Joe Rogers.

"You guys better pipe down," said Jimmy Pappas.

"If the champ hears you, you'll get a busted nose."

Nobody said anything. Mandl took out a cigar-case and passed it around. In the silence that followed the lighting of the cigars, they heard a crash inside the house.

"Lordy, champ," they heard Ruby Hall saying, "I didn't see you sitting there."

"Well, by God," came Coke's voice, "you better get your eyes open and pick up your big flat feet or something's liable to happen to you. Get the hell out of here!"

Ruby appeared on the front porch.

"Man!" he said. "The champ sure is raring!"

Joe began to laugh, but Jimmy got up and went inside.

"I never seen him sitting there," said Ruby. "I just walked through the room and fell over his feet. It was dark. I ain't no cat."

"Never mind," said Mandl. "They just got him all upset, that's all."

"Yeah," said Ruby, "and I'm telling you that man ain't two-fifths of what he was. He gets tired in the legs."

"Will you shut up," said Jeff.

"It's all right between us," said Mandl. "Let's hear it. I'm already up on the champion some. So what's the difference?"

"Me, too," lied Cahill.

"We ain't giving out no information," said Jeff. "The champ looks good to me, that's all."

"What he needs is Regan," said Mandl.

"By God," said Cahill, "that reminds me. Have you guys heard the latest?"

"Yeah," said Mandl, "it's good. But I wasn't gonna say nothing with Coke here."

"Me, neither," said Cahill.

"What's George been doing?" Jeff inquired.

"He got pinched for drunkenness and assault and battery," said Cahill, laughing. "It took Tim Morgan and half the big shots in town to get the case squashed. Ain't that good? Tim's trying to keep it out of the papers, but it'll get in."

"Hell, that's nothing," said Jeff.

"Yeah," said Mandl, "some wise guy down at O'Keefe's camp started wisecracking Regan about playing both ends against the middle, and Regan popped him. Oh, it was good!"

"Hell," said Jeff, "you should have seen the time out in Leadville when a gang of toughs tried to mob Coke and the referee, because Coke licked one of the local boys. Some of the guys tried to bust in the dressing-room door. George got himself a chair and opened the door. The first two guys in got the chair over the head. The other guys stayed out."

They all laughed.

"Yeah," said Joe Rogers. "Ever since I was a kid I've heard my old man talk about George Regan. The old man knew him out in Omaha."

They sat silent for a while, all of them intent on their cigars. Then Mandl said:

"Well, all kidding aside, I feel sorry for Regan. He says he hates Coke like poison, but he don't. Funny! But let me tell you one thing, if Coke ain't in A-one shape he's gonna have his troubles with O'Keefe, because Regan knows Coke from the ground up, an' he's killing himself coaching O'Keefe."

Jeff sighed and stared at the lighted end of his cigar.

"Rattler'll never lick the champion," said Joe Rogers. "It ain't in the cards."

"I think you're right," said Mandl. "But I wouldn't take no affidavit to that effect."

"O'Keefe's as strong as an ox," said Cahill. "But he's easy to hit especially around the body, and that's the champ's long suit. It all depends."

"Well," said Mandl, getting to his feet, "we might as well be getting back. What do you say, Bat?"

"I'm ready."

Mandl stood silent for a moment, then he said:

"Jeff, run in and tell the champ we're going and ask him if he wants us to do anything for him in town."

Jeff got up and went inside. Mandl took a couple of yellow-backs out of his pocket and handed them to Ruby and Rogers.

"There's some chicken feed," he said, "keep me posted."

Ruby looked at Joe, who stared back at him. Ruby shrugged and slipped the money into his pocket. Joe did the same.

"Yes sir, Mr. Mandl," said Ruby.

Jeff came back.

"He's asleep," he said.

"All right," said Mandl. "So long."

"I wouldn't say nothing to him about Regan," said Cahill.

"No," said Jeff.

VI

There was a big crowd watching Coke work out with Ruby Hall. Ruby was in wonderful condition and was dancing on his toes all around the champion, who followed him flatfooted, his chin on his chest, scowling. Ruby leapt in, played a tattoo on Coke's ribs and got away without a return. The newspaper men glanced at each other and smiled. Ruby repeated this maneuver and made Coke miss a long right. Coke's timing was bad. But Ruby was overconfident now and, wanting to make an impression on the crowd, he tried to slug with Coke. Coke took a couple of hard clouts to the head, but he didn't back up. He never did. Then he landed his famous left hook and Ruby arched his body. Coke swung his right and missed. Ruby tried his rushing tactics again and Coke landed another left hook. Ruby didn't like it and backed away. The bell rang.

"It's all he's got," said one newspaper man, "but it's enough. O'Keefe's easy to hit. Six of those hooks'll kill him."

"Yeah," said another reporter, "but the champion looks off color to me."

"Well," said the first reporter, "I don't know. This is the first time he ever entered the ring as a favorite. He's clumsy. You can't tell nothing about him."

"He's a toe-dancer compared to the Rattler. This is gonna be some fight."

Coke worked a round with Joe Rogers, who was fast as lightning, then Jeff climbed through the ropes. Jeff was a good, honest fighter. He was aggressive and could take punishment, but he couldn't hit very hard. For the first sixty seconds he looked like the champion instead of Coke, but presently Coke began to land his body punches and Jeff slowed down. Most of the newspaper men didn't know what to think, but they all agreed that the champion looked fat, that he seemed slower than usual, and that his timing was not up to the mark.

In the dressing-room Coke said:

"My legs is tired, Jimmy."

Pappas grinned.

"Don't let that bother you, champ. You're coming around fine. You got to quit worrying, champ."

"All right."

Coke dressed slowly. It was hot, and before he got into his clothes sweat was dripping from his forehead.

"Look at me sweating," said Coke. "I oughtn't to be sweating like that."

"Say," said Jimmy, "don't hunt things to worry about. You ought to be glad you can sweat."

Coke broke a shoe lace. He pulled off the shoe and flung it across the room.

"There's a jinx on me, by God!" he cried. "Everything goes wrong around the goddam place. Listen, Jimmy, this morning when I was out on the road with Joe and Jeff a black cat run right across in front of me. I tried to head him off, but he was too fast for me."

Jimmy retrieved Coke's shoe, put a new lace in it, and, bending down, put it on for him and tied it, but said nothing.

"Are you superstitious, Jimmy?" Coke inquired.

"No," said Jimmy. "That's all bunk. Only one thing. I don't like busted mirrors."

"Well," said Coke, "maybe you ain't superstitious, but I am. My father was, too. So's George Regan. I used to get him going by standing behind him when he was playing poker."

He laughed, then his face fell.

"Anyway," he said, "I don't like black cats. Jeff was gonna take a stone and kill the cat, but I wouldn't let him. It might be some kid's cat."

"Sure," said Jimmy.

Joe put his head in the door.

"Champ," he said, "a couple of newspaper guys want to see you. How about it?"

Coke leapt to his feet.

"No," he cried, "I'm sick of 'em! The hell with 'em. Why don't they go see Lewis? Why don't they go see Tim Morgan? No, I don't want to see 'em. They never write what you tell 'em, anyway. They might just as well stay home and make it up."

"I'll talk to 'em," said Jimmy. "Only what'll I say, champ?"

Coke stared at Jimmy, then he burst out:

"I wish to God there was somebody around this camp that knew something!"

"I'll take care of 'em for you," said Jimmy.

"Tell 'em I'm in wonderful shape," said Coke. "Tell 'em I'll win by a knockout. And then tell 'em to go to hell."

He went into an adjoining room, banging the door.

"Whew!" said Joe.

Jimmy just shook his head.

VII

It was nearly ten o'clock but Coke was still sitting on the front porch, showing no signs of getting ready for bed. Jimmy was sitting on the steps playing his mouth organ softly. Ruby was lying in a hammock, snoring.

Coke sat looking out over the lawn toward the sea. The moon was up and between the two big poplars he could see its reflection on the water. He felt lonesome. Joe came out and sat down beside Jimmy, who began a new tune. Joe started to sing:

> "Moonlight and roses,
> Bring wonderful mem'ries
> Of you...."

"Say," said Coke, "I wish you guys would lay off them sappy songs. Why don't you sing some good, lively song?"

Jimmy stopped playing and they sat in silence. Coke got up and went out on the lawn where he stood looking at the far away image of the moon on the water. He liked to look at the moon. When he was a kid his mother used to tell him it was a big balloon. It looked like it, only it had a picture on it, a man's face or something. Funny! He turned and came back.

"Jimmy," he said, "I'm gonna take your Ford and ride around a little."

"It's about your bedtime, champ," said Jimmy. "Wait till tomorrow, and I'll take you right after supper."

"No," said Coke, "I just want to ride around a little by myself. I'll be back in a half hour, then I'll hit the hay."

"Well," said Jimmy.

"For God's sake be careful, champ," said Joe.

"I'll be careful," said Coke. "It'd be my funeral, wouldn't it?"

He climbed into Jimmy's Ford and started down the road.

"You suppose he's heading for town?" Jimmy demanded suddenly.

"That's my guess," said Joe.

"He's worried about that wife of his," said Jimmy, "and I don't blame him. She plays 'em all. I used to live a couple of doors from her. I knew her before Coke ever married her. She never could see me, though."

"She can put her shoes under my bed," said Joe.

Coke himself didn't know what he intended to do till he had driven through Ash Harbor. But an hour later he stopped in front of his apartment hotel and went in. The clerk was surprised to see him and rather confusedly told him that he didn't think his wife was in although he hadn't seen her go out.

"Never mind," said Coke. "I got a key."

But as soon as Coke got into the elevator, the clerk called his apartment. Coke unlocked the door and went in. Rose, in a cerise kimono, was standing in the middle of the living-room. She looked flushed and rumpled. She ran over to him and kissed him.

"Well, papa," she demanded, "what are you doing here?"

"I got lonesome for you, honey," said Coke. "Why don't you never drive out to the camp to see me?"

"I been awful busy," said Rose, pushing him into a chair and sitting opposite him. "Anyway, Paul told me I better stay away from camp, it might upset you."

"Yeah," said Coke. "He's right there, I guess. But you ought to call me up, or something. I get lonesome as the devil out there."

"Just stick to it, Coke," said Rose. "There ain't much time left. How you feeling?"

"Fair," said Coke. "But there's a jinx on that camp."

Rose laughed.

"I'm telling you straight," Coke went on. "Everything goes wrong."

"You ought to have your friend George Regan running things," said Rose.

"Well," said Coke, "I'll say one thing for George: he can sure keep things moving at a training camp."

"I guess you haven't heard the latest."

"About George?"

"Yeah," said Rose, and she told him about Regan's escapade, adding to it a little on her own account. "Yeah," she went on, "and it took everybody in town to keep him out of jail."

Coke sat staring at the floor.

"A fine boy, that friend of yours," said Rose.

"We ain't friends no more," said Coke.

"No," said Rose, "and you ought to be darn glad you're not. He's gonna get himself in an awful mess some day. If it wasn't for Paul and me you'd still have that poolroom bum ordering you around like you was some palooka instead of the champion."

"George sure is a bossy guy, that's a fact," said Coke.

Rose sat playing with the sash of her kimono, and Coke glanced at the clock.

"God," he said, "I ought to be in bed. Them guys out at the camp'll have the police looking for me."

"Yeah," said Rose, "you better get started."

Coke was looking at Rose. There was something about the way she acted that puzzled him. She didn't seem like the same Rose. Before he had gone to the camp they used to sit and talk about fighting and things, and she'd look at him as if she was taking a big interest. Now he felt like he was talking to somebody he didn't know very well.

"Yeah," said Coke, "I guess it was kind of silly to run in here like this, but I got lonesome."

"I know," said Rose.

"You been lonesome, too, honey?"

"Why, sure," said Rose, but she didn't say it as if she meant it.

Coke got up. He was sure there was something wrong but he didn't know quite how to go about mentioning the fact. What could he say? He said nothing. Rose got up and put her arms around him.

"You ought to've called me up," she said, "and I'd've had a little lunch ready for you."

Coke grinned.

"Much obliged," he said. "But I ain't eating at night now."

He glanced apprehensively at the clock.

"Coke," said Rose, "are you sure enough in good shape? Paul says he don't know."

"He don't know nothing," said Coke. "He's a hell of a manager. I got to do all the work. Sure I'm in good shape. I'll lick that Irishman till he begs for mercy."

"Good," said Rose, kissing him.

"Well," said Coke, "I guess I better be hauling myself back. I wish to God I could stay in here all night with you, honey."

"I do too," said Rose. "But that's against the rules."

"Yeah," said Coke, smiling. "Well, see you after the fight."

"All right, honey," said Rose, holding the door open for him.

She seemed in sort of a hurry to Coke, but he didn't say anything. He kissed her again and went out. When he left the elevator he saw Riley and a couple of his friends standing in the lobby. Riley turned and said:

"Well, if it ain't the champion himself. What you doing out this time of night? I thought they had you buried down in Ash Harbor."

Coke shook hands with Riley and the other men, both big gamblers. Riley asked him if he wouldn't sit and talk to them for a little while as they were waiting for some women and had some time to kill.

"I got to be getting back to camp," said Coke. "I just run in to see my wife. She ain't been feeling well."

Riley winked at the men behind Coke's back.

"That's too bad," said Riley. "Sit down, champ. Let's have a session. We ain't had a good jaw together since you left Chicago."

"No," said Coke, "that's a fact!"

They all sat down. Coke felt guilty and from time to time looked at his watch, but one of the gamblers, Joe Stein, kept telling one story after another and they were all funny. Coke laughed long and loud, for the first time in weeks. He began to feel very friendly toward Mr. Stein, a man who could tell such funny stories with such a solemn face. The other gambler, a Texan named Ray, had nothing to say and sat staring at his shoes, smiling slightly at Stein's stories. Forty-five minutes passed before Coke could prod himself into going. Finally he got to his feet.

"Going?" Riley inquired.

"Yeah," said Coke. "The boys out at the camp'll be turning handsprings."

"Say," said Stein, "if you wait till the women show we'll drive you out. We can go for the ride."

"What's keeping 'em?" Coke wanted to know.

"It's like this," said Stein. "They're show girls and one's got a husband and the other two have got red-hot sweeties they got to ditch. So we just have to be patient."

They all laughed.

"Well," said Coke, "I got Jimmy Pappas's Ford out here anyway. I'm going. I sure did enjoy the session. I ain't laughed like that since I can remember. Drop out to the camp and see me, all of you."

He shook hands all around and left them. As he was passing the elevator, the doors opened and Lewis stepped out. Seeing Coke, Lewis made a slight, convulsive movement as if to climb back into the elevator, then, smiling, he held out his hand.

"Well, champ," he said, "this is an unexpected pleasure."

Coke kept his hands in his pockets and stared at Lewis. He was in a very bad humor. The transition from his mood of a moment ago, a mood induced by the stories of Mr. Stein, was so abrupt that he wasn't sure just why he felt like hitting something hard, like arguing loudly and disagreeing violently. His irritation fastened on Lewis's clothes. He was wearing a big, floppy panama with a narrow black-band, his suit was made of some summer material, gray with a white pin stripe, the coat was double-breasted and the trousers full and long. He was carefully shaved and powdered, and his black sideburns were so symmetrical that they looked as if they had been cut out with scissors and pasted on.

"Well," said Coke, "you sure are dressed to kill. Where you been?"

Lewis smiled and touched Coke on the leg with his cane.

"Is that a nice question?"

Coke stared at him.

"I might know where you been," he said. "Fooling around with some woman. Don't you never get sick of that?"

"Well," said Lewis, "that's my weakness."

"Yeah," said Coke. "Some day somebody's gonna ketch you at it and then they'll bury you. Why don't you leave Mrs. Wills alone?"

Lewis seemed very much surprised.

"Why...!" he said.

"Don't try to lie to me," said Coke. "I know all about it. Ain't you ashamed of yourself acting that way? I don't see how you can sit and talk to Marty the way you do and then act like that."

Lewis smiled and swung his cane.

"You seem to know so much about it," he said. "I won't say a word."

"No use lying to me," said Coke. "I know. I got the dope straight."

"I'm not saying a word," said Lewis.

Coke stood looking at Lewis for a moment, then he said:

"Well, I got to be moving back to camp."

"Yeah," said Lewis. "I was wondering what you were doing out this time of night."

"That's my business," said Coke, looking for trouble.

"Certainly," said Lewis. "I'm not arguing with you. I just wondered."

"I came in to see my wife," said Coke. "I got lonesome."

"I know just how you feel," said Lewis. "I don't blame you a bit."

Coke shifted, feeling better now, then he grinned.

"Well, Paul," he said. "I'm on my way. Want to ride downtown in a Ford?"

"No," said Lewis, "I got a taxi ordered."

Coke turned to go, but Lewis put his hand on his shoulder.

"By the way, champ," he said. "You got rid of Regan at just the right time. He got himself in an awful mess the other night, and they tell me he owes everybody in town."

"I know," said Coke.

Coke and Lewis walked out of the hotel together.

Lewis's cab was waiting. He offered his hand and Coke shook it.

"I'll be out tomorrow afternoon," said Lewis. "We'll talk things over."

"All right," said Coke. "So long."

He tried to make his voice sound friendly, but he didn't succeed. Lewis irritated him with his immaculate sideburns, his carefully pressed clothes, his oily manner. Lewis wasn't his kind. He climbed into the Ford and stepped on the starter.

"Damn dude that's all he is," he said. "Just a damn dressed up dummy always playing around with somebody else's women. He better never get funny with the wife or I'll slug him good and proper, and then where'll he be with his pretty hair!"

He spun the Ford in the middle of the street and was cursed by a taxi driver, who scraped fenders with him.

"Get out of your cab and say that," yelled Coke, but the taxi driver didn't even look back.

When Coke got out of the heavily travelled district, he pushed the accelerator to the floor, thinking that it was a good thing the boys at camp couldn't see him. He thought about Tim Morgan and how sore he'd be if he knew that his prize drawing-card was hitting fifty miles an hour at this time of night. Out beyond the city limits, he passed several roadhouses surrounded by parked automobiles, a little further on, the estates of the rich began to appear with their tall mansions set back from the highway. Coke glanced at them in passing, slowing down for a mile or two.

"Some day I'm gonna have me a dump like that," he said. "Then maybe Rose'll be satisfied."

For no reason that he could discover, a sudden suspicion crossed his mind. He tried to shake it off and laugh, but it was no use, it clung. Why had Rose been so flushed and mussed up? Why had she been so anxious to get him out of the apartment? Why had Lewis tried to step back into the elevator as if to hide? He remembered all of Regan's insinuations, and as he drove along, slowly now, he went back over all that Regan had ever said to him about Rose. He recalled their quarrel after the Prince Pearl go, when Regan had said something about a part-time boy-friend and he had been on the point of slugging him. He recalled Regan's repeated warnings of what would happen to him if he took Rose back. He thought of the many times that Rose had gone out with Coon and Lewis, of how one night he had said to Mrs. Lewis "them guys are playing tag with my wife" and Mrs. Lewis had replied that they had been doing it all evening. He recalled seeing Lewis and Coon arguing in his apartment one afternoon, when the rest had gone, and how, even at the time, he had thought that it was queer for a millionaire like Coon to be arguing over money. Still there was Mrs. Wills.

When he drove into camp, Jimmy Pappas was sitting on the porch alone, softly playing his mouth organ. Coke parked the Ford and climbed the stairs slowly.

"Well," said Jimmy, "I was just getting ready to send the police out looking for you."

Coke sat down on the steps.

"I went in to see the missus," he said.

"We figured maybe you would," said Jimmy.

Coke looked up at him, but said nothing.

"Yeah," said Jimmy, "we wasn't worried much. We figured you was getting pretty lonesome for the missus."

He paused, but as Coke made no comment, he added: "She's getting better looking every day."

Coke sat silent for a while, then he got up and went into the house.

"Goodnight, champ," said Jimmy. "How about tomorrow morning?"

"Regular time," said Coke.

"O.K.," said Jimmy, then he started playing his mouth organ again, more softly than before.

Coke undressed and got into bed, where he lay turning from side to side. He remembered the night in Chicago a few days before the Prince Pearl go, when he had lain awake half the night, thinking about Rose. He had her now, but here he was lying awake just the same.

"Funny," he said.

He began to feel drowsy, and in the midst of this drowsiness a comforting thought came to him. It was the training. When he was training he always looked on the dark side of things and was inclined to be suspicious and irritable, to be bothered by attacks of the blues.

"That's it," he thought, relieved. "It's the training, that's all."

In a few minutes he was snoring.

VIII

Coke, in a sweater, an old pair of pants, and a cap, strode up and down the room, while Jimmy Pappas, Ruby Hall, Jeff Davis and Lewis argued. One said Coke ought to take it easy the first few rounds and wear the Rattler down, another said he ought to try for a knockout in the first part of the fight, as the Rattler was a limit fighter and tough as they make them, Lewis had qualifications and suggestions no matter who was talking, and Ruby Hall declared that nobody knew anything, implying that he was the one to be consulted. Coke listened with growing irritation. He remembered Regan's curt orders and the silent way that they were received by the other men. Regan was bossy and pigheaded and hard to get along with, a drunkard and a tough guy, but he knew his business, and if anybody tried to tell him what to do he shut them up. Coke looked at Lewis. There he sat in a white flannel, double-breasted suit, his panama at just the proper angle, languidly tapping his foot with his cane, and occasionally making an indecisive gesture with a manicured hand. Regan would have been dominating them, ridiculing them, laughing in their faces with a dirty straw hat on the back of his head and his shirt open at the neck. Coke stopped and stood listening to the clamor for a moment, then he hit the table with his fist.

"Watch your hand," said Jimmy, starting half out of his chair.

"Shut up," said Coke. He looked at each of them in turn. "Listen, you guys, you might just as well cut out this arguing, because I'm gonna fight to suit myself. What the hell do you birds know about it, anyway! This is all just so much wind. I'm going in there and lick this Irishman to a stand-still. If it takes two rounds, all right, and if it takes ten, all right. Now get this through your heads: I'm running this show and I'll fight to suit myself."

They all sat looking at Coke: Ruby Hall sulking, Jeff stupefied, Jimmy Pappas hurt, and Lewis indifferent.

"Well," said Lewis, "you're the champion and you ought to know your business."

When the meeting broke up, Lewis shook hands all around, handed out twenty-five cent cigars, and went out. Ruby Hall sat sulking, but Jeff and Jimmy followed Coke out into the backyard and sat with him. Coke said nothing. Jimmy took out his mouth organ and began to play, Jeff tried to sing, but was afraid of annoying Coke by singing loudly, so he compromised by muttering. After a while, Ruby Hall joined them.

PART VIII

I

Coke sat in his street clothes with his knees apart and his forearms resting on his thighs. He felt tired. Beyond the dressing-room he heard the clamor of the crowd. Jeff was sitting across from him, getting the bandages ready, and Jimmy Pappas, nearly unnerved, was walking up and down smoking a big cigar. Tim Morgan put his head in the door.

"Hello, champ," he said, grinning. "Great crowd. We're gonna turn away a couple of thousand. Better get your duds on. I don't think either one of these next bouts are gonna go the limit."

"I got plenty of time," said Coke, yawning and stretching.

Tim withdrew his head and shut the door. Coke got to his feet, hesitated, then sank back on his chair.

"What's the matter, champ?" Jimmy anxiously inquired.

"Nothing!" shouted Coke.

Jeff and Jimmy exchanged a glance, then Jeff went on unwrapping and rewrapping the bandages, and Jimmy paced up and down.

"Listen, Jimmy," said Coke, finally, "throw that cigar away and sit down. You're getting on my nerves."

"O.K., champ," said Jimmy, stamping out the cigar and sitting down.

Coke got up and began to undress slowly.

"Goddam, it's cold in here," he said, as he pulled off his shirt.

"Cold," said Jimmy. "I'm sweating."

"You would be," said Coke. "But I'm cold."

There was a prolonged roar from the crowd, and the walls of the dressing-room vibrated slightly. Coke thought of Chicago and the Prince Pearl go. He fell back into his chair, half-undressed.

"I don't know what makes me so tired," he said.

Jimmy looked at Jeff, who glanced at Coke, neither of them spoke.

"Hell," Coke exclaimed, leaping to his feet and stripping off his clothes. "I got to snap into it, or it'll take me five rounds to lick that dub."

This was bravado, and Jimmy knew it, but he was relieved all the same. Jeff went on with his work. Coke got into his togs and stood in the middle of the dressing-room working his arms like pistons, then he shadowboxed for a moment.

"All right, Jeff," he said.

Jeff put the bandages aside and Coke climbed up on the table and lay down. Jimmy got up and began to pace the floor again, but remembering what Coke had said, he sat down and flexed his fingers. Coke lay quiet with his eyes closed, while Jeff lightly massaged his muscles. Lewis came in, looked down at him, and said: "O.K.?" Coke nodded and Lewis went out.

"Hell of a manager he is," said Coke.

Nobody said anything.

Coke wanted Regan. He lay there worrying about the fight, wondering what would be the best thing to do. Should he try to hook O'Keefe to hell and back during the first few rounds, like he had Larsen, or should he hold off, stall, like he had done against Prince Pearl, and wait for a perfect opening? Should he give O'Keefe all he had with his right or should he wait till he was tiring? What made his legs feel so funny? And why did he feel slightly sick at his stomach? Maybe he had eaten some bum food, maybe somebody had put something in it. He had heard of that. He lay there worrying, at one moment anxious for the fight to begin, then fearing it would begin before his legs began to feel normal.

"Feeling O.K., champ?" Jeff inquired.

"Yeah," said Coke. "Give my legs a good rub."

He felt alone. Jeff was faithful and hardworking and dependable, but dumb. Jimmy was excitable and nervous. Coke had the full responsibility for the conduct of the fight. Jimmy, as chief second, wouldn't be able to help him any. The best thing he could do was to rush inside O'Keefe's left and murder him. If he could hit him with half a dozen hooks squarely, he'd have him. But how would O'Keefe fight? Some stalling way, you could bet, with Regan managing him. Coke wanted to confide in somebody, to ask advice, at the very least to talk the fight over, even that would have been some relief. But he said nothing and lay with his eyes closed, while Jeff rubbed him.

There was a prolonged roar from the crowd. Joe Rogers came in.

"Ruby won by a knockout," he said.

Coke sighed and envied Ruby Hall. He was all through for the evening, and could go back to his dressing-room with not a thing on his mind except maybe a good steak and a stein of beer. Or else he could get his clothes on and sit, without a worry, watching the other boys in the ring.

"How you feeling, champ?" Joe inquired.

"O.K."

"All right," said Jeff, tapping Coke on the shoulder.

Coke got up and put on a sweater and a bathrobe, as Regan had always made him do. Then he sat on the rubbing-table, swinging his feet. In a few minutes Regan came in to watch Jeff put on the bandages, while Jimmy went to O'Keefe's dressing-room to watch McNeil. Regan was drunk, had a two day beard, and looked haggard.

"Hello George," said Coke.

"Hello, Coke," said Regan. "They tell me you're in A-one condition."

"Yeah," said Coke, "I had trouble with my weight, but I'm all set now."

"Well," said Regan, "a pound more would have cost you. You better try the lightheavy class after the Rattler gets through with you."

"I been thinking about it," said Coke.

"Yeah," said Regan, "you can lick anybody in that division with the right kind of management. Unless O'Keefe tries it. He had trouble with his weight himself. He's got big bones. He ain't like you."

"I can lick O'Keefe and not half try," said Coke.

"That's what the wise money says," said Regan. "But the wise money ain't always right. Riley's betting on O'Keefe."

Coke got red in the face. "Shut up," he said. "Don't try none of your tricks on me."

Jeff looked at Regan, who, to Jeff's astonishment, said nothing. When the bandages were wrapped and O.K.'d, Regan gave Jeff a push and said:

"Beat it and take the lightweight with you. I got private business with the champion."

"It won't look good, George," said Jeff.

"The hell with that," said Regan. "Beat it. I don't care where Rogers goes, but you stay outside the door, Jeff, and don't let nobody in."

"I don't like it," said Jeff.

Coke hesitated, then said:

"All right, Jeff. Do what George tells you."

Jeff and Rogers went out. Regan waited until the door was closed, then he pulled up a chair opposite Coke and sat down.

"Get it over, George," said Coke. "We ain't got all night."

Regan took a blackjack out of his hip pocket, put the leather loop around his wrist, and sat tapping the leg of his chair with it.

"Coke," he said, "I got something I want to tell you that you won't like. You're a pretty hot headed guy in some ways and pretty husky, so I ain't taking no chances." He held up the blackjack. "See this? That ain't just a bluff. You get funny with me before I get through with my story, and I'll put you out before O'Keefe does."

Coke stared at Regan. He noticed that Regan's eyes were unsteady and that his hands were shaking.

"George," he said, "you're drunk, that's what's the matter with you. You better put that jack away and go lay down someplace."

Regan laughed.

"Well," he said, "I paid enough for this jag, I better be drunk. Boy, them bootleggers cut liquor something awful in New York. Worse than Chicago."

Coke sat looking at Regan, who kept tapping the blackjack against the leg of the chair.

"Coke," he said, "remember the time we had that little argument down at The Viennese and you beat me to it with a one-two punch?"

"Yeah," said Coke. "George, I'm sorry...."

"Wait a minute," Regan interposed. "I don't give a damn about you being sorry. That don't help you none. Listen, Coke. Remember what caused that fracas?"

"Yeah," said Coke. "You was shooting off your mouth about the missus."

"All right," said Regan. "Get all set, because you're gonna hear some more of it."

Coke flushed and jumped down from the rubbing-table. Regan got hastily to his feet and stood waiting for Coke to rush him, the blackjack set. But Coke didn't rush him, he stood looking at him.

"What's the idea, George?" he demanded, wearily. "Are you trying to get me all upset so maybe O'Keefe'll have a chance to get a draw?"

Regan laughed and took a letter out of his pocket.

"Take a look at this," he said.

Coke took the letter and tried to read it, but the writing was so peculiar that he could only make out a word or two. He turned to the last page and looked at the signature. It read: "yours truly, Louise Lewis."

"I can't read this stuff, George," he said. "Why don't you wait till after the fight?"

Regan laughed.

"My God, but you're dumb," he said. "I got a boy waiting over across the corridor that's gonna be the next middleweight champion of the world. It's time we had a champion that ain't tied to a woman's apron strings. Listen, you big sap." Regan turned to the middle of the letter and began to read: "...since you insist, I will tell you. Yes, I am going to enter suit against my husband, Paul Lewis, for a divorce. He has never been anything but a woman chaser. He has spent all my money on other women, and made me a laughing stock. I have enough evidence against him to get a divorce in any court, and I am going to name Mr. Mason's wife, whom you inquired about..."

Regan threw back his head and laughed.

"There you are, boy. There's the noise in black and white. You wouldn't believe friend George when he told you, would you? Oh, no, I was a liar and tough and not fit to associate with. You had to get high society people like your wife and Lewis."

Coke dropped his hands helplessly.

"Is it straight, George?" he demanded. "You ain't kidding me?"

"Kidding, hell," said Regan. "How do you suppose Rose got such a good part in Martin's show. Course she's got the stuff, but they ain't handing out parts like that to strangers. I'll tell you. First, because she was the champion's wife. Second, because she was Lewis's fancy woman."

"I thought maybe that was it," said Coke.

He stood weaving from side to side, rubbing the palms of his hands against his thighs, an expression of acute misery on his face.

"Yeah," said Regan. "You thought right. Listen, why do you suppose Coon left town so sudden. He was scared out. He spent too much time with your sweet woman. You didn't give a damn, but Lewis did, and he made it so hot for Coon that he decided to take a trip around the world. Get the idea? Lewis played the freeze out game. He's got a strong yen for your woman, and he ain't letting nothing stand in his way. You're the next freeze-out."

Coke made a sudden movement that Regan misinterpreted. He raised the blackjack, but Coke sprang past him and flung the door violently open. Jeff looked startled.

"Jeff," said Coke, "go get Lewis. Bring him right away."

Jeff rubbed his hands over his face.

"Champ, I don't like this business," he said.

"Get going," said Coke.

Regan took a flask out of his pocket and tipped it up. Coke came back and stood in the middle of the room, staring at the floor. Jeff had left the door wide open and loiterers were peering in. Coke turned and closed the door. He flung off his bathrobe, his face was a dull red. He clenched his fists and hit them together.

"I'll kill him, George," he said. "Just as sure as you're here, I'll kill him."

"Go as far as you like," said Regan.

There was a noise in the corridor. Tim Morgan came in followed by half a dozen of his employees. Lewis came in a little behind them. Jeff edged his way through the crowd. When he saw the expression on Coke's face, he hurried over to him.

"What the hell's going on in here!" Tim bellowed. "What you think this is, Regan? You get the hell out of here or I'll throw you out. I've had enough trouble with you, you damn drunk!"

Coke walked toward Lewis. Jeff took hold of Coke's arm, but Coke threw him off and rushed at Lewis, who cried: "Hold him! Hold him!" and made for the door. But Coke caught Lewis before he reached the door and knocked him into the corridor with a swishing uppercut to the jaw. Tim Morgan, Jeff and Morgan's men grabbed Coke from behind and held him, while he cursed and kicked back at them. Lewis lay unconscious in the corridor. His panama was jammed over his face and his cane was lying broken at his side. One of Morgan's men went over to Lewis and raised his head. Lewis began to bleed from the mouth. Jeff shut the door.

"Well," said Morgan, "I been in the fight game for twenty years and I never seen nothing like this."

Regan laughed.

"Just one of George Regan's shows," he said.

"Yeah," said Tim, "and this is the last show George Regan'll ever put on in New York. The Commission's gonna take action on you tomorrow. Soon as this fight's over."

"I've heard all that stuff before," said Regan. "Tomorrow morning I'll be the manager of another champion, then what you gonna do?"

He went out. During the opening and closing of the door, Coke, who was sitting on the rubbing-table, saw two men lifting Lewis to his feet. Lewis had his head bent and his hands over his face. Coke jumped to his feet and ran to the door before anybody could stop him. Jeff was the first to reach him, and grabbed his arm from behind, but Coke made no effort to get away.

"Lewis," cried Coke, "if I ever see you again I'll kill you. You get the missus out of my apartment."

Lewis nodded without looking at him. Then Coke went back and lay down on the rubbing-table. Jeff bent over him.

"Are you all right, champ?"

"Yeah," said Coke.

Jimmy Pappas and Joe Rogers came in and stood staring at Coke. There was a long roar from the crowd. Tim Morgan took off his hat, mopped his brow with a big handkerchief, and said:

"My God, what an evening!"

One of Morgan's men put his head in the door. "Ready for the main-go, boss!"

Tim Morgan nodded and walked over to the rubbing-table.

"Mason," he said, "are you all set?"

"Yeah," said Coke, "only I got to have my right mit bandaged again."

Morgan turned to the man at the door.

"Get O'Keefe out," he said. "It won't hurt him to wait a minute."

The man went out. Morgan sat down beside Jeff and watched him rebandage Coke's right hand.

II

When Coke climbed into the ring O'Keefe was already in his corner, leaning back against the ropes and talking to McNeil with a grin on his face. Coke mitted the crowd without raising his eyes and then sat in his corner staring at the canvas. The ring was full, newspaper men were in a circle around Regan, who was laughing, talking, and handing out cigars, Tim Morgan and the judges were in a neutral corner, talking loudly to make themselves heard. When the referee, Leo Harness, climbed into the ring there was a long burst of applause from the crowd.

Because of the confusion in the heavyweight ranks, due to the retirement of the champion, the lightheavy and the middleweight divisions had taken on an importance they had never had before. The O'Keefe-Mason match had drawn a record crowd. The Ball Park was packed, and a disappointed mob milled outside the ticket windows. The crowd had come to see Coke Mason work. His reputation as a slugger drew them. Most of them didn't concede Rattler O'Keefe a possible chance, but that didn't matter. They wanted to see punching, and for days the newspapers and magazines had been assuring them that "when Coke Mason fights something always happens." They had seen him flatten Larsen in two rounds, they had seen him score a technical knockout over Mike Shay, who had never been off his feet before, badly beaten, they had seen him spurt up in the final rounds and win a unanimous decision over Joe Savella, when Joe was still good, they had seen him batter Cahill to the canvas in three rounds, and they had yelled themselves hoarse at his sensational victory over Soldier Bayliss, who had dynamite in either hand and landed repeatedly only to be outslugged and outgamed.

The radio announcer told his audience that:

"The Iron Man looks surly, friends. I'd hate to be in O'Keefe's shoes."

One of Morgan's helpers called to Coke and handed him two envelopes. Jimmy Pappas opened them for him. One was a cablegram from Coon. It read: "We figure you can't lose. Best regards." The other was a telegram from Rose. "Get it over quick and come home to mama. Will be listening in. Love." Coke tore up the two messages and threw them out of the ring.

"Are you O.K., champ?" Jimmy inquired, noticing how Coke's face had darkened.

Coke nodded.

While they were tying on the gloves, Regan talked to Coke, who paid no attention to him. O'Keefe came across the ring and put his arm around Coke.

"Champ," he said, "we'll be at it in a minute. That handshaking before the go don't mean nothing. Let's shake hands now."

"Get the hell away from me," said Coke.

"Naughty," said Regan.

A score of flashlight pictures were taken, then the referee ordered the ring cleared. A long hush followed this order. Coke got up, pushed his stool out of the ring, and rubbed his feet in the rosin. O'Keefe followed his example. They were both on their feet leaning against the ropes when the bell rang. Then just what the crowd was waiting for happened. Coke leapt across the ring, his chin on his chest, crouching, like a predatory animal, caught O'Keefe coming out of his corner and drove him to his knees with body punches. O'Keefe weathered the first rush, got his balance and clinched, but Coke clubbed him, forced him to the ropes, and landed repeated, stinging blows to the body. Before a minute had passed, O'Keefe was fighting entirely on the defensive, ducking, sidestepping, swaying, blocking, parrying, back-pedaling, tripping over his own feet, even covering up so long that the crowd booed. Coke was all over him, swinging punches from every angle, wide open, stamping around the ring, panting like an animal. O'Keefe seemed bewildered, absolutely unable to cope with the most violent and homicidal attack seen in the ring since the Dempsey-Willard fight. When the bell rang for the end of the first round O'Keefe went toward Coke's corner, but Coke turned him around and gave him a shove. The crowd cheered.

"Well?" Jimmy demanded.

"He's tough," said Coke. "I licked Bat Cahill with less than that."

"Don't you think you better slow down a little, champ?" Jimmy inquired. "That's a hell of a pace you're setting."

But Jeff winked at Jimmy and shook his head. Coke said nothing.

At the beginning of the second round O'Keefe leapt out as fresh as ever, grinning, with his long left out as far as it would go. He was taking no chances this time and met Coke in the center of the ring and stopped a rush with his left. Coke took a hard left on the forehead without wincing and bored in. But O'Keefe arched his body away from body punches, leaned forward from his hips up, and drove a hard right to the side of Coke's head and followed it with a smacking left. Coke kept coming and took two or three more hard blows to land a stinging hook that sent O'Keefe into a clinch. Coke clubbed him all over the ring, landing one blow that looked very much like a rabbit punch. The referee warned him. O'Keefe landed with a left that smacked all over the Ball Park. Coke missed a counter and, off balance, was hit with a right which turned him half around, but he landed a lucky punch straight from the shoulder at this angle and O'Keefe went down. Resting on his hands and knees, grinning at Coke, he took a count of nine, then leapt into a clinch, and getting a hand free, hammered Coke about the head. The ringside was in an uproar and hats sailed into the air. This was no murder, this was a contest. At the end of the round O'Keefe danced to his corner. Coke swaggered across the ring and was cheered by the crowd.

"Yours by a mile," said Jimmy.

"Yeah," said Coke.

But he was thinking that O'Keefe was just about the toughest boy he'd ever fought. His legs were tiring. He wondered if it wouldn't be a good thing for him to stall. Let O'Keefe, who seemed willing enough, set the pace for a while. He said nothing to his seconds, but he decided to stall for a couple of rounds and maneuver O'Keefe into a series of left hooks. He had two knockdowns to his credit already and even if he lost the next two rounds he'd still be even.

But O'Keefe crossed him. At the beginning of the third round he began to stall, and run, refusing to lead. Coke, as champion, had to carry the fight. He rushed O'Keefe and hammered him, but O'Keefe had a way of arching his body that made him hard to hit. Coke was at a loss. O'Keefe clinched frequently and hung heavy on Coke, whose legs were tiring. Once or twice he was lucky enough to get a hand free and make the going tough for O'Keefe when he clinched. But in general O'Keefe stalled successfully through the third round, also the fourth and fifth, never leading, hanging on, taking a good deal of punishment, but able to stand it, worrying Coke with his arched body, and occasionally landing a stiff counter. Coke began to lose confidence in his own generalship, and when he went to his corner at the end of the fifth round he said to Jimmy:

"How does it look?"

"Well," said Jimmy, "you've got every round so far. But from the crowd it must look pretty bad. He's tying you up, Coke. How's the legs?"

Coke hesitated, then said:

"Getting tired."

Jeff looked at Jimmy. They said nothing.

"What do you think I better do?" asked Coke.

Jimmy didn't know what to say.

"What do you think Jeff?" he demanded.

"Well..." said Jeff.

"Good God," said Coke, "you guys ain't worth a damn. I'll just go in and kill him, that's all."

"Don't talk so much," said Jimmy. "If your legs are getting tired, maybe you better try to finish it."

The bell rang. Coke bounded across the ring as he had done in the first round, caught O'Keefe by surprise and landed a hard left hook, followed by a terrific right to the head. Coke had seen Prince Pearl and Mike Shay drop before these two punches, he thought the fight was nearly over. But O'Keefe grinned and bored in. Coke clinched and thought: "Christ, I must be losing my steam!" The referee pulled them apart and Coke rushed in to try his favorite punches again. But O'Keefe shot his left down at the angle that had worried Cahill so much, and Coke went back on his heels. Cursing and panting, he went after O'Keefe, driving him all over the ring, landing on his biceps, his elbows, his gloves, but failing to connect with one clean blow. Toward the end of the round, Coke maneuvered O'Keefe into a corner and peppered him, but O'Keefe, timing Coke's right correctly, sidestepped it and Coke fell into the ropes. O'Keefe took advantage of this break and kept Coke on the ropes, beating him about the body. For the first time in the fight, Coke covered up. At the bell he was on the defensive and taking a beating.

People in the crowd began to look at each other in surprise. What had happened to the Iron Man?

The radio announcer told his listeners that O'Keefe had shaded the champion in the sixth round.

Coke sat in his corner staring across the ring at O'Keefe, who seemed fresh and was grinning at someone in the crowd. Coke hated this tough, freckled kid. He wanted to see him stretched out bloody and helpless on the canvas. Suddenly he thought about Rose. He'd never see her any more. She and Lewis would live together now and give him the laugh. Mrs. Lewis would get a divorce, there would be a big scandal. Everybody would be laughing at the champion who wasn't man enough to hold his own wife! At the champion? Champion no longer if his legs didn't improve or if he didn't knock O'Keefe kicking in the next round. A fine mess he'd made of things. He was alone, alone. Tears of rage came to his eyes. The bell rang.

Coke leapt out of his corner and attacked O'Keefe with all the ferocity he had shown in the first round, but O'Keefe weathered the rush easily this time, sidestepping, clinching, countering, his head high and his left ripping up for the body. Coke began to tire. Even the radio announcer noticed it and communicated his discovery to his listeners. Coke clinched and held on, his legs wavering. The referee pulled them apart time after time, and warned Coke again about the rabbit punch. But Coke was fighting for his life now, and paid no attention. The referee warned him repeatedly. But Coke was all fighting man now and was out to win, no matter how it was done. The referee didn't know what to do. He couldn't disqualify the champion, the crowd would mob him, but he couldn't let O'Keefe get the worst of it. O'Keefe solved his problem for him by using the punch himself. The referee sighed with relief and let them rabbit-punch as much as they pleased. O'Keefe, noticing the look on Coke's face, was fighting his best. He had been warned to watch out for Coke when he began to tire, or seemed beaten, for at such times he was more dangerous than others. Coke was landing his hook now, and although it had lost some of its steam, he was hurting O'Keefe, who once flinched very noticeably. Toward the end of the seventh round one of Coke's rushes was stopped by O'Keefe's straight left. Coke staggered. O'Keefe saw his advantage and rushed in, landing a right to the head and a left to the pit of the stomach. Coke turned sideways, took a right on the chin and fell. The bell rang.

Coke leapt to his feet and swaggered to his corner. The crowd cheered.

McNeil worked fast over O'Keefe, whose body was covered with big, red splotches.

"Best boy in the ring," said O'Keefe.

"Shut up," said McNeil. "You got him. He's about all in."

Coke had a cut over his right eye and blood was trickling from a split lip. He lay back on his stool gasping for breath. Jeff knew he was licked but Jimmy was so excited he didn't know anything. He got out the courtplaster and fixed the cut over Coke's right eye.

"Put some over my other eye," said Coke. "Don't you know nothing?"

Jimmy obeyed without understanding.

"You want to make a target for him," said Coke.

When the bell rang for the eighth round Coke rushed O'Keefe, but there was not much violence in the rush and O'Keefe fell into a clinch. Coke tried to punish him with a free right hand, but he was arm weary. O'Keefe got away from him and hit him with a light right and a hard left. Coke fell into a clinch to rest his arms, but he found that his legs were wavering. In a sudden excess of rage he wrestled O'Keefe all over the ring, O'Keefe scarcely resisting, except to keep Coke from getting an arm free. The referee pulled them out of the long clinch and warned Coke about the wrestling. O'Keefe landed a light right and then a glancing left which hurt Coke, who followed him flatfooted, trying for a knockout. O'Keefe tried to feint Coke into a right lead, but Coke wanted to land the left. O'Keefe rushed him, but Coke crossed him by sidestepping with an agility that surprised O'Keefe, who was thrown off balance. Coke saw his advantage and landed a right swing that swished through the air. O'Keefe was flung across the ring and into the ropes. The crowd stood up and yelled. But O'Keefe, cursing, bounded out of the ropes and rushed to the center of the ring, where Coke met him. O'Keefe, like Prince Pearl, Bat Cahill and Mike Shay before him, lost his head and stood slugging toe to toe with Coke, who landed his left hook cleanly at last and followed it with a right which glanced off O'Keefe's head. O'Keefe kept his feet and hung on, groggy. The bell rang. Coke staggered to his corner, cursing. It was all over. He'd missed his chance. If O'Keefe came up fresh for the next round, he was through. He sank down on his stool.

"You got him, champ," cried Jimmy. "You got him sure."

Jeff put his hand on Coke's shoulder and smiled at him.

"Best round you ever fought, Coke," he said, but Coke paid no attention. He kept repeating to himself a single phrase, "I shot my bolt, I shot my bolt." O'Keefe was too tough for him, toughest guy in the world. He had landed enough clean punches to lick Cahill, Savella and Larsen rolled into one. The kid just wouldn't drop and stay down. Coke glanced across at O'Keefe. He was already sitting up on his stool, grinning. Coke felt a sudden lassitude, he felt old and worn out. He wished it was all over, then he could go home and lie in the dark. That's what he wanted to do, lie in the dark. He glanced up at the powerful white light over the ring. Beyond that was a cloudy, summer sky. He could see the flash of matches in the far off dark bleacher seats. He glanced down into the ringside. Men were staring at him with set faces. Did they know it was all over?

When the bell rang for the ninth round, a damp wind sprang up, and it began to drizzle. Coke came out of his corner with his chin on his chest, bobbing, weaving, scowling. He saw that O'Keefe was cautious, and didn't seem anxious to mix it. A sudden hope filled him with strength. Maybe he would win, maybe he could pull this one out of the fire. He'd done it before. But there was that freckled kid with the big shoulders and the little legs, young Fitz they called him, dancing in front of him, grinning, moving about as if it was the first round instead of the ninth. Coke rushed in wide open, panting and stamping heavily on the boards, but O'Keefe met the rush coolly, stepped back and to the right and landed his left. Coke staggered. His legs were giving out. There wasn't a good round in them. O'Keefe hit him with his right, then his left and right. Coke staggered and turned slightly sideways. O'Keefe hit him a right uppercut and suddenly the ring turned a somersault. Coke reached for something, the ropes maybe or O'Keefe's arms, but missed and felt the canvas under his hands. He heard a long dim roar and glanced up, but the light hurt his eyes. The roar continued, getting closer. He heard someone saying: "Six, seven, eight." Christ, he was being counted out! He felt water on his back. What was that? Rain. "Nine!" He leapt to his feet and put his arms around a blurred figure in front of him. But the blurred figure jerked away from him, he staggered forward two steps, then something hit him a terrific smash on the jaw. He felt the canvas under his hands again, heard the dim roar which gradually came closer, felt the rain on his back. "Nine!" By God, they couldn't count him out. He got to his feet and began swinging his fists, one of them landed. But he couldn't see. How come he couldn't see?

Something reached out of the darkness and belted him on the jaw. He felt the canvas again, but under his back this time, he heard the dim roar but it was receding now, and the rain was falling on his face. "Nine!" Hell! Up again. Wouldn't this round never end. But somebody had him by the wrist, pulling him to his feet. The fight was over.

THE END